Steelflower

Steelflower

Lilith Saintcrow

A Samhain Publishing, Ltd. publication.

Samhain Publishing, Ltd.
577 Mulberry Street, Suite 1520
Macon, GA 31201
www.samhainpublishing.com

Steelflower

Print ISBN: 978-1-59998-642-5
Digital ISBN: 1-59998-438-5

Editing by Angela James
Cover by Anne Cain
Illustrations by Josh Z. Carter

First Samhain Publishing, Ltd. electronic publication: March 2007
First Samhain Publishing, Ltd. print publication: September 2008

Dedication

To Teri Smith
Go, blithe spirit. You were a joy to know.
And I look forward to seeing your smile again.

Try to Look Innocent

I woke from a fuzzy trance with my mead-filled head ringing and four Hain Guards seeking to separate said head from my shoulders.

In strictest point of fact, they did not seek to kill *me.* They sought to kill the barbarian whose pocket I had picked last night, and I dove into the fray without realizing it, still half-asleep. The case could *further* be made that things became a general mess because of one small reflexive action.

I am not my usual charming self with my head pounding like Baiiar drums and my mouth full of foul Kshanti camel-piss, and I was a bit more enthusiastic than twas necessary. As I wiped my *dotanii,* after the last Hain lay flopping and gasping on the floor, I finally had a chance to look about me.

I had killed three of them, two with short thrusts and one with the piri-splitter cut, carving half his face off. He drowned in his own blood.

The tavern's commonroom was full of patrons who had either slept through the fray or pretended to. Nevertheless, there was a wide space around the table I had used—leaping atop it to gain the high ground, while smashing a Hain on the head with a crockery tankard—and I remembered a general scurry from the vicinity as soon as my eyes opened and my sword cleared its sheath. It says something for my reputation that I am allowed to sleep in a tavern commonroom unmolested—and without *my* pocket being picked.

I dropped down to the rough, splintered floor of the commonroom, my *dotanii* sliding back into its sheath. I considered spitting as I strode for the door, decided against it.

My mouth tasted foul, but spitting here might start another fight.

"Off so soon?" A low male voice with a strange guttural accent, behind me. My mind automatically catalogued it—*barbarian.*

Which only meant the speaker was not of any race or language I knew offhand. There are many in the wide, wide world.

"Go and bugger yourself," I tossed back over my shoulder, "unless you want the same done to you as those poor bastards."

"Ye saved me life, wench, after ye picked me pocket last night. Even enough. So where are ye off to?"

I turned on my heel, and my reply died in my throat. *That* barbarian. The *huge* one.

He bore a startling resemblance to the puppets of giants traveling Tsaoganhi use in their shows. Frizzy ginger eyebrows and a huge bushy beard, blunt fingers wrapped around an axe haft, and a bloody bandage around his even-bushier ginger head completed the picture. He had been left unmolested with his tankard last night, except for my quick fingers as he brushed past my table. The small blade fitted over my finger had cut into his trousers, and I had nimbly picked his pocket clean, without even knowing quite why I bothered.

I drew in a deep breath. "I desire a bath, and I need some kafi, and I wish for peace and quiet. So *go bugger yourself.*"

With that, I turned and stamped out the door, doing my level best not to flinch when the early-morning sunlight speared my skull. It reminded me of S'tai, and fighting with the Sun in my eyes, the screams of the wounded...

I shook the memory away, stepped over the threshold and out onto the street—

—right into the path of a full cadre of Hain Guards.

We stared at each other, one tired, hung-over sellsword thief and fifteen Hain Guards in full leather armor, with pikes, crossbows, and swords, not to mention daggers.

"Oh, Mother's *tits.*" I put my palms together and gave a correct little bow. "A good dawning to you, Dogs of the Most Beneficent Sunlord."

I received no answer but the sound of blades ringing free of their sheaths. There was a roar from behind me and the ginger-haired barbarian charged the Hain Guards. He had the grace not to knock me over as he passed me.

I was about to turn and walk away.

No, really, I *was*.

Then I drew two knives, and flung them both. The two crossbowmen fell. Waste of good metal now if I did not finish the fight.

I picked my moment and dove in. I received one nasty bruise on the right thigh from a stray kick, but the ginger-haired mountain bellowed like an ox and smacked *that* luckless Guard on his helmet with the butt-end of his axe. The Guard dropped like a stalled calf, blood dripping from his nose and mouth. I took two with quick fencing strokes, one with another short thrust to his lungs, the third was a good fighter and it took two passes before I could carve open his sword-arm, laying him open for the killing blow.

I punched another Hain in the face, a short sharp strike finishing upward and driving his broken nasal bone into his brain. He dropped like a stunned ox as well.

When it was done, I worked the second thrown knife back and forth against the suction of muscle in the crossbowman's throat. I *hate* leaving knives behind, especially ones filed down to achieve the proper balance on. Good metal that does not need filing is a rarity.

I faced the barbarian, breathing deeply, my ribs flaring. My sword was at waist-level, the blade slanting up, a guard position taught to me on a drillground in the dim dark ages of my childhood. In that long-ago time I held a wooden blade far too big for my hands, and my head ached far worse than now. The sharp thrill of combat had washed some of the pain from my mead-abused body.

He stood with his axe hefted easily, and belched—a long resounding sound; I could almost taste his last night's dinner. "Guards." He peeled the bloody bandage off his head. There was a nasty scrape along his right temple. It looked half-healed, but painful. "Want t'bet another cadre's not on its way, lassie?"

I would not lay odds on that, barbarian. "What do you

want?"

"T'get off this street and somewhere quiet, and get to know ye." His eyes glittered under the bandage and the gingery hair. "Rainak Redfist, Clan Connaiot. And ye?"

Did I not tell you to go bugger yourself? Still, I had drawn blood on his behalf, and he looked spectacularly unfit for passing unnoticed here in Hain. "Kaia," I said. "Come this way. And try to look innocent."

A Flawed Crystal

I lay on my stomach, eyes closed, while Ch'li's iron fingers worked down my back, easing out tension and knots. The massage oil was fragrant with linwood and citron, and I heaved a sigh. After a pot of kafi and a light breakfast, a bath and a massage was the perfect start to an otherwise unsatisfactory day.

"I dinnae see how ye can stand that." Redfist's voice boomed across the tiled room. Water splashed from the fountain in the corner.

"Barbarian," Ch'li said, in singsong Kshanti. "Big red pig barbarian." She sniffed, a sound of quiet disdain.

"Quiet," I said in Kshanti, repeated it in commontongue. "He cannot help it, Ch'li. I paid extra. Now cease your chattering, both of you."

A good massage, ruined. But when I finally rose from the table, the barbarian was asleep, slumped against the wall. I thought I would leave him there, decided not to, and prodded him with a foot after I dressed. Ch'li had disappeared. I would have to pay her double next time, to make up for having a smelly pig in the room.

Kshanti are fastidious about everything but their liquor.

"Come, Redfist." I prodded him again. "Get up. Tis time to leave."

He groaned, and I kicked him for the third and last time. "I can very easily leave you here. Now *come*." I heard thinly veiled impatience in my own voice, bit it back with an effort.

He hauled himself to his feet, the wooden bench groaning as his weight left it. He almost knocked his head on the pretty porcelain lamp hanging from the roof. I snorted, and led him out through the bathhouse. The staff here knew my preferences, and did not cavil when I took the back way out—into an alley smelling of refuse. I set off at a brisk pace down the alley toward the Street of Delights. "I know a place we can rest you for a day or so. Then we shall take you from the city. Is it a bargain?"

He made a short belching noise that might have been an affirmative.

"I shall even refund you the contents of your pockets," I added, charitably. The bath and massage had left me in an excellent mood, not to mention the light breakfast served at Ch'li's bathhouse. *And* a pot of kafi. Fine stuff, even if it does smell of old socks.

"Noble of ye, lass. Do not you e'en want t' know what it *is*?" He sounded surprised.

The contents of your pocket? Nothing of import, my fine red one. I reached the end of the alley and peered out onto the Street. "A lightmetal chain with a flawed crystal. Some streetseller's gaud, no doubt. And a stunning array of ten copper sundogs, plus three silver *kiyan*. A key made of iron. Tis all you had in your pocket."

He laughed. "Aye, to those dinnae know how t'look. Ye can keep it, I mun well glad to be rid of it."

"Rid of what?" I pushed him back into the alley. A cadre was clattering in our direction, Sun gleaming off their high-peaked helms. "More Guards. Good gods, what did you *do*? Try to look inconspicuous."

He rolled his green eyes. His skin was like uncooked dough under the hair, and I wondered what it was like to see that paleness in a mirror. Or to have little Hain children point at you and giggle behind their hands. My own skin is an even caramel, closer to the Hain than his, and I still received my fair share of giggles. Mostly when I opened my mouth to speak, for my Hain was accented with the liquid vowels and sharp consonants of my homeland. I do not have the mouth-of-mush the Hain seem to prize.

"Ye doan pass any more than I do, lassie," he growled. The guard clicked by, marching in formation, their red-tasseled pikes raised. "Where d'ye hail from? I'm Skaialan born an' raised."

"I can see that." I peered after the Guards as they vanished around a corner. Now that he had told me, I could see the ruddiness and the clumsiness. I had never seen a Skaialan before, but everyone has seen streetplays with puppets of the giants. "Come, tis safe now." I led him out onto the street. "And I repeat, rid of *what*?" I felt the hilt of a dagger with my left hand—something I only do when nervous. The smooth hilt is comforting under the fingers, and I have lived long by being close to steel when needed.

"Rid of the cursed thing. That's twice ye've fought at me side, lassie. Makes us shieldbrethren."

"None of your barbarian customs for me, thank you." The Street was crowded, but the Hain knew better than to point here on the Street. Too many barbarians with quick swords and hot tempers. The Guard would find out we had been here anyway, tales carried on air. Better to concentrate their attention on the Street of Delights than where I was truly bound.

I took him to the very end of the Street and through a metalworker's shop, ignoring the protest of the thin, scar-seamed Hain man—protests that stopped as soon as I tossed him a square Hain coin and a straight level stare. The man blanched. I did not look away, he finally dropped his eyes.

My gaze has that effect on some people, especially here on the Lan'ai Shairukh coast. They consider strangecolor eyes unlucky, and hence dangerous.

The barbarian was stumbling by the time we reached the docks. I eased the door open and led him into the small room, then closed and bolted it safely. I pushed aside a cunningly made table masquerading as a pile of wooden splinters. Twas actually held together by glue and varnish, and rolled away from the trapdoor with a protesting groan. When pushed to the side, it half-hid the trapdoor and gave me enough room to escape if anyone discovered any of the other exits. "Do you have the darksickness?" I asked in commontongue. "The fear-of-close-spaces?"

"Lass, every space is small here." He wiggled his busy eyebrows. He had taken advantage of a sponge bath at Ch'li's, but he was still ripe. The Hain smell of garlic and hot peanut oil; this man smelled of leather and a reek too foul to be horse. Old sweat and meat, perhaps.

I nodded and motioned him closer, to the back of the tiny shack set between mounds of decaying rubble, far out in the ruin of the docks after the last great fire. The trapdoor opened smoothly, and I dropped down. He landed heavily after me.

"Good." I examined the room. Everything as it should be. "You may sleep here. I shall bring food. I suppose you eat like a horse, eh?"

"Like a bull calf, lassie," he replied, already yawning. "Ye've done me a fair turn, ye have. I'll not forget it."

I shrugged. *As if I should have left you to die in the street. It seems the least I can do after picking your pocket, to offer you a safe berthing.* "Tis a mystery to me why I am taking this much trouble. Try not to snore. I shall bring some food."

By the time I shimmied up through the trapdoor he was breathing deep, sprawled upon the sleeping-pad I had carried down here a moonturn ago and scattered pungent fislaine around to keep the rats away.

Crouched in the tiny shack above the hidey-hole, I dug in my purse. Drew out the sundogs and the *kiyan*, and the key. The *kiyan* were stamped with a crude figure of a wolf-headed goddess. The sundogs were etched with something chariot-shaped. They felt like good metal to my experienced fingers. In this part of the world, foreign metal is easy to exchange.

I bundled them and the key neatly in a square piece of cotton from my clothpurse. The only item remaining was the necklace.

I thought I had stolen from him because he was big and blundering. It had been an absent-minded training exercise, almost; but the truth was I had picked his pocket without knowing why.

As if I had been compelled. My fingers had shot out, divested him of his valuables, and flicked back almost against my will. And I had compounded my error by fighting on his behalf, as well as bringing him here, to the safest bolthole I had in Hain.

Kaia, you are a fool.

I held up the cheap lightmetal chain. The thumb-sized

crystal had a zigzag flaw, darkness cracking in its heart. It glinted, coolly, as I swung it back and forth.

I slipped the chain over my head and nestled the crystal between my breasts. It was set in cool cheap alloy, too light to be real metal. It was chilly before it warmed to my flesh.

You are a fool. You do not know who this man is, or why he is so far from home.

I had to pay extra for my bath and had killed a good nine people today without being paid for it. He owed me.

And if he became a problem, well, I had killed more dangerous prey. One stupid barbarian would surely not be so much trouble.

Food and Shelter

I returned with enough food for three barbarians, by circuitous routes to make certain I was not followed. Hain seethed under the late summer heat, a glass bowl over the city. The Guard was everywhere, poking into every corner, and I contemplated leaving the city as soon as possible. I could leap ship for the Clau Islands, perhaps, except there was no business out there. I would do better up the coast, near Shaituh. I could make enough to take me through the winter with a few assassinations, and the Thieves Guild operated there. No shortage of work with the influx of trade taking advantage of the recent lowering of tariffs by the Shaikuhn and the God-Emperor. Here in Hain, there was no thieving to be done worth my while, and assassination was beginning to look a little more complex with the Guard after the barbarian, who was now connected to me.

What had he *done*?

What have you *done, Kaia? He is a stranger. And a barbarian.*

He was also far from home, like me. He was alone.

I dropped down into the hole and was met with the sight of Redfist sprawled on his back, breathing softly through his nose.

"I brought food." *That* piece of news managed to wake him. "I could only carry one wineflask. The entire city is roiling like a poked anthill. What exactly did you *do*?"

"And a good dawnin' to ye, lassie Kai." He sat up and yawned so widely I was amazed the walls did not cave in.

I tossed him the hank of cotton holding his coin and his key. "I shall be keeping your cheap gaud. Unless it has some sentimental value."

"Nay, damn thing's bad luck," he grunted. "Won it at dice a full Moon ago and been sour ever since. Did I hear food?"

I squatted down next to the bedroll and undid the parcel. "Some Skaialan sausage and hard Ch'li cheese. I thought you might like a taste of home. There is flatbread too, and you may have one of the cirfruit."

He had the two arm-length sausages before I could blink, and tore into the first with vigor. "Fine of ye, lassie," he said through a mouthful, and I handed him a whole piece of flatbread. For myself there was more flatbread, rice balls, and pickled fish I rolled with the rice in the flatbread. It was good, even without piri sauce. I finished by eating the other cirfruit and took a few swallows of wine, handed him the flask. He drank in noisy gulps, then wiped at his cheeks with his blunt fingers. "Fine of ye," he repeated, his green eyes dropped to the floor, and it struck me that he sought to offer thanks.

How long have you been away from home, large red one? Do you wish you could return? It was uncomfortable, this interest I was taking in his predicament. I had already involved myself too deeply. Yet I could not leave him to his own devices, it was increasingly clear he would never escape Hain alive. He was just so...*huge.* "Welcome you are to it. So why exactly are the Guards after you?"

"I doan know," he said through a mouthful of cheese. "The necklace. Red-eyed bugger chasing me e'er since I won it, an' tha' made the Hain mad. Killed three of their'un, an' I think they thinks we be partners, the red-eyed bugger an' me. That, an' the Sun festival."

"What red-eyed bugger? Be a little easier with your meal, friend Redfist. You will choke." I took another swallow of wine and then rose up out of my crouch, moved to the little cupboard set on the side. There was a flask—the water tasted leathery, but was still good.

"Red-eyed bugger wit' two swords. I think th' sorry bugger who lost the necklace stole from him."

"Who would steal something this cheap?" The crystal was sharp and warm against my chest. Why, exactly, was I wearing it? Why would I keep something so shoddy? I had not worn a piece of jewelry for nigh on ten summers. Not since the ear-drops I had stolen in my first city, so long ago.

Now *that* was an unpleasant memory. I quelled a shudder.

"D'nae know. Ye stole it too, din ye, lassie?"

"My name is Kaia. Not *lassie.*" I sounded ill-humored, even to myself. "I shall sleep on the floor tonight."

"Nay, lass. You take the softie, I had'tall day." The rest of the sausage vanished down his gullet. It was amazing to see so much food vanish so quickly.

I shrugged. It had been a long weary day, and my head still hurt from mead. "It makes no difference. I merely hope you have no fleas. And I warn you, I *will* kill you if you try any bedgames with me."

He rolled his eyes, and let out another amazing belch. "A l'il thing like you's no proper wench. I had want one I wouldnae squash, lass. Doan trouble yerself."

"No trouble." I am actually taller than the Hain, and a hand taller than most other G'mai women as well. The G'mai call a taller woman *s'tatadai,* a marshcat, and I had been compared to a marshcat before: ill-tempered, lethal, and invisible before striking. "Tomorrow I shall take you from the city, and we may part ways."

"Aye." He nodded sagely. "Unless ye be wanting work. Two of us better than one."

"You are far too conspicuous to make a good thief, and the only war for mercenaries is half a continent away. The Danhai are still rebelling against the Shainakh Empire. I wish no more of that war. The tales the newsmongers sing are awful enough."

"Ye mun fair wi' yer pigsticker there, K'ai." He indicated my sword with a jerk of his chin. It rode my back as usual. Easier to draw. Not like the Hain, with their short flat blades at their belts.

"If I carry it, I should know how to use it." *How am I going to remove you from the city? If this was a freetown we could simply choose a direction and go, but the Hain like their cities locked tighter than a whore's cashbox.* I rubbed at the back of my neck, smoothing away tension. The only trouble with Ch'li's massages was how quickly the relaxation faded.

"Th' red-eyed bugger chasing that prettybit, carrying blades tha' shape." He nodded sagely, again. I wondered if he was simple, or if he was so used to other people thinking him stupid because of his size that he had begun to act so.

I mulled over his words a moment. *Dotanii* are long and slightly curved, slashing blades with oddly shaped hilts meeting the hand differently than other blades. The shape is fairly distinctive. “Other than the red eyes, what does he look like?”

“Taller than ye, lass, with yer type o’hair. The blueblack, not the redblack. Short hair, an’ a scar on his throat.” He demonstrated, drawing a thick finger across his own throat. “So, and so.”

My skin prickled with gooseflesh. So. Perhaps a man had stolen G’mai blades—or bought them, though we do not sell steel outside our own borders. Still, twas possible. *Anything* is possible, once one leaves one's native land. “Well, he shall not find us here, and we will be gone by morning. Better sleep. The chamber pot is there.”

“Ai, I know, lass. Nice little cottage here.” He hefted himself to his feet, licking his fingers. I winced, looked away, and brushed the crumbs off the bedroll, settled down gratefully. I would sleep lightly tonight. The hilt of a dagger poked into my ribs, but I ignored it. I had learned quickly to take what sleep I could, wherever I could. Before the barbarian finished his...

I was asleep.

A Lucky Thing

By the time I had my knives drawn, I was beginning to wake.

I thought I would have to kick the barbarian, but at the sound of metal leaving the sheath he rose to his feet with far less noise and far more speed than I thought possible.

I pointed to the other side of the bedroll and made a shoving motion with my hands, knives glinting in the dimness. Redfist nodded and knelt on the bedroll carefully, pushed at the wall. It folded aside silently, revealing a short staircase leading up to another trapdoor—a one-way escape hatch. I had learned the trick of making them on a ship one winter with a half-drunk Rijiin carpenter.

The same winter we fought off pirates all the way across the Lan'ai, another unpleasant memory.

The barbarian squeezed himself up the stairs while I waited. Cool predawn air filtered down to me as he sought to open the hatch quietly.

Another sound. A step that did not try to be silent against the creaking floorboards of the shack overhead. I had deliberately chosen this hut because the floor was noisy, the best assurance against thieves and assassins.

The one above us knelt at the trapdoor.

I made it up the stairs, stopping only to throw the small clay ball behind me. I heard it shatter on the floor in the hole, the navthen trapped inside mixing with ortrox coating the outside. Chemical reaction would produce a short-lived but very hot burst of flame, and the floor was highly flammable.

Learning *that* trick had almost cost me three fingers. I am most emphatically *not* an apothecary.

Redfist waited above, his axe held ready. I ran past and he followed, running with more stealth and speed possible from someone of his size. The shack would be ablaze in moments, but the wasteland of already-charred land around it would not threaten the rest of the city with a conflagration.

I led Redfist through a merry patchwork of alleys and streets until we came to rest just out of sight of the West Gate. The larger gate would open at dawn, when the horns rang, but the postern—if I could bribe the guard—could be opened for us. I took in great heaving gulps of air. The barbarian sweating smelled even riper. I wrinkled my nose and bent over, rubbed at my eyes to clear the nightsand away.

"Wha' was it, lass?" Redfist gasped finally, when we both could breathe.

"Someone searching the shack above us." My aching bladder protested sharply. "Stand watch."

"Uhn." An affirmative grunt, the same in any language.

I pissed behind a pile of rags set out for the ragpickers and made it back to his side, tying the laces on my trousers. "You mean you ran all this way without knowing what I did?" My lungs were easing their burning, and my legs did not feel quite so shaky.

"Ye're nae stupid nor coward, K'ai." His green eyes shone like a solemn child's. "'F ye stand up wi' yer eyes full of fire and a dagger in each fist, Rainak Redfist will nay disagree wit' ye."

Well, that is a comfort, I suppose. "I do not know who our intruder was, but he is probably dead now. I would not be surprised if the entire shack burned." I settled myself against the kiln-fired bricks of the wall, glad of the support.

"Uhn." Another affirmative grunt. "Mayhap the red-eyed bugger?" His ginger hair stood up wildly in spikes and clumps. He was simply too *big*, I could not hope to talk him past a gate-Guard.

"Mayhap," I agreed gravely. "You have no idea who he is?"

"Nary, lass."

I believed him. Small bits of my hair had slipped loose from its complex mass of braids. I tucked a strand behind my ear

and peeked around the corner.

"Ah. Luck is with us today, Redfist. The gate is open early, and the guard just ducked into his hut with an exceptionally enterprising streetseller. Come now, quick and quiet." My thigh burned with the fantastic bruise the Hain had gifted me yesterday. I would stiffen again if I did not stretch and allow myself some time to heal.

Soon enough, Kaia. Move now and worry later.

We reached the gate and slipped through the postern, nobody the wiser.

Once outside the Hain city walls and through the maze of shanty dwellings spreading out from the larger redbrick warehouses and the fantastic, red-tiled wall, I relaxed a little. We moved with the steady, ground-eating lope most mercenaries and sellswords develop after a time, a pace most of us can keep for a full two days without rest or food. *Mother grant me that is not needed here,* I prayed, and when we cleared the shantytown and moved out into the clearcut plains before the coastal forest, I called a halt.

We drank from a stream trilling through waist-high chedgrass, and I splashed my face. "Well. I think we may be safe enough now. No gear, and no bow...we shall have to live lean for a space. True?"

"Right enough, lass." Redfist's mouth pulled down glumly.

A smile spread over my face. "Not at all. I've a cache around here somewhere. Two bows, some gear. Wish we had a horse. I could steal one, given half a chance. But you are too big to ride."

"Aye. Except a Skaialan draft, an' they be few and far between here. Mayhap south?"

"You may go south, if you wish. I am bound up-coast to Shaituh." I trailed my fingers through silky chedgrass heads, the seeds plump and fat like little pearls. "I will give you a bow and full quiver, and you should be able to—"

"I'll nae leave ye, lass. That's thrice ye've saved my life."

I made a small sound of annoyance. "I cannot drag a barbarian in my wake. You are too *big*. People will *talk*. I make my living doing things I do not wish spoken of."

"So ye're a thief." His ginger-haired lip curled. "I ken. I can earn honest coin, ye can steal what ye like."

His tone managed to nettle me. "I make my living by being *inconspicuous*. Tis hard to do as the only G'mai in a city, but I manage. I took you out of the city, I saved your life, now you may go where you like and leave me to my own troubles." I had my hands on my hips by now. What I *really* desired was another bath, a chance to re-braid my hair, and some fresh clothes.

What I had was one large furry barbarian problem and someone possibly chasing us. Someone with red eyes, and with two swords, shaped like mine.

That does not make a pretty tale, and I like it even less after this morn's events.

"Rainak Redfist goes where he pleases, lass, and I'll thank you not to forget it. I go wit' ye until I've paid me debt." He folded meaty arms across his massive chest and stared at me with green barbarian eyes. "So I've sworn."

"Oh, Mother's *tits*." Disgusted with the entire conversation, I took my bearings and turned, trotting off for the forest. I had wanted to practice my woodscraft—but not like this.

He followed me, of course. Lucky Kaia, with a new barbarian pet.

"I dinna think any of the Blest People came over th' mountains." He was behind me, moving more quietly than he had any right to.

I rounded on him. "What would you know of the Blessed People? You are a *barbarian*. You are trouble I do *not* need. Is that perfectly, undeniably clear?"

"Ye be Gemerh, then. Elvish. I wondered, I did."

"Oh—" I could not even curse, I was so distempered. No G'mai likes the term *elvish*, tis usually pejorative. They use it when they wish to call us something less than human, and therefore easier to think of killing. "Do not force me to draw my sword, large red one. I am not what you think. Come."

He had the sense to shut his mouth, and followed me across the rolling plain.

Try to Keep Pace

I found the cache about mid-morning, as the Sun climbed to her zenith. Everything was wrapped in a sewn oilcloth, which also doubled as a pack. I strapped on the first of the two bows, my favorite, and a full quiver of arrows as well. I examined the dried meat and journeybread, thankfully still good. And the dried cirfruit. Enough for a few days. Yet I had the barbarian to feed, too.

Well, at least my practice of having a cache was proving useful. Again. If I would but cease being tossed out of cities or fleeing the authorities...but what else is there, when you are a sellsword and thief? It is not work recommended to give one peaceful nights.

I hardly remembered what I had buried here. There was a travel-kit too. I belted it on and sighed. A full purse; I opened it and saw silver Hain sequins. Not as good as *kiyan*, but good enough. I divided them as evenly as I could by eye, and gave the barbarian half. "Here. A hedge against trouble."

He nodded. "Not many folk would do so, K'ai."

"*Kaia,*" I corrected. "I have rescued you from the Hain Guard twice now, and from your red-eyed bugger too. I suppose I might as well cap it by giving you half my coin. At least you are not boring." *And if this red-eyed bugger is chasing us, you may make an excellent shield against him. It is not unlikely that you are the one he seeks.*

"Uhn." He grunted, but there was a twinkle of amusement in his green eyes. I wondered if the Hain made ward-signs on catching his gaze, as well.

On the fringes of the forest, the trees were merely scrubwood but still growing quickly in the warm clime. I gave the oilcloth pack to Redfist and surveyed the lay of the land. “We shall have to hunt tomorrow. For now, let us put distance between ourselves and the Sunlord’s city.”

“What about tha’ red-eyed bugger?” Redfist looked relieved, his eyebrows wagging so hard I almost felt the breeze. The bandage on his head was much the worse for wear, dirt and old blood marring the linen.

I shrugged, the familiar weight of bow and quiver settling into my shoulders and back. “We shall go a little further into the forest. Is the crystal something important to him? Do you know?”

The barbarian looked surprised. “I doan know, lass.”

“I have a sneaking suspicion we shall find out.” I eyed him, gauging how long he was likely to last at a punishing pace. “Try to keep pace.”

“I hae not fallen behind yet,” he said stiffly.

I set off, deeper into the coastal forest. The barbarian followed me.

Lucky, lucky Kaia. With a new barbarian pet, pursued by a red-eyed bugger.

A Barrier to Evil

At our nooning, taken in a small glade with a stream chuckling through, I sat atop a large flat rock and ate journeybread with a dried cirfruit. The barbarian contented himself with dried meat and bread. This clearing had a small whitebark tree in the very center. Sunlight filtered down, edging each leaf in gold and glowing on the paper-white trunk.

I stared at the tree for a long while, thinking. Whitebark is generally held to repel evil.

What are you contemplating? I chewed my cirfruit slowly, drank from the filled water flask. *What can you possibly be planning, Kaia?*

Simple enough. If twas another G'mai—this far from G'maihallan twas not likely, but still—his *adai* would be with him. Probably waiting in the shadows. Did someone steal an *adai*'s necklace? Surely an *adai* would not send her *s'tarei* after such a trifle? Unless it was a Talisman. I would not know a Talisman if it bit me. I avoided Power, having none of it myself.

Maybe a capricious *adai's* pocket had been picked, and she had sent a *s'tarei* after it? Why would an *adai's* necklace be in her pocket if twas not a Talisman? And why would a cracked crystal on a cheap chain be a Talisman?

The more I dwelled on it, the more uneasy I became. I had never heard of a red-eyed *s'tarei,* nor of any red-eyed ghosts in the tales of my youth. My own eyes are a clear dark gold, unusual enough among my dark-eyed people. I was doubly strange, I had no Power. Was this the ghost of the *s'tarei* I might have had, if my mother had not let me be born lacking?

I pushed the thought away as soon as it rose.

Only *s'tarei* carried double *dotanii*. So it was impossible, unless someone had bartered or stolen for G'mai swords. But red eyes...perhaps a ghost?

A *hungry* ghost, mayhap. Just because there were children's tales of such things did not mean they did not exist. The world was wide indeed, and I knew better than to think I had seen all its horrors.

I shivered, hopped down from the flat rock and washed my hands in the stream, rinsed and filled my flask. "Are you rested?" The first words I had spoken since our stopping sounded strange in the clearing.

He scratched under the soiled bandage. "Rested enow. What makes ye so grim, young lassie?"

"Thinking on your red-eyed friend. It seems passing strange."

"Oh, aye, it does. What d'ye think, then?"

I levered myself to my feet and approached the whitebark in the middle of the clearing. Sunlight fell down unbroken, warming my shoulders.

I slipped the chain over my head and hung it on a convenient branch. The Sun glittered through it, sending one hard flash winging outward. As if it cried out as it left my hand.

Strangely, the crystal felt heavier. It certainly bowed the half-finger-thick branch I looped it over. The setting did not look so cheap now, and when I looked closely it seemed worked out of a larger piece. I saw the faint wavy lines of something in the metal. The flaw did not look as large, and the chain more supple. Had I not known differently, I would have sworn it was true silver instead of lightmetal mix.

"How very odd," I said, quietly. "Very well, then, red-eyed thing. Take your Talisman back, and be satisfied." I thought a moment, dug in my purse, and laid three silver sequins at the foot of the whitebark. Silver and whitebark—traditional barriers to evil.

Ah, well. I had done it now. *Best not to undo what is already done*, a proverb older than my people.

"Ye're a-going t'leave it there?" He sounded shocked. The sound of water and wind rose, a comforting backdrop; I decided I had taken my fill of cities for a time.

When I was hungry enough, I would want a city again. I would want noise and excitement and different food. But not for a long while. “Perhaps he wishes its return. Even if he chases you for some other reason, it still means no loss to us. You won it at cards, and you've half the coin I own. *And* I saved your life to boot. Do not ill-mouth your luck, barbarian. Either way we are free of a burden.”

“It’s got a fair mun o’ Power. We could sell t’a magicker—”

Twas like being pinched hard in a tender spot. *I would not go near a witch or a conjurer if you paid me.* “I would not know of Power, and I do not deal with ‘magickers’. I have a faint idea of what your red-eyed friend may be, and I do not wish him or anyone else tracking me. Now, sunlight wanes upon us, Redfist. Let us travel while we may.”

He did not ask again.

Kaia's Dream

We were deep among the trees by the time dusk fell, deep enough that I chanced a fire. The travel kit included a flint and steel, and I thanked the Mother as I coaxed a tiny blaze into starting. Redfist came back with an armful of deadwood, and—lovely surprise—a brace of coneys he had trapped. We were near a small stream, so I cast around and found a bed of starchy meatroot, and we had a fine stew in the small pot I had thought to store in the travel kit. He found some pungent baia and I stumbled across some walcress. Altogether twas a satisfactory evening, with journeybread and stew more savory than usual.

After our sup, he scoured the pot with sand. At least he was not a witling in the woods.

I settled down by the fire with the comb that never left my purse, and began rebraiding my hair. "Tell me. What is a Skaialan doing here in the Middle Kingdoms? I thought your kind never left the Highlands."

He poked at the fire with a long stick, making the dusky shadows dance. "An' I thought yer kind never left the Blest Country, so we're both a-treading far from home." His face turned soft, reflective. Even with skin like uncooked dough, he had a rough sort of charm. "M'clan—Clan Redfist Connaiot Crae—is dead. Was wiped out by the black-hearted Longwalk Ferulaine Crael and their bastard lord Dunkast. Was a fair battle, but I was sent to take news to our allies, and by the time I returned...no clan remained. Wha' else does a Skaialan do? I took to the road. No clan to demand weregilt." He shrugged, his eyes distant and reflecting the leaping flames. "And ye, lassie? Why are you so far from home?"

'Twas fair enough, I had asked first. Still, I disliked saying it again. "I have no home. I am outcaste among my people, Redfist. I was born without something they never lack, and so..." My shrug was easy, loose, perfected over several tellings of an exile's tale. "It appears we are both clanless. My House threw me out as soon as I passed my *k'yaihai*—my womanhood ceremony. They let me take my sword, at least."

"I heard th' women of the Blest only use the dagger and the sorcery they learn."

I shrugged again. "Tis an oversimplification. Swords are not necessary for most of the *adai*—the women of the People. They have their *s'tarei*—their twins—to carry *dotanii*. Since I was born without a twin, having no Power, I was cast out. It matters little, I have done quite well for myself. When I was five summers high I set myself to learn the sword."

"Aye, ye have doon a fine fair job o'that. Ye must hae been a fine little lass."

Not fine enough to keep. I tied off the end of a braid and started unraveling another. G'mai women past their adulthood ceremony do not usually braid their hair where anyone but their *s'tarei* can see—it is custom, a private thing. But I was no *adai*, so it did not matter despite the strange feeling of almost-shame I suffered whenever I twisted my hair in public.

It took a long while, and we spoke back and forth, desultorily. He fell asleep with his back propped against the large round rock I had built the fire near, to block the fireglow in at least one direction. By tomorrow we would be gone, the campsite cold.

I took the first watch, sometimes singing to myself as the Moon rose in the sky. She was waxing, almost full, and the light was excellent. Good odds, if anyone chanced upon us here. Also bad odds—we could be seen, and the reading of smoke in a clear moonlit sky was not beyond a *s'tarei*. Would our ghost have tracked us to the whitebark? Our trail was clear, and the whitebark would glow under the Moon's light.

Silver and the whitebark are powerful deterrents to any illcraft, I knew that much of witchery. I did not care to learn more, and would not unless forced.

With one problem potentially solved, I set my attention to another. I had left most of my gear in Hain. It was safe enough with Jebbel, he dared not rid himself profitably of it unless certain of my death. But I had planned to move the Skaialan safely from of the city and double back to pick up my gear before taking ship for Shaituh.

Restlessness made me shift uncomfortably. If the barbarian would not go his own way, I could not return for my gear. I would have to outfit myself again. Another harsh expense.

The crystal returned, nagging at me. Had I ever heard of a Talisman like it? It seemed vaguely familiar, and yet, not at all. I was brooding on it far more than I should. Why *was* it so familiar? Something teased at me, behind the locked door in my memory. Everything to do with *adai* lay behind that door. I wished it to remain there.

Perhaps an *adai* had left it somewhere, bartered or lost it, and some poor *s'tarei* had been asked to track it down. Perhaps it was a Talisman, and it went where it willed. Why had I felt oddly like I was leaving behind a part of myself, hanging in the whitebark tree?

It would get better. The only cure for anything magical was to move as far away from it as possible. It had been a relief to leave G'maihallan and find people living without Power to waste on the most trivial of things.

There was my skill with a sword—at least being G'mai was good for something.

At least there was that.

I would soon steal enough to find a quiet corner on a trade route, and buy an inn. A simple little six-room travel-house, maybe with a stable. I would settle into serving beer to travelers and changing sheets the rest of my days, and when I died perhaps an apprentice in the trade would build me a pyre.

It was an old dream of mine, to have an inn, and I amused myself in the long reaches of my watch planning it inside my head. I would scour the wooden floors and have a copper kettle singing on the hearth. I would have chai-bushes in the back garden, and make my own chai. I would hang the linens in the Sun to dry, and I would make a stew each night to feed the travelers who paid their good coin in my inn.

The night wore on. I began to sing softly again, the old Lay of Creation. Twas soothing, especially in G'mai, with rising and falling cadences. I had not allowed even the oldest or simplest of words from my native tongue to cross my lips in so long.

The breeze stirred the forest as I sang. I broke off, listening, and the wind died.

Puzzled, I started again. I sang of how the Moon pulled the tides with silver chains, looked into the ocean swinging below, and fell in love with Her reflection. She pulled Her reflection forth from the water and lay with the Silver One, Haradaihia. From the love of the Moon and the Silver One a bright rain of spirits became All That Is.

The First Folk were the first spirits to move among the trees, and in time they became the G'mai, the Blessed Ones, the People, closest to the gods.

I ceased my song again. The branches settled into stillness. I gaped my mouth, my breathing soundless, and waited.

Nothing. Merely the common noises of a forest night—a rako bumbling through the branches, the far-off sound of water from the stream, the faint soft cough of an owl's wings. The death-scream of something caught by the owl, a deer, stutter-stepping through the brush, avoiding our fire.

Nothing out of the ordinary. Yet I was restless.

"Six rooms and seven waterclosets," I murmured. "A bedroom on the bottom floor. Linens hung in the Sun."

I flipped out one of my nightknives, a thin, dull-finish blade, almost a *stilette*. I started to flip it over my hand, in a game most G'mai boys learn early. The trick is to roll it over your knuckles and catch the hilt as it rockets past, moving your hand as little as possible.

I made five passes before the knife dropped to the side. My thigh ached dully where the Hain had kicked me. Clumsy, I had been clumsy, I had to be more careful. The *s'tarei* were meant to engage in combat while protecting an *adai*, so I had been required to modify some of the forms. The lessons I gained once I passed the borders of my own land had been no less quick and harsh. Had I not been lucky and fast, I would not have survived.

Luck, Kaia. Merely luck. Carrying a big red barbarian with you is no worse than anything else. Admit it, if only to yourself—you are glad of the company. Too long traveling alone turns even the most solitary sellsword into a bushel of strange fancies.

I picked up the knife again, flipped it over my hand, started a complicated doublepattern with both hands. Flip the knife, catch it, flip it again, using the momentum of the first throw, double snap of the fingers, catch it in the opposite hand, roll it around my fingers twice, three snaps, catch it in the opposite hand. Twice around while the other hand snapped, change hands while the knifeblade blurred, snap.

It passed the time.

I woke the barbarian when the night was just past its highest point, and curled into a ball on the other side of the fire. It was uncomfortable, I would be sore on the morrow and stiff from sleeping on the cold ground, but I fell asleep immediately.

A Night Duel

The sound was familiar, metal chiming against metal. I woke, swordhilt in hand.

"Briyde protect us!" It was the barbarian, scrambling to his feet.

I gained my own feet, leapt across the fire, and put my back to the big rock. It was the best we had. "You were asleep," I accused.

"Nay." His axe glimmered in the dull glow from the dying fire. "Resting me eyes."

I replayed the sound inside my head. Knifeblades, chiming together. Knifeblades? I blinked the sleep out of my eyes, and inhaled sharply, tasting the air. "Something is not right."

"Oh, aye?" He sounded sharp and sarcastic. "Truly, wise one?"

I ceased speaking, straining my ears to catch the sound. I could *feel* someone listening. A silence I knew all too well, from growing up among the G'mai.

There is nothing like the direct approach. "Come out!" My voice sliced the breathless quiet. "Come and face me honorably, coward!"

"What are ye doing?" the barbarian whispered fiercely.

"If tis an animal, it will be scared off unless it has the water-sickness. In which case we need it where we can see it," I whispered back. "If tis an assassin, his secrecy is gone. If tis our red-eyed ghost, we may be dead anyway. *I* would rather die fighting." I raised my voice again. "Come and die, if you have the courage!"

The branches rustled to my right, ignored. An *adai* would be capable of misdirection.

The shape stepped out on my left side. Indistinct in the darkness, taller than me, a confused impression of motion.

Now, Kaia. Now.

I launched myself, sword held to the side and coming in low. I am fast, greater speed a consolation for my smaller frame, but my fightbrain had already taken in the relative size and shape and announced he was slightly bigger than a regular G'mai male—which meant he had a full handspan and a half of height more than me and several pounds of muscle; G'mai women are generally built slight. How I had cursed my slimness until I found out it gave me an edge in pure speed.

Metal clashed and slithered. He had only one sword out, and it was a *dotanii.* Either he had stolen it, bought it from someone who had, or he was a *s'tarei.*

If he was a *s'tarei,* I was dead.

The voice of the warmaster resounded inside my memory. *A cornered animal has nothing to lose. Be cautious of a trapped opponent.*

He deflected my next blow, barely. My eyesight *shifted,* and I could see. It was the fightbrain taking over, showing me the world in darkness as my pupils expanded to take in every available shred of light. G'mai are excellent night-fighters, and I have done more than one assassination with the help of my night-vision.

He parried again. Metal rang. He gave no answering strike. It destroyed the rhythm of combat. Why did he not attack?

I retreated three steps, careful to keep the fire to my side. He could not walk across it, my flank was covered—if he was a *s'tarei,* where was his *adai*?

The stranger spoke. "Peace." In commontongue, then repeated in G'mai. "I offer no attack. I alerted you to my presence."

My ribs flared. I took in deep even swells of breath. "Tis the middle of the night. Why would you be here if you intended no harm?" Alert for any twitch presaging attack, I spoke in G'mai without thinking. "Where is your *adai,* hmm?"

He stilled, the absolute stillness only a *s'tarei* can use. "Do you not know?"

I retreated another few steps, cautiously. If he came at me, I would kill him. I was faster, and the onrush of his attack would make him vulnerable. *He has been following us, and he has a* dotanii. *Is this Redfist's ghost?* "What do you *want*? I returned your gaud bit of trash. Now leave us *be*!"

"I will travel with you." No doubt about it, he was G'mai. His accent was too true for anything else. And a *s'tarei*. Here. Outside the borders of the Blessed Land.

How?

"Where's your *adai*? Bring her out and have her swear on the Moon you will not kill me in my sleep." It was highly impolite, but I was in a temper.

His shoulders stiffened, his eyes glittering darkly. "Can you not guess? In the sight of the Moon, can you not *guess*?"

"Guess *what*?" I almost screamed, losing hard-earned patience. I switched to commontongue. "Redfist, unlimber your bow."

"I already have, lass," he said grimly. "Tis *him*."

I had guessed so, but hearing the barbarian say so was different. My heart coney-ran inside its cage of ribs, so hard and fast individual beats blurred together. "I thought his eyes were red."

"Tis an *expression*, lass," Redfist replied. "Red-eyed bugger. Hae you ne'er heard it before?"

"Oh." I tried not to sound baffled. The man's eyes were not red—they merely glittered, as all eyes do at night.

The G'mai man took this in. His silence was like a living thing.

This is a riddle I do not care for. "Where is your *adai*? Huh? Where is your twin, *s'tarei'sa*?"

He sheathed his sword. Why had he not drawn his second blade? "Since I see no other G'mai, I am forced to conclude *you* are my *adai*."

I had thought I would never feel that sharp bite of shame and anger mixed again. "Go bugger yourself," I snarled. "I am no *adai*. I have no Power. Go on your way, and be quick about it."

"I shall travel with you." He moved, slowly, over to the fire and folded himself down. He sat cross-legged and straight-backed, and I saw the shape of his features. A G'mai face, high cheekbones and a strong jaw. I could not see what color his eyes held, just a faint shine from the banked fire's reflection. The hilts of his *dotanii* rose fluidly over his shoulders. "*In'sh'ai.*"

"*In'sh'ai,*" I replied automatically, accepting the customary greeting. It meant while he was at my hearth, he would offer me no violence. I watched him for a few moments, slowly sheathed my own sword. "Well," I said, in commontongue. "Redfist, lower your axe. He will not kill us. Not yet, anyway..." How could I explain? "He thinks he is to go with us."

"I doan trust this, lassie," Redfist growled deep in his chest.

He's G'mai. And from a House, by his accent. He will not slaughter us in our sleep, not after offering to share our hearth. "Nor do I. Keep your bow handy. Shoot him if he draws a blade." I backed away, closer to the giant barbarian. "If you fall asleep and he kills me, I will haunt you."

"D'ye think he will try't?"

"Not yet." I sank down to the ground beside the barbarian, watching our visitor. Had a full troupe of Kshanti acrobats appeared from the darkness juggling gold balls and ringing finger cymbals, twould have been less of a marvel. "I need sleep. Wake me when the birds start dawnsong."

"I will, lass." Redfist yawned, but he held the bow steady, an arrow loose-nocked.

I took a deep breath, curled up beside him, shifted to get a rock out of my side. The G'mai across the fire appeared to be watching me, his gleaming eyes fixed through darkness. "What is your name, *s'tarei'sa*?"

"Darik." It meant *dagger* in the G'mai name-tongue. "And yours, *adai'sa*?"

"Kaia." It was a shortening of my full name, but since he had not given me his, I was not required to give mine. "Where is your *adai*?" I could not let go of it. If she was waiting in the dark to kill us—

—why had she not struck? Was he alone? He could not be.

I was the only G'mai who traveled alone. The sharp bite of shame returned. The last I had felt of it had been before I left the borders of my country.

The gods will smite him if he breaks the law of the hearth. There was some comfort in the thought. Yet if he was here, alone, he may well have shaken off the prohibitions of a life spent in G'maihallan.

I have not. Should I think he has?

"Rest," he said. "I shall keep watch. Sleep, Kaia'li."

It was a pun meaning a small, sharp, precious thing, like a decorated hairpin *stilette.* I had forgotten what it was to speak in G'mai, with the puns, the cadences and nuances, wordplay and poetry. I almost wasted breath telling him not to use my name for his play.

Instead, I eased into an uneasy doze.

A Seeker, Found

Redfist was snoring when I woke, stiff and cold. I pushed myself halfway up, something small and hard in my left hand.

I held it up, my fingers tangled with a thin chain.

It was the necklace. Or—not the same one. The flaw was much smaller, and the setting was truemetal, not cheap alloy. The chain was serpent-supple, fine silver. Twas worth the value of the metal and a bit for the craftsmanship as well, if I was any judge of such things.

Across the fire—it was built up and burning now, welcome warmth in the mist and dew of an early morn—the G'mai sat, his eyes closed. Twin *dotanii.* He was definitely a *s'tarei.* He carried no travelgear, and there was no *adai.* I was fairly certain of it. She would have come to the fire.

What was he about in this trackless forest without travelgear?

I held up the necklace, glittering sharp in the morning light. Was it the same one?

It could not be. And yet, it seemed so like.

The G'mai had put it in my hand as I slept. As the barbarian slept, too. And now, the G'mai had retreated to his side of the fire.

I rolled up to my feet, slowly, cursing under my breath. I left the gaud behind. If the G'mai wanted to gift me something, I would inform him his leaving my presence would be gift enough. I kicked Redfist, hard enough to hurt but not enough to bruise, on his meaty left leg, and strode away into the trees to relieve myself behind a chana bush.

When I returned to the fire, Redfist was rubbing at his leg and grimacing between huge lung-emptying yawns. "What di' ye do that for, lassie?"

"You were to *keep watch*. Barbarian." I stalked away in the direction of the stream.

I washed my face, shivering at the icy water, and the back of my neck under my hair. Shook my hands free of water and turned back toward the clearing.

Once on solid ground with a fair bit of room, I laid the bow aside, planted my feet and drew in a deep breath. I raised both hands, loosely shaping the air. My entire body protested, stiff and sore.

The forms for unarmed combat are coded into the deepest regions of my brain by almost-daily practice since I reached my third summer. As an orphan I was held in common by House Anjalismir, and was taught the unarmed forms, as are all *adai*.

When I was five summers high, my mother died. Two moonturns past her death, I was tested in the old traditional way, and found to have none of what makes a G'mai woman worthy of the People.

That was when the shunning began.

The other G'mai would never be unkind—not even the children, most paired into twins by the time of their Tests. They simply would not speak to me once the Yada'Adais had finished my Test. Nobody ever spoke of my embarrassing lack. They were simply, kindly, unavailable. Silent. The Yada'Adais herself would often send for me, and bid me, by pointing one long elegant finger, to wait in a corner of her room while she Tested others. She made me watch how their Power showed, glittering and swirling in the air around them as she sat in her thronelike chair, her hands held just so, a black glassy Testing Stone clasped between them and turning phosphorescent.

I remembered no such glitter in the air around me during my Test. The lesson was explicit and silently delivered, as are most lessons among the People.

I developed excruciating headaches from sobbing myself to sleep each night. And when I reached six summers, I refused to go to the customary *sh-yada'adai*, where they learn how to control the Power. Instead, I presented myself at the drilling ground with a clumsy practice sword filched from the armory. I followed the motions as best I could, my small hands sweating and slipping on the grip. The practice blade had been far too large for me.

It took a good four moonturns before the warmaster—a tall, spare *s'tarei* related to my mother—would stop and watch as I followed along before barking a correction. He would occasionally correct my grip, then step back and say, "*A'vai.*"

Again. And again, and again, until I performed correctly.

I stopped using the rooms provided for me, my mother's chambers. She had died of a rare fever; her death had killed her *s'tarei,* for among us one does not live without the other. Two deaths, both my fault. If I had Power, I might have given her something to live for. Perhaps shame had killed her. After all, she had birthed a flaw in the pattern of the G'mai. Had she been able to tell even before the Yada'Adais Tested me?

I finished the basic hand-to-hand forms; my sword hilt was in my hand. The blade cleared with a soft *shing.* The first simple form I had ever learned unreeled before me.

It was a pleasure to feel my muscles loosening, the blood flowing quickly through my fingers, my breath in deep round swells like the sea under a ship's belly. The basic forms flowed away, and I started one of the more advanced forms—the third, one of my favorites. I loved the piri-splitter, the starstrike, the minstrel's plea. I leapt into the stag's strike, the hind's leap, the swinging-strike.

My booted feet shuffled and leapt as I switched from the two-handed strikes to the one-handed, working for speed and precision, every contact marked with a sharp huff of breath. *Cannot breathe, cannot fight,* I heard the warmaster yell, felt the sting of a slap delivered by a thin cane. Corrected my angle, spun on one foot, patter-stepped to the side, avoiding the strikes of my invisible opponents.

The knife was in my hand, reversed along my forearm to act as a shield, and I started to work in earnest. I needed the clarity of thought that would arise from warming and loosening the body. I *needed* the calm.

Besides, a sellsword always needs her practice.

By the finish I was sweating lightly, warmed and loosened,

and much calmer. I stretched down to touch my boot-toes, let the complex braids of my hair fall forward. It felt wonderful. My right thigh felt a little better, less sore, though I favored it a bit.

I bowed, slightly, to the four quarters and raised my arms briefly to honor the Unseen, and returned from my warrior's trance to find Redfist and Darik both watching me. I scooped up the bow, my hands moving habitually. "Is the fire doused?"

Redfist nodded. "Care for journeybread, K'ai?"

Alas, not all problems can be solved with a bit of warm-up. "A little, and some of the dried cirfruit." I accepted with a scowl, filled my flask at the stream and took a long drink, filled it again.

Redfist approached, cautiously handing me the bread and the dried fruit. "He din seem like a threat. Ye would nae be sleeping if he was, lass."

"True." *But that does not excuse sloppiness. Though I was a fool to trust the watch to you.* "The next time you sleep during a watch, no enemy will have to kill you." *Or perhaps I will merely leave you in the woods.*

He nodded. "Fair enow, lass." He scratched at his linen shirt under the huge leather vest. I wondered briefly if the leatherworkers had used a whole cow to craft it. "I would be liking a bath."

"There is a freetown up–coast, before we reach Shaituh. I know an innkeeper there, and we have coin enough for a few nights." *And I will be leaping ship, leaving both of you behind. This is too much trouble even for me.*

The G'mai—Darik—said nothing, watching me. I brushed past him, ready to turn and strike if he made any move, and he fell into step behind me, slightly to my right.

The very place a *s'tarei* would walk.

Heat rose in my cheeks. I rounded on him. No, my temper was not smooth this morn. "Exactly what do you think you are *doing*?"

"My duty." Calmly, matter-of-fact.

I took a closer look at him.

Dark hair, the same blue-black as mine, cut short like a *s'tarei* but a trifle shaggy, as if he had trimmed it himself. High, balanced cheekbones, like mine, an even, relaxed mouth. He had the kind of harsh beauty most often seen among the noble Houses of the G'mai, and he had it in spades. Even among us he would be considered exceptional.

Except for a ragged band of scar tissue across his throat as if someone had tried to take his head with a garrote. Twas an awful scar. I certainly would have remembered it had I ever laid eyes on him before, and anyone singing a tale of him would mention it.

His eyes were dark, too, wide and liquid. We are a beautiful race, the First Children, the G'mai. After the Darkness was defeated and Beleriaa journeyed to the Halls of the Gods, the Silver Ships came from the stars, bearing gifts. The legends say the G'mai were taken into the ships and changed by the will of the Moon into the loveliest of the world's children. The Elders in the Silver Ships had charged the G'mai with protection of the Blessed Land, and we do not fail in that defense.

I found myself examining his face as I had studied no other G'mai. I had learned long ago in my childhood not to look directly. It hurt too much, to see them walking two by two while I was always alone.

Say something, Kaia. You are staring. "Your eyes are dark, not red. I expected an evil spirit, from Redfist's description. Why were you following him?" *Not so incidentally, what are you about without an* adai*? You are at least as old as I, and should be well bonded by now.*

"I did not follow him. I followed *this.*" He held up the new necklace, with the smaller flaw and the finer silver. Its sharp glitter speared my eyes—perhaps a random ray of sunlight. A silver wire, threaded directly into me.

No. I closed away the sudden feeling of greed, of *wanting* it. "What befell the first one—the lightmetal gaud?"

He shrugged. "This is the only one I have, *adai'mi.*"

Rage and terrible pain squeezed my heart. "Do not ever name me thus." The killing quiet was in my voice. "*Ever.*"

He nodded, not surprised or frightened. "What would you prefer? Kaia'li?"

I stopped the betraying little twitch. It was only a use-name. He had no idea how close he was. "Merely Kaia. And you are Darik." It was not a question, but it left my mouth as one, changing in midair.

He bowed his head a little, accepting the name. Again, no offer of his full name or House.

Good. It meant I did not have to give him mine.

I watched him a few more moments, searching for something sharp enough to say. Nothing edged enough to draw blood arose from my confusion. Finally I turned away, hitching the bow a little higher on my shoulder.

"Kaia." He used my name as if he knew me. As if it sat easy in his mouth.

I half-turned. Redfist watched with much interest, his busy eyebrows reaching up to touch his hair, giving him the appearance of a wrinkled old puppet.

I thought of cursing, let it go.

Darik held out the chain and crystal. It glittered in his hand with something far more than the misty sunlight should wring from a piece of jewelry only fit for a streetseller. The world was quiet around us. I smelled wet earth and my own sweat, the exhalations of trees and the bruised grass.

"It belongs to you. Take it."

I considered it for a long moment. "What if I do not wish to?"

It made no impression. "You are G'mai. You know better."

He was correct. Twould be rude to refuse it, especially since I had returned it once already and he had shared my fire last night. Sharing a hearth made him my guest, and twas rude to refuse a guest's gift to a host. My childhood rose under my skin, the codes of behavior bred into every G'mai.

Even flawed ones.

"What is it?" I sounded more like a petulant child than a fully grown sellsword. I firmed my chin, eyeing him.

"A gift," he said, patiently. "It belongs to you. Please, Kaia."

Politeness and childhood training warred with hard-learned caution. "Do you swear by your *adai* it means no harm to me? And that *you* mean no harm to me, or my traveling companion?"

"Of a certainty." He wore dark G'mai travel gear, brocade

worked into the fabric of his overshirt. Trousers, G'mai boots, finely made even for us. From a House, then. A G'mai nobleman, his word worth the air it was printed on and a great deal more. "I swear by my *adai*, this gift means you no harm. *I* mean you no harm. I will even swear that I mean your traveling companion no harm. I saved him from death at the hands of the Hain, but he did not stop to thank me. Rather rude."

I measured his little speech, took the necklace from his fingers. Twas cold, and I slipped it over my head again. I dropped it down the front of my shirt and shivered a little as the metal and crystal met my skin. But it warmed quickly, and I considered him again.

His shoulders relaxed, slightly. That was curious.

The whole *situation* was absurd. My luck had turned sour. Or had it?

"I do not know what this means," I told both of them. "And I do not like this turn of luck." I strode away, my boots sliding in damp loam.

There was silence, but they followed me.

I was beginning to wish they would not.

Battle-Rage

I set a slow pace until midmorning, when the urge to stretch my legs took me and I shifted to a ground-eating mercenary lope. I bore northwest, planning to strike parallel to the twin roads leading to Shaituh. I did not like the roads—either the inland *or* the coast road, too easy to find a pack of bandits—but I would have to use one as we came closer to Arjux Crossing. I was contemplating this choice when my nostrils flared, and I ceased all movement between one stride and the next.

Woodsmoke.

Moss-hung trees lifted to the sky; here in the coastal forests the trees robe themselves with green and gray because of the rain coming in from the Lan'ai. The ground was soft, rich black under a carpet of fallen leaves and needles. In the old forests the relative lack of underbrush makes travel easier. There was no slashwood to bar our passage.

A tingle at my nape flared into life. Woodsmoke in this quarter meant travelers or bandits. Most travelers took the roads in groups and caravans, hoping swiftness and more weapons would throw the road-wolves off. This deeply in the woods, the chance was high it was bandits.

Lovely. My lips stretched in a wolf's grin.

I sniffed. Wind from the coast, more due west than northwest now. Two days or so out of Hain by foot...

Is it worthwhile to steal a horse?

I was reminded of my companions. The G'mai could ride, but the barbarian, no. Too big for any of the small wiry horses the bandits would have; shaggy Hain ponies unfit for anything other than packing about baggage.

"What is it, lass?" The barbarian broke his quiet, shifting his considerable weight. A stick cracked sharply under his feet.

I lifted my hand, asking for silence. Stood thinking.

The risk outweighed the benefit. But twas nice to know where the encampment lay. If we were cautious, they need never know we were about. "Bandits. That way." I pointed. "We must go silently, and quick."

"They have horses," the G'mai said.

I suppressed my irritation, that his thoughts would follow mine. "Not one Redfist can ride. And I do not wish another battle right now, I wish to reach the next freetown in one piece and without undue delay. I wish for a bath, and the barbarian could do with one too—"

The wind shifted, and I dropped to the ground without thought. Actually, I was *knocked* down after I had already shifted my weight to drop. Knee-high ferns rustled as bloodlust combed the air. I heard the whistle of the arrow and found myself pinned to earth by the G'mai, who rolled away as I shoved him. Redfist cursed. The arrow had come from the left, my fightbrain juggled sound, distance, trajectory—and returned a probable location.

Lucky twas not a crossbow bolt. Even the G'mai's speed would not have saved me from that. My shocked body suffered a brief flare of nausea, training shoved it away. I could not afford coney-fright, freezing into immobility by narrowly escaping death.

Running footsteps, light and almost impossibly quick. I rolled onto my belly and peered up from the grass to see Darik running.

Toward the arrow's birthplace.

I gained my feet and leapt after him. He had saved my life—and was about to commit suicide chasing down an *archer*. The fool.

I saw them, six men in the dappled shade. Four had straightswords, one had dropped a bow and now had a blade in his hand, and the last had a pike. Darik ran for them, and they returned the favor with long easy strides. Why the archer had not simply *shot* him as he ran I could not guess, unless the archer was indifferently trained and stupid as well.

Darik met them with a clash of steel, and I almost stopped in confusion. He had both swords out, and wasted no time. He killed two of them in the first pass, taking out one man's throat and carving the archer's right arm off with a solid speedstrike.

Mother's tits, he's fast.

He engaged the other four with a form I had never seen. Twas similar to the ones I had learned, but this was the double-*dotanii* style, a wonder to behold. He moved like a whirlwind through the bandits, metal clashing or tearing through flesh, and when he finished all six sprawled on the ground. Even the archer, who had gone into shock as he lost his arm. He thrashed and gasped weakly, the song of a death approaching.

Darik flipped a dagger out and sent it blurring into the man's eye, easing his passage. The hilt glittered.

His blades flashed in a complicated pattern, blood shaken away, and were re-sheathed. He bent down, worked his dagger free, and straightened, wiping the blade on the archer's overshirt.

I had stopped short when he killed the last one, having no more need to run or unlimber my own bow. The barbarian was behind me, thundering to a standstill. My lungs burned. Not only had Darik reacted with G'mai speed, but he fought with a fury I had rarely seen.

I was lucky. He could have killed me during our nighttime duel.

Why had he refrained?

I took a deep breath as he glanced at me, a brief passage of his dark eyes from my boots to my hair. The words spilled free, a cascade of ire. "You thrice-damned *idiot*. What possessed you to run them down? They had an *archer*. You should have let Redfist and me return their arrows with interest instead of running yourself ragged like a bloodcrazed *fool*!"

He bowed his head, accepting the rebuke. It was a gesture I had seen from several *s'tarei*. For some reason, it only made me angrier.

"He dropped his bow. I was angry. Forgive me." He spoke in G'mai, and the term he used was a touch more than *angry*. It was the literal word for *battle-rage.*

My heart ceased its knocking in my throat. I could not take him to task—he was only a G'mai man unrelated to me, not my *s'tarei.* My breathing began to even out. Blood steamed, sinking into moss-laden earth. *Mother Moon, all three of us still alive. What luck.* "See if they carry anything of use. Redfist, are you hale?"

"Just sorry t' miss the fight, that's all," he grumbled. "He fights mun well, that Gemerh."

I am in no mood to hear you sing his praises. "Mun well indeed." They all had purses, no doubt full of stolen coin. I subtracted another flint and steel from the archer's limp body. Flies gathered, drawn immediately by death. I wrinkled my nose; trees continued whispering in the soft breeze. The edges of the sawlike ferns were dewed and dripping with blood, Darik had shown no mercy. *Now I know his measure as an opponent. Tis worth something, is it not?* "Let us hope they were not an advance party."

The barbarian began to say something, but a curious look crossed his face. "Aye, lass. Let us hope. If ye say so."

I clicked my tongue. "Messy." I emptied the four purses onto a larger piece of cotton cloth I found tucked into the pikeman's belt. "Bandits with *pikes.* Mother Moon. What next?"

The purses yielded a fair bit of *kiyan* and plenty of square Hain copper sequins. I flipped the Hain currency off to the side—their copper sequins were mixed and of little value—and concentrated on the rest. *Kiyan,* a few sundogs, and several Shainakh coins, heavy dark russet gold. "Look at this. Shainakh red Rams. How nice."

I divided the coin into three roughly equal piles, put one of the piles in my purse. "Here, you twain. Take your share, tis as even as I can make it. Any other usable gear?"

"Some smoked leather," the barbarian said. "A few gold chains."

"You keep those. G'mai?" It took an effort of will not to call him *s'tarei'sa,* the honorific for an adult male.

He stood next to me, his head up, scanning the forest. Standing guard, I realized. That sparked fresh irritation—I should have thought of it. "Nothing I need. Tis meant for your purse, Kaia'li."

I shrugged. "If you wish it." If he was to give me coin, I would not complain. I had lost all my gear leading Redfist out of Hain, and I had both of them to feed as well.

If I do not simply leave them both when I take ship. Why have I not slipped free of them? Twould be simple enough.

Redfist scraped up his part. "Ye be mun fair, lass. I did nae earn this."

"Most people do not earn what they suffer. Tis only luck. We could lose it all tomorrow." *Just like I lost all my gear in Hain.* I sniffed. The air smelled clean of danger, and my nape had stopped its prickling. Still, I did not like the leaf-touched silence.

"We should go," Darik said. Softly, but with an edge. Did he feel the same uneasiness?

Well enough. I stood. My thigh ached. I had not looked at the bruise since the bathhouse, and it had been rapidly darkening then. "Are there more?" My tone was just as quiet, and just as edged.

"Almost certainly." He glanced down at me, smiling faintly. It looked like a grimace of pain, on him. "My apologies, Kaia'li."

I took a deep breath of air tainted with death, wished for a wind from the sea. Wished to be on a ship, bound anywhere but here, wind in the sails and the rigging singing me to sleep. "For what?"

"Acting the fool. I am new to this." His dark eyes were a little easier now, something flickering behind their screen of politeness.

I shrugged. "See if you like the feel of his bow. Have you practiced archery?"

"Of course."

Ridiculous. Of course he had. Every *s'tarei* did. The mystery deepened. Where was his *adai*? Was he like me—without a twin? If so, why was he here? And what had the gaud of a necklace to do with him?

Cease your thrashing, Kaia. Worry later, move now. "Let us be gone. This way."

We left the carcasses behind and went due north. I strode

silently, thinking furiously, and only stopped when the Sun was low in the west and it was time to make camp. We had left the bandits far behind, though we had no doubt left a trail.

Redfist cleared a firecircle and I gathered deadfall. Twas a little damp, and I was not sure if we would be able to make fire. I wished I had thought to pack a tinderball or two in the cache. *Ah, well. Next time. If there is a next time. Though twould be easier if I could stop losing gear.* I crouched down, striking sparks and cursing my luck.

"Are you *i'yah'adai*?" Darik asked quietly.

I stared at him. After a moment he gestured at my hands. "Too tired to use Power?" he repeated in commontongue, as if I did not speak G'mai. Three fat, limp coneys dangled from a strap.

A dinner that flies to the stewpot. Then again, this was the best season for small game, even without traps. Coney-hunting with a bow was a highly skilled art.

"I was born without Power." *And thank you so much for reminding me, s'tarei'sa.* I was even beginning to *think* in G'mai again, a thorny pleasure at best. I had not allowed that language to cross my tongue in so long, except in late-night singing of songs so old their words were like the hiss and creak of water under a keel, barely noticed.

Darik's dark eyebrows drew together. "You..."

The sparks finally caught. I blew on the smoking tinder, gently, willing it to burn, and the barbarian stared at me from where he was untangling some brush that looked relatively dry.

The sticks began to crackle. I glanced up at the white curl of smoke rising and cursed internally. If we were remarked by other bandits we would have trouble, and while I thought we were more than equipped to handle startled and stupid road-wolves I did not cherish the idea of a melee. "Damn," I whispered. My gaze fell on the G'mai again, his loose easy grace and the *dotanii* above his shoulders. "Get those skinned and into the pot the barbarian carries. I will find meatroot."

"There is some, twenty paces that way." He tipped his head a little to indicate direction. I had chosen a thorn bracken to one side, merely to cut down on the approaches to our camp. "I may—"

By the gods. "No. Redfist, watch the fire. I wish some quiet, I shall return with meatroot."

The G'mai nodded. His hair fell forward over his dark eyes. I could not stop looking at him, stealing his face. It was such a strange, hurtful thing to see another G'mai, the bones so similar to mine, hear another G'mai voice after so long.

Hurtful, but pleasant in its own way. Like lancing an infection.

He did not belong here among the moss-hung trees and the velvet-covered boulders, the sword-edge ferns and the shades of gray and green. He belonged in a House, in silks and velvets, against the arching, beautiful architecture the G'mai love.

I tore my eyes away and stood. Redfist brought the pot, Darik paced over to the other side of the thorn bracken to skin the animals. He would have already gutted them away from the camp. The skins would sell in Vulfentown—fat sleek coneys were always in demand.

I found the meatroot and dug up four large ones, leaving plenty for the patch to replenish itself. I washed them in the stream, singing a little chant of thanksgiving, and washed my face. The water was cold, and felt good.

I made my way to the camp, seeing firelight through the trees before I could smell the smoke. Salt-freighted wind came in off the coast, too, twould carry the smoke and alert anyone inland to our presence. There was nothing to be done for it.

Had I been *adai* I could disguise the smoke, or surround our camp with confusion. Had I been gifted with even the smallest touch of—

I shook my head, angrily, the necklace moving between my breasts. I had left that part of myself behind—the part that wished I had been born with Power. The part that sobbed to sleep every night, the part that begged the gods for some measure of belonging, some mark that I was worthy to be one of the People.

"No." I held my hand out. Felt the lash of the warmaster's cane against my fingers, a correction and chastisement. It hurt as much as it ever had. "*No.*"

My hand throbbed. I made a fist, and my fingers ached. I shook them out, picked up the meatroot I had dropped. Stalked back to the fire, my boots landing with more force than necessary. Why bother stepping lightly?

The pot hung on a makeshift tripod over the fire that would bear careful watching. I dropped the meatroot in front of Redfist. "Well done," I said. He had used rawhide thongs, probably taken from the bandits, to lash the tripod together.

"Aye. Your *cor'jhan* there—"

"Corszhan?" I tried to accent the word as he did. Twas always good to pick up words where one could; sometimes they were better than gold.

"Word for a..." He was at a loss for the proper term before his face lit up. Perhaps he was not stupid, he was only unused to the trade-language of the Lan'ai Shairukh. "A suitor! A suitor. A betrothed."

Oh, Mother's tits. "He is only a G'mai. I have no intention of doing anything other than sending him on his way as soon as possible. Just the same as you." I stared at the barbarian, knowing my eyes would reflect the firelight with gold. "Both of you are annoyances I will be well rid of very soon."

"Oh, aye, no doubt, lass." He picked up the meatroot, cutting and dropping them into the incipient stew. One of them had added baia, the plentiful, pungent herb called *poor man's woundheal.* "Well rid of two problems. Aye. Anyhow, he—your Gemerh—put this 'un."

"Kind of him, to be sure. He has probably run off with the skins and his purse." I was warming to this theme when Darik melted out of the gathering dark behind Redfist. I shut my mouth, ashamed and furious at the same time, the crystal a warm lump against my breastbone. "*Both* of you are annoyances, and I will take you far as Vulfentown. Then you may go where you wish, together or apart, I care little. But you shall travel no further with me."

"We may go where we like when we reach Vulfentown?" Darik sank down by the side of the fire. He had a handful of pipriweed, and he threw some into the bubbling pot. It began to smell savory. Even more annoying, my mouth filled with water at the scent.

"As you like." I settled my chin on my hand. Ferns rustled as the wind rose, dusk sending invisible streamers through the trees. "As long as you leave me in peace, I care little."

Darik nodded. "I heard you sing last night. The Lay of Creation."

A graceful change of subject, worthy of a G'mai. I nodded, pulled my knees up and hugged them, staring into the fire. The damp wood burned amazingly well.

Redfist looked at Darik, and then dropped another handful of chopped meatroot into the stew. "Ye were nae chasing me, then?"

Darik shrugged. "I was chasing a *dauq'adai.* I had no choice."

My heart thumped again, sourness rising in my mouth.

"If it belongs to the lassie, why were ye chasing it? And what's a dawukaddaye?" The barbarian's ginger eyebrows drew together.

"Excuse me." I sounded polite enough, though all the breath had left me in a rush. "A *dauq'adai*?"

Darik nodded. "So it is." He turned his gaze to Redfist. "A *dauq'adai*—"

I tore it off over my head, almost catching one of my braids in the process. "This is a Seeker? *Is it?*"

Darik nodded again. "Yes, Kaia'li. Tis a Seeker, and I—"

"Take it from me." My hand was shaking. The flawed gem danced at the end of its chain. "*Take it back!*"

"I cannot. You know better. You are G'mai, you *have* to be, there is no other explanation. You know the forms, you have a *dotanii*—and I see the stamp of a House on you. I cannot tell which one yet, but give me time."

"*Take it back!*" I made it to my feet, the words pitched just below a scream, my throat aching with the force of it. The chain bit my fingers, I had clenched my fist so tightly. And why did it seem heavier, like true silver instead of cheap lightmetal?

"Twas beginning to crumble when I came to Hain." He spoke deliberately, quietly, as if I were a wounded animal in need of soothing. "It slipped from my hand in a city street. I searched, in something of a panic, and finally found a streetseller had found it and given it to her pimp. The pimp was knifed, the Seeker taken by a petty thief, who bartered it to a barbarian in a game of cards. And then, a G'mai *adai'sa* picked the barbarian's pocket—"

"*Stop it!*" I screamed. "*Stop!*" My voice bounced and echoed off the trees, the wind bending treetops. Leaves fluttered down to the forest floor.

"Now, lass," Redfist said, tentatively, "no need t' get—"

"*Take it back!*" My throat swelled with the enormity of the shout.

Darik shook his head, solemnly. "I found it hanging on a whitebark branch, three silver Hain sequins underneath. Yet it had begun to heal itself. The moment your flesh touched it, life began to return to the *dauq'adai.*"

The crystal hit him in the chest, its chain slithering, and his face changed slightly. I had seen irritated *s'tarei* before. He certainly looked the part now, his black eyes narrowing and his mouth firming.

My aim is true, I thought blankly, part of an old teaching rhyme. My hands shook. I wanted a swordhilt to steady them, restrained myself with a massive effort that left me sweating. "You will *not* say such things to me," I informed him in the coldest tone I possessed. "I am not *adai.* I was thrown from of my House because I have no Power, and I have done quite well for myself. You may sleep at my fire tonight, but the morn I wish you *gone*, and if you are not, I will leave you both to die in the woods. I *do not care.*"

Darik held the necklace up. Its glittering speared my eyes. I wanted it back in my hand, the feel of the silver against my flesh. "Take it, and I will leave you be. Tis not polite to throw a gift at its giver. You were taught better manners."

My stomach revolved, thank the Moon I had not eaten anything since morning. *I want it. I want it, I will not take it. I cannot.* "Tis a *dauq'adai,*" I said tonelessly. "It has nothing to do with me."

His face did not change. Did not he *understand*? "Perhaps not. But tis healing itself, Kaia. You can see as much. Perhaps it is a flawed Seeker. Such things happen." His tone was reasonable, soothing, he spoke in G'mai. The words sounded silken in his mouth. "Pardon me, I do not seek to anger you."

I took in a deep, coughing breath. Sat back down, heavily.

Redfist stared at me, his eyes wide and green in the firelight. He was dying to ask the question again, could not quite bring himself to do it. "Tis a Seeker." Pointlessly, in commontongue, the explanation felt strange to be giving to a barbarian. "Meant to find an *adai*—a twin—for a *s'tarei*, a G'mai man, when he reaches his adulthood and has not found a twin inside his House or at the festivals, but has not died either. Tis a powerful piece of magic, and it acts as a northneedle, guiding the *s'tarei* to the *adai*. They are called *dauk'qa'adaia*—the Everstars—because they guide with a constant light. Still, they fade after a while if they do not find what they seek."

I did not tell him the rest. The failing of the Everstar means the failure of a *s'tarei's* life as well. The songs and poems that praised the Seekers also spoke of their doom, time slipping away, and the searching and longing each *dauq'adai* contained.

Redfist dropped a last handful of chopped meatroot into the pot. He grunted. I found it absurdly comforting that he cared so little.

I found my voice anew. "Obviously this one is so weak, the presence of any G'mai female would have triggered it. Take it back, Darik. You are many long leagues from home, I would suggest you go back to G'maihallan and find your twin. You have waited long enough." My voice faltered a little. *I am not adai. I am not. I will not think of it.*

He said nothing.

He watched the fire, light caressing his face. He did indeed have a full share of beauty. It hurt to see, deep in my chest where the worst pain always lodges, that of a heart-wound.

"You should go back. *S'tarei'sa.*" I used the inflection that made it an honorific again, the one used for any *s'tarei* by G'mai girls before their adulthood ceremony.

He flinched slightly, as if struck. His fingers spasmed shut around the necklace. "I wish to gift it to you. Please." He used the formal inflection in G'mai, the one that was not—quite—a command. But twas close. Very close, as if he was accustomed to commanding and only stopped himself with an effort of will.

I swallowed bile. The wind had slacked a little, but still carried a breath of the sea. "I am not *adai*."

As often as I said it, the words still tasted of bitterness and shame.

"Nor am I." His mouth twisted humorlessly. "Yet I carried it. Are you afraid?"

"Of course not." It was reflexive, to answer his challenge. "I fear nothing." *I have faced much worse than you,* s'tarei'sa.

"Then you can prove it, can you not?" It was the oldest trick, and one I had fallen for many a time as a child. But I was too old to fall prey to it now.

Truly, I was. "That will *not* net me, G'mai."

"Then perhaps this will. Take it, or be responsible for my death. I am oath-bound, Kaia'li." He did look at me then, dark eyes in the firelit darkness.

"I know you are." I shook myself. "But I *cannot.*"

His jaw set. He was determined. "You must. Unless you wish to kill me yourself."

"I am too weary for swordplay tonight." I yawned to prove it, a pantomime of exhaustion. "Mayhap tomorrow."

Darik tossed the necklace, a passionlessly accurate throw. It landed near my boot, and I had to look down to see the crystal glittering as soon as it came near me, sparkling and flashing. *Now who is tossing gifts, G'mai?* But I did not say it.

"Briyde." It was a long breath of wonder from the barbarian. "Tis nae the same bit o'metal."

"It is," I said dully, and *knew* it was. I had thought it might be a *dauq'adai,* and I had kept it anyway. I had been unable to give it back to the barbarian. A piece of G'mai; no matter how I told myself I was no longer of my people I still hungered for it. Still ached for the feel of it. "If I accept it, he will follow me and I will *never* be free of this annoyance."

"Is nae such a bad thing to keep a pair of swords for using," the barbarian pointed out. "And ye could steal more wi' him watching yer back."

I considered the G'mai man. "Can you steal? Are you a thief?" *Why does he not take offense? No* s'tarei *would cherish being spoken to so.*

"If necessary," he said. "If you demand it."

I looked down at the necklace. My voice stuck in my throat, finally worked its way free. "I will not wear it. Tis for an *adai.*"

"Keep it until..." Darik stared intently, as if trying to read my face. "Until some better plan for its use arrives. Tis embarrassing to give a woman a *dauq'adai* and have it thrown back."

What would you know of embarrassment, G'mai? "Equally embarrassing to possess no Power and have a G'mai *s'tarei* give you a Seeker," I flashed back. "I cannot wear this, Darik."

He did not look away, kept studying my face. "You are not required to. Tie it to your sword, I do not care. Just keep it for a short while. Until Vulfentown, perhaps."

"Then you will leave me be?" *I sound like a child.*

"I will give you peace. I swear it. *Insh'tai'adai, s'tarei, ai.*" It was the most serious oath a *s'tarei* could swear. "Simply keep the Seeker for me, Kaia'li."

I could kill him. But for what? I shook as if with cold, my fingers numb. He had not sought to bring harm to me, for all that harm had been brought.

I dug in my purse and retrieved a single Shainakh Ram. "I will give you this, then. *Luck*. Tis the only thing I know. Face, I take the *dauq'adai* and find your *adai* for you. Haunches, I leave you in Vulfentown and you swear never to follow me again. Will you play?"

His eyes were sorrowful, but sometimes G'mai look sad. It only adds to their beauty. "Have the barbarian toss. I will play."

I threw the coin across the fire. "Toss it, Redfist. Face or haunches."

The barbarian caught it. "Are ye certain, lass?"

The only thing I am certain of is that I wish you both gone. I bared my teeth in what could have been a grin. "Of course. Luck."

"Luck," he replied, and tossed.

The coin spun, circling, and I watched. *Haunches,* I whispered to the coin. *Haunches. Haunches.*

Long ago I learned the trick—if I whispered in just the right way, luck would fall as I wished. I learned to concentrate in a peculiarly fierce but relaxed manner, my entire world narrowing to the fall of the dice or the coin. It stood me in good stead once or twice, though I *had* been accused of witching dice. An accusation I always replied to hotly, with steel-sharp words or steel itself.

It is no witchery to whisper a coin into falling. It is, after all, only a whisper, and seldom used in any case.

The coin flashed, came to rest in Redfist's hand. "Luck," he repeated solemnly, looked down at it. I felt my heart twist with relief. It would be haunches. I *knew* it.

"Tis the face of the Ram." He offered me his hand so I could look for myself. I bolted to my feet and stalked around the chuckling fire.

It *was* the face. The ram's head of the God-Emperor of Shainakh, deeply stamped into red gold. I had seen the coin flip in the air. It should have been haunches. I was lucky with haunches. Had the trick failed?

But the trick never failed me—*ever*. I had once been reduced to my last three *kiyan* in the great city of Taryak, under the gaze of the priestesses of Taryina-Ak-Allat. I gambled them all and won several times, and when I left Taryak I rode on a new horse bought with my winnings, with new armor—and a new bow, and a full purse swinging by my side. I had been laughing like a gods-touched fool.

The trick had failed.

I swore so vilely in commontongue Redfist's ginger eyebrows rose.

I looked at the G'mai man. He was far too beautiful for a deserted campground and a simple fire. No, he deserved something else—a House, one of the singing stone palaces that fill the Blessed Lands. He deserved the tapestries woven by the singers of K'maisharan, graceful Clau furniture, and an *adai* to match.

I could set myself to finding a way to send him home. It would be my penance, my punishment for daring to touch a *dauq'adai*. "Very well," I said through a throat full of sand. "I shall aid you in finding your *adai*. Then you will leave me in peace." I turned on my boot heel and stalked to the edge of the circle of firelight, looked out into the dark.

He said nothing.

Redfist cleared his throat. "I would nae hold ye to that promise, lass, and he shouldna either."

"He does not have to," I cut him off. "So I have sworn, so I will do. Luck."

"Luck?" the barbarian said.

"Yes." My eyes were fiercely dry. I would *not* cry. "Luck. Stir that stew, it had better not burn."

He grunted in reply, evidently determined to leave me to my fate.

I heard the G'mai move. He was behind me, making no attempt to be silent. Heat rising from his skin touched my own, he stood so close. His hand came over my shoulder, dangling the necklace. The crystal flashed, an intermittent wink of light somehow expressing distress.

"I wish I could crush it." My voice was throat-full. "Throw it in a fire and burn it, and be *rid* of you."

His tone was gentle. "I am sorry. Truly, I am. I am late, and for good reason."

"Should you not have been at festivals, searching for your *adai*?" But the thought of him watching a G'mai girl, of the ceremony to celebrate the twinning...no, that hurt me too.

"I will tell you the tale, if you wish to hear."

"I do not want your excuses," I said, bitterly. "Save them for your *adai.* I suppose this means you wish me to return to G'maihallan." *To go back and be shamed anew.*

"No, Vulfentown is good enough. Shaituh is better. I think she travels long and far, this lonely *adai*, and she is not likely to cease wandering soon." He took a step back, another, leaving me my space. I was grateful for it. "I go with you."

"Suit yourself." I slipped the necklace over my head again. Dropped it down the front of my shirt. It was warm this time, and settled against my skin as if it belonged there. I cursed again, softly but with great force, an oath I had learned in mercenary service during the last skirmish on the S'tai Plain against the Danhai.

I had been so sure it would be haunches. The trick had never failed me before. Had he used Power to affect it? I would never know, would I?

What had gone wrong? It seemed getting sotted in that Hain tavern had twisted my entire life off course. Maybe this was all a mead-soaked nightmare, and I would wake with my head on the tavern table and my pockets empty.

I could hope, could I not?

Night-Hunting

His hand closed over my shoulder. "Kaia." An urgent whisper. "Wake."

I sat straight up, my hand curling around a knife-hilt. The G'mai crouched right next to me. "Someone moves on our fire." His mouth barely moved with the words.

It was the dead dark time of night, the midst of third watch. I saw the glitter of Redfist's eyes across the banked fire. He lay on his side as if asleep, a man-mountain strangely still. "The barbarian woke me," Darik continued. "He will play sleeping tarn. I am for night-hunting. You?"

"I shall play tarn too," I said softly. He had to lean close to hear, and I smelled him; leather, cloth, oiled steel. Male. "The better the bait... Take care."

He nodded, and his white teeth showed in a smile. "I shall."

Now why did I say that? I did not care if he was cautious or not...but I had taken the *dauq'adai.* According to custom, I was responsible for him.

As if I were an *adai.* His *adai.* My heart leapt bitter into my mouth.

I lay down again, on my back. My sword lay next to me, I curled my fingers loosely around the hilt. Pulled a few inches free, so it could clear the sheath in a moment.

No. Something tickled my nape. The feeling of danger was too intense. I had not lived so long as a sellsword thief by ignoring that sensation.

I rolled up and took my sword with me, buckled it on so it rode my back as usual. I faded into the trees, moving silently over mossy ground.

I told him to take care. Why?

Do not think on it, Kaia. Think on the business at hand. I strained my ears. Nothing but the ordinary noises of the forest at night—and an almost-silence, the peculiar not-sound of the G'mai man slipping through the trees.

How? How could I *hear* him? He was not clumsy, nor did he make noise. Yet I felt him. Felt his movement, his presence.

The almost-silence stopped, waited—coiled and deadly. I felt faintly queasy. I quelled the feeling, my stomach twisting and releasing.

I was uncharacteristically afraid. Of what?

Motion, stealthy through the forest. I found my nightknives in my hands, their blades painted dark. Two men, less than five paces from me. I smelled them, rotten leather and smoke, the reek of bandits.

Now, Kaia. Now.

I moved without thought. Took one from behind, slitting his throat and stepping away, fading into the trees again. The Moon was shrouded in cloud, better for me. I would lay odds on my night-vision, not theirs.

The second man whipped out his shortsword. I sighed silently. Worse for work in the dark, the gleam of the blade would give him away. On the other hand, he had more reach than my knives now.

I contemplated this, watching him chop the air wildly, and a lick of fire raced across my right arm.

I stumbled back, slashing with a knife in counterattack. The blade cut through empty air.

Nobody there. But who cut me?

What was *happening*?

The bandit, alerted by the sound of a stick breaking under the ball of my foot, leapt for me. I threw myself back, rolled, came up with the knives gone and my sword whipping out of the sheath, meeting his strike. The sound was a sudden smithy's clatter in the hush.

I killed him with a halfmoon stroke, grimaced, and whipped the blood off my sword. Then I ran, silently, in a line straight for the fire. My arm throbbed fiercely.

I heard Redfist bellow and burst out into the clearing. The barbarian's axe smashed down, carving into the head of a squat frog of a man. The sound was a woodsman's axe striking cleanly through a log.

I met another bandit carrying another shortsword, engaged him with a clash. Then it was a straightforward fight, as far as the chaos of any fight can be considered straightforward.

I found my back to the fire, facing down three separate men. I showed my teeth in a feral grin. My right arm hurt, phantom blood sliding down from a phantom slash. I paid no attention. "Who wishes to die first?" I spat in commontongue, my blade held steady in the high-guard.

Two dropped, blood spraying. The stench of a battlefield rolled out around me. I engaged the last one with a side-downsweep, he blocked and slashed in—then fell, his face amazed, mouth gaping open and eyes swiftly darkening with death.

Darik resolved out of the dark, his face full of bloodlust and his swords bloody as well. He twisted his second *dotanii* free of the body savagely, turned to survey the clearing.

My heart pounded like Baaiar drums. For a moment I had been ready to engage him, for the rage in him did not look easily controlled.

Redfist leaned on his axe. "Is tha' all?" His green eyes were lit from within with something chill and fey.

"I believe so." Darik sounded just as savage. His right sleeve flapped a little as he moved, a restless twitch of rage tightly reined.

Blood. A slash high on the arm, on the pad of the shoulder. My heart throbbed high in my throat. "Oh, no." I wiped my sword on a fallen body to clean it, automatically, and slid it back in its sheath.

"I thought you were to play sleeping tarn." Darik wiped his own blades clean. "Douse the fire, barbarian. We do not wish to stay here."

"That wound needs cleaning." I could not stay silent.

"I will not catch the woundrot. I am G'mai." He looked at me, and sudden concern wiped away the cruelty of battle. "You are pale, Kaia'li. Are you well?"

"Hale enough." The ache in my arm intensified. I could *feel* blood dripping, soaking my shirt. It took all my willpower not to clutch at my arm. I knew I was whole, unwounded.

If I am not adai, I should not feel his pain. Is it truly his pain I feel?

I discarded the question as useless. "I will not leave here until that wound has tending. You will slow us, even if you do not catch woundrot."

He bowed his head, looked at the bloody slash. "Tis nothing. I was clumsy, that is all."

I put my hands on my hips to disguise their shaking and glared at him. "Find baia, Redfist. I will bind a poultice on it, and then we shall take our leave."

"Aye, lass." Quietly, with no trace of anger. "Are ye sure ye're nae wounded? Ye're whiter than a Rijiin hoor."

"I am well *enough*. Fetch me baia, and quickly. Young leaves, small ones." *I do not wish either of you guessing I feel this in my own flesh. It should not be so.*

He blundered off, and I faced Darik. "Let me see." I stepped through the chaos of limp bodies. There were at least seven of them in the clearing. Redfist had been busy.

At least I will not be worrying about him in battle, he is able enough.

Darik submitted, stepping away from the bodies and closer to the fire so I could have a clearer view. I peeled the torn sleeve away, peered underneath. "Mother Moon," I breathed, in G'mai. "Tis only a scratch. You will live."

His dark gaze was a weight on my bowed head. "I hope so." Quietly, soothing.

I dug in my clothpurse for a square of silk and a smaller piece of cotton. I folded the cotton, wishing we could spare the time for hot water to bathe the cut. "We shall have to sew your sleeve." I half-sang it, in G'mai, seeking to soothe him. Like a child, or a frightened animal, though he needed no soothing. He was completely calm.

Except for the tension in his shoulders, and the smell of bloodlust clinging to him. I knew that smell, and it was oddly comforting. It takes a short while for combat-madness to fade, and I have smelled it on many a fellow sellsword. And on myself.

"I think so. Are you well?" The concern of any G'mai man toward a female, reflexive, meaning nothing.

"Hale enough." I feigned more interest in his wound. "You had all the ill-luck of that fight." I felt his eyes on me, more physical weight on my shaking shoulders. I hoped he could not tell.

"I was engaged with two of them, the third came from the side. Sloppy of me. What is your House?"

I shrugged, pressing with my fingers, a little above the cut. My own arm responded with a flare of pain. I drew in a sharp breath through my teeth. "I have no House. They threw me out."

"Are you certain?"

As if I could be uncertain of such a thing.

"I returned from practice to find everything missing from my room," I began, and Redfist came back into the circle of low firelight. He had a fistful of baia, and something my nose identified as woundheal. "I count myself lucky they let me take my *dotanii*. I left without a word. What could I say?"

"Ah." The G'mai had no pat reply for that.

I took some of the baia from Redfist. "My thanks. And woundheal. How did you find that?"

"Follow m'nose," he said, gruffly. "Tend to him, I'll strip tha bodies."

I nodded, and took the baia in my mouth to bruise it. The pungency of the herb tore at my eyes, hot water rising to fill them. I stripped the leaves from the woundheal while I chewed, bruised them, and applied them to the slash. The resulting flare of pain made my eyes water even further, but I could pretend it was the baia. One tear trickled hot down my cheek, another.

I spat the baia paste onto the square of folded cotton and pressed it to the wound. Hissed again at the flare of pain.

"Tis only a scratch." Darik shifted his weight, fretfully. Did he find the pressure of my fingers annoying? "I have had worse."

"Hold this." I took his left hand and pressed it over the

cotton. The stinging of the baia and the woundheal burned in my own arm as a brand. I snapped out the piece of silk, tied it to his shoulder. *A fair field-dressing, Kaia, even if not one of your best.* "There."

I found his face inches from mine. He watched me closely; he was sweating, too. I felt the water on my own skin, and let out a pent breath. "You will live," I repeated.

He held queerly still, still as a stone. "I certainly hope so." No trace of sarcasm. Merely quiet politeness. "My thanks, Kaia'li."

I killed the smile seeking to reach my mouth. The fiery hurt in my shoulder eased a little. The woundheal would help with the pain, and baia was deadly to sepsis. Even if he was G'mai, it was never wise to take chances with woundrot.

I took a cautious step back. He stayed absolutely still.

His eyes held mine.

Tis not possible. It is not possible, not possible, impossible, no. There was simply no way it could be possible.

I had never broken my word before. Now I thought of it. I could escape them easily enough, I was sure. In Vulfentown, I could take ship for anywhere on the Lan'ai.

The longer I traveled with them, the more I would feel bound to him. If I felt his pain in my own flesh, just as an *adai* feels her *s'tarei*'s hurt—

No. It was *not real.* The *dauq'adai* had to be causing this newest complication. I was sorely tempted to leave him behind. Tied to a tree, if possible. Or simply *behind*, away from me.

But what if the *dauq'adai* also triggered twinsickness? I had no desire to die of longing and fever, and if the Seeker could force me to feel his pain it could certainly also force me into the sickness of an *adai* whose *s'tarei* was absent for too long. Now that I had met him and taken a Seeker from him, was it too late?

I am not adai. *There is some mistake. It is a fluke, a chance accident. Nothing more.*

I turned on my heel. Breaking the hold of his eyes on me caused a small, sharp pain, like a needle going into the skin. I was surprised there was not a sound—a snap, perhaps, or a ringing cut short like a chiming blade sinking solid into flesh.

I set about the task of checking the dead for useful items, though Redfist had already. I tried to tell myself to cease dallying, to keep my mind on what was occurring around me, to stop acting like a silly little spoiled G'mai girl. I would *not* lose my head because a man looked at me. He was a G'mai man, a *s'tarei* seeking an *adai*, and I was not what he wanted.

It was *impossible.*

How could I explain feeling his pain? Or the unsteady panic I felt at the thought of leaving him behind and perhaps falling victim to a lost twin's wasting sickness?

I cursed under my breath and ripped my mind from that line of thought. I would not let it be possible. I would search for an *adai* for this man, and hand the Seeker over to her when I found her. She would be a slight, beautiful G'mai girl, stranded through some quirk of fate and fortune. She would look up at him with large, dark, grateful eyes, and thank him in fluid G'mai while she clasped his hands.

I swore again, kicked a limp body—the frog-shaped man. They possessed nothing of consequence, and they were dead, breath and life both wasted.

Sometimes I hated life at the sword's edge.

Wordplay

I set a punishing pace for the rest of the night, but I heard no complaint. In fact, Redfist seemed to enjoy it. He even whistled a little once dawn broke, a sad little Skaialan air I set myself to learning. Twas beautiful, if a bit crude, and I could imagine it played on a strinlin or a pipe. Darik said nothing, simply kept up, our pace enough even for him.

We stopped near noon, and I chewed a piece of flat journeybread while perched in the branches of a moss-cloaked toak tree. The barbarian and the G'mai conversed in low voices near a shrouded rock, and I did not try to hear what they said. They shared rations, and once there was low male laughter.

I had longing thoughts of strangling them both.

Once I was finished with my journeybread, I hopped down from the tree, landing softly, and set off again. They followed, and I moved faster.

I made for the coast road. I was confident we could handle bandits now, and the road would take a full day off the journey. There were tiny hamlets scattered along its narrow ribbon, fishing towns and the like, each with its charter declaring itself an independent entity, free of the Shainakh or the Hain. I could buy thread at one of them, to repair Darik's shirt. If perchance someone had a tub and some hot water for rent, I would dearly love a bath. And some kafi—I missed kafi in the mornings, the smell of it, at least.

Arjux Crossing might even have a healer. Doryen Innkeeper would know. I could pay a healer to take the cut from Darik's shoulder.

As soon as I realized what I was thinking, I increased my pace.

I was soon running, leaping fallen logs, flashing through the forest, my entire mind taken with the problem of moving at top speed and avoiding pitfalls that could break a leg. Twas a relief, yet soon enough I was forced to stop, leaning against a tree, sweating and gasping and smelling my own sour scent.

I reeked of fear, a scent I associated only with the people I killed.

The forest here changed, the moss less verdant green and more smoky gray, hanging in long strings. Slashwood boiled up, a sign of clearing left to grow back. The undergrowth would make further travel difficult until we reached the road.

I closed my eyes, breathing deeply. Sweat soaked through my shirt, chilling my skin. It was a cloudy day, the air still and hushed as if a storm approached. The air was full of salt and the green promise of rain. Of course, in this part of the Lan'ai Shairukh it rained six days out of ten, we had been lucky to escape a downpour so far.

Why was I afraid? I had only promised to find his *adai*, I had not promised to travel alone with him. I could look for his *adai* anywhere in the world. I would not fall prey to twinsickness. He was not my *s'tarei*. Twas as simple as that.

If I had any Power the *dauq'adai* might have spoken to me, and told me where to find his blasted *adai*. Then again, if I had any Power, I would not have met him at all.

Or would I? Maybe at a Festival, our eyes would have met, and maybe he would have offered me his hand.

How still and silent it was. Had I lost them? I had not meant to, I had simply bolted. Blindly as a coney chased by bellhounds.

My breathing lost its harsh tearing quality, and I shivered. The air was absolutely still, cold creeping into my skin.

This deep in a dark part of the forest, tall trees reached toward the sky, swordfern and milkyweed carpeting the space beneath between the smaller hunched shapes of slashwood peppering the forest floor. Great boulders thrust up, each cloaked with moss and fallen leaves.

I kept my back to the tree and waited.

Eventually, I heard the near-silence of Darik's approach. He appeared, followed by Redfist. The barbarian's eyes were ringed with dark smudges, and he moved stiffly. I felt a burst of guilt, strangled it. I had not *forced* them to follow me. I had told them to go away and leave me be.

I was not responsible for either fool.

I set my shoulders, seeking to ignore the small voice that informed me they were simply seeking to act honorably. I had saved Redfist's life, or so we thought at the time.

Darik looked much the same, except he was pale, and the sleeve of his shirt flopped, caked with stiffened blood.

They came to a stop, and Redfist coughed a little. "Well, are we resting here, lass? I think I smell water."

I pointed. "That way. I was thinking deeply, and did not hear you fall behind. My apologies."

"None needed." Redfist waved it away. "Well, then, let's find a streamlet t'fill our flasks and a good bivouac, eh? I wouldnae mind some food, either."

"I will hunt." It was the least I could do. "Make a fire, I will find you."

Redfist nodded, prodded at Darik. "I can hunt," the G'mai man said, his dark eyes on me. "You look pale, Kaia."

"You are wounded, I am not," I said shortly. "Besides, tis my turn to bring a few coneys or a treeleaper. Find a defensible place, if you can."

He nodded a little. "The wound is a small matter."

I glared at him. "If you do not wish to do as I say, you may choose another path to travel. Clear, Darik'aan?" It was a pun on his name, meaning *stubborn.* A word often used for balky beasts and children.

"Very clear, Kaia'li'ta."

He meant to put an additional pun on what he already had called me, *Kaia'li,* a small, sharp precious thing. The inflection he used made it into "temperamental," the word for a high-strung horse. Still, I started, as if pinched in a sensitive spot.

"Merely Kaia." *Kaialitaa,* brave little beauty. The name my mother had given me. It was a beautiful name. *Kai* could mean sharp, or brave, and the extra *a* added the "beautiful" meaning.

G'mai are addicted to poetry, wordplay, exchanges of sharp insults, and pretty turns-of-phrase.

I did not wish to play this game with him. I turned away.

"Why do you not ask my name?" he asked in G'mai. "Are you afraid?"

I did not answer. I did not trust my tongue.

Never Push a Pinquill

I found the stream, broad and deep enough for troutfish, and spent a chilly half-candlemark or so with my arms submerged, tickling them out of the water. I lost two, cursing inside my head and quieting, before I caught four beauties in a row. I gutted them and sang my short prayer of thanksgiving. I found a handful of long grass and improvised a strap to tie around their tails, carried them back to where a curl of smoke rose from a well-laid fire.

I did not have to seek very hard; I could hear Darik's presence like wind in the trees. I was quickly growing accustomed to it.

I had to halt this soon.

Could I?

When we find his adai, *he will go his way and I will go mine. If I grow fevered 'twill only teach me not to be silly. I have suffered fever before, and always survived.*

Yet I was G'mai. What if, after so long spent away from my native land, I had fastened onto the first *s'tarei* seen? I did not know if such was possible, and I had no one to ask.

A familiar quandary.

I found a small stand of pipriweed and another small stand of curya, took a little bit of both. I was growing heartily tired of meatroot.

I stepped between two boulders, greeted by the sight of Redfist sprawled on his back, fast asleep. Darik had a flattened piece of toak bark and some meatroot he was tearing the small roots from to prepare for cooking. "I thought you would bring fish. Tis a large stream."

"It is," I agreed. "More meatroot. I am glad it is in season."

"It likes the damp." He glanced up at the sky. "It may rain."

"As long as tis not raining swords." I made the traditional swordseller's reply, laid the troutfish down next to him. The pipriweed and the curya followed. "I weary of being attacked."

He made an affirmative sound, setting the meatroot on a smallish flat rock they had built the fire against. It would cook them nicely, and if he put the troutfish atop the toak bark and I could find another piece of it, we could broil the fish between with little effort.

He held up another piece of the bark. "I found it." Quiet, a restful voice.

I swallowed what I intended to say and retreated to the other side of the fire, a welcome warmth working back into my stream-chilled arms.

Tis not possible. The voice inside my head repeating it so loudly and often now seemed thin and unsure. I sighed, lowering myself down. There was long grass here too, the huge boulders ringing this campsite kept the trees back enough to make a clearing. The canopy of branches overhead might block a light rainfall too. All in all, a good place to spend a night.

I slid down to lay on the grass, with a sigh. My leg hurt. I did not wish to see what the bruise looked like now. I grimaced a little, and let out another sigh. Sometimes the rest is worse than the moving, after a battle.

"Your leg," he said. "High up. When did that happen?"

"A Hain. Kicked me during a fight. Tis nothing."

He nodded, laid the fish down with finicky care, and balanced the toak bark atop the meatroot. He placed the second piece of bark on the top, weighted it all down with a handy rock. Then he added another piece of deadfall to the fire, making it snap and hiss. "What is your truename, Kaia'li?"

"You will not tell me yours. Why should I tell you mine?" My tone was sharper than necessary, a warning. If there was a fragile truce between us, it could still break with the wrong word.

"If I told you mine, you would be forced to tell me yours. I wish to avoid forcing you." He examined the fire critically. They had made a good job of it. Smoke and heat would make the troutfish a delicacy.

"You could not force me. Tis not possible." *I am Kaia Steelflower. I am not* forced, *not if you wish to remain breathing.*

He shrugged. "Still. There is a saying in G'mai: *never push a pinquill, or an* adai."

My teeth gritted together. I knew that saying, and hearing it in commontongue obliquely unsettled me. "I am not *adai.* I cannot be. I was born without Power."

"Are you so certain? Who is your mother?" He returned to G'mai. It almost hurt to hear the pure language used so softly. The way he spoke it was close to a caress.

I set my teeth to endure it. "Dead," I informed him, curtly. "I tire of this." Yet I had spoken in G'mai, and used the wrong inflection—the personal, instead of the communicative.

As if I was an *adai.* His *adai.*

I am weary unto death. It makes no difference.

He smiled, something wonderful to see. No, he did not belong in the trackless forest. "Rest, then." His inflection was the most intimate one possible. "I will keep watch."

"You are wounded." I stifled a yawn. I forgot to change my inflection again, still spoke as if he was personally known to me.

"A scratch. Not worth your worry, Kaialitaa." A singsong, so soothing I almost missed my truename being spoken. As it was, I only felt a faint alarm.

"How did you..." I was warmer, and sleepy, and the smell of cooking was wonderful too. A sellsword learns to take sleep where she finds it, especially after a night battle and a day of hard travel.

"Not hard to guess, you looked so amazed. Tis a beautiful name." It seemed I could feel his eyes, even when I closed mine. "A beautiful name for an *adai.*"

I. Am. Not... I began, once again, to think something I did not believe. I fell asleep halfway through.

Hunger Is the Best Sauce

"Food, lass," Redfist said, and I sat up, rubbing at my eyes.

"How long did I sleep?" The sleepsand was not bad but I still felt groggy, as if I had just achieved dreaming and been rudely shaken loose.

"I do nae know, K'ai, I was asleep meself. D'rik woke me." The barbarian had washed his face, but still looked worse for wear, his linen shirt limp and leather vest darkened with sweat. His trousers were distinctly dirty.

I did not look any better. My braids were full of leaves and dirt, and blood marked my clothes. My fingernails would have been grimy if not kept so ruthlessly short. I smelled now of sweat, blood, dirt—and fish. A more unappetizing bouquet would be hard to imagine.

Redfist handed me a baked meatroot and a handful of walcress. The main course was troutfish, broiled almost perfectly, lying on a bit of toak bark. All other considerations became secondary.

We ate with good appetite, near the warm fire. Redfist settled down to my left, and Darik to my right. Darik ate slowly, chewing thoughtfully, but I wolfed mine. I did not care that I ate with my fingers. Some of the fish was a little too hot, but I cared little for that either.

"I know tis only fish," Redfist said finally, after chewing and swallowing at least as fast as I did. "But tis the best fish I think I've had for a season or so."

I made a wordless sound of agreement, because my mouth was full. I swallowed, and took a long drink from my waterflask. "All it further requires is a cask of mead." I smiled, for once not thinking of walcress stuck in my teeth. "And a roaring fire, and a clean bed—"

"And a bath!" Redfist finished, over my laughter. Twas a companionable sound. Even Darik smiled.

I juggled the meatroot from hand to hand to cool it, my hunger abated a little. "Watch. Now you see—" I tossed it in the air, "now you *do not*!" I laughed, and Redfist's eyes were gratifyingly wide. I leaned over, plucked the meatroot from his ear. "Ah, what is this you have? A fine earring, m'lord barbarian."

"How did you—" His eyes widened even further, their green light and merry.

"You should see me toss knives." I broke the meatroot open, a puff of steam escaped. I took a little of the curya Darik had scattered over the fish and stuffed it into the meatroot, blew to cool it. "I was the best in my House at the tossgames. Quick hands, you see."

"Aye, I can believe it," Redfist said. "And you, master Gemerh?"

Darik made a short clipped sound. "No time for games. Too busy training."

I glanced at him. He paid attention to his food, eating neatly. I felt a little ashamed of my lack of manners, then angry because I should not be shamed. I had done very well for myself. I was famous on the Lan'ai Shairukh coast as the queen of thieves and a sellsword worth red Shainakh gold. So what if this G'mai who had probably never seen Antai thought me a mannerless lout?

"I wish I had, though." Darik's tone turned wistful. "I would like that gift. It seems a gentle thing."

My anger shamed me further. "I could show you how." A grudging marker of the truce between us. "Tis not so difficult."

"Would you? Perhaps once we reach the town?" He brightened visibly.

My shame intensified. He sounded like a child promised a treat. "Perhaps." I sought another subject. "This is a true feast."

"Hunger is the best sauce." Another G'mai proverb, but delivered hopefully.

I restrained the urge to spit. How could he sound so…well, placatory? "I hope we remain undisturbed. I may lose my patience." I scanned the trees, as if bandits might leap forth at any moment.

"I would hate t' see that," Redfist grumbled, and I gave him a look that could have chipped a stone. "How much longer to a town, lass?"

"Another day to Arjux Crossing." I settled into thinking aloud. "Tis a fishing town before that, I think. Maybe more than one. If we could have gone a little farther today we might have found one, but tis not likely to find an inn this far from the Crossing. The coast road is near, we shall make good time. The Crossing has an inn I know, and I will stay there at least a night. Vulfentown is another four days beyond, mayhap two by horse…but you cannot ride any shaggy pony they are likely to have in the Crossing; not enough market for horseflesh there unless you spend more coin than I would like. Perhaps you could find one in Shaituh, or further inland at Pesh."

"Where be ye headed after Vulf'ntown?" Redfist split open his own meatroot.

"I cannot tell." *Tis truthful enough.* "Eat, large one. I want a full night's rest. Between the three of us, it means shorter watches and more sleep."

"True," Darik broke in. "Who takes the first watch?"

"I will," Redfist said. "I'm rested."

"Good. I will take second." Darik did not look at me, staring instead into the fire. The light was kind to him.

"Leaving the last watch for me. Very well." I was not thinking *Very well.* I was thinking something more like, *Perfect.* That would give me a start.

I had already decided, waking from a short sleep with my course planned, as often happens. The risk of twinsickness, if I stayed near him and the *dauq'adai* convinced me I was somehow his *adai*, was enough to make a treeleaper's quick panic under my ribs. I could not endure much more of this.

After dinner, Redfist buried the bones a fair way from the fire, and I settled down in my little grassy hollow. Darik moved to sit at my feet, ignoring my glare. "You are kind to the barbarian," he said, in G'mai. "Why?"

I shrugged, yawning. Fishbreath. Ugh. I could barely wait to buy a packet of toothpowder. *Why indeed. Can he not guess?* "I am akin to him. Both of us alone, without clan, House, or country, living by our wits. Not so long ago I was as lonely as he seems." Another yawn took me. I was comfortably full, oddly warm, and safe for the moment.

Good enough. I have snatched sleep in far worse places—in a saddle, during a slashing sleety rain while patrolling a gods-forsaken stretch of the constantly shifting border between the Danhai and the Shainakh Empire. The tribesfolk seemed able to hide behind a single stalk of grass; you could never tell when a bolt would come winging from the dusk or dry noon. Still, it was possible to snatch moments of rest in the saddle. The constant picking-off of scouts and patrols began to seem like the hand of luck or the gods, plucking sellswords from the face of the earth.

I was, at least, lucky *not* to still be an irregular in the God-Emperor's army.

"You seem lonely still." His voice had the singsong intonation again, and the personal inflection. My shoulder throbbed—his must be hurting.

I surfaced from unpleasant memory, blood and grass and thirst even in the cold rain. "You speak in the wrong inflection," I told him, formally.

He nodded as if I had said something profound. "Mmh." Neither an agreement nor an argument. "Do you wish to know my name, Kaialitaa?"

"No." I closed my eyes. It took a long while before I fell asleep. My arm hurt with his pain, and I cursed us both.

* * *

I did not wake until morning, opening my eyes with a faint sense of something awry, confused when daylight greeted me. I sat up and stretched, yawning, and tasted my mouth with a grimace.

Darik sat next to the fire, asleep, his back propped against a boulder. Redfist paced back and forth at the other end of the camp.

I looked at the G'mai man, his eyelashes making two perfect charcoal arcs against his cheekbones, and my entire chest twisted. *Why could I not have been born with some Power? A small crumb, for others had enough and to spare.*

I thought this, as I had not since I was sixteen summers high. He was unshaven, and just as dirty as we were. Yet still, he seemed a statue, each line and curve made for maximum aesthetic effect.

The wind rose a little, tossed the branches, and I felt wetness touch my cheeks. Was it raining? That was all I needed, rain *now*. I would catch lungrot before we reached the Crossing.

I wiped tears away, angrily. The movement caught Redfist's eye. I waited for him to speak, but he did not. "So he sleeps. Who took my watch?"

"We shared it, lass. Ye looked so peaceable, we decided t'let ye rest. Done ye good." The ginger-haired man nodded smartly. "Ye were right pale last night."

"Just lack of a proper bath, and being run out of Hain by the Guard. And a pack of bandits." *Tis your fault, large one.*

It did not trouble him in the least. "Aye."

Darik opened his eyes, immediately awake. "I thought I heard you." He stretched, turned the stretch into a graceful movement bringing him to his feet. "How do you feel?"

He spoke in G'mai, the personal inflection, again. The very tone a *s'tarei* would use with an *adai*. Anger flared red in my chest, died away.

"Very well, thank you," I answered politely, in commontongue. "If we go quickly today, we may well be in an inn by sundown."

"An' I would thank me gods." The Skaialan stretched with a gusty sigh. "Let us break camp, lass?"

"Do as you please." I was hard-pressed to keep a civil tone as I gained my feet in a graceless lunge. "I wish to wash my face. Then we shall see what the road holds."

The Whitegull

The lights of Arjux Crossing glimmered through rainy dusk. I was too wet, cold, and tired to care. We splashed through the freetown's mercifully clear streets, the storm having driven most of the citizens inside their houses and taverns. Half-height walls were manned by crossbowmen in huts built onto the walls themselves, a remnant of the Blood Years when the former God-Emperor had tried to extend his borders to this stretch of coastline. The freetowns had disputed hotly, a loose federation that nevertheless banded together for common war and made the God-Emperor reconsider before his death.

His successor Azkillian afterward turned his attention to the Danhai plains, and the freetowns were allowed to go on their way, some with tax and trade agreements with the Empire, all with a prickly sense of civic pride and freedom that caught like fire all up and down the coast. They quarreled with each other more than anyone else, but woe to the foe who attacked a freetown; for the others would come to their neighbors' aid. It was too dangerous for all to allow a foreign power to intrude on even one of their ilk.

Doryen's inn—the Whitegull—was a comfortable three-story brick and wooden building, very near the wharves but remarkably clean and peaceful. We came through the door into a blast of damp heat and noise that was the commonroom, and I stamped mud off my feet on the thick wovenraff mat. "Doryen!" My battlefield-bellow cut through the noise. I was in no mood to be tactful.

"Who the blasted—" Doryen was near the roaring fireplace, mugs of beer in either hand, setting down the drinks for a group of scream-laughing, worn mercenaries. *Bound for Shaituh.* I noted the *kiyan* one of them tossed to the innkeeper, their hilarity bespeaking much mead. *Tis the only place they could be bound for. Is the Shainakh Empire planning another war? As if they can afford it, Danhai is bleeding them dry.*

"Ah!" Doryen was an exceedingly round, red-faced man with the dark hair and yellow face of a half-Hain. He had acquired unusual height from his mother, a Pesh slave. He saw me, bedraggled and dirty as I was, and his face lit up. "Lady Kaia!" he yelled. "The Iron Flower herself! An honor, an honor!"

He made it across the commonroom the moment Darik entered behind me, then Redfist, soaked to the skin and shivering. He had taken a bad spill in the street, and was coated with mud.

Doryen stopped, his red cheeks going pale. "Ai, lady, what did you bring me? He looks to be a giant!"

"He is," I said, humorlessly, "but even giants need beds. Two rooms, Doryen, bath, and board, for at least three nights. Eight *kiyan*."

"Eight? *Eight?*" He puffed up. He loved this part of the game. "Three Shainakh reds, and not a sundog less. I am not running a hospice!"

"No, last I looked you were running a flea-bitten ramshackle inn. Ten *kiyan*." I was not in the mood, but the barter had to be played. My tone, however, was so sharp it could have cut meat.

"Ten..." The look of disbelief he gave me was practiced and innocent. "Two Shainakh reds or twenty *kiyan*."

"Twelve kiyan, and a Shainakh red if you find me two good horses by tomorrow afternoon."

"Fifteen *kiyan*, and a red for the horses. I will find you fine horseflesh." He rubbed his fingers together to indicate how fine of horseflesh he could find me.

It was too much, but I had taken my fill of walking in the rain. I did not care if it was expensive, I wanted a bath and a bed. And when we left the Crossing, I wanted to be a-horseback.

I held out my hand. "Done," I said, and he touched my fingers with his. "Two rooms, with a watercloset between them."

"Oh, yes. I have always room for my friends." He turned

and led us through the commonroom, up a flight of creaking stairs to the second floor. The pouring rain outside was muted to a soft low sound here, and the occasional burst of noise from the commonroom hardly penetrated once we made it to a far corner of the building. "Timon Taxcollector was asking about you, Lady Kaia," he said soberly, once he was sure nobody else could hear.

I yawned, rubbed at the back of my neck. "What the *drosh* for?" I had no business concerns in the freetowns; the Thieves Guild operated in some of the larger ones but only respectfully. There would be no reason for a tax-collector to speak to me.

"The time you paid the taxes on the inn. With the Ponstahken holding the Maior this season, Timon's head is too big to fit through a decent door, being Ponstakh-kin. He even bought a Pesh bondgirl." Doryen stopped, unlocked a door. "Here is the first room."

What does a tax-collector and a slave have to do with me? But Doryen was an inveterate gossiper, like most freetowners, for any usable piece of information they will give you four of no use at all. I motioned at Redfist and Darik. "Go. Take a bath—I shall be along."

Darik looked as if he wished to speak. He was gaunt and splattered with mud, but the glitter in his eyes and the beauty of his G'mai bones shone through the dirt. The twin hilts of his *dotanii* made him into a grim picture.

Redfist grunted and ducked into the room. "My thanks," he growled over his shoulder.

"Do not think on it, m'lord," Doryen said nervously.

"Is there a door between this room and yours, Kaia'li?" Darik, in G'mai, his tone unwontedly serious.

"There should be." I replied without thinking in the same tongue. "What of it?"

He nodded, and then half-bowed to Doryen. "My thanks, innkeeper." His commontongue was lilted with G'mai, it was a pleasure to hear him speak. A pleasure I scolded myself for.

Doryen looked too shocked to reply.

"Oh, go." I motioned at Darik. He stepped inside the room, I closed the door behind him. "So, Timon is causing you trouble about the cache of coin and gem I left with you for safety. And he has taken the inn apart to find it more than once, and come up empty." *Since his kin are ruling the Maior council this season, you cannot gainsay him, either. There is nothing more galling than a petty freetown bureaucrat.*

"Well, yes." Doryen continued down the hall. He unlocked the next door.

"You lost it." It was the only explanation. "To Timon?"

"Well..." Doryen looked as abashed as it was possible for a round freetown innkeep to look. "The stable-girl, lady. The one with the nasty gleam in her eye."

I remembered her, a sharp thing with curling hair and a tongue that could flay a man in seconds. For all that, she was gentle with horses, even if she did scold their riders for mistreating the beasts.

"The curlyhair wench? I liked her. Come in, Doryen." I dug in my purse, pulled out three of the Shainakh reds by touch. Handed them over as soon as he passed the threshold. The room was just as I remembered, down to the faded bedspread worked with roses and the lead-glass windows. "Will that aid in the payment of your taxes?"

Doryen's jaw dropped. "I hid it in the stable. Under the—"

"And the stable-girl found it, and you've not heard of her since. Well, at least she has some sense." *Even if you have precious little.* I found myself yawning. The heat was delicious after the penetrating rain outside. "If the tax collector comes again while I hide here, I shall make certain he troubles you no more."

Doryen bowed, flushed with relief. "I still have your armor, lady, and your travel-packs. Saddlebags and gear. Tis all stowed safely."

Well, that is good tidings and better luck. "Good. I may need to leave here quietly, Doryen. It is good to know I can trust you."

"Trouble on the road between here and Shaituh. Talk that the crazed flea Azkillian is fighting with the Danhai again. Yet the armies are massing to move south and east." He waited, having been bursting to tell me this.

A few more pieces of gossip clicked into place inside my head. "Pesh. Tis news, that is. Why would he do so?" I dropped down in a hard wooden chair—the mud clinging to me could be cleaned off it with little trouble, and Doryen gave me a grateful look. "By the way, the bandits plaguing the coast road have met with a bit of bad luck. Especially the ones running near Hain with a man who looks like a frog."

"Hm." Doryen nodded. "Tis news too. You are the sixth pair of G'mai I have seen in the past moonturn." He handled the glottal stop better than any other non-G'mai I had ever heard.

Why do I feel I will receive the worst of this conversation? I stared openly at him, my jaw dropping. "Five pairs of G'mai and me?"

Doryen's eyes were bright with interest. "Your man in there is G'mai. Is he the prince?"

"What prince?" I felt a complete idiot. My brain had turned into soup, between the rain, exhaustion, and the relief of finally being inside. Warmth unloosed my shoulders, I heaved a sigh of relief as it reached the small of my back.

"The prince the G'mai are seeking?" Doryen repeated, slowly, as if I was a lackwit. "Never seen you with a captive before. You seem sure of him."

"He is no captive." *If anyone is captive here, tis me. Shackled to a G'mai who thinks I am* adai *and a barbarian without enough sense to come in out of the storm.*

"Then is he your twin?" He knew a little about my people, having run his inn for long enough to collect all sorts of information. Besides, he had asked me once.

I had been drunk enough to reply, that night. Mead breeds truth and loosens tongues.

A sharp, short pain lanced through me. "I am no man's twin. I am to help him find his *adai*, tis all. What prince?"

"The prince the G'mai have left their land to seek," he said, slowly. His eyes were on my face, sharp, missing little. "You mean you have not heard?"

"I do not concern myself with the G'mai. I have other concerns—the first of which is getting the mud out of my clothes. So the G'mai are seeking a prince?" *What prince? Why would one of the Houses leave G'maihallan, and why would five pairs of G'mai be looking for him? Unless he is outcaste, or a kinslayer.* For a moment I felt cold; but I could not think that of

Darik. He could not be a kinslayer, it was not in him.

As if I knew him.

Why was he outside the borders of the Blessed Land, then? It made no sense.

"Survived an attempted palace coup and disappeared without a word. The G'mai are frantic. They sent their own over the sea to find him." Doryen folded his arms. More than food or drink, he loved gossip, and this was juicy.

Palace coup? That means Dragaemir. But there are no Dragaemir princes. "A palace coup? But the only palace is..." I paused. "Someone rebelled against the Dragaemir? How is that possible?"

"Apparently not very successfully," Doryen said dryly. "The rebels must have been crushed, for the prince to be sought so."

I shook my head. It defied imagination. Rebelling against the queen was akin to misusing a *dotanii,* such things were simply not done. I yawned again, rubbed at my forehead, mud crackling in my wet braids. "Is there aught else?" I sincerely hoped not.

"Not that I can bring to mind. If more G'mai come, what shall I tell them?" Doryen wiped his hands on his apron, a rare show of nervousness. But then, I made him nervous the way few other mercenaries could. He owed me favors.

"Nothing. Tis not your task in life to tell them tales of me." Rain brushed the walls, and I was endlessly glad to be hearing it from this side. A bath, a real bed—I could hardly wait.

"As you like, lady. I think some know your reputation by now, though. There is a fair amount of talk."

I groaned, with feeling. "Oh, no. Do not say such things—a minstrel?" Another thought occurred to me. "No. Not *that* one."

"Yes, returned he has, and he has a new song. Full to the brim of the Iron Flower and the King of Thieves." Doryen's eyes sparkled, his mouth twisting as he fought to contain a smile.

I dropped my head back against the chair. "Oh, *no,"* I groaned, again. "You are *jesting.* I thought nobody believed that story!"

"Tis a stirring tale, and delivered with such grace one can hardly help but believe, lady." Doryen retreated to the door, grinning like a dog hearing its master's voice. "I will have a pair of horses for you. The giant cannot ride, though."

I waved a hand. "A saddlehorse for me, and a pack-horse for them when they go on their way. My thanks, Doryen Innkeeper. Tis a great pleasure to find I can still rely on you. If more G'mai arrive, you will warn me?"

He nodded, his hair flopping forward over his eyes. "I shall. My thanks, lady."

"And you have mine, innkeeper." I smiled at him, through the mud and exhaustion. "Just keep that buggering minstrel away from me. Send up some food, if you please."

He grinned even wider and retreated. I rose with a little difficulty—soreness already settling in—and crossed to the window. We were on the wharf side, looking out onto docks, warehouses, and the bay's heaving glimmer. The room was comfortable, rough but clean, and Doryen had good service here. At least I would not be throat-slit in my sleep.

Rain beaded against the diamonds of leaded glass, requesting an entrance that would be denied. Twas lucky we had gained shelter before the worst of the storm.

A G'mai prince. Startling, but not impossible. I was of a noble House myself. But I had not known of a prince among the Dragaemir. He was older than me, how had I not heard of him?

If he *was* Dragaemir, and not of a rebel House. I could not see him as a kinslayer, but I could see him—just possibly—as a rebel. He had a stubborn streak, this G'mai.

One does not rebel against the queen. It is simply not done. So why do they seek him?

I paced to the door of the watercloset between our two rooms, knocked, and entered.

The blue-tiled room glinted under the lights, a privy in its enclosure, a washbasin, and—thank the gods—a fallwater.

Nobody was there, another boon. I stripped down, put my clothes in the basket set in the corner, and selected a bathing-robe. I piled my weapons on my bed and used the tiled fallwater, scrubbing the worst mud off. Wrapped in a freshly laundered robe patterned with kingflies, I sighed as the clean cloth touched my skin.

I went out through my room and down the long red

carpeted hall to the communal bathing room, unwinding my braids as I went.

It was time for a long, hot soak, and some brooding.

A Prince's Name

I lolled against the stone rim of the sunken tub, hot water easing aches and pains I had barely known existed. The bruise on my right thigh was the size of my spread hand, turning a deep unwholesome purple. Stone was slick and warm with the heat of constant baths, steam hung in the air. The walls were mosaics of the Shelt, fishes and artistic treatments of other sea life in the freetown style, elongated and interlocking. Other tubs sat behind screens; the lamps glowed mellow.

Twas close to paradise.

My eyes closed, and my hair unraveled on the surface of the water. Communal bathing is one thing I have always been fond of, even among the G'mai. When everyone was drowsy with hot water, nobody was busy shunning me. It was the one time I had been able to relax among my kin.

Someone else slid into the water. Heat lapped my skin. I opened an eye to see Darik settling back on the opposite side of the circular tub, sighing in relief. "The barbarian should be along. He is scrubbing at mud. Perhaps he will choose another tub, if they have one large enough."

"He might squeeze into this one." Color rose in my cheeks. Twas only the heat. I have bathed with hundreds of people, men, women, eunuchs, children. One more was nothing to make me blush.

I watched Darik under my lowered lashes.

His hair plastered to his forehead, strips of darkness, and the wound on his shoulder was closing well. G'mai are quick healers. He had shaved, and the scar across his throat flushed. A palace coup? A rebellion?

"An'Anjalisiman Kaialitaa imr-Anoritaa, Anjalismir-hai," I said formally in G'mai. "A pleasure and honor to meet you." I used the inflection reserved for greeting royalty. It was as close to an accusation as I could tread without open rudeness.

His face went through surprise, embarrassment, and finally settled on something I could not name. "Tar-Amyirak Adarikaan imr-dr'Emeryn, Dragaemir-hai. An even greater pleasure to meet you, *adai'mi.*"

He used the same inflection. The way a royal *s'tarei* would formally address his *adai.* I stifled the bite of annoyance.

"You should have spoken of your House." I tried not to sound hurt.

The lamplight touched his slick dark hair, ran over his shoulders. "Tis a long, complex story, we had not the time. You were intent on our survival."

It was reasonable, I supposed. And I had not wanted to tell him my own name. "Who *are* you, then? I never heard of a Dragaemir prince born of Emeryn—she was the queen's sister, no?" I could only guess, since the queen had only one sibling, and she had died in my childhood of the same summer fever season that took my mother. I vaguely remembered hearing of the mourning...and whispers of something else, that the queen's sister had not died of the rampant fever but of poison.

Twas merely rumor. We do not kill *adai.* It is the greatest sin imaginable.

He shrugged, his jaw firming and something suspiciously like well-banked anger flickering in his eyes. "The queen disliked her younger sister. I was not allowed the Dragaemir name until four summers ago, at the K'nea Pass." He was back to the intimate inflection. It really was more like singing than speaking, in G'mai. "The Hatai attacked, and I helped to drive them back. I was allowed to carry my name afterward. My mother would have been pleased." His mouth turned down a little at the corners.

Adarikaan. It meant *shining blade.* A fine name for him.

"Adarikaan." I tried the name, in the formal inflection. "A fine name for a prince."

His eyes half-closed, whether from heat or wanting to hide his anger, I could not tell. "Kaialitaa. A fine name for an *adai.*"

"I am not your *adai.*" The *dauq'adai* made a liar of me, shimmering under the water as if I was. The traitorous warmth of it pulsed against my skin.

"What would you lose if you were? I wish never to see the palace again, Kaia'li. I could spend the rest of my life as a sellsword, if you liked. I am valuable, trained in strategy and tactics. Perhaps I could even thieve."

It was a faint comfort, to know he had set his mind so. "I have no Power. I am not even properly of the People."

He sighed, a long weary sound. Our voices bounced off tile, parted the billows of steam. "Are you so certain? What happened during your Test?"

I shrugged. Ripples slid through the water. Every move I made would brush his skin. The intimacy was unwelcome, and I could not help wanting it. "Nothing. Absolutely nothing. The Yada'Adais bade me stand and watch other Tests—I saw all the glitters and stirrings in the air around my agemates. Nothing happened during mine." Old hurt rose in my throat, I swallowed it.

"Is that what you think? The *adai* cannot see the light, when she is in the Test. Only the Yada'Adais can. If she let you see the Tests of your agemates, she was perhaps grooming you for an apprenticeship. How could you think otherwise?" He sounded eminently reasonable. "You have Power, Kaia'li. The Seeker would not heal itself otherwise. It was fading when you took it, and you have kept it whole and well, even reversed its fading. Can you truly say you have no Power?"

The languor induced by hot water and finally being clean faded, along with my good temper. "I am not interested, *prince.* I have my own life, I have my own sword, and I neither need nor want a Dragaemir *s'tarei.*"

"It matters little," he returned, with a shadow of annoyance finally tinting his voice. "I do not *need* a hotheaded noble *adai* with a tongue sharper than my *dotanii* and foul as a foreigner's, as well."

"I did not ask to be saddled with your Seeker. Why have you done this to me?" The pleasantness of the bath spilled away. I never thought to see the day a *bath* could be ruined.

An attendant glided into the room. A welcome distraction.

"I did not *ask* for this either," he said softly, using the intimate inflection. "I was ready to die. But the gods have other ideas, it seems."

"Pardon, lady," the bath attendant said in commontongue. She wore the short white tunic of the baths, belted with a white cord. "Doryen Innkeeper sends word the table is laid in your room."

"My thanks," I replied in commontongue. The syllables felt harsh and grating in my mouth, after the fluidity of G'mai. I moved from the stone seat, slowly, half-swimming, my hair raying out behind me. I thought perhaps I should cut it, chop it short like a Pesh bondslave's. *That* would be a sight.

A G'mai woman rarely cuts her hair, except for mourning. What would I be mourning if I sheared myself now?

Darik moved, following. Had the man no sense? "I wonder what the barbarian does now."

"Perhaps already at dinner." I yawned again, reaching the stone steps, too tired to keep ill humor for long. Water sluiced free of my skin. "Chewing at the table. Perhaps he does not like baths." *Take this truce, prince. I will not offer it again.*

"Why did you pick his pocket, Kaia'li?"

I took a drycloth from the attendant, submitted to her chafing at my hair with another cloth. Perhaps he would grow weary and leave me to myself. I could afford that hope. "I was drunk. If I knew this was to happen, I would have left his pockets unplundered."

"Then I am glad you did not know."

I could make no reply to that without striking him. So I let it be.

The Barbarian Sacrifice

Redfist had waited for us, at the table set in the room the two men would share. He shifted uncomfortably on his chair—it was the only one large enough to accommodate him. "Ye twain took long enough. I near starved t'death."

The room held two beds, a table and chairs, a fireplace with a cushioned chair, and a few floorpillows. A Baiiar rug hung on the wall, cheerful reds and oranges accenting red Shainakh bedspreads.

My hair lay against my back, a heavy damp weight. "Ha-ya, barbarian, begin your feast. The fare is good here. My thanks for your courtesy." *I am surprised you are not taking chunks out of the table to whet your hunger, friend.*

His green eyes traveled down my short robe, touched my legs. The edge of the bruise from the Hain guard was visible under the white cotton hem. Darik had seen it too, and said nothing. "Briyde's tits, lass, where did ye find that mark?"

"A Hain. One of the cadre sent to fetch you. Twas only a kick, he was dead soon enough." I settled myself on a stool and reached to pour a cup of wine. I would perhaps visit the commonroom later, and have a losing duel with a tankard of mead. If a drinking bout started this madness, a drinking bout might end it. "By the by, why were the Hain after you?"

"I think twas a festival of theirs I disturbed. How was I to know?" He shrugged, picked up a poppadum, slipped it into his mouth. Chewed with great and noisy relish.

A number of things became clear. "Are you the one that ran about bellowing during the Sun's Beneficence?" Laughter bubbled up, I sought to swallow it. "Naked and painted *blue*, twas how the rumor ran."

"Ye would yell too, lass, if ye had found yerself a'the mercy of a bunch of Hain bent on sacrificin' ye to their dark god." His face darkened like the god of thunder's. "Drugged me beer, they did, an' when I woke up—"

Curiosity took advantage of me. "How did you know they had drugged your beer?" *This is a fine tale.* I swallowed more laughter, composed my face. "What did the priests look like?"

"Little black-robed things—" He stopped, mystified, when I put my head down on the table and laughed fit to choke.

I could guess the tale now. He had run afoul of the Dark Sun sect. One of their myths was the slaying of primal giants by their Sunlord. Perhaps they had drugged him, or more likely he had been dead drunk when they took him. The idea of six or seven short stocky Hain seeking to maneuver the barbarian's limp body through the streets, perhaps on a horsecart, was enough to make me fair die with mirth.

"Tisnae funny, lass," Redfist said stiffly, which only made me chuckle harder. I sounded like a girl again. "I could hae died. They were about to start with me *stones*."

I waved my hands, helplessly. That story had been the cause of a great deal of merriment among taverngoers. No wonder the Hain were chasing him. Disturbing the Sun's Beneficence would have been tantamount to spitting on their god. The thought of a Redfist streaked blue with Hain ritual paints and bursting out of a Dark Sun temple to bellow in the streets was too much. Then, if Darik had killed the Guards responsible for hunting down the barbarian, things would have rapidly run out of hand.

When I finally calmed, wiping at my streaming eyes, both of the men were staring at me. "Well." I picked up a pair of eating-picks. "Let us break our fast. Tis a wonderful story, Redfist, for reasons I shall tell you later." I scooped up a rice ball and some pickled fish, and took a dish of fried stretchlegs as well. "*Much* later."

"Why did ye attack the Hain in that tavern, lass?" Redfist set to with a will.

I shrugged, savoring my rice. "I was asleep, and by the time I woke, I was already fighting. I did not stop to ask questions." I picked up some pickled fish with the eating picks, dipped it in the piri-sauce. Heavenly. "I did pick your pocket, it only seemed fair to do you a good turn."

"Am right glad ye did, too."

Darik was too busy eating to make much conversation. We settled down to drinking the wine and filling our bellies. Most of the food was simple—rice, pickled fish, poppadums, a sheksfin soup, a dish of mushrooms cooked with barley and garlinroot—but there was no shortage, and it was well seasoned. There was a dish of fresh baia, too, reminding me of Darik's shoulder, hidden under the robe. The gash was already healing, itching in my own flesh.

At last, comfortably full, I settled back on my stool and took a long draft of wine. Darik watched me, holding his goblet gracefully, and the Skaialan belched and continued eating poppadums. "Wonderful." I blinked, tasting the garlinroot again. At the moment, clean and warm and with a full belly, there was nothing more in life to want.

A sellsword's pleasure, maybe, but born of too many nights spent hungry. It is a clean pleasure, and a safe one.

"Very good," Darik said. "I have not eaten this well since Garmindor."

"You came through Garmindor?" My ears prickled to hear that name. "Is there news of a town called Sidai?"

He shrugged. "I spoke to none in that city. Why?"

"I did some work there." I remembered the shrieks and the cursing, the crack of a whip, and the gold coins in my hands, slippery with blood. *And* the stench of the beast in the cave. "Tis perhaps not safe to return yet. I simply wondered."

"Ah." He nodded, as if he understood. His hair had started to dry, looking less slick and more like silk. Black silk. "What comes next, Kaia'li?"

I stretched, yawning. "Next, I go change into some real clothes, and perhaps visit the commonroom. I have not played at dice for a good moonturn, my luck should be ready for me." *And if I win a few rounds and get drunk enough, I might be able to forget all this. Or wake up in Hain and find it all a dream.*

"I'm for bed," Redfist said. "As soon as I finish me dinner."

How could you eat more, large one? I swallowed the words,

kept them back with a pained smile. The barbarian did not notice.

"I shall accompany you." Darik pushed his chair back, as if to stand.

I shook my head. "Your clothes will not be dry until tomorrow, unless the staff has grown witches while I was away. I have nothing to fit you, either."

His jaw had turned to stubbornness itself. "Then I must ask you to remain here. We have much to speak of. Please."

I felt the anger rise, strangled it. "We have nothing to speak—"

"We do." His eyes were level, dark and intent. "*Please,* Kaia'li."

I shrugged. "Very well." I could not say it gracefully. I rose, the legs of my stool scraping on the floor. The crackling of the fire suddenly sounded very loud. Now that they were clean it was faintly pleasant to be in the company of men again. "Bring the wine. Safe dreaming, Redfist."

"Aye, lass, and yourself," he replied. He looked highly amused, and at my expense too.

I had a faint idea of what was coming, and braced myself for it as for any storm. Still, I would not have minded a few more days of grace.

Oathsworn

I found Darik had moved his weapons into my room, and was about to protest when he made the first cointoss. “As long as I travel with you, I do so as your *s’tarei*. You would not ask your *s’tarei* to sleep in another room, would you?”

I searched for something appropriate to say, found nothing, and settled on, “I do not *have* a *s’tarei*. Therefore, you are not my *s’tarei*. I thought twas clear enough even for you.”

“You still insist?” A humorless grin stretched his mouth, and his hands were tense. I wondered if he would try to strike me, discarded the thought. A *s’tarei* did not behave so. “You try my patience.”

“And you try mine, G’mai,” I returned harshly, snatching up my purse from the bed and scooping out my comb. I dropped onto the cushioned chair by the fireplace and began to work at my tangled hair.

Darik watched this, standing across the fireplace, his back to the window. I worked at a particularly bad tangle and hissed a sellsword’s curse.

The struggle for his temper filled the room with crackling silence. Finally, he mastered himself with a long, deep breath. “Kaialitaa, do you deny me as *s’tarei*?”

The question was formal and archaic, part of the legal code. I stopped combing and stared at him. For him to ask meant that he assumed I was his *adai*; indeed, that he had acknowledged me as his twin. My heart leapt into my throat.

Why could you not have come to me with such a question years ago, G’mai? It was utterly useless.

"I am not your *adai.*" I spoke as gently as I could. "You must be mistaken." *Leave me be, princeling. What have I done to earn this pain from you? I gave up the Blessed Lands, I gave up my House and my birthright, I even gave up my name. Who are you to offer me what I cannot have?*

"I am *not* mistaken. The *dauq'adai* chose you, and I have seen enough to know you are honorable—" His cheeks flamed, his eyes glittering. He looked shamed. Good. Perhaps he would become angry and leave me be.

No, my luck with him was running bad. "I *am* honorable. I cannot guess why you choose to play such a cruel game with me. Answer me this, Dragaemir, what happens when you meet your true *adai*? How will you extricate yourself from that thornpatch? From what Doryen says, there are G'mai searching for you, spreading the story of a prince who survived a palace coup and disappeared—"

His voice cut across mine. "I *'disappeared'* because as I lay in bed feverish and suffering, I was granted the *ilel'adai.* When I recovered from fever and the vision of my twin, I went to the Yada'Adais of the palace and requested a *dauq'adai.* I was given one at Dravairehai Temple, because any fool could see the geas was upon me. The Seeker led me here, to the edge of the world, to a G'mai *adai* who talks like a noble one moment and a guttersnipe the next—"

I do not think he realized he was shouting. The window threatened to rattle under the force of his voice.

"You have not answered the question," I reminded him silkily. Or as silkily as I could while shouting myself. "*What happens when you find your true* adai?"

"If I am wrong in this, I will let you kill me or I will take the *sadaru.*"

I believed him. There was no reason to lie. His face was pale under its tone and drawn as tight as I had ever seen it. He half-turned, stared at the window as if it offended him.

Mother's tits. How could this get any worse?

I sat back in the chair, working at the tangles in my hair. When I had them finally combed out, I began the braids I would loop around my head in a coronet. It was a sloppy compromise between the braids I needed and my exhausted longing for a real bed. The fire crackled, and I suddenly wished for my solitude back with such a vengeance I half thought I would throw him out of the room. Yet that would require energy to stand, and I did not think I had enough.

When I could speak without my voice shaking with anger or frustration, I did. "I am willing to believe you do not do this for cruelty. I do not wish to see you commit ritual suicide either, princeling. You will make some G'mai girl a fine *s'tarei*. Do not throw your life away on me."

"What cruelty is there, if you think me so fit? I doubt it is a throwing-away, too. In any case, tis my life to do as I please with."

So stubborn. He would indeed make a fine *s'tarei*. "You are *Dragaemir*. Your life is not your own."

It brought him back to face me. His hands did not curl into fists, but I thought they perhaps wanted to. "I was never allowed to bear my own name until the queen needed my support as the warleader who held K'nea Pass. She struck a bargain with me: the Dragaemir name and my mother's tomb restored, in return for my support in council and on the field. She no longer needs my support—her Heir is old enough, and her Throne is secure. In any case, I have a perfect right as a *s'tarei* to seek my *adai*, and she can no more stop me than she can stop the Ma'Tar." He had fallen into the personal inflection again, watching me braid my hair. "Where are you bound for next, Kaia'li? Where will you take your *s'tarei*?"

"I wish you would not say such things." There went all my plans of leaving him and the barbarian behind. If I accepted Darik as a *s'tarei*—which I was implicitly doing by leaving the legal question unanswered—then I was honor-bound to take him with me if I left a place. I could not slip out a window and leave him behind as a cast-off serpent's skin.

"Kaialitaa, do you deny me as a *s'tarei*?" Again. Quietly. As if it was no large question, one to make my chest tighten and my eyes fill with water.

He would make a fine *s'tarei*. Guilt prickled behind my wet eyes.

I opened my mouth to say *Yes, I deny you, I deny you in truth*, which should have been my ritual answer. This was a cruelty waiting to happen to me, and I have not survived so long that I walk blindly into such a trap.

Instead, I heard myself say, “No. I do not deny you. I accept your oath if you choose to swear it, Dragaemir.”

Fool. You are a fool, Kaia. What will you do when he abandons you as your House did?

He actually rocked back on his heels. I was just as astonished. Silence stretched between us as I continued, mechanically, to braid. My fingers slipped through the strands and plaited them as they had done every other night of my adult life I had leisure to perform this little ritual.

He was determined, though. I finished braiding and had just dropped my hands when he was on his knees in front of the chair. That put his face almost level with mine. “I accept you as my *adai,* Kaialitaa of House Anjalismir. *Insh’tai’adai, s’tarei, ai.* It is done.” His hands gripped the chair-arms, his fingers sinking into the padding over the carven wood. I thought in that moment that he might have snapped the chair like firesticks if I provoked him. A *s’tarei* in a rage can do wondrous things, between their training and the Power that is the birthright of every G’mai.

Every G’mai, that is, except me.

I sighed. “I suppose I must, then. I accept you as *s’tarei,* Adarikaan of the Dragaemir. *T’adai assai.*”

That simply, it was done. I had given my word, and now could only wait for the worst. Mother Moon, what have I done? I would hardly put it past him to do something rash if I denied him. *I will simply not hold him to it when his true* adai *appears.* I sagged back in the chair, as exhausted as if I had just finished a duel. “You have made a grave mistake. Gods grant it does not kill you.” *Or break me. I cannot stand this.*

“Gods grant.” He watched my face, studying me intently. “I simply regret I did not find you sooner.” His black eyes were lit with something I did not care to name.

“You could have come to festivals.” My tone was not conciliatory in the least. “I attended them until my sixteenth summer, before I ceased believing in miracles and children’s tales. Get the weapons off the bed, except for those you wish to sleep with.”

“I was barred from attending festivals, by order of the

queen." His voice did not alter.

I was so shocked I actually spluttered. "Wha—why? The *law*...she *cannot*—"

"Oh, she can, and she did. Since I was past my Test and had no *adai*, she had custody of me. I am told my mother raved and threatened before she died, and her *s'tarei* spoke to the queen's *s'tarei*, but twas no use. The queen could not risk me finding an *adai*—and possibly breeding—before her own Heir bonded. She is bound and determined only her daughter shall rule. Once my cousin was twinned, I was a little freer, but I would suspect you were already gone from G'maihallan by then."

I nodded, blankly, and repeated the story with its usual accents. "I left eleven summers ago. I came back from a practice to find everything in my room gone. Thankfully I had my sword with me." I was queerly light-headed, exhausted. What more could happen now? All I wished for was sleep, and plenty of it.

He was already moving to clear the bed of weapons and gear. Doryen's staff had brought my belongings up, to my intense relief. I hated traveling as we had been, with nothing resembling proper gear.

"Why would they do so, Kaia'li?" His voice was so gentle, I could not stop myself from replying.

"Because I reached my sixteenth summer without a *s'tarei*. And I have no Power. They threw me out." I realized I was using the personal inflection too, and cursed myself. "I am half-dead with exhaustion. At least let me sleep before you inflict more cruelty on me."

"What is there in this of cruelty? You should rest. It has been a long road."

I wish nothing more than to sleep for a moonturn. I hauled myself up, muscle by muscle. Stood staring at the fire, watching the flames lick the wood. "Darik?" I licked my lips, assayed the question. "Do you mean it? Do you think I have Power?"

"I do not doubt it." No hesitation.

The relief was sharp enough to turn my anger at both of us. "Then you are a fool. I am a fool too." I stalked to the bed, threw my robe down onto the wooden floor and dropped down into softness, pulled the blankets up. The sheets were fine Shainakh linen, and I luxuriated for a long breath before Darik snuffed the two oil lamps. Firelight flickered, a dull glow. Tension invaded my body.

I heard the bed creak as he settled on the other side, above the blankets.

“Do not seek to touch me.” *If you do, I will feed you a knife, G’mai or not.*

“Of course not, Kaia’li. You are not ready.”

That annoyed me so much it took almost a half-candlemark to fall asleep. He said nothing, pretending not to notice the tears I gave to the pillow as silently as I could. He would betray me just as surely as my House had.

It was idiocy. For I found now, in the deepest part of me, that I did not care. I was so hungry for a piece of my home, my kin, my people. Once he found his *adai* I would be cast adrift again.

I fell into darkness wondering how I could stand it a second time.

Sharp Memory

We left Arjux Crossing three days later. I rode a pale gray gelding, and there was a packhorse loaded with purchases. I spent a good deal of our coin outfitting us properly. There would be sellsword work in Shaituh to repair the hole in my purse, as well as whatever I could steal.

I was very interested in what the tavern gossips had to say about the G'mai searching for a wayward prince. I was equally interested in what the gossips were currently saying about Kaia, the Iron Flower. My reputation would not exactly suffer if I appeared in the company of a Skaialan giant and a G'mai prince, but I was known for working alone—had insisted on it, several times at swordpoint. So twould be valuable to the Thieves Guild, as well as the Shainakh God-Emperor's Blue Hands or anyone else in the trade of information, to find out who accompanied me.

I was fairly certain I could avoid being thrown into a donjon—after all, I had never been accused of anything *illegal* in Shaituh, there were merely some things *rumored* to have been my work. Like the jewels from the collar and cuffs of the Shaikuhn of Shaituh while he was in the embrace of a courtesan—in the same room. That had bought me entry into the Thieves Guild.

I still spared a smile for that story.

Or stealing the treasury of Tak-Himor half blind, and casting the money to the poor on Slumstreet where the wickerwork baskets that passed for houses rattled in the desert wind. Or the shipboard fight with Ylar, the pirate. I had been fevered once again, the sea heaving as much as my illness making me unsettled, and I had...what had I done? The song said I had taken his ship with only one sword, but I remembered I had only disarmed one of his crew, magnanimously refusing to throw him overboard. I was merely taking ship from Hain to Antai during the usual winter lull in sellswording. I spent the rest of that trip sleeping with one eye open, though none of them had tried to kill me. At least, not after I had gutted the coxswain.

Thinking of that winter made me feel sick again in the saddle. I had leapt ship in Antai and sailed to Vulfentown after hearing whispers of work available, entering Shaituh in the company of a band of street performers. People paid good coin to see me exhibit my swordwork, and I attracted the eye of a Shaikuhn's son. For three moonturns he pursued me, throwing the coffers of his father's house over my companions. I tried to take nothing, and gave his gifts back as soon as he sent them. He had sought to buy my dinners, and invited me to stay at his father's house while I recovered from the *tai* fever. I refused, and he tried to have his Guard drag me. The songs said I was a frigid beauty, who gave the boy one night of pleasure and left him until his obsessed grief drove him to madness. In truth, sick and blind and fevered, I fought him off until his Guard came, and escaped while he howled that he had paid for me, and he would *have* me.

I do not know whom he thought he had paid, or in what coin.

That winter had culminated in a duel. Snow, ice, one sick, half-frozen G'mai girl running for her life and finally turning to kill the madman who thought he owned her. Afterward, I spent two summers as a mercenary irregular on the Danhai border. Once I was officially in the army, the Shaikuhn could not duel me in revenge.

I would have hated to kill both father and son. They prize their sons, these foreigners; not unlike the G'mai prize their daughters.

It had been irrelevant, the father had died of *tai* fever the next summer. By then I had been embroiled in the morass of the Danhai plains.

I did not care to think too deeply of that, ever.

We crossed the Bridge at sunup, the great span and causeway arching over the Aijan River, stone pilings sunk into the slow-moving, silt-laden waters. I paused mid-span, as was my custom, and gazed down to where the River poured into the ocean. I looked, feeling the call of the sea that bowed away to a distant horizon, the tide spilling out, and finally urged the gelding on.

I patted the horse's neck as the Sun mounted higher, morning creeping through gray veils of ocean mist. Darik walked alongside, and Redfist led the packhorse. I should have left the barbarian in the woods, gone back to Hain, spent the autumn doing little bits of thievery and taken ship elsewhere for the winter. Maybe a caravan out across the Y'kani Waste. That would have been interesting, and more to my taste than *this*.

Darik said little. He had said little since I had accepted him as my *s'tarei*. Perhaps he did regret his rashness.

I hoped so. I sought a graceful way to break the oath or find a mousehole in the laws, but nothing came to mind. In the cold light of morn, my exhausted inability to fend off his attention shamed me even further. It was not his persistence but my weakness I cursed.

I spent most of the morning in the saddle watching the road change under the horse's hooves. I thought of nothing that did not require me to break both G'mai custom and godlaw, and that I could not do.

Could I? The G'mai had thrown me out...but the Moon had not. Her laws still bound me.

Darik avoided speaking to me at all.

I did not know whether to be pleased or even more irritated.

The Sun brought out blue lights in his hair, and since I had repaired his shirt and had his weapons-harness oiled, he looked a little more princely. I could now see the echo of the Dragaemir in him, the shape of his black eyes and the curve of his cheekbones. We are beautiful as a rule, the G'mai, but the Dragaemir are known for harsh beauty, the kind that settles onto the bones later in life, a kind of loveliness that hurts to see. My House—Anjalismir—is known for both temperamental stubbornness and a fragile, tensile beauty my mother was said to embody.

She had been very gentle, my mother, while I seemed to have inherited only the stubbornness she had not. None could ever have called me fragile—or beautiful. I had seen my own face in mirrors and found it nothing special, just a G'mai woman. Nothing out of the ordinary at all except my strange golden eyes.

Cursed eyes, to match the rest of me.

Hooves clopped on the road. My head slipped forward, I thought so deeply. He did look like a Dragaemir. I wished I looked more like an Anjalismir. Some of my agemates had been so lovely, the blossoming of our House. Even now, the faces I had grown up with were so clear in my memory. Tormentingly clear.

"A sundog for your thinking, lady," Darik said, just as I shook the thought away. "Your face is full of sorrow."

"You look like a Dragaemir." Why could I not keep my silly mouth shut?

"So I have been told." His eyes were very dark, catching a gleam from the sky as he glanced up at me. "Does that please you?"

I shrugged, watching the road ahead, curving now between coastal forest on one side and a long sloping fen leading down to the seashore on the other. Salt filled the air, and I heard the distant breathing of the waves as they touched the shore. It was a sound I had sorely missed. "Must it please me?"

I heard a low gruff sound from the barbarian, twisted in my saddle to look back at him. He waved a broad blunt hand at me. "Just me throat, lass. The air here." He tried unsuccessfully to smother a grin, coughed again.

I turned back to the horse's ears and scowled. Such an expression would make me look even less of an Anjalismir, and I scowled even harder.

"Now you look even more sorrowful. What is it, Kaia'li?" He spoke in G'mai, damn him to Pesh hell, and I liked the sound of his voice too much. Far too much.

I shook my head. "I am seeking to compass how I am to feed you twain. There is work for sellswords, but tis dangerous, and I cannot thieve with both of you bumbling about."

"I can thieve, if necessary." His jaw set again, a stubbornness to match my own. "Should you require it."

That managed to prick my pride. I took a deep measure of

salt-laden air, wishing I was on a ship, the deck thrumming underneath me as canvas snapped in the wind. "I do not wish you to steal for me. If thieving is required I shall do it on my own, thank you."

"I thought one of a noble House would not stoop to such things." He stopped short.

Angry heat prickled along my cheekbones. "I do not steal for the *money*, princeling. I steal for the challenge. And I share what I steal. I only keep what I earn, or what I need to stave off starvation, thank you very much. Those I steal from can afford it." I realized I spoke in G'mai, using the personal inflection. Again. It seemed he would not speak to me in aught other than my native tongue. "I must eat to live. There is no shame in that."

Amazingly, he nodded, his hair falling over his forehead. "Agreed. You must have been hungry, when you left your House." His voice barely reached me over the sound of wind through dune-grass and trees, the distant roar of the sea.

We merely continued traversing from one subject I did not care for to another. *What do you know of hunger, princeling? Have you ever thought of selling your body for a warm bowl of soup?* "No more than usual. They did not look for me, my precious kin. I might have starved from their neglect had I stayed, who knows?"

Twas not strictly true, and we both knew it. I would never have starved within the borders of my land, no matter how shunned. Daughters are simply too precious.

Even flawed ones.

"How do you know? I seem to remember hearing of the Anjalismir losing a daughter ten or twelve summers ago." He had a hand on my horse's bridle, and looked up at me. "She was the Heir to the House, as I recall. The Yada'Adais sent to the queen to ask for a tracker, but the girl had covered her trail too thoroughly."

"I do not know the Heir," I lied. "I was too busy practicing on the drillground." I looked down at the top of his bowed head. "May we speak of something else? If it would not *trouble* you."

He refused to take offense. "As you like, Kaia'li. We are for Vulfentown?"

I nodded, one of my braids swinging forward to tap my right cheek. "We may find some luck there. Doryen told me two pairs of G'mai came through less than a nineday ago, following the others and heading for Shaituh. They should be well gone by the time we reach the freetown, but you may wish to be discreet." I wished I could see his face while I mentioned the other G'mai. His reaction might tell me something. "Can you be so? I am assuming you do not wish to be found."

He tilted his chin up and eyed me, amused. "I survived many summers under the queen's scrutiny because I *am* discreet; almost painfully so. I am finding it a habit difficult to break." The corner of his mouth lifted a little, a smile that warmed me though I tried not to be warmed. "For example, I think I might have found you sooner if I had not been too discreet."

"You were not seeking *me*," I reminded him, my hand coming up to touch the hard lump of the necklace under my shirt. The leather vest I had left at the Whitegull thankfully still fit me, and its laces were loose enough to be comfortable. "You sought an *adai*."

"You are my *adai*. Hence, I sought you."

I had to bite the inside of my cheek to keep from screaming a curse at him. That would not make the situation better. "You *must* stop," I hissed at him, in G'mai. "I cannot bear it. I *will not* bear it."

He said nothing, then, looking down at his boots against the hard-packed dirt of the road.

I tasted blood, shook him free of the reins. "I will scout ahead."

"Kaia—" he began, and the kindness in his voice was enough to stab me to the heart.

I touched my heels to the gray gelding's sides. The horse sprang forward, eager to show his paces. A trot lengthened into a canter, I rode to the top of the next rise. Pulled the horse to a stop and gazed at the vista presenting itself.

The road ribboned along the rises, following a belt of solid ground between the shifting marsh and the equally shifting forest. Twould follow this course until Vulfentown, and in Vulfentown I would make a clearer plan. One that hopefully involved me free of this increasingly untenable conversation with a G'mai princeling.

What truly angers you, Kaia? This man, or your shoddy hunger for a bit of G'mai magic, no matter what it costs you?

Like all uncomfortable questions, it had no answer I was willing to voice.

I waited, the gelding stamping and blowing as I watched the world fill with sunlight. The storm had passed, and the weather would hold for another two days or so. Like as not, we would be in Vulfentown when the next rainstorm moved in. Twas the season for swift changes, though; soon the trees would begin dyeing their leaves for the harvest festivals. We were lucky to be traveling during harvest, food would not be so scarce.

Darik and the barbarian finally caught up, and Darik caught at the gelding's bridle. "I would speak with you," he said formally, in G'mai.

I shrugged, patting the horse's mane. "Speak, if it pleases you so much," I replied in commontongue. "I do as I please, Dragaemir." *Most of the time. Or I do what I must, and no more.*

"That is very well." Still in G'mai. The barbarian said nothing, watching us both. His green eyes were glimmering with something like amusement. I suppressed the urge to dismount and offer to teach him why it was not wise to look at me so. "You should not seek to leave me behind. You could kill me, *adai*, and that would not be comfortable for either of us."

"I am not truly your twin, despite your idiotic oath." Clearly, in commontongue, enunciating each syllable. "Twas a moment of weakness. You *know* this. And yet you persist."

"It makes no difference. I have sworn my oath to you, you are my *adai*. Do not seek to leave me behind. Tis dangerous." His jaw was set, and his black eyes glittered.

I shrugged again. I felt like a child, being taken to task by the Yada'Adais. Except she had never taken me to task, only silently shown me why I could never be a part of the G'mai—why I could never be a true *adai*.

Why I could never have him, or anything else from the Blessed Land. Not even a taste, or a touch.

"Please," he said. Faultlessly polite, and pleading. Why had he chosen to inflict this on *me*? What had I ever done to him?

I ground my teeth together, searching for something to say and failing completely. Stared down into his black G'mai eyes, my hands sweating and my stomach roiling uneasily.

The silence stretched, broken only by the low, faraway song of the sea.

"Pretend," he said, finally. "Can you do that much, Kaia'li? Can you *pretend* you are my *adai*, to help me?"

I found my voice. "I do not like to pretend. But until we find your *adai*—"

"No." He shook his head, and I did not imagine the flash of anger in his Dragaemir eyes. I had pushed him into losing his temper.

Good.

"You *are* my *adai*, Kaia'li. And if you wish to dispute that, we shall come to the dueling ground, you and I. I am *more* than happy to teach you not to dismiss me." His voice dropped, so soft it was almost a courting-tone. If the steel underneath the softness had not flashed, an onlooker might have thought he had just complimented me.

"Do you challenge me, then?" I tried not notice the way my heart fell into my feet. He was better-trained, even if I was faster, and I had already seen his skill. I would meet him on the dueling-ground if I had to—honor required nothing less—but I would also avoid it, if I could.

I have killed men aplenty in my time. But to kill a Dragaemir *s'tarei* trained by the finest warmasters of the Blessed Land was another matter.

"Only if you force me, Kaia'li." Did I imagine the sudden comprehension on his face? Perhaps I did. He ducked his head, his hair falling down to hide his face, and when he looked up, the expression was gone.

I shrugged and looked ahead, over the Road. "The sunlight wanes, *prince*. With your permission, I would like to reach Vulfentown in this Cycle." I made the little half-bow that was all I could do on horseback. "If it *pleases* you."

"What would please me is a little consideration from my *adai*." His teeth were clenched no less tightly than mine. "If that does not please *you*, I crave your pardon, but I can do nothing to ease that."

"Do not make yourself my enemy. You will not survive such a trick." *This is a mead dream or a mad witching laid on me. I am not having this conversation with you. The gods have a strange sense of humor, saddling me with a mad G'mai man.*

"I might not anyway," he shot back, almost as soon as I finished. "You could kill me with a careless word, child. Perhaps you were never taught how to treat a *s'tarei*."

Twas a low blow, and I at least had the satisfaction of watching him turn pale as soon as he realized what he said. I let my faint smile widen, looking down at him. An angry man made mistakes. I had provoked enough angry men to know.

I chose commontongue, and made my tone as dismissive as possible. "Come. Sunlight wanes." I flicked the reins. The grey gelding walked forward, so Darik had to follow, let go or be dragged along. We picked our way down the gentle rise. Yet I could not rest until I had the last word. Tis one of my failings. "If I am not the *adai* you wish for, why do you not leave, and find another?"

He looked up at me, smiling, and I bit furiously at the inside of my cheek again. "Of course not, Kaia'li. You are all I could have wished for."

What does he mean by that? I shook my head, my braids shivering as salt-laden wind touched them, and cursed my own stupidity. Why had I prodded at him, engaging in an empty battle of words? I was not behaving like myself.

You are all I could have wished for. A pretty sentiment.

He did not mean it. He could not mean it.

Still, I turned it over and over inside my head as we continued on, polishing the sentence like a jewel. At least I would have the memory of it, no matter what happened.

An Unflawed Jewel

Twas a pleasure to have a proper camp at night, and we made good time to Vulfentown. There was no trouble, though we did catch sight of a few figures in the woods, mayhap bandits eyeing us, wondering at their chances. The barbarian did not fall asleep on watch again.

I managed to avoid another show of petty temper by reducing my words to single syllables or barbarian grunts. Darik did not speak again beyond giving information or mentioning food.

Twas highly satisfactory.

The sky was clouding ominously by the time we rode through the South Gate and into the walled freetown. Vulfentown harbor was a furnace of gold, the Sun sinking into the sea and Sun-gilded ships bobbing on the waves. We rode into a crush of people and horses, waggons straining and people cursing.

The horses—and the barbarian—gave us fractionally better time through the mess, and we turned off on Inn Street, slightly less crowded since it did not lead directly to the Great Market, where ships would dock and spill the wares from their holds, trade coursing like hot blood through the town. Darik cuffed a pickpocket and I caught his shoulder, leaning down from the horse, tossing a *kiyan* to the dazed and scrawny boy who had tried to separate the princeling from his purse. "Be a little gentler." My tone was not gentle. "He is in my profession, after all."

The boy scooped the *kiyan* out of the air and stared at me with huge owlish dark eyes, his tangled dirty hair falling forward over his forehead. He wore an indeterminate-color rag passing for a shirt and a pair of frayed leggings, and was barefoot. A twin to every other street urchin in any other freetown in the wide, wide world.

"As you like, Kaia'li," the G'mai said between clenched teeth, and I smiled. Not even the pet name he had adopted for me or his practice of sleeping next to me every night could dampen my glee at the fact that he would, almost without exception, do what I told him, when I spoke at all.

It was, after all, a *s'tarei*'s duty to do so.

I had not used this novel and utterly delightful power irresponsibly. I barely used it at all. It was not for lack of opportunity—I simply had not found the best way to use it to rid myself of my two problems.

The urchin rolled the *kiyan* in his fingers and stared at me, his jaw agape and eyes aglow. I nodded to him and moved on, the gray's hooves clopping comfortingly against paving-stones.

"Bloody stinking town," Redfist muttered behind me. "An' *crowded*."

"Tis." I would have liked more time in the quiet of the forest, too. Time to sort out the problems fast closing in on me, time to think of a solution, time to perhaps find some way to stop my heart's half-guilty leap inside my ribs each time I looked at Darik. "But we shall be able to catch a caravan from here to Shaituh. Safety in tribes, my barbarian friend. I have gossip to sell, and gossip to buy as well. We shall stay for two days and find a caravan going out onto the Road by then."

"Aye, lass," Redfist said. "An' what will I be doing during this time?"

I twisted in my saddle to grin at him, my mood lightening. "You will find a corner in a tavern I know and keep your ears open for me. I wish to know a few things, and you are the perfect man to find them for me. I give you a bit of what I earn when I sell the information, understand?"

"Of course I understand. Ye be the captain of our crew, and a finer one I canna remember. What of D'rik?"

What of him? "Darikaan will stay in his room like a nice little princeling. We do not wish any G'mai paying attention to him—or finding him here in the company of a woman who appears to be G'mai. Tis valuable information, and I wish it to stay valuable. And what, pray answer, is the most valuable information?" I tossed one of my braids back over my shoulder.

"Th' information nobody else knows, aye?" Redfist surprised me by chuckling. "Oh, aye, lass."

"I cannot stay in a room if you go traveling, Kaia." Darik had been silent for far too long.

I looked down at him. "You will do what I ask of you, *s'tarei.*" I did not bother to smooth the jagged edge from my voice. "Unless you wish to be shipped back to the Blessed Land in the company of the G'mai sent to drag you back to the palace for a reason you have not told me of yet."

He shook his dark head, setting his jaw, and I wondered if these were the signs of trouble coming. Traveling with a man will show you the measure of his temper, and I suspected I had severely strained his. As it was, I turned off Inn Street into a familiar little avenue, and was greeted by a long trilling whistle.

I whistled back, three short blasts, and Jettero appeared out of an alley to my right. "Ha-ya, woman, seen any of the Guard yet?" he called.

I had to laugh, twas an old joke between us. *Seen any of the Guard yet? Why no, unless you count the one right behind you.*

I pulled the gelding to a stop and waited while he stepped up to meet me. I caught his hand. We squeezed, twice, in the manner of the Thieves Guild, then he went back to smoothing the gelding's neck. "Not even the one behind you, Jett. How is business?"

"*Cha,* much less interesting since you left, Iron Flower, but you leaving means more for the rest of us." Jettero was a lean dark thief, a long face and a shock of greasy red-black hair. He had the uneasy complexion of a single Pesh ancestor among the Hain of his family, and a little bit too much height to be pure Hain. He wore loose dark clothes, the dusty attire of a sellsword or a thief, and the sword riding at his side was no more than a rapier. He made his living by thieving, not fighting, and I had never seen him draw the rapier. Instead, he used knives. He sewed the sheaths into his clothes and was a cool, vicious opponent, since the only fighting he did was for position in the Guild or quiet knifings in alleys. The rapier seemed for appearances only.

Still, it was wise not to count the rapier merely for show. Those who underestimated Jett rarely did not regret the occasion.

"You never have any trouble finding business. I am bound for Kesa's."

He nodded. "*Cha!* Thought so. She has a few rooms. Care to grant me a sundog? You are gossip nowadays, Iron Flower, and some of it *interesting*."

I dug in my pouch and held up a *kiyan*. "Dinner tonight? I have trade, and I wish to know what so interests you. Worth a moonwheel, *cha*?"

Jettero's eyes fastened on the silver coin. Half his mouth curled up into a smile. "Be careful, Kaia. Some of your kith and kind have appeared. They ask after a prince of theirs, but a pair of them came through yesterday and spoke of the Iron Flower. Teyo Keynat's-kin gave them a bellyful of song, and they left next morning." Jett shrugged his thin shoulders, interest printed over his lean dark face. "Ah, and I see you travel with company. When did this happen?"

I would have been lucky to have nobody notice. "Ask not. They attach like *sha'laia*. People keep following me around, and I have to kill them to make them cease." I gave a sunny, wide smile, and noticed with satisfaction that he paled a little. "Must be my luck."

"Must be," he agreed.

Darik had edged behind the horse—probably useless, since Jett had more than likely taken a good long look before whistling to me. Still, I appreciated the effort.

Darik's hand curled around my ankle, I felt the tension in his fingers through my boot. I restrained the urge to kick him. *What are you so worried about now, princeling? That I will throw myself in Jett's arms or suddenly vanish?* "Tonight." My good humor faded a bit. "We shall have a feast. *Cha*."

"*Cha*, Flower." He used the word that made up half my nickname in commontongue, the word for a cut flower. It was also slang in Vulfentown and Shaituh for young, well-dowried girl seeking a rich husband. The "Iron Flower" business had come about because of a pun made on my name—*Kaia* was the only name I had ever given, no clan, no town, and they had been forced to play with it. It is not only the G'mai who are addicted to pretty wordplay.

Jettero sauntered back into the dark alley and disappeared. I blew air out between my teeth and looked down at Darik. His black G'mai eyes met mine. "What are you about?" It was hard to keep my tone level.

"Staying out of sight. And should you need Power, I was ready to supply it. As a *s'tarei* should."

"Take your hand off me." I nudged the horse forward.

"Is nae valuable information now," the barbarian said from behind me. "Or is it?"

I shook my head. "I need a pot of mead and a hot bath to make sense of this. How would *anyone* know enough to ask about a G'mai prince and my own sweet self?" I sighed. News travels fast, faster than horses. *Even the air carries rumors,* the freetowners said. "We are almost home, my friends."

Twas true. If I had a home on the Lan'ai Shairukh coast, twas right around the corner and a few steps inside.

Hamarh Street cut away from Inn Street, and I followed, thinking deeply, until we reached Kesamine's inn—the Swallows Moon, named so because the sign held a picture of three swallows under a full Moon. There was a low open gate on one side, and I rode straight into the courtyard, the gelding's hooves clicking over the stone paving. I sat and waited for perhaps ten heartbeats before the door set in the side of the high white stone building was flung open.

Kesamine Drava's-kin put her hands to her hips and regarded me, her long blue Clau eyes accentuated with black lines and her curling gold-red hair pulled severely back. Her lips were stained red with kav juice, and she wore gold in her ears and at her throat and wrists, heavy Clau gold that was pure yellow instead of the Shaituh red gold. Despite several tankards of mead and several endless nights—a few spent sharing the same bed whenever I came through Vulfentown—I had never found what brought her so far from the cold islands of her home. She had been taken into the Drava kinhold about ten summers ago, whether by gold or favors nobody knew.

"*Alhaia!*" Kesa called. "You come back to my door again,

Kaia-naa." It was her private joke, something to do with her native tongue. I did not speak Clau, so I did not know what it meant. "You must be troubled indeed."

Her commontongue was more song than speech. Somehow the musical nature of Clau language rubbed through. I dismounted and tossed my reins to a small Hain stable boy who appeared out of thin air. "*Cha,* Kesa-li, tis merely to see your pretty face." I strode past Darik to meet her in the door.

She held out her arms, I hugged her, and she kissed me—a long, deep, melting kiss, her usual greeting. She smelled, as always, of spice and dusky tradewinds, and the salt of the sea. She was soft, almost as tall as me, and the material of her full colorful skirts wrapped against my trouser-clad legs. "Mmh." She finished her greeting, and held me at arm's length. "You are grim-faced and tired and too thin, Kaia-naa. Who are your friends?"

"The tall one answers to Redfist. Skaialan. I did him a good turn, and am punished for it." I clicked my tongue against my teeth. It smelled of *chaabi* stew inside, and fresh flatbread. "The dark one is G'mai, and I am punished for that too."

It was too close to the truth for me to say it lightly.

Her strange Clau eyes managed to look through me. Kesa knew well enough to tell when I spoke of something that pained me. She would ask me later, or not, judging by my mood and her own. "Ach. Come in, then. Your room is empty, and I add the one next door for half price. *Cha*?"

"Agreed." I kissed her smooth cheek. "Jettero will join me for dinner. Do you care to make it a festival?"

"Do you have news?" Her eyes began to glint. "Trade or pay?"

"For you, Kesa-li, trade." I was rewarded with her broad face breaking into a smile. "Of *course.*" I brought out two of the Rams I had left and pressed them into her hand. "No business right now, *lya-ini.*" I used the G'mai term for an agemate who was a particularly close friend, for Darik was right behind me. He was dusty, and his *dotanii* and knives made him into a dour picture, helped by the dark expression on his Dragaemir face.

"*Cha.*" She breathed out slowly, examining him from head to toe. "A pretty piece, Kaia'naa, not your usual type."

I managed a laugh, but Kesa was not fooled. Then she inspected the barbarian, who stamped his booted feet on the stone to knock away road-dust. "And that one. He looks too big for a bed."

I saw the speculation in her blue eyes, was not convinced. "I would not know. He says I am too small for pillow-play."

She laughed and chucked me under my chin, lightly. "Ah, come in, come in, why do I keep you waiting? You need a bath, and a massage. A'lian will be pleased to see you."

I let out a sound that was half a groan. "Oh, I cannot wait. Lead on, lovely one. I am weary and hungry for your kindness." I half-sang the line, from an old ballad. She grimaced, pulling me into the inn's dark warm interior. The sky overhead rumbled, a warning of weather to come. A roar of conversation spilled out behind her. This passage led directly to the commonroom.

"*Cha*, not that old song," she sniffed, and I smiled, my mood lightening as it always did around Kesa. She slid her arm around my waist and I let her lean her golden head on my shoulder, ignoring Darik's silence. It would do him good to see he was not anything to me.

The barbarian came behind Darik, ducking his head, and I glanced back over my shoulder at him. "You would not happen to know where I could buy a Skaialan draft-horse, Kesa'li?"

"No." The thought evidently amused her. Laughing, she brought us out into the commonroom. I scanned the room habitually and felt my heart drop into my belly and pound like wardrums.

I stopped dead, and Kesa smoothly swung me around so we faced Darik, who stopped short as well. "G'mai," I said, softly. "Two of them, by the fireplace. Kesa, I cannot have them see me."

"Oh." She stopped for a moment, thinking, her head against my shoulder. "Well, there is no other way up to the room, my darling." There was a burst of laughter from a bunch of traders, all clustered around a low wooden table groaning under the weight of an early dinner.

I cursed under my breath. "Very well. Darik, walk on the other side of Redfist. And do so *quietly*. They speak to each other, we may pass unnoticed. I thought they had left?"

"They returned," Kesa murmured. "Trouble on the road between here and Shaituh. They would say no more. What is it, Kaia'naa?"

"He cannot be seen either." I indicated Darik with a slight nod. "Could be unpleasant for me."

Kesa, as usual, did not question. "Very well. Come, walk with me, and hide that pretty face of yours behind your hair."

Twas too late. One of the G'mai—the slender, small woman in the indigo dress—had seen us. She reached us just as Darik glanced up at Redfist, shrugging, and her gasp was loud enough to make me whirl, Kesa suddenly behind me and my hand on my knife-hilt. I was strung far too tightly, my nerves stretched like an acrobat's wire.

A *s'tarei* was suddenly at her side, watching me with eyes as black as the velvet between stars. "*In'sh'ai, adai-sa,*" he greeted me. He had the long face of a Tyaanismir. Twas a shock to see another G'mai man. Eleven summers had I gone without hearing a voice or seeing a face from my homeland, and now I was faced with three of them. He wore G'mai clothing too, and the *adai* was in a long beautiful dress of the deepest evening-sky. There were lilies patterned into the fabric, and she looked every bit as lovely as an *adai* should. Twas a double shock to see her, this woman who could have been one of my agemates.

I thought I had escaped them, the G'mai. I had grown accustomed to a world without them.

Darik had not caused me such an instant flash of vertigo. I took a step back, crowding Kesa, and stopped when Darik's hands met my shoulders. "*In'sh'ai,* Tyaanismir Atyarik. It is good to see your face again." He spoke in commontongue.

The *s'tarei* stared at me, up at Darik's face, and back at me again. "Your Highness." It would have been hard to imagine a man looking more shocked. "This—you have—ah—"

"A moment, if you please." Darik's voice changed. It was the tone of a man accustomed to command. His hands shifted on my shoulders. "Kaia?" He meant to turn me to face him.

I swallowed, hard. Stepped away, shaking his hands from me. He let me. I half-turned, saw Kesa's face, blank and carefully uninterested. They all watched me, from the *adai,* her perfect mouth half-open in shock, to the barbarian, who looked grave and dark-eyed. The crowd was avid, staring at me again.

"Come, Redfist." I nodded to Kesa. "We have returned the princeling to his people. I wish for a bath and a pot of kafi, if you do not mind, *lya-ini.*"

I started across the room, my footsteps unnaturally loud.

"Kaia." Just the one word, Darik's tone half a question, half a plea.

It was the plea that fired my anger, I tried to tell myself. *Make the cut quickly, Kaia. They have found him, they will take him to another G'mai woman, and you will be left in peace. You knew it would happen. Save a scrap of your pride and thank the Moon you have not done anything ridiculous.*

My heart scalded and rang inside my chest. It was useless. I had no choice. "No thanks are necessary, *prince.* You are where you belong now." There were plenty of people in Kesa's commonroom, staring at me while the fire crackled. I *hate* being the object of this attention. Travelers and freetowners gaped at me, and a tide of whispers raced through the room.

Kesa saved me. She fell into step beside me, sliding her arm around my waist. "A prince? Oh, *dalai'al'al'alai wahana,* Kaia'naa, you *have* risen in the world. Last time I saw you, you were with that acrobat."

"Very funny." My heart cracked. "I was merely traveling with him. Besides, he was a boy-lover."

Redfist walked behind us, and for once I was glad of his bulk, shielding me from interested eyes.

"To what do I owe this honor?" Darik sounded cool and calm, but my fists tensed. I had to look down at my hands to see them loose and easy at my sides. Why did I feel someone else's fingers wanting to knot into fists?

I knew why. *Refused* to know why. As soon as I escaped on a ship, I would toss the Seeker into the depths of the Shelt, and I would hope that with it went the feel of his wounds in my flesh.

Kesa swept me aside, up a flight of stairs leading to her own suite. Redfist lumbered up after us. "Lass?" he said, once we had reached the top of the stairs.

"You stay in the room next to mine," Kesa answered in my

stead. There was a long hall, lit by skylights of the thick glass Vulfentown was famous for, mosaics of sea waves and monsters on the walls. Kesa opened a smaller door to one side and motioned to Redfist. "Will this do, Skaialan?"

"Oh, aye." A cursory glance inside, his attention elsewhere. "I'm more worried about yon lassie there."

I looked up at his broad, ginger-furred face. "I am hale enough, Redfist. Tis a shock, seeing so many faces from G'maihallan after so long. I thought I would be better prepared." My lips pressed together, I settled for nodding sagely. "Dinner tonight, with us?"

"Nae." His broad shoulders slumped, and I saw how weary he must be. "I think I mun well sleep, t'clear m'head. Dinnae be too hard on the Gemerh, lass."

I shrugged. "He is where he belongs, with his people. Now I must find a lonely giantess for you, and my work is done."

The barbarian turned, and fixed me with his strange green eyes. "I would nae draw my axe on ye, lass." It seemed he clenched his teeth, though through his hair I could not be sure. "Do nae sharpen yer tongue at m'expense."

"That is enough." Kesamine bowed to the barbarian—slightly, I noticed, but definitely. "I shall care for her, tall one. Enjoy your room. Pull the rope on the left side of the door should you need aught. Dinner will be sent up, tis a private bath and watercloset through that door." She pointed.

"My thanks, lady." He doffed an imaginary cap, bowing deeply. There was a rough sort of grace to the gesture, and I thought wearily that I had misjudged him.

Kesa ushered me down the hall, and I heard the door close behind us. "There now." Her skirts made their familiar low sound. "Is that not better? *Lahai wakana lawai*, eh?"

"I do not speak Clau, sweetness. I need some kafi and perhaps a real meal. Was that *chaabi* I smelled?" *Speak of food, Kesa. Let us not speak of what you just saw.*

She pushed open the door to her private chambers, and I saw white linen and yellow silk. "*Cha*, thinking with your stomach like any sellsword." Her skin was pale, too, like Redfist's. But what was uncooked dough on him was white satin on her, and something familiar tightened under my breastbone.

Yet I thought of black eyes, and callused hands, and an even mouth. A band of scar tissue across a throat, a band I wanted to trace, and ask how he had received the wound.

"You have redecorated," I said, without seeing the room through the haze in my eyes. "Tis beautiful."

She laughed, pushing me down into a chair by the fire and tossing a handful of sweet incense into the flames. "My thanks. You always did have a good eye. Remember those candlesticks?"

I groaned and began to work my boots off. "I suppose you have not forgiven me yet." I dropped the first boot, pulled my stocking off, and grimaced at it. The second boot followed, and the second stocking. I rubbed my feet against the red Shainakh rug.

"Not every day I walk into my own bedroom to find a dead assassin, half my linen shredded, and my candlesticks broken." She dropped down in the seat across from me. "And a bloody, exhausted Kaia'naa in my bed. T'jai will bring up your gear, and we shall have a long chat. But for now, I think a bath is what you need, and some fresh clothes."

"I am leaving for Shaituh early on the morn," I heard myself say. "With the gray gelding. I will leave the packhorse and a purse for the barbarian."

Run, Kaia. Run. See how well I flee my fears.

"Kaia." Her red mouth pursed, and her blue eyes sparkled. She crossed her legs under her skirts—they were a savage pattern of green and red and yellow, and her top was patterned with red diamonds against a yellow background. "I have never seen you flee from trouble. Why begin now?"

I leaned my head against the back of the chair. Outside, thunder rolled and boomed. A storm coming in off the sea. Twould be a harsh one, and there would be no ships leaving the harbor anytime soon. Pity, that. I could have leapt ship to Antai. There was always enough work in *that* city, even for me.

"I am not fleeing," I lied. "That was a problem, rather neatly solved by others. Now there will be a new round of rumors about me and another man. They must think me the most successful streetseller in the history of the Lan'ai Shairukh coast." I sighed theatrically.

Kesa laughed, a brilliant golden sound that made my own mouth twist up a little. She folded her white, white hands. "So he is a G'mai prince, this man. What makes him unpalatable, the G'mai or the prince?"

A knock at the door, and a young girl dressed in the tunic and leggings of an inngirl entered, carrying a tray with a pot of kafi and two porcelain Shainakh cups.

"Kafi, Kesa." The girl was a young Shainakh, her long red-black hair braided back in a thick rope reaching her waist. "The lord who came with Lady Kaia is downstairs. Sitting in a corner by the fireplace, willna accept wine or food. Says he waits on her."

I all but cringed. "Let him wait," I muttered, but Kesa shook her head.

"Tell him he needs a bath before he sees her, she shall be at dinner with me, and he is welcome to attend in two candlemarks." Kesa winked, and the girl set the tray down on a handy table. "*If* he wishes. Tell him also we are honored a prince of the Blessed People is in our humble inn, so on, so forth." She waved a hand, lazily.

"Kesa—" I began, but she lifted her white hand to me, gold sliding down her wrist to chime sweetly, and I bit at the inside of my cheek to keep from screaming. Kesa poured kafi, her black-rimmed eyes intent on the cups.

"Take him to the west room, the finest one. Give him whatever he wishes." She nodded at the girl, who dropped a pretty courtesy. "How long did he speak to the other two?"

"*Cha*, they were pleading with him about something. He didna listen. Just watched the lady leave the room and walked away while the Lady Gemerh still spoke. Should have seen their faces! He went to the fireplace. Staring at the staircase now, Kesa." The girl cut her dark eyes at me, and I closed mine. She would see nothing on my face except weariness.

So I hoped.

"Thank you, Vavakha." Kesa sounded amused. The girl left, gliding along the polished wooden floor.

"Very unkind of you, Kesa-li." Even to myself, I sounded unsteady. And far more bitter than the occasion warranted.

"Have I done aught to displease you?"

"Come now, Kaia. If you leave tomorrow morn I will have a mad Gemerh tearing down my inn." Kesa made a short sound of annoyance. "You are generally more intelligent, *Iron Flower.*"

"Oh, by the Moon, stop." I failed to still my reflexive protest on Darik's behalf. "He might drown himself in the bay, but he will not tear your inn apart."

"Are you so certain? Gemerh are mad, and if what I hear is any indication, this one is one of the maddest. Here, have some kafi, and tell me what ails you."

I opened my eyes, stretched my legs out in front of me. It felt good to be motionless, and I saluted Kesamine with the cup. Twas beautiful, eggshell-thin porcelain, a pleasure to hold something so well made. "I picked the barbarian's pocket."

"I have never known you to pick a pocket without reason." She blinked, slowly, giving me the full force of her pale blue gaze. "So?"

I hardly know, myself. "A training exercise. Actually, I was compelled."

"Ah." She sipped at her kafi, tucked one sandaled foot behind the other. "So you were witched to pick a pocket? What did you gain?"

"Hain sequins, an iron key and a necklace." I shuddered at the thought of witchery, stopping the reflexive ward-evil sign with an effort. The instinct of other sellswords, rubbing off on me. "A flawed Seeker."

"Flawed Seeker?" Her golden eyebrow raised. She set her cup down and reached up, unwinding her hair. I sighed. My own head suddenly seemed very heavy.

"Tis meant to help a G'mai man find his twin." I retrieved the chain from under my linen shirt and leather vest, pulled it over my head and tossed it to her. It flashed sharply as it left my hand. Kesa plucked it out of the air, a sheaf of hair like liquid light falling over her shoulder.

She examined it while I sipped my kafi. Her blue eyes came up to mine. "Tis flawed?" She tossed it back to me, and I caught it without thinking.

"The crystal." I held it up.

Her eyebrow raised. She crossed her legs, the silk of her dress sliding sweetly. “My eye may be off, but I see no flaw in that gem, Kaia’naa.”

I set my cup down. It made a thin chattering sound against the inlaid tile of the tabletop, my hand shook so badly.

The crystal was no longer a crystal. “Mother’s *tits*,” I breathed.

Now the chain was fine G’mai silver, supple as a serpent’s back. The setting was a silver wingwyrm, curled around a glittering diamond. I have stolen a fair number of jewels over my long seasons away from G’maihallan, and if this was not a diamond I was no thief.

The Seeker had indeed healed itself. “Kesa…I swear by my sword this was a cheap streetseller’s gaud on a lightmetal chain when I first saw it. Less than a tenday ago it still held a flaw as large as a Shainakh palace.”

“Sorcery.” Kesa shivered a little. The Clau do not mind witches, but sorcery they fear mightily. Their gods take a dim view of a sorcerer's habits of sacrifice and secrecy.

“But I *have* no Power,” I said blankly.

“Oh, you do not?” She laughed, a bell-clear sound. “Oh, come now, Kaia. You are a witchling if ever I saw one. Why, that time you won against Faverro in my very own commonroom—*he* was witched, you know. Bought a charm from that woman outside the city walls, the one with the birds.”

I shivered too, rubbing my soles along the floor. I always stayed far away from the northwest edge of Vulfentown, using the East Gate and swinging around to reach the road through a shallow belt of marshland. The only time I met the birdwitch outside Vulfentown had not been comfortable for either of us. I like witches little, and they seem to have an aversion to me as well. “He was witched by that one?”

“Paid a pretty penny for it, too. Won against everyone—except you.” Kesa took another ladylike sip of her kafi. “He returned and laid siege at the witch’s door. She told him the only thing twould not work against was a more powerful witch. Said she had given him no surety against other witches, merely luck with dice. He threatened to cut her and she threatened to curse him. Set her birds on him.” Kesa laughed a warm caramel laugh, imagining the scene. I could almost see it myself. "*Cha,* Kaia, how can you say you have no witching in you?"

Everyone but me thinks I have a G'mai's Power. I should be grateful; then again, those outside Blessed Land cannot tell. If I had Power I would not have been thrown from my home. I shrugged helplessly. "Mayhap I need that bath now." In other words, *this discussion is closed.*

"You cannot tell me you did not know." Her bracelets chimed again, earrings tinkling faintly as she moved. "Oh, Kaia."

I shrugged again. The weariness of travel settled deep in my body, familiar but painful all the same. "I have no sorcery, Kesa'li. The G'mai have been working with Power since the Moon was made, if I had my share they would never have cast me out. I was shunned from my fifth summer on; ten summers later I came back to my room to find all possessions *gone.* Vanished. I had only my sword and the sweat in my clothes to leave with."

Kesa watched me, her pretty mouth pursed. I had never told her this tale. I stared at the diamond dangling from the fine silver chain that had somehow found its way into my hand, stared as if it could tell me the future. "Now I am faced with a G'mai man who thinks I am his *adai.* He will be lucky if his true *adai* does not shun him for consorting with me, once he finds her. Which I gave my word to help him do." *And I do not think I can live with this small crumb snatched from me again.* "Gods, Kesa. What a mess."

"You are ridiculous." Thunder rattled again, faraway. Storm from the sea, and we had just missed being caught in it. "Is it so outlandish to think you might be mistaken?"

I kept my silence, staring at the gem. *Not outlandish, Kesa. Terrifying. Yes, that is the word.*

Kesa sighed. "Finish your kafi, Kaia'naa. Then we shall have a nice long civilized bath, and you shall dress properly for dinner. Jettero will wear his best. You do not wish to disappoint him, do you?"

"I have never cared much for Jettero's disappointment." I watched the diamond swing back and forth.

"Then," she answered lightly, "think of mine."

Proof and Tidings

I left my hair down.

Twas childish. G'mai *adai'sa* braid their hair. Always. There are poems of a *s'tarei* watching his *adai* twist her hair; love-poetry, of the bittersweet taste G'mai adore.

I did not want any reminder of G'maihallan. And so, unbound hair, an insult at worst, a deliberate flaunting of polite convention at best.

Over Kesamine's objections, I wore a fresh suit of travel clothes. The only concession I made to style was a pair of silver and ruby ear-drops I stole from a Taizmiri lord in my very first days of traveling. Twas a miracle I had not since lost them. They rather suited me, even if it did hurt to have them in my ears again. The G'mai do not wear such things.

Still, their weight reminded me of stealing them, and of surviving an unpleasant experience. I had traveled far enough from that memory to transform it to strength instead of a fearsome thought.

I chose a black linen shirt, my second leather vest, and a nice pair of black Shainakh silk trousers. I went barefoot.

My hair was a trouble, since I could sit on it when unbraided. But I had decided, and twas too late now. So I gave the soft knock required by politeness and strolled into Kesamine's dining room, fresh from the bath and with rubies swinging against my cheeks.

Jettero sprang to his feet. "Ah, Kaia—" He stopped in confusion, eyeing me in my unbraided glory.

I smiled sweetly. "And good evening to you, Jettero." I bowed, a lovely, courtly bow, if I do say so myself. My hair fell forward over my shoulders and I winced internally at the thought of tangles.

Kesamine's dining room was reached through her sitting room, done in blue Kshanti silk and graceful Clau furniture looking far too delicate to withstand the use I knew it could. I once hit an assassin on the head with a spindly little Clau folding stool, surprised when it killed him. Of course, I had been bleeding from the mouth, the shoulder, and the leg at the end of that fight, and I never dreamed I would be rescued by a *chair.*

A row of windows looked out on the harbor. As I glanced out, a flash of diamond lightning speared darkness, and thunder rattled the sky. I returned my gaze to Jettero. "What a marvelous instinct I have for making entrances." Twas the right thing to say, self-deprecatory and amusing.

Jettero had, true to Kesamine's prediction, dressed like a lordling. Crimson silk shirt and trousers, loose and elegant, and a finely worked leather swordbelt too. His hat, with a huge sweeping feather, lay tossed on a low Clau couch, the kind with only one pillow at the end, done in blue satin.

She has such exquisite taste, my Kesa.

Any other time, I would have dressed to match him, even borrowed a gown from her. But tonight, no. As it was, my plainness set him off to advantage, and he preened.

Darik rose slowly from a fragile-looking Clau chair. Kesa must have dressed him, because he wore black silk in the Kshanti style, a high-collared tunic and loose trousers. It suited him. His *dotanii* rode his back as mine did, and his eyes glittered black. I could not guess if twas fury or embarrassment that made his gaze so bright. His face, when he registered my unbound hair, was priceless. First his eyes narrowed fractionally, then his mouth firmed just a little. His shoulders were rigid under the black silk.

A deep and nasty satisfaction welled up inside me, too sharp to be clean.

He looked every fingerwidth the prince. His hair was silk, all trace of dust gone, and he moved with the unconscious grace of someone drilled in the publicity of royal life.

Jettero regained himself. "Indeed you do, Iron Flower.

Come, we have had a fascinating discussion. Your friend knows nothing of your fame. I have taken it upon myself to remedy that." Jettero's lean face split into a smile.

I almost lost my temper. If I cuffed Jett now we would have a sharp, vicious fight, and Kesa would never forgive me. I would never forgive myself.

"You are filling him to back teeth with ridiculous bits of minstrelsy, you mean." I made a little *tsk-tsk* sound. "Pour me a cup of wine, Jett, and *do* stop being a fool."

Darik gave me a correct little half bow. "I had no idea you were so famous, Kaia'li," he said, in commontongue.

"Hardly." My smile fixed upon my face. Jett poured wine from a smoky glass bottle into a silver goblet. "Jett likes to lie to the naïve. Tis his only real hobby."

"Oh, you are harsh." But Jett's tone was mild, as if he realized now was not a fine time to bait me. "*Cha*, sit down, and give me some gossip. I've a few pieces to make that lovely hair curl."

I moved across the room. Rain splashed the windows—a downpour I was more than happy to witness rather than bear. Storms moved in from the sea at the end of harvest season and sometimes continued during the lean winters. Vulfentown was on the main southern road to Shaituh, so it still received trade income that way, but a storm so early in the harvest season spelled bad luck. Not only would trade suffer, but if it stormed more, I could not take ship for Antai.

I would be in Shaituh for the snows. Again.

I took the goblet Jett offered me and smiled.

Darik's chair had its back to the wall housing the fireplace. He must have arrived first, since Jett would have taken that place otherwise. Since Kesa's customary chair had its back to the other wall, Jett had chosen the chair across from Kesa, to Darik's left, with its back to the bank of expensive windows. That left me with my back to the door, highly uncomfortable. So I took the small, thin-framed Clau chair and moved it at an angle to the table. Kesa would only see a slice of my face, but she would understand. If I could irritate Darik enough that he left the room, one of us could take his seat. I had to pull my hair aside gracefully or risk sitting on it.

Once settled, I took a sip of the wine. Baiiar, a nice white, very sweet. *Kesa must be seeking to sweeten my disposition.* My palms were damp.

Why?

Damn the G'mai. He had robbed me of the pleasure of a long dinner spent gossiping with friends. The *dauq'adai* was warm and hard against my skin. I saw Darik's eyes drop—he could not tell if I wore the Seeker, the chain was hidden under my shirt. "Jett, my dear." I leaned back against the chair. "What's the Guild up to these days? Any dues I should know of?"

"Business before dinner?" Jett raised a single eyebrow. His hair was freshly washed, and he had a braided bit over his right eye, tied off with red thread. For luck. Thieves are a superstitious group. "*Cha,* love, you know I cannot do that."

I turned my smile on him. "Oh, *cha.* Let us finish the boring things, so we may enjoy dinner." I tucked a flyaway strand of hair behind my ear. "I hear the High Shaikuhn lowered tariffs. Trade goes well, then?"

"Ah." Jett shrugged. "Not as well as it could. They doubled the tax on rice and flour. And salt." Jett swirled the wine in his own goblet, his long horse-face thoughtful. "Now why, do you suppose, is that?"

"Orders from the Emperor." I wriggled my toes against the hardwood. "Old Azkillian is planning another war."

"They are already bled dry over the Danhai." Jett's eyes flicked over the table, a habitual movement. "New offensive?"

Darik said nothing, simply watching me. The table was set for four, and there was the traditional dish of salt, as well as two graceful Clau glass candlesticks with white candles burning, Kesa's little joke. When our hostess came, the appetizers would arrive.

I could barely wait, famished as I was. I shook my head, settled back in my chair. "Pesh." I felt great satisfaction in being able to give the news. "Tis simple, Jett. Sellswords are heading to Shaituh in droves, if you have not noticed. Low tariffs to bring in metalwork, taxing the peasants for staples—and Azkillian cannot take the freetowns, the Blood Years convinced him as much. The freetowns are worth more in trade than he could ever get in tax, and he uses them to corral the Shaikhuns on the coast. No, tis Pesh he has his eye set to. Rich, used to slavery, will bring in tax revenue to balance the Danhai drain, and will rid him of troublemakers in the army. Unless Pesh puts up a savage fight, Azkillian cannot lose—unless of course the Holy City revolts and forces him to change his policy, and tis as much chance of that as there is of me singing in a Rijiin *harbara.*"

"Ah." Jett's face lit with comprehension.

"Your grasp of politics never fails to amaze me." Kesa, at the door. I rose to my feet and, after an embarrassed moment, the two men did as well.

She wore white, contrasting with the satin of her skin and the golden floss of her hair. I smiled, and wondered which one of the men she was after. Probably Darik—Kesa was little able to resist adding a prince to her list. The dress was long and floating, trailing sleeves, a low neckline revealing more of her milky, beautifully clear skin. "You began the gossip without me," she chided gently.

I gave Jettero a reason to stop needling me, and Darik a reason to stay silent. "Merely uncomfortable business before dinner, so we may enjoy the storm and the table at the same time. You look beautiful, Kesamine Drava's-kin."

She accepted the compliment with a courtesy, her skirt pooling on the floor and her elaborately curled ringlets bobbing. "I bought the material from Tanyas Spicetrader. She brought it from Clau." She straightened, and pulled gently on the rope next to the door. That was the signal for the inn staff to start bringing up dinner.

My hair was still damp, despite the attentions of the bath attendant. A'lian had pummeled me on the massage table, scolding me for being too tense, and he had clucked over the bruise on my thigh. Twas healing quickly—by now a deep ugly yellow-green with purple spots and still a little tender, but not so bad. "Lovely," I murmured. "Tis close to a pattern I saw in Tak-Himor."

"It is." She looked pleased. "Very flattering. You were speaking of Pesh? Jettero, pour me some wine. Prince, tis lovely to see you. Thank you for accepting my invitation."

"How could I resist?" But his eyes were still on me. Black

eyes, hot with something unnamable. He lowered himself into his chair slowly, and Jettero dropped into his after pouring the wine. Kesa sank down gracefully, arranging her skirts, and I sat too, gingerly. Kesa sipped at her wine.

"Azkillian is planning an offensive against Pesh." I took up the thread of our former conversation. "Tis the only logical explanation. The man is crazed."

"Well, *that* much is certain." She clicked her tongue against her teeth, a decisive sound. "What made you think so, the tax on staples?"

"No. Although tis the deciding factor. He will have riots to deal with before long. The peasants will not take kindly to a new tax. They already carry the burden for the Danhai war—and that morass has lasted a decade. You would think a God-Emperor would *learn*." I blew out through pursed lips, beginning to forget Darik was there, staring at me. Between Kesa and Jett, I could relax and eat without worrying about where the next meal would come from.

"Sellswords," Jettero said thoughtfully. "Hmmm. Kimon Leatherworker—you know, the Hagat's-kin, the tall one—told me the sellswords passing through are asking for leather armor and light chain. Good for plains-fighting. Lots of horseflesh, too. One cannot buy a horse at the markets, all the horseflesh is bound for Shaituh."

"*Cha*, I know," I groaned. "I had to pay two Rams for the two I bought, twas in Arjux. I stayed with Doryen. He lost a stablegirl—the brat made off with my cache. He hid it in the stable to keep it from the tax collector."

Kesa laughed. "Doryen. No wits at all."

"Oh, he is plenty of wit, but very little *sense*. So, what gossip, Jett?" I spun a *kiyan* across my fingers and tossed it into the air. He caught it on its descent, made it disappear into one hand. "Nice. I almost missed your fingers."

"Tis what they all say." He grinned, shaking his hair back. "You are a subject of much interest in the marketplace and in the taverns, pretty Flower. The Shainakh remember you and might be wanting to conscript you for their war. Word just arrived from Hain you are wanted for questioning. The entire city's in an uproar. What did you do?"

"Rescued a barbarian." I hesitated a moment, then told the story of Redfist's escape from the Dark Sun sect. I spoke of picking his pocket, and waking up to face the Hain guard, slaying two before I was even truly awake.

Kesa was laughing, and Jett had his hands clutched over his stomach. Tears streamed down his face. They were still chuckling helplessly when appetizers arrived.

The food was, as usual, superlative. Deep-fried whitefish, sweet rice balls, poppadums. We set to with a will. Darik said nothing, and ate only enough to be polite. It began to feel normal to be watched so closely. Or I set myself to ignore it, as gracefully as I could.

By the time the first course arrived—sheksfin soup and *chaabi* stew, with puffy flatbread, served with a clear tart Ambiij wine—we were deep into a discussion of the gossip Jettero had heard about me.

"So the tale is," he finished up, "you and the one that calls himself the King of Thieves have declared war on each other."

I wiped tears of laughter away. "Why would I? He is far too petty a bandit, I take no such small prey. Is it that minstrel again?"

"I know not, but tis a song making the rounds—" He whistled a snatch of a melody I had heard before. "Full of the Iron Flower dueling the King of Thieves."

"I am going to *kill* that minstrel," I muttered. "What of our fine princeling here? I am curious, you understand."

Jettero leaned back in his chair, took a long draft of wine. "*Cha*, Kaia, what is *not* said of him? The Gemerh search for him—something about a palace coup, and him being an Heir to something. Tis a reward for any news of him, and double the reward if there is news of him with a woman. Word just arrived in the market—suddenly the Gemerh are asking of you, too. Apparently one of them was curious, asked for a description, and decided you could be of their ilk." Interest was bright and reigned behind Jettero's muddy dark eyes. "Teyo sang them a few songs, and seemed to interest them. Particularly your name. But the most *interesting* piece of gossip is about a commander in the Shainakh army. He came back to Shaituh half a year ago from the Danhai border, and let it be known anyone who can carry a message to you will be richly rewarded.

Guess who it is."

I sopped some flatbread in my *chaabi*, chewed thoughtfully, took a swallow of wine. Finally I shook my head. "I served out my time in the irregulars. I cannot think of a single commander I would be interested in."

"Does the name Ammerdahl Rikyat mean anything to you?" Kesamine said.

Ah. My spine prickled, as always when I thought of the plains. I leaned back in my chair. *Rikyat? Why would he be asking for me?* "Ah. A commander? Tis more luck than he ever had."

"Well, the Danhai keep killing them," Jettero said practically. "Advancement is fast on the battlefield."

You do not know how correct you are. Memory turned my skin cold for a moment. "He seeks me?" I chewed at my bottom lip. "How certain is this?"

"Certain enough," Kesa said. "I've heard from the travelers coming from Shaituh—the ones that can reach us. Tis some trouble between here and there, but nobody knows quite what. Even the Gemerh cannot go through."

Uneasy news, that. "Odd. You would think the Shaikuhn would keep the road clear. What species of trouble?"

Jettero shrugged, spreading his hands. "Ask the Gemerh."

I would rather ask the wind. I sighed. "It matters little. Shaituh is where I am bound. I must find work. I have been dropping coin all over the barbarian. And if Rik is asking for me..."

"Old lover?" Jettero wiggled his eyebrows. Darik said nothing. I felt his gaze on me.

I sighed, rolled my eyes. "Fellow soldier, rode patrols with me out where the plainsfolk hide behind grass and pick off Shainakh like a Pesh picking boyflesh." The wine was bitter in my mouth, my voice softened. "He saved my life on the S'tai Plain—the last battle I fielded there. Took a crossbow bolt for me. I carried him on my back through the battlefield to the healer's tents. It was..." I looked down at my bowl, losing my appetite.

The S'tai Plain. Blood soaking into the long yellow grass, screams, the moans of the wounded and dying. The yells of the

Danhai as they took heads from the fallen—war prizes. Lancing pain in my side as I carried Rik's limp body through the bloodslick grass, slipping and falling to my knees, cursing steadily to keep from weeping. And the dust, dear gods, the dust, *rising to choke every breath.*

Dust, and heat, and the Sun in my eyes. The carrion stink of death on my skin, and my heart playing racehorse as I staggered, and slipped, and cursed still more. And heard the hoofbeats behind me—

I shook my head, took a long swallow of wine. "So. If he calls for me, I should at least go visit. He may have a commission for me. As long as tis merely an assassination and not the Danhai, I would be willing."

"Life at a sword's edge." Kesa shook her golden head. "I am glad I am no sellsword."

"I share that gladness." I pushed my hair out of my eyes. Why had I left it down? Twas more irritating than I had bargained for. "I would hate to have to duel you, Kesa'li."

It was a pale joke, but she laughed anyway. The shadow of the Danhai blew away; I was grateful to see it go.

Twas the fourth course—delicacies, fried stretchlegs and moonshells, tamburin fried in butter and garlinroot, sweet tarka in wine sauce—when we became serious. I finally asked the question. "So what is the real news, Jett?" I plucked a tamburin from the pan with my eating-picks. The discomfort of travel was long forgotten.

Jettero cast a nervous glance at Darik, who had just taken a drink of wine. For the fourth course it was a dry white freetown vintage, just vulgar enough to balance out the delicate tastes. "Why does your princeling not tell you, Kaia? I am certain he knows by now."

My eyes, compelled, met Darik's. He set his cup down, moved it along the surface of the table. Shrugged. The cut on his shoulder was mostly healed, I felt no betraying twinge in my arm when he moved. "It makes little difference. I go where Kaia goes."

Let us not tread that road again. I set my own winecup down with a click. "The G'mai have given you a message, I warrant. What is it? The queen's found you an *adai*? Or just pines for your pretty face?"

His gaze pierced me, a level stare more suited to a battlefield than a dinner table. "The queen's Heir is dead, her *s'tarei* died defending her against the Hatai. The queen has named me provisional Heir until she has more issue. Which is not likely, as she is past childbearing age and the Heir—my cousin—was her only child."

Shock loosed my fingers. My eating-picks clattered against my plate. "Well. That *is* news." I retrieved the picks, my eyes dropping to my bowl. "Tragedy indeed for the house of Dragaemir," I murmured, in G'mai. "Accept my compassion."

Kesa was very still to my left, and Jettero watched my face avidly. The silence began to grow predatory. When I could raise my eyes, I did.

"When do you leave?" I asked in commontongue. "And do you wish your Seeker returned to you?"

A muscle in his cheek twitched. "It is bad manners to mock at bad news." He spoke still in G'mai.

Kesa's face changed. She looked for all the world as if she was trying to keep from laughing, or gasping in shock. Jettero took a noisy gulp of wine. It did not break the tension.

"I have already told you," Darik continued in commontongue, "where you go, I go. The palace means nothing to me. Let them have their halls and hangings. They did not lift a hand to aid me or my mother when I was young. Why should I aid them now?" He shrugged, Kshanti silk moving over his shoulders. "You interest me far more than any empty Throne."

My throat closed. *Gods. Why does he continue with this farce?*

"That is truly wise of you." Kesamine's pale face was thoughtful in the candlelight. "But tell me, my lord prince, why do you follow the Iron Flower?" She was about to add aught else, but the look on my face must have stopped her.

Darik glanced at her, consideringly. "Do you really wish to know?" A slight smile touched his lips.

"Curiosity consumes me." Her blue eyes glimmered through the black traced on her lids. "I have never seen a man chase Kaia for long. Her tongue is so sharp she has no need of a sword to keep them away."

Darik shrugged. "Push your chairs back a little, then. I shall show you."

Kesa and Jettero complied, scraping their seats back along polished wooden floor. I stayed where I was, frozen in place, staring at him. What was he thinking?

If I was truly his *adai*, I would know, would I not?

Without flinching, Darik held his hand out over the table. Directly over the candleflame, an arm's length above.

A spot of warmth bloomed on my left hand. I set my jaw. His eyes locked with mine. "There is a drawback to being *adai*," he said, calmly. "The *adai* feels the wounds of her *s'tarei*. Tis a reminder, not to be careless of her twin." He moved his hand down slightly, and the warm spot in my palm grew hot.

"You cannot be serious." My throat was shuttered, the words were a hoarse croak.

"I am." His hand dropped. The spot on my palm became scorching hot.

I fought to keep my fingers loose and relaxed. "You would cripple your hand to seek to prove a point?"

"I will not be harmed." His tone was intimate, as if we were the only two in the room. "My *adai* would not allow it."

He dropped his palm down into the flame.

Kesa gasped and stood up, her chair squealing along the floor. Jettero let out a curse.

I found myself on my feet, leaning half over the table, my fingers around Darik's wrist. I had shoved his hand out of the candleflame and flung it back at him before I knew what I did. My left palm throbbed, spikes of agony forcing their way up my wrist. I had not moved quickly enough.

I swept my hair back, away from the flame. Looked at Kesa, looked at Jettero. And finally, I looked at Darik, cradling his left hand in his right. His swords looked up over his shoulder, twin accusers. And his eyes—

I had expected pain, in his black eyes. Shame. Instead, I saw triumph, and a fierce pride. His face was harsh in the soft light, and his jaw was set. The full beauty of the Dragaemir was upon him, and I saw how he would look in twenty winters or so, when time settled on his bones and brought him fully into his prime.

"You see?" He lifted his left hand. There was a red patch in the middle of the palm, but no blister. Perhaps I had been fast enough after all. "My *adai.* Tis not in her nature to allow me to suffer."

I shook my left hand out once, briskly, snapping my fingers. "I will not have you continue—"

"Kaia," Kesa snapped. Her eyes sparkled, an overflow of some emotion I could not name. "Sit down. I will have no more of this at my table. You are rude."

"Oh, Mother's *tits*—" I began.

"Sit down." Her tone brooked no disobedience.

I will face sellswords and assassins, I will duel in the ring, but I would not cause Kesamine any shame at her dinner table. I was raised better. And I value her peace.

I dropped meekly into my chair. My hand gave one last livid flare, settling to a dull ache. No real damage, merely pain. "Kesa," I managed, weakly. "Please." *You have no idea what this will do to me, when I lose it.*

"We have not had sweetmeats yet." Her earrings jingled as she raised her chin. "Thank you for that...*illuminating* spectacle, Your Highness. And I *do* mean that. Kaia never speaks of her people."

He shrugged. His eyes never left me. Dull anger woke in my bones.

I grow weary of being watched so closely, princeling.

Jettero took another gulp of wine. "Amazing," he said, as Kesa drew her chair back up to the table. "If you are wounded, she feels it?"

Darik nodded. "Tis the curse of the gifts we are blessed with. Kaia'li has more than most." He picked up his wineglass, took a sip. Calmly, as if he were at a banquet and not about to ruin my entire life.

"This is mere callousness," I said tonelessly. "When you find your true *adai* I will be left to wander alone again. You should not toy with me so."

"Kaia—" Jett began.

Jett, if you make a snide remark now, I will call you to the dueling circle. I am angry enough. "Leave it be." I made it to my feet again, slowly, like an old woman.

Kesa stared up at me with a strange expression. Thoughtful and curious all at once, and tinted with...what? Regret? Envy?

Sometimes other races envy us. They do not know the heavy price of the twinning, or the pain when it is broken.

I did not dare meet Darik's eyes. He had proved his point. "I will meet you on the dueling ground tomorrow, Dragaemir. Two candlemarks past dawn."

I turned on my heel and paced across Kesa's dining room. Silence thickened, vibrating with tension. The storm, forgotten by us all, stroked the sky with thunder and lashing rain. I could imagine ships at anchor swaying under the force of that wind. Wished I was on a ship, hauling on rigging, battening down, too busy with canvas and hemp and shouted commands to worry for anything but the next moment, and the next.

I put my hand on the doorknob. My palms were slippery. I did not fear him, did I?

No, I did not fear him. I feared what I might become in his eyes; and when he met his true *adai*, it would kill me to give up the dream of being a true G'mai, a daughter of my people.

A daughter of the Blessed. The girl I was before I left the borders of my land and became Kaia Steelflower.

"Do you truly wish to duel me?" Darik's voice hit the walls like a slap. It was the second time he had raised his voice to me, and I could not feel satisfied that I had provoked him. Chair legs scraped against the wooden floor again. Had he risen? Was he prepared to come after me?

"No, I do not." My throat felt thick, full of unshed tears. "But you leave me no choice, Tar-Amyirak Adarikaan imr-dr'Emeryn, Dragaemir-hai. You leave me no choice at all."

With that, I escaped through the door, shutting it quietly but firmly. I had the last word.

I could not feel victorious, though. I only felt emptiness. The dream was over.

I would never be a true G'mai. Best just to end it quickly.

Death Tomorrow, Talk Tonight

"Ye did what?" Redfist's deep voice slurred with sleep. I had picked the lock on his door and brought most of my gear in silently, locked the door again, and tilted a chair under the doorknob. By then, I felt as if I could breathe again.

Perhaps.

"I duel Darik tomorrow, two candlemarks past dawn." I poked him on the shoulder. "Wake *up*, barbarian. I go to meet my death tomorrow, the least you can do is give me some little conversation."

The room was pale rose and cream, with a flower motif. Kesamine liked her rooms in themes, and her taste was exquisite. There was a simple Kshanti vase of palest blush porcelain on the mantel, with a spray of *maati* flowers made out of silk with stems of twisted cotton and wire. A wallhanging of pale embroidered risinflowers hung over the small table where Redfist had eaten dinner alone.

I envied his solitude.

Redfist sprawled bellydown on the bed, his hands dangling off on either side. His ginger-furred face was turned into a pillow, but I heard his groan clearly enough. "What have ye done *now*, lass?"

I ruined a perfectly lovely dinner and probably made Kesa very angry. "I just insulted the Heir to the Dragon Throne and challenged him to an open duel. Tomorrow." I restrained the urge to poke him again, or shake him.

Redfist groaned. It was a sound loud and weary enough to move the bed. "Lass, why did ye do that?"

I tore a blanket out of its roll and spread it on the rug next to the fireplace. Picked up a saddlebag full of clothing and tossed it down to serve as a pillow, then slipped out of my swordharness and snuggled myself into the ready-made bed. I rolled over, curled myself around the aching hole in the middle of my belly. Darik had slept next to me for the past few nights, and I had not awakened in the middle of the night with my heart pounding and my hand reaching for a weapon.

No, I had slept as deeply and trustfully as a child. Now I found myself missing the silent warmth of him, just close enough to touch. "I do not know, Redfist."

I was no stranger to men. I was no stranger to playing the game of conquest and courtship; I was no stranger to maneuvering the treacherous waters of breaking off a liaison. So why could I not break off this liaison before it started?

Because he is not merely a pretty princeling. He is G'mai. You told yourself your blood means nothing so often you almost believed it, until he came to remind you. If you must give up that dream again, Kaia, you will begin to bleed inside once more. This time the bleeding will not stop.

Redfist let out a disgusted snort. "Ye're a spoiled child, K'ai. Always having to have yer way."

"I saved your life." *You ignorant, smelly, halfwit barbarian.* But I could not be cruel to him. He had merely been a coincidence. The hand of Luck lighting on me at last.

"An have bossed me aboot like me mums since," he grumbled. "Now let me think, lass. Sleep if you like, but let me think."

"Very well." I closed my eyes. Sleep refused me. I shifted on the hard wooden floor—at least there were no rocks or thorny bushes here. And the fire was warm.

Very soon, Redfist began to snore.

Dinner curdled in my belly. A snoring barbarian. I wanted a deep bed and Kesa's arms around me, the whispers and giggles of us sharing jokes and stories, maybe Kesa teaching me how Rijiin courtesans lacquered their nails, maybe me teaching her the proper way to throw a knife. Perhaps sharing gossip, perhaps more.

Instead I had a duel with my avowed *s'tarei* in the morning, and I had been unforgivably rude to Kesa in her own dining room. I would have to steal her a nice present to make up for it.

What had I done?

The Prince—no, the *Heir to the Dragon Throne.* Challenged him to a duel because...

Because if I allowed myself to think of him as mine, I would not be able to let him go.

Think of something else. Of Jett selling this tale to a songster. Jettero, curse him, would sell and sing the story of the Iron Flower losing her temper before the sweetmeats course. A welcome bite of irritation bloomed inside my head. Another Frozen Flower song. If I lived to hear it sung.

I was not certain I could push Darik's control enough to make him kill me. I also was not certain I could make a lucky strike and kill *him.* Nor did I wish either outcome. I had told the truth: I did not wish to duel him.

I wanted what I could not even name to myself.

Thunder rolled and boomed. The rain began in earnest, sweeping in heavy waves like the sea's fingers combing land's fringes.

Footsteps sounded in the hall outside. Probably Jettero's, they were a man's boots. Walking deliberately.

"I have done well for myself," I whispered, squeezing my eyes shut and ignoring the warm trickles down my temples, vanishing into my hair. "Six rooms and seven waterclosets. A bedroom on the bottom floor. Linens hung in the Sun."

I lay there, turning the words into a humming song in commontongue. *Six rooms and seven waterclosets. A bedroom on the bottom floor. Linens hung in the Sun.*

Is that what you wish for? I imagined I heard Darik's voice, a cool murmur, right next to my ear. Speaking G'mai, of course, his voice shading the words intimately, comfortingly.

I sighed, rolled over, presenting my back to the fire. I could pretend the warmth was his. *I do not know. I wished to stay in G'maihallan. I would not have left, had they not thrown me out. I longed for Power, for any scrap of it.*

Why? His voice again. It was just my imagination. There was no harm in imagining, was there? *You have enough to make the trees dance in the wind, enough to kiss a pair of dice into rolling the way you wish them to, enough to make a coin land the way you wish. Enough for a* s'tarei, *Kaia.*

He would never say such things to me. They were not *true.*

I scrubbed at my eyes with my fists like a child. There was wetness on my fingers. What had I done? The rain beat on the wall of the inn, as if it intended to wash the town away. I was using my own facile tongue to dupe myself into thinking I was truly G'mai.

Shhh. It was comforting, his imaginary voice, far more comforting than I probably deserved. *Just rest, Kaia'li, little sharpness. All will be well.*

I do not know what I want. Relief crashed through me like waves against cliffs. I was moontouched, crazy. I was imagining voices. Maybe G'mai without Power went insane, and I had been saved from that fate by shunning. Saved until I brushed against other G'mai, felt the Power in their eyes, heard the song of my native tongue again.

I fell asleep, cradling my *dotanii* in my arms. Twas strange, but I seemed to hear someone singing as if to a child. It was a familiar tune, the Lay of Creation, in a male voice. A G'mai voice, one that knew the right accents.

I slept.

A Little Hunger

Dawn broke over the harbor in a glory of red. The inngirl Vavakha brought a tray of kafi to Redfist's room. I was in the watercloset, and watched her set it on a table and look at the sleeping barbarian. She snorted, flipped her hair impatiently and stalked out.

Light leftover rain misted down from an infinite sky. The storm's fury had been spent last night. It was a good omen, if one believed in such things.

I stepped cautiously out of the watercloset, crossed to the kafi pot, and poured myself a cup. It might well be the last cup of kafi I ever drank.

"What is tha' disgusting smell?" the barbarian rumbled from the bed. "Lass, I would hae ye take th' softie."

He was not such a bad sort, after all. "The floor was well enough. At least there are no rocks. Will you be my second in the duel?"

"Duel?" The ginger-furred man pushed himself upright, blinked at me. "Were ye serious, then?"

"I was." *Have you ever known me not to be, even on such short acquaintance?* "Two candlemarks past dawn. One of which you have already slept away, while I've oiled my sword and prepared my deathsong. Come, have a drink of kafi."

"*That's* kafi? It smells like burned stockings." He rubbed at his face, then blinked and peered at me. "Did ye sleep here last night, lass? Ye must have. Ye must think me a right bastard."

"Do you know you snore?" I smiled thinly; I felt a little more myself, with my hair rebraided and a duel to look forward to.

Facing Darik over sharp steel. A little flutter touched the bottom of my belly. Nerves. Not unexpected, and I ignored them. Well, maybe not precisely ignored them. Tried to ignore them. I took three sips of kafi and smiled at the barbarian.

He blinked his green eyes at me. "Ye look fair glowing, lass."

"A good fight to look forward to. I've had precious little challenge since I left home. I hope I have not become rusty."

"Briyde's eyes, what did he do?" Redfist yawned again. I watched him behind the mask of my smiling face and set the kafi cup down. Three sips was all convention allowed before a duel, to avoid the use of stimulants.

I shrugged. "Tis complex, Redfist. Did you know he is not merely a prince, our red-eyed bugger, but the Heir to the Dragon Throne of G'maihallan? His cousin is dead in a frontier battle and he is wanted at home. If he follows me about, he leaves the Blessed Country without an Heir. That could mean disaster. The Council will be open to infighting, and—"

"Why do ye nae go back wit' him then?" Redfist asked. "Ye may see yer kith and kin again."

I shook my head. My hair was braided back in complex loops, secured for battle. I could fight through an entire campaign with these braids in. My *dotanii* was oiled, I had already done my stretches.

I was as ready as it was possible to be. "I cannot return, Redfist. They will shun me again." I shivered to think of it. "He was given a flawed Seeker, and so ends the tale. If he returns to G'maihallan, perhaps he will find a true *adai*." I took a deep breath. "All I must do now is avoid being killed and provoke him into returning home." *Easy. Except for that pride of his.*

"An' how de ye propose to be doing that?" He gaped and stretched again. "Yer pardon, lass, but I need t'piss."

"Ease yourself." I tried not to sound amused. He rolled up out of the bed, making it groan, and rumbled toward the bathroom.

I had suspected he was covered in hair, but it was another thing entirely to see it in reality. I pursed my lips, denying laughter, and looked over at my packs. If I died, Kesa would sell all my gear the barbarian could not use. Then she would send him on his way.

If he wished to go. I had no doubt work could be found about the Sparrows Moon for a barbarian as strong as an ox. His size alone would stop trouble in the commonroom.

And Kesa would probably make certain I had a pyre. If she ever forgave me for ruining dinner.

Drops of mist beading on the window, running down, growing fat again. A heavy seaward mist, not the best weather for fighting. But for dueling—*ah, there is no good weather for dueling,* as the proverb says. Tis dangerous no matter what.

Redfist lumbered out of the watercloset, blinking against the light. He found his breeches and nimbly stepped into them, a sudden grace surprising in one of his size.

It was time. "I am bound for the dueling ring. Come down if you like. If not, wait here, and someone will come tell you what happens."

"Lass—" Did he actually look *concerned*? Did he have so little faith in my skill?

Then again, I was facing a fully-trained *s'tarei*. We had both seen Darik fight. I was fey with the thought of a duel, Redfist was feeling the caution I should have.

I shook my head. "I would recommend you watch, at least. Two G'mai dueling is likely to be a spectacle you will not soon see." I stalked for the door.

"Ye are determined, then. Well, I owe ye two lives, I'll come an' second ye."

Gods bless you, barbarian. You are more honorable than most. "Ask anyone where the dueling ground is. They will be happy enough to guide you, tis considered lucky." I stepped out into the hall and closed the door, leaving a half-naked furry barbarian standing in a square of moonshell light from the cloud-shrouded Sun.

I found my boots in Kesa's room, worked my feet into them. Kesa had not thrown them out into the hall, which meant she probably was not *that* angry.

I perched in the chair in front of Kesamine's fireplace, pulling my second boot on. Kesamine breezed through the door, her red and yellow dress fluttering. She stopped, put her fists to her hips, and glared at me.

"Kesa," I began. The first of many apologies, I was sure. "I crave your pard—"

"*There* you are. Do you know I've made more this morn than in the last moonturn? *Cha!* The Iron Flower and her suitor, a duel at the ground outside the Sparrows Moon. Rumor travels on air." Her blue eyes were unreadable, her hair pulled back so the purity of her bones showed through. Her gold—ears, wrists, throat—glittered like the Sun despite this cloudy day.

I leaned back in the chair, though not far enough to lean against my sword. "Jettero."

"Oh, yes. *Jettero*. There are two more pairs of G'mai here, paying good coin. You are a draw for business, Kaia'naa. Even if you *did* ruin dinner last night." She cocked her head. "Well, what have you to say for yourself?"

I stretched up out of the chair, the soles of my boots gripping the floor. Already I was in the dueling-ring, thinking of my opponent, wondering. "I *do* crave your pardon, Kesa. I did not seek to mar the enjoyment of your feast."

"You did not. Jett and I ate your sweetmeats. Your prince left, waited outside your door all night. Vavakha nearly tripped over him this morn, and he has been closeted in the room I gave him since, preparing for the duel, I warrant. The most exciting thing since your last visit here." Amused and furious in equal measure, she eyed me from under her black-smudged eyelids.

"Twas not my fault. They were bandits." *And ten on one is bad odds, twas to my good luck I had a bow. I remember that knife-wound, I thought I would die lying outside the walls. If that caravan had not happened by, I would have been saved all this trouble and been singing in the Moon's shadow all this time.*

"*Cha*, bandits." Her mouth pulled down, her skirt rustling as she shifted her weight. Abruptly sobered. "Kaia, you felt his pain last night. I saw it."

I shrugged. I was naked without my knives, but I was only allowed the largest of them as well as my sword in the circle. "I have no choice, Kesa. The barbarian is my second. If I leave the ground on my back, I expect you to put me on a pyre."

She grinned, her eyes twinkling. "You may leave the dueling ground defeated, but that man will not kill you." Her teeth were very white. She reached up, rubbed at her forehead with delicate fingertips, and shook her head. "I suppose you will not eat breakfast."

I shook my head. "Too much in the belly means a lost duel. I fight best a little hungry. Besides, tis against convention. Too many lordlings dosing themselves beforehand."

Kesa crossed the room, took me by the shoulders, her hands pale and cool against my linen shirt. She shook me, sharply, twice. "You are a fool, Kaia'naa. A twin for you, something all your women have and you were raised to expect. And what do you do, *wahana laia laiawaha*? You wish to kill him!" She laughed, and the sound was far more serious than any sob. "You are *kawahana'laha'naa*, stubborn as a k'wahana bird. Do you know the k'wahana bird will not leave a beach where its mate has died? It will starve to death crying on the sands. Who are you crying for, Kaia?"

Not for Darik, certainly. Perhaps only for the girl I was, or what I have become. I reached up, touched the hilt of my *dotanii*. "I cry for no one, Kesa. Just as I trust nothing but steel."

I had not meant to sound so cruel.

For a moment I thought Kesa might slap me. I saw the betraying twitch in her arm and braced myself. I would not have blamed her. I bit my lip and waited for the blow.

Instead, she took a step back. "Good luck." Her cheeks had gone pale.

"I do trust you, Kesa. Truly, I do." *You have had far too many opportunities to slip a knife twixt my ribs, my Clau darling. And you have not. That is worth something.*

That made her drop her blue eyes, still regarded as bad luck in some places. "Luck," she repeated.

"My thanks," I returned, gravely. "Watch me fight?"

"No, I do not think I will." Her mouth turned down at both corners, pulling against the rest of her face.

Not after I've just made a complete ass of myself, you mean. And the Clau consider duels foolishness. "Kesa—"

"No." She turned away sharply, her skirt belling out in her haste. "Luck, Kaia. Tis all I wish you today."

Wingwyrms Circling

The dueling-ground lay below a wide round thatch roof, dripping from last night's rain. I approached the edge, watching a young woman with bare feet scattering sand on the stone.

It was bad luck to get to the ground before the duelers did, so there was often a pushing and shoving for position at the very last moment. I leaned against a post on the south side—the challenger's side.

Twas a cool, rainy morning, the Sun shining through the clouds in bursts. Under the roof twas light enough, and the sand was fresh. There is no central pillar in a dueling-ground, the roof is supported by long flexible bantha poles; in some small towns the dueling-circle is merely drawn at need in the ground with a sharp stick.

I waited, my hands loosely clasped before me, leaning against the post, breathing in the smell of a rainy morning. The wind came fresh off the sea, full of salt and the cries of gulls. Deep draughts of its cleanness, *breathe in, breathe out*, tuning my mind to a blank readiness.

"Are you certain you wish to do this?" A woman's voice. Speaking in G'mai.

Oh, Mother's tits. *I hoped to escape this.*

I half-turned. The *adai* I had seen yesterday wore forest-green velvet, a G'mai gown, patterned with the design meaning the Everstar in our symbol-language. Long oversleeves brushed the ground, and her boots were stamped with leaf-shapes. She wore emeralds in silver at her throat and wrists, and rings glittered on her slender fingers. Her braids were intricate, but much shorter than mine. Younger, then. She *was* very young, more than I had thought.

"What do you wish of me?" I did not sweeten my tone, and I did not speak in our native tongue. I could not use G'mai for this girl.

She shrugged. She had a lovely face, the delicate loveliness speaking of extreme youth. I might have looked so once—but not as beautiful. Not so beautiful at all. She appeared a Gavridar, one of the lowland Houses that have not bred harshness into their children. I have seen Gavridar at festivals, and they all look too unearthly, skin too flawless, faces too soft. "It pains me to see a sister so unhappy."

I let out a low derisive noise. "I am no sister of yours, *adai'sa*. I was born without Power, I am *sharauq'allallai*." The word meant "outcaste", and was the word for murderers, kinslayers, those the G'mai cast away.

Like leavings after a feast. Like rubbish.

She shook her head, those liquid dark eyes on me. "No. Rather I would say you have too much. The immensity of your gift would make you difficult to train, and you are past the age of easy learning. Adarikaan needs no more battles in his life, sister. He has had enough." She used the same inflection she would use with a royal *adai*, refusing for her part to speak commontongue, and helpless anger curdled in me.

I will not feel guilty, you little chit. What do you *know of battles?* "He is determined to battle me. I have given him every chance to leave me be."

"The *dauq'adai* found you." Stated as a given fact, as if she had been present and knew. "Yet you deny him."

"I merely wait for his true *adai* to appear." *Argue with that, girl. It is not wise to bait me before a duel, anyone who knows of me can tell you as much.*

"He may not be so gentle if you step into the circle with him." She tilted her lovely head back to look up at me. Abruptly I felt tall, graceless, and awkward compared to this beautiful doll of a G'mai girl. Anger speared me, anger at myself—and oddly enough, at her. Had she ever struggled, ever starved because she lived by her sword, ever had to fight off the Hain guard or a Shaikuhn's son? Had she ever been sick, and cold, and hungry, and alone?

"Little of my life has been *gentle.*" I managed to keep my tone civil, but only just. "This should at least be familiar."

She clucked her tongue at me, the sort of sound G'mai mothers use to express weary wonder at a child's antics. "Darik may well be the only Heir the queen will have, now. You are his *adai.* Will you deny our people? Have we been so cruel to you?"

"I am *not G'mai.*" Through gritted teeth, slowly and clearly so she could understand. "I have not *been* G'mai since I was five summers high. I was tested for Power, and found to have none. This does not concern you, *adai'sa.* Today I either go to death or freedom, and I thank you to leave me be. I have a duel to think of."

Amazingly, she laughed, a carefree sound. Her *s'tarei* leaned against the inn's wall, watching. Of course—I had a sword and an uncertain temper, and I was within reach of his *adai.* No wonder he was edgy. "You are a fine match for him." She shook her head, her braids swinging. "Both of you too proud and stubborn. I look forward to this."

I gave a noncommittal noise and turned my back on her, gazing at the freshly sanded circle. Rainwater dripped steadily from the border of the thatching. Gullcries seemed far away, the sea even further. *What I would not give to be on a ship right now. Bound for Antai, bound for anywhere.*

I touched the hard lump of the *dauq'adai* under my shirt. A flawed Seeker and a flawed G'mai. What a perfect pairing. Poor Darik, driven halfway around the world by a miscarriage of G'mai magic.

Do not pity your opponent before the duel, Kaia. Pity him after, when you have finished with him.

Redfist appeared, eased up to my side. He wore—finally—some freshly laundered clothes, linen shirt, a leather vest. The sight of him, hunching his shoulders and blinking against the rain, was absurdly comforting. His axe swaggered, strapped to his belt. "I have nae seen a duel like this before, lass. What is it ye need of me?"

Tis enough that you are here, barbarian. I had ceased to think of him as a halfwit, precisely when I did not know. "Merely watch, to make certain he does not cheat. Though I do not think he would."

He grunted.

Make your amends now, Kaia. "I crave your pardon. I was harsh to you. You do not deserve the sharp edge of my tongue."

"Aye, I do not. Though I think I would die of astonishment should you cease using it." He tapped blunt fingers on the haft of his axe. "Thank ye kindly, lass."

There was nothing more to say or do. We lapsed into quiet, the Skaialan and I.

Despite the ill-luck, people drifted into the courtyard early. I caught a few excited whispers, and the betting started. "Can you find what the odds are?" I pitched my voice low, merely curious.

He slipped away and came back, moving far more quietly than I thought a giant could. "The current line is three to two, yer favor. The Gemerh, he's unknown, but they're canny fighters."

"Pfft." I made a small noise. "I am accustomed to better odds."

Darik appeared. He resolved out of the gray rainy day next to the northernmost pole supporting the roof. I let my face take on its dueling-mask.

Some will laugh and shout before a duel. Others will sit quietly in the circle, pretending to meditate. Others will bluster about, trying to unnerve their opponent before the fight.

I bent down, touched the freshly scattered sand. Twas grainy and cold, and reminded me of other duels. I brushed grit from my fingertips and stood, gazing steadily across the circle.

He was slightly taller than the other *s'tarei*, and every bit the G'mai. The two swords strapped to his back watched over his shoulders, and he wore the shirt I had repaired for him. Black trousers, black boots, a blot of darkness on the fresh-washed morning. He stood, quietly, and the *s'tarei* I had seen yesterday reappeared, with his *adai* at his side. Tyaanismir Atyarik.

I had not asked the name of the silly little so-young *adai*. I did not wish to know.

The *s'tarei* appeared reluctant, but Darik merely looked interested and pleasant. It was the same mask his face held during most of the time we had traveled together, and I found I preferred his jaw clenched with fury and his eyes glittering-deadly.

My heart began to pound.

Two candlemarks past dawn.

I stepped into the ring. People poured into the courtyard. There was betting, and a close press to the thatched circle. A dueling-ground is seven or ten bodylengths in diameter, and freshly sanded before each bout. It can go unused for weeks, but should always be kept well-thatched with chedgrass. The sand should be fine and white, though in the desert they sweep the stone floor clear before a bout. Enough blows onto the stone during the duel to give traction.

Excited whispers rose. The Tyaanismir *s'tarei* murmured to Darik, and the prince shrugged. He made a single low reply, and the *s'tarei* paled. The Tyaanismir cast one venomous glance at me, bowed shortly to the prince.

Darik's black eyes met mine.

If it was the first blow of the duel, I was not the worse for it. Yet I felt it, a shock against my entire body. My nape tingled. He drew himself up, and I truly saw the Dragaemir in him.

The crowd stilled, taking a collective breath. There was a frenzied whisper around the man taking bets. Had the odds just changed? I allowed myself a small smile.

Darik stepped into the ring.

We faced each other finally over four armlengths of sand. I had not lost his eyes once. His face was set. The beauty of him—a Dragaemir, his chin lifted and his mouth firm—was enough to make my breath hitch.

"You have only one blade," he said in commontongue. "I wish no cries of cheating."

There was a shadow under his eyes—sleeplessness? I hoped so, twould give me an edge. I drew my longknife, reversed it along my left forearm. The blade went from my wrist to my elbow, fine Gavridar steel with the characteristic dappling on its bright shine, carried with me from my homeland and about to serve me now. "Enough of a blade for me, princeling."

His lips thinned before he spoke. "Are you so determined? I warn you, I am close to losing my temper, Kaia'li."

I reached up, drew my *dotanii* from its sheath. Stepped back a little, just out of range. Anger tinted the air, the rage of a *s'tarei*, kept carefully reined but still sensed, a heatless incense under the salt and rain. "Your temper does not frighten me at all, princeling. Did the palace teach you any fighting, or did they only teach you pretty words?"

His jaw set, and his black eyes lit with anger.

Good.

He drew a *dotanii*, his stance shifting into one I recognized, the first of the three battle-poses. "I may not be gentle."

I nodded, slowly, taking him in from head to foot. Taller than me, he would have weight and reach. I was certain I had speed on my side. "Save your gentleness for an *adai*." I held his gaze with my own, knowing my eyes often disconcerted opponents. "If there is anything left of you to find her after I finish rolling you in this sand."

"You are my *adai*," he said, softly, in G'mai. Intimately.

It only fueled my anger.

We circled. I saw his hand move a little, countered it with shifting my weight. Silence spread over the crowd.

I answered in commontongue, another deliberate insult. "Your flawed Seeker found a flawed G'mai. There is still time for you to leave with your pride intact, prince."

"My pride is too deep for you to injure it, Anjalismir." Brittle, courteous and infuriating.

I swallowed rage, set my jaw.

He moved in, fast and light, a flurry of strokes. Metal clashed, slithered, sang, and the familiar fierce enjoyment of a duel began to beat behind my heart.

I heard the gasp of wonder from the crowd, ignored it. Nothing mattered now but the bright metal and the dance.

He moved forward, testing, a flurry of strikes. I parried them all—barely. He was well-trained, and *fast*, faster than any opponent I had encountered outside of my native land. It was a joy to see him react, to see the purity of his form, to feel another G'mai fight.

Sweat trickled down my back. A few passes of real combat wear worse than a whole day's worth of training. Darik only

looked patient, cautious, his black hair beginning to dampen against his forehead. He moved in again, and I gave ground, slashing and feinting.

I attacked.

I do not think he expected it, and I do not think he expected me to strike to kill. I attacked with all my speed, and the crowd cheered—*Kaia! Kaia! Kaia!*

He retreated, pushing my strikes aside. It felt good to use all my strength and speed, felt good to *use* myself, forgetting everything but the man in front of me and the blade's sharp length.

He struck, I warded the blow aside with the knife laid along my forearm. It would bruise—my arm gave an amazing flare of pain and went almost numb.

My blade snaked through his defenses. The star-strike—I had first blood, a ribbon of red up his sword arm. The danger was, I felt it. There was a gasp from the assembled crowd. My arm hurt, but I shoved that aside. I dripped with sweat now. So did he. A salt different than the ocean stung my eyes. We closed, and his strength would have told had I not used the knife-hilt to punch him in the face.

My head snapped back, I almost saw the bright pinpoints of light from a stunning blow. I retreated, saw the ribbon of blood threading down from his mouth. His cheek would bruise, and his right eye almost immediately began to puff closed. Phantom blood slid down my own chin, I fought the urge to wipe it away.

We circled. Step by step, each locked into the other's rhythm now, no retreat possible.

No quarter asked. None given.

Darik's face was set, a muscle along his jaw flicking. He reached up and drew his second *dotanii*, his hand closing lovingly around the fluid hilt.

I bared my teeth. So I had managed to anger him. He smiled as well, and my heart leapt into my throat to hammer there before I forced it down. In that one moment, I felt as if the man I faced understood me completely. A rare gift, to be *understood*, comprehended fully, to have your enemy reach into your heart so that it is not fighting but *dancing*, and not even that. It is a heart, each chamber echoing the other's beat; the two halves of the lungs working in concert, salt in the water that carries it.

For just that moment, it was thus. And if he understood me, if I felt so completely *known*, could I not also say I comprehended him?

Someone yelled in G'mai. Probably the *adai*. I ignored it.

Darik moved in, and I saw again his speed and strength. He was better-trained, and stronger. Yet I stayed one measure ahead, just out of reach.

Ah, Kaia. You have seen him. Now you must out-dance him.

He closed in, I had all I could do to keep his steel from me. Finally, he did not hold back. I led him a merry dance around the circle. Sand flew. Now that he pursued, my speed gave me some breathing room.

Stop this, I imagined him saying. *While you still can, Kaia'li.* His voice caressed me, and I shook it aside. I could no more stop now than he could. Desperation demanded I fight him with everything I had. There was no room for anything other than the truth.

When he leaves, it will kill me. It will tear the heart from me to give up G'maihallan again. I cannot.

I chose my spot with care—in the east quarter of the circle, between two support posts. Then I turned on him with all the anger I still possessed, the spell of comprehension still lingering between us, both caught in the pattern of *what would be.*

Sparks flew. Metal rang and sang as it had on the anvil that made it. The silence enfolding us—a prince and a flawed G'mai woman—was absolute. None spoke. None cheered.

I closed with him, my knife flicking out to scrape across his knuckles. He did not drop his sword, but the echo of his pain in my own body told hard on me. I would not have the strength much longer.

Now, my fightbrain shrieked.

I dropped my blades and leapt.

Twas a spin-kick, and a beautifully done spin-kick at that. The chiming of my blades hitting the ground caused him a split second of hesitation—it was not enough, his right-hand *dotanii* flicked across my arm and scraped down my ribs before my boot connected. The kick sent him flying back—I had gauged it just under rib-snapping force. He flew out of the dueling-circle between the two support posts, boots skidding against the stone.

Forfeit. The crowd gasped, turned into one being for that brief moment. Melded into an instrument I had just played, a tide I had just directed.

Darik regained his balance and stopped, gazed uncomprehending at me. The crowd stilled.

Blood trickled down my left side, down my left arm. I picked up my *dotanii* and my knife, slowly. Then I turned to the crowd and lifted my blades, pain tearing into my side through a screen of numbness.

An instant of silence, then Redfist bellowed. The sound made several people start, and the swell of the crowd filling the courtyard cheered.

I had won. Once he left the circle, Darik was in forfeit. I had won without killing either of us.

I had *won.*

Now leave me be, let me alone. Leave me to suffer in peace.

The crowd filling the courtyard chanted my name. I was pummeled on my shoulder—the unwounded one—and my hair was touched, people converging on the dueling-ground to pick up handfuls of sand. Twas scuffed and cast about, and lucky to boot. A duel to remember. Kesa would make a sundog or two from the thirsty afterwards.

He had not killed me, and I had not wanted to kill him, but I had indisputably won. I was free. We were quits, the prince of the G'mai and me. There was a duel finished between us, and all debts were canceled. All promises set at naught.

I began to believe I was still alive. I drew a ragged breath into living lungs. He was still alive, and I was free. Cheated my way out of Death's bony grasp, once again.

Not for long, a deep voice warned me. I knew that, as well.

Redfist bellowed, hoisted me up out of the crush of the crowd. I had re-sheathed my blades and now smiled, nodding to the crowd, my right hand up, when the tension and blood loss suddenly combined to turn the world gray. Redfist's hands clamped around my knees—he had set me on his massive shoulder like a Kshanti acrobat. He carried me through the crowd's loud chanting of my name. Rain kissed my hair, my face. I swayed, kept myself upright, smiling. Someone wept aloud of the odds. Another yelled of the fight—*like wingwyrms circling!*

I grinned. It *had* been a beautiful duel, I wished I had seen it instead of participated.

Redfist carried me back into the Swallows Moon. As soon as we reached the door he hefted me off his shoulder like a sack of meatroot. "Can ye walk, lass?"

"I cannot tell." My teeth locked together, the words difficult. "I will walk. I merely cannot dance." My boots touched the ground. "Did you bet?"

"Aye, lass. On you. Made a pretty sundog too. As soon as the crowd saw him, the odds became five-two, his favor." The barbarian laughed. It was the sound of a bear chuckling.

"Fickle crowd." My voice sounded watery. The commonroom—Kesa's commonroom—spun underneath me, deserted.

"Oh, aye. Lass, yer pale."

My face was on fire, and my right arm ached. My left arm bled, and my shirt was sopping, stuck to my ribs. My breath came fast and shallow.

I lifted my left arm a little, showed him what lay under. The leather vest and linen shirt were both cut, and the sword had bit around the front of my ribs and torn down. I was lucky to miss a cut bowel. He had struck me cleanly. "Collect your winnings soon." I pushed Redfist's hand away—had he thought to steady me? "I will walk."

The barbarian grunted. "Aye, certainly. But me knees are weak, lass. Ye've to help me. I thought it sure he had killed ye."

If you only knew. Maybe he did. "He may well have." The world spun away under me, returned.

I pushed away from him, made it halfway across the commonroom before blood loss and relief conspired to knock me to the floor. Redfist caught me, and bellowed something loud enough to make the entire inn shake.

Twinsick

I opened my eyes to see a beautiful face, black G'mai eyes and a lush mouth, the shorter braids I remembered dimly. The *adai* who had spoken to me before the duel peered down at me from her great height as a flame of scalding coolness washed through me, the agony of cut flesh melting in a wash of something prickling and alien.

"What?" I croaked. My throat was dry.

"I have offered you healing." Her lips shaped each word, gave it beauty, set it free. Even commontongue would sound beautiful coming from her. "You sorely need it, sister."

A flare of sharp, lifesaving irritation boiled through me. "Keep your healing to yourself." Cold, so cold my teeth chattered, I was so *cold*. "Leave me be. Kesa?"

"Here." Kesamine's blue eyes, her hair pulled sharply back, filled my eyes. I blinked. Why did she look so fuzzy? "Kaia, you are delirious. Let her help. You've a fever—the rain, and the wound."

"No." I closed my eyes. "Leave me alone. Better. Kesa..." I could not speak to tell her what I needed to tell her. "How...long?"

"A full day since the duel. Sunup to sundown." She answered me far too gently.

Sunup to sundown. He was safe now. I had survived a full day. No bloodguilt would attach to him. He could go back to G'maihallan with a clear conscience, and be free of all flawed things.

"What does she say?" A familiar voice, accented with G'mai. I closed my eyes.

"Since tis been a full day, sunup to sundown, you are free of bloodguilt. She won the duel, but you are free should she die." Kesa sounded grim. "If you've aught to say to her, say it quickly."

There was a moment of crackling silence. I heard a fire burning, and the breathing of five people, my own harsh gasping for air.

My skin flushed with fire. That was a bad sign. Cold, then hot—I had traveled in the rain and was now wounded, caught a fever.

But G'mai never caught woundfever. A gift of the gods, our antiseptic blood, proofing us against some accidents of fate and disease.

What could this be? Not *jai* fever, I had caught *jai* once and survived, one did not catch it twice. Being G'mai had meant I caught only the lesser of the two fevers, not the greater *jai* from which precious few returned.

Still, I had been prey to strange fevers all my life. I had always recovered, before.

"Get out." Darik's voice, an iron-cold fury to it. I would not have disobeyed that tone. I heard shifting, people's boots resounding, the crackle of the fire.

"I would finish the healing—" the *adai* began, pleading.

"Get *out.*" Darik did not need to raise his voice.

More shifting sounds. The door, closing, latching shut.

The lock on the door, shot home.

Had he left me in here to die in peace? Good. I would perhaps thrash with the fever, grow delirious, lose control of my tongue. Say what I should not, and have it pass unheard.

He sighed, nearby. I sought to open my eyes again. Could not. The darkness was too heavy.

His fingers touched my forehead, smoothed stray tendrils of my hair back against slick feverish skin. The touch was cool and dry, and helped calm the spinning weakness.

"Kaialitaa," he said, and though I knew it was the same voice it was difficult to believe. No harshness, no fury, just the sound of a weary man.

I sighed, fretfully. Tried to turn my head away. Could not

move. His touch simply felt too good against my skin. Comforting. I had not felt comfort in so long, I had forgotten it.

"I hunted the length of G'maihallan for you," he said quietly. "I learned long ago not to surrender too easily. But even my own *adai* will not have me. Tis enough to make a man question living."

He stroked my cheek, traced my dry lips with a finger. I sought to move my head away.

Softness against my forehead, against my cheek. His lips. "Tis *jada'adai*," he whispered, his mouth moving against my skin. "Twinsickness. Too long spent fighting me." He sighed, and rose to his feet. I heard him moving about.

I gathered the little strength I had and tried to speak.

"You are…free." My voice cracked. "Go *home*. Occupy your Throne and leave me be."

"The queen did not want me before, she may have the gift of my absence now." His tone was sharp. "Cease this idiocy."

The bed creaked as he slid into it. I was too weak to roll away. My stomach roiled, settled as he slid his arms around me. He pulled me close against him, and the feeling spilling over me—a kind of stillness, almost peaceful—was so new and unexpected I sighed. I had not felt peace in so long I had forgotten what it was.

"Shh," he said in G'mai. Still using the personal inflection, too, the inflection he would use with his *adai*. His voice was gentle. Not at all the furiously cold tone he had used on everyone else in the room. "Tis done. Whatever game you were playing is over. We shall start again."

My voice slurred, the ramble of a dreamer. "Take ship for Shaituh or Antai. Be *rid* of you."

"You would die of *jada'adai* before a moonturn, and condemn me to death as well. It was too late the first night you spent in my company, Kaia." He shook his head, his hair sliding against the pillow. "I am not so bad. Perhaps you will grow accustomed to me."

My left arm and my side were a furnace of pain. I tried to struggle, tried to move.

No use. The *dauq'adai* was a lump of scorching against my skin. They had not stripped me—I could still feel my trousers against slick linen sheets. A rough bandage lay against my ribs. That sparked another thought.

"Your face," I whispered.

"I took a healing from Atyarik's *adai*. She is gifted with such things, and has closed the worst of your wound as well." He rested his chin atop my head, my forehead against his throat. I felt his pulse and let out a sigh. My own heartbeat might start to mimic his. "Next time, I will ask you for the care of a wound."

"I cannot heal." Twinsickness. Caused by the *dauq'adai*, or could it be that I was an *adai*, however flawed?

You cannot afford to believe so, Kaia. It will hurt you.

"Once she trains you, you will. You have Power, Kaia. Tis why you suffer so. Think on it. Now that you have a *s'tarei*, your Power is awake and far more active, and brought on the twinsickness. Janaire swears you have far more than she does, and you are a danger to yourself and others until you learn to use it."

"No." Yet I rested my forehead in the hollow between his throat and his shoulder. Comfort, curious feeling that it was, wrapped around me.

"I begin to think you need careful handling. Perhaps the queen did me a service in teaching me discretion."

I would have replied with a curse, but I was too weak. I shut my eyes and wished for darkness to take me. I did not have to wait long.

Détente

"Tis a song in the taverns." Kesa stroked my cheek. Her fingers were cool and dry. "About the Iron Flower and the Dragon Prince. Rumor is thicker than a Rijiin's rouge."

"Oh, Mother's *tits*." I blinked. "How did that happen?"

I was still weak and shaky. Twas not woundfever. Darik said *jada'adai*.

What would he know? The symptoms—cold sweats and fevers, pain, weakness—made sense. My left side burned, healing. My left arm too—marked in a duel. I would bear scars from this. More scars to add to the collection.

At least I healed quickly, there was enough G'mai in me for that. I would not blame or praise the young *adai* for my recovery.

"Well." Kesa shrugged. "Tis a minstrel—a lanky Pesh boy, once a bondslave unless I miss my guess—rolled into town early enough to see the duel. He seems transported by your skill."

I groaned, propped up on pillows in a western room of the Swallows Moon. Kesa had given this room to Darik, and apparently I was expected to stay here too. Redfist had slept in Kesa's chambers for the past two nights.

Slept, or otherwise occupied his time. Kesa certainly had dark circles under her eyes and an unwonted smile.

Darik stood by the window, looking out on Hamarh Street. He had not left my side—or more precisely, he had not left the room—for two days. He said little, slept near me, and spent his time going over the travel-gear, repairing and oiling and generally conducting little tasks of maintenance.

I sought to ignore him. Especially when I saw him running through the weapons-forms in the morning, each movement skilled and precise. Or when I saw him glance at me during the day, as if I were an ill child who must be watched.

"Has not someone chased him from the town yet?" I struggled to sit upright, gave up.

"*Cha*, no." Kesa straightened, stroked my hair, and stood. She picked up the tray, set it on the small table next to the bed. Poured me a cup of kafi. "They buy him rounds for singing that song in the Sparrows Moon. Someone always buys an additional round or two of ale as well. Twas the best duel we've seen in a good ten seasons."

"So dies my career as a discreet thief," I muttered, accepting the kafi. "My thanks, Kesa. You should not be serving me so. I do not deserve it."

"I know," she agreed cheerfully. "You are ridiculous. But you are *so* good for business, I shall forgive you. Do you know how much profit the Iron Flower has brought us? I shall be able to expand the inn if you stay here much longer. Or buy a ship."

"Expand the inn and buy some property. Ships are dangerous, not very profitable." There were little sweetcakes. I picked one up and bit into it. Sugarcake. The delicacies used to tempt an invalid were paraded in front of me. I would be fat as a ratbird before long. "Lost at sea, pirated, grafted by employees...No, Kesa. Not a ship."

"You sound very certain." Darik spoke from the window. Kesa poured him a cup of kafi, and he accepted with a nod. He sniffed at it, cautiously, and took a sip. His eyebrows raised, and he looked at me. *Is this what you drink? It tastes awful.* He sounded mournful.

I thought he spoke aloud, the words were so clear. "Tis an acquired taste." I rolled my eyes at him. "I have spent enough time on ships to know how profitable they are. Too much luck involved even for me."

"Hard to believe." Kesa was merry indeed, and at my expense. "Now I shall return to the commonroom. We have a room or two opening up today, and the bidding will be fierce. Your barbarian's useful—not even Jettero will cause trouble while the big red one is here."

"Miracles do occur," I murmured. "Thank you, Kesa."

She nodded. Crimson stained her lips, and gold winked at her ears. She wore yellow and green today, bright colors mixing uneasily, and there was a yellow ribbon around her slim throat. It suited her, since she was Clau. "*Cha.* May I let the other Gemerh in? They have been asking to speak with the pr—ah, to the lord Gemerh, every hour."

I looked at Darik. He sipped at the kafi and made a slight face. I strangled the urge to laugh, the expression was so fleeting and sour. He said nothing.

"Well?" I prompted, finally.

His black eyes came to rest on my face. He had trimmed his hair again, short as a *s'tarei.* And he had apparently received more G'mai travel-wear from somewhere, probably another *s'tarei* staying at the inn. "I will not see them, if it displeases you. It is the least I can do, for my *adai.*"

"Mother *Moon.* Very well, Kesa, send them up. What does it matter?"

Darik's face did not change. Of course not—he must have learned how to hide his emotions, growing up as the queen's discarded and marginalized nephew, a threat to her succession and a constant reminder of danger. He must have been schooled in diplomacy since the cradle. I almost regretted insulting him with the palace of his childhood.

Almost.

Kesa shrugged. "I shall give you a candlemark, and send them up with your nooning. Today tis soup and fresh bread for you, Kaia'naa."

I sipped at my kafi. It had cooled enough to be drinkable. "My thanks, Kesa. When may I have dinner with you?"

Her sandaled feet whispered over the wooden floor. "*Cha,* when you promise not to ruin it with your temper," she responded smartly, and danced out the door, leaving behind only her laughter.

Darik settled into the chair she had vacated. He took another sip of his kafi and made another one of those small faces—just a quirk of the lips and his expressive eyebrows lifting a fraction. On him, it was like a shout—perhaps because I spent so much time watching his face. *It is not so bad, simply very bitter*, he said. *I can see why you would like it.*

"Tis not bitter. Merely a different taste." I stopped. His lips had not moved. Yet I had heard his voice, as clearly as if he had spoken.

Did he speak before, or did I simply hear him?

I stared at him. My heart gave one last leap, then dropped down as far as it could without ripping free of its moorings.

The G'mai called it *taran'adai*, the Power to speak within.

Twas true, then. Proof even *I* could not argue with.

He sighed. It was a heavy sound, the sound of a man finally free of a burden.

I gazed down into my kafi cup, not seeing the porcelain and the dark aromatic drink. "Why have you done this to me? Why?"

"Blame the gods, not me."

It did not help that he was right. "You gave me the *dauq'adai*. Tis flawed. You tied yourself to a flawed..." Kesa was right, I was being foolish. Maybe I had only weak Power—too weak to be seen by even the Yada'Adais.

Hope. Ridiculous hope. Still, I had taken it into my breast, like the adder in the old story. Now I was subject to the mercy of its poison.

He took another sip of kafi. "I think I could learn to like this. Tis not *that* bitter."

I felt my mouth stretching up into a smile despite myself. It was a peace offering, and worthy of all the grace I could muster to accept it. "Why do the G'mai ask to see you? What do they wish of you?"

He shrugged, set his cup down, and regarded me. "I think they wish to meet you." He managed to keep his face composed and say it seriously. "The *adai* of the provisional Heir—can she be bought? What is her House? Will her kin rise to prominence now? Where do her loyalties lie? You may alter the balance of power in G'maihallan, and they wish to know. One or two of them may even be friendly. Or simply curious."

I made a small sound of disbelief. "I cannot imagine them *friendly*. They will shun me as everyone else did."

"Did Anjalismir shun you? I cannot think of why. All

adai'sa are precious, Kaia. Every girl-child is a gift." He looked down at the blue woven bedspread. Kesa did not like this room, only because the blue she had chosen for it was a pale color. Yet it was soothing. The stone walls held blue tones as well, and made the entire room a reflection of sky.

"Of course they shunned me. Why do you think I left? None would speak to me."

"Perhaps you shut them out, Kaia'li, the same way you have sought to shut me out." He offered it gently, but the thought still made me glare at him.

"I did not." My jaw set, I stared into my kafi cup.

"Have you ever sought speech with an *adai* whose Power is focused on silence? Especially yours. Tis almost like the silence of a *s'tarei*." He rubbed his chin thoughtfully. The twin hilts of his *dotanii* watched me as well. His face had lost little of the gauntness haunting it. "I think perhaps—just perhaps, Kaia—Anjalismir did not know how to reach or train you. Instead of having no Power, perhaps you have too much." He picked up his cup again, took a sip. "You are right. This kafi—the taste grows on you."

"Just as moss does," I muttered, and saw him smile.

"Indeed."

Speak of something else, Kaia. "As soon as I recover, I must go to Shaituh. Rik needs me." I stifled a yawn with the back of my hand. "Or he just might be curious. I left Shaituh on the wings of a bit of ill-luck."

The light from the window slid over his face, caressed it. I did not think I would ever tire of looking at him. "Hmm. If Shaituh is where you are bound, then Shaituh is where I shall go."

"What of G'maihallan? And the Dragon Throne?" He would be a fool to give that up, a fool to walk away from it. Though even I am wise enough to know thrones are notoriously heavy burdens.

He shrugged, a fluid graceful movement. "They may keep it, it will not pursue us."

"But do you wish to return?" I studied his face. The scar on his throat—who had done that? It looked like a garrote, how had he survived? *What* had he survived, to make him willing to give up G'maihallan and settle for a flawed *adai*?

He made a small, dismissive movement. "I was trained to be the Heir should anything happen to my cousin. Trained on the one hand, and taught to disregard the training on the other."

His cousin. The Heir, the queen's daughter. I had seen her once at a Festival, a slim G'mai girl dressed in cloth-of-gold, her face very serious under its newly done adult braids. Since she was the Heir, she had taken her womanhood ceremony earlier than most girls. She had been seated, motionless, under a canopy while the prospective *s'tarei* had been assembled, each hoping he would be the Heir's twin. Or *not* hoping, the position was hardly an easy one.

So he had been trained to take on the succession, and just as harshly trained not to expect it. A dichotomy that could drive a man mad.

The Heir had been so serious, sitting utterly still. She had been in her tent when the dancing started, and I had thought of her motionless in the dark, hearing the music and unable to participate because of the weight of decorum. I myself had stayed on the fringes of the crowd, only watching, never joining the games or the dances, sometimes nervously touching my own hair in its two child's-braids.

It reminded me of my hair, half-undone and messy. "Will you fetch me my comb?" I asked, and began to untangle my braids. Darik unfolded himself from the blue-painted chair and retrieved my comb from my purse, lying on the table near the fireplace. The fire—Kesa had built it up when she brought the kafi—snapped and popped.

He handed it to me. "I must admit," he said, softly, "the thought of returning to the Dragon Throne is not appetizing. The jockeying for position, the lies that must be told to keep G'maihallan safe...but were I to go, Kaia, I would need your help."

I made a slightly rude, disbelieving sound. Yanked at my hair. "I doubt that. You seem to do everything perfectly."

He smiled. It was a genuine smile, different from his usual faint ironclad grimace. "I am glad you think so."

I started working at the tangles in my hair. He watched,

and when I hit a particularly bad tangle, he winced. "Be a little gentler with yourself, Kaia'li."

"I do not wish to be. What will they do when they arrive, Darik?" I heard the wistfulness in my own voice, hated it. So. I had a *s'tarei* now. Why was I not happy? I had given him every chance to leave gracefully, and he was still here.

"They will be courteous, at least. Or I shall throw them out of the room. I think the *adai* will want to speak to you, they seem very interested."

"The same way peasants are interested in bloodgames and duels," I muttered darkly, and he shrugged. He was made for the G'mai clothing—loose and practical, with its brocade pattern worked in black thread against the soft material. He was wearing his boots, too, and I felt my own bare toes against the linen. I stopped combing my hair—twas too tangled. I wore a linen shirt and my bandages, hardly proper receiving-garb. "I should dress myself, then. Twill not do to become rusty with bed rest."

He retreated to the window. The rain continued, a sloppy trailing species of mist beading up and rolling down the glass. The nights rained a little harder, but I felt the storm losing its force. Tomorrow would bring fairer weather, I was certain of it. And with the Sun, traveling. I had not had time to inquire of a caravan, but at least one would leave at dawn tomorrow if the weather broke.

"We shall travel to Shaituh, then?" he inquired, as if he cared little.

I finished my kafi, pushed the sheet and blankets back, and swung my bare legs out of the bed. The bruise on my right thigh had faded, yellow-green and sickly now. My ribs hurt, but the flesh had closed with alarming speed; nothing was broken, and I had escaped a cut bowel. I was lucky. "I am bound for Shaituh. If you are so determined to come, I cannot stop you."

I did not mean to sound so harsh. Or did I?

He turned and looked steadily at me. I left the comb on the bed, made it on wobbly legs to the heavy wooden cloth-stead holding my laundered and repaired clothes—and his as well.

My clothing would begin to smell of him.

I found I did not mind, and blushed. I had not blushed

since girlhood.

"I would like it better if you were not so sharp with me, Kaia'li."

I shrugged. Twas his own fault, for seeking to make me into an *adai*. I was not even truly G'mai. Flawed and broken, I was no fit *adai* for him, no matter how well we understood each other. "I crave your pardon." I surprised myself. "I am new to this, D'ri. It has never..."

He said nothing, but when I looked back over my shoulder, he had closed his eyes and smiled gently. "This is new to me too, Kaia'li."

The smile was good to see. He was the image of all I could have wished for in a *s'tarei*. If I had not been flawed, that is.

I opened the cloth-stead, took out a shirt and trousers. My vest was ruined—I would have to repair it or find a new one. I escaped to the watercloset with a fistful of clothing while I still could.

A Queen's Plea

Darik drew the comb gently through my newly untangled hair just as a knock came at the door. "G'mai," I said. "Maybe I can escape out the window."

"Not until your arm is better." To his credit, he merely sounded practical and unsurprised. "Enter, if it pleases you." This was pitched loud enough to go through the door as he handed my comb over my shoulder. I sat on a three-legged Shainakh stool in front of the fireplace, basking in the warmth. "I shall finish this later. I may manage a braid or two, with some practice."

I do not think I wish an amateur braiding my hair, princeling. I held my peace.

Vavakha carried in a tray with soup and fresh bread. "An' good nooning to you, lady." She lifted her chin slightly. The duel had given her a high opinion of me. "The Gemerh approach. Right glad they are too."

I felt my lips pursing. "My thanks, Vavakha. Do you suppose I could throw myself in the harbor from here?"

She laughed, set the tray down and took the kafi-tray away. "I would not worry, lady. You are prettier than any of them, and fair with a blade too." She winked, her triangular Shainakh face wrinkling with amusement. I sighed and looked at the soup. It was broth, as if I was an invalid.

I could not *wait* to set myself to a pot of mead. Or two. Or ten. "I thank you for the compliment."

She straightened, self-consciously, starting to re-make the bed. I considered telling her not to bother, I would be crawling back into it as soon as I could. Twinsickness drains G'mai women. Twas difficult to move *or* think. I was still a trifle shaky, and exhausted by the effort of crossing the room. My fingers accomplished the first separation of my hair for a braid, quick habitual movements.

Darik looked as if he wished to say aught, visibly thought better of it. "Thank you," he said gravely to the inngirl, who fluttered a little, tossing her red-brown hair back over her shoulder. I bit my lip.

Jealousy is not allowed, I told myself sternly. *He will see his mistake soon enough.*

Darik's black eyes met mine. *There is no comparison, K'li.* His mental voice was shaded a little darker than his speaking voice, and had a peculiar flat quality—no echo, as if he spoke through a silk curtain. *Inngirls do not interest me.*

You are eavesdropping! I do not know which was worse, his reply—or the fact of his hearing my private thoughts.

He shook his head and staggered, his boots shushing over the hardwood floor. The inngirl was too busy pushing and pulling the bed into order to notice, but I did, and stared at him as he turned pale. My hair slipped through my fingers.

"Not so loud, Kaia'li." He spoke in G'mai. I was becoming accustomed to hearing it again, the liquid cadences, sharp consonants. "You could be heard in the next city, if you wished to be."

I began to braid again. The routine comforted me as few other things could. I found myself speaking in G'mai too, my inflection matching his. "I doubt it, but I thank you. Do you really think—"

"Yes," he replied, without hesitation. "I really do. I am a judge of such things, Kaia."

I opened my mouth to say aught else, but there came a polite tap at the half-open door. I turned to the fire and wished I could throw myself out the window.

"There." Satisfaction at a job well done stood evident in Vavakha's self-conscious straightening. "The other Gemerh. I'll be going now."

"My thanks," I replied automatically in commontongue, and continued braiding my hair, weaving a bit of black velvet ribbon in. It would not take long to have it all up out of the way.

"*In'sh'ai,*" Darik said, quietly. The room filled with the soundless hum of G'mai. I hunched down further on my stool and stared into the fire. If I pretended not to notice them, they could shun me with little effort. "Gavridar Taryarin Janaire, Tyaanismir Atyarik. You are known to me. The rest of you, *in'sh'ai.*"

The politeness in his tone made me hunch in my seat. He greeted the two G'mai I would know of, having seen them face-to-face. It was part of the codes of etiquette, a courtesy to his *adai.* I finished one braid, tied it off, and began another. If I was very still and silent, they might not notice me, despite the insult I offered by braiding my hair in public. Shame bit below my breastbone, I pushed the feeling away.

"*In'sh'ai.*" The word was murmured. I listened. Six voices. Three pairs of G'mai. And Darik.

I could leap out the window right now, I thought, longingly, as quietly as I could. *Tis only a two-floor drop onto stone. I could make it. I know I could.*

Silence stretched around me. I finished another braid. If I ignored them—

"Kaia. My *adai.*" Darik sounded very far away, as if the room had grown. "She is recovering from *jada'adai.* I will speak for her."

"So tis true." An *adai*'s voice. I shut my eyes. The weight of Power in the air sparked against my nerves, filled the air with lazy swirls. G'mai, here, close to me after so long. A tear trickled down my right cheek, thankfully hidden because my face was to the fire. I watched the flames twist and lick the wood. "You've an *adai. K'asai'adai,* Your Highness." Her voice was accented like Anjalismir, but with a faint lisping intonation. Mountainfolk, then, not part of a House. Anjalis-kader, perhaps, or the heights above Siyara. I could see it so clearly, the shapes of the mountains cradling my home rising to knife at the sky, their harsh beauty scoured by wind and snow, each crag and rock fixed in memory.

"Please, enter, be at ease." Darik was faultlessly hospitable. I finished another braid. Three more to go. My fingers flew. "You must be Hadarik. *In'sh'ai.*"

"*In'sh'ai.*" Male. A *s'tarei,* gruff and older, with something close to Darik's accent. From the land around the Dragon City, then. "Saw you on the practice ground once or twice. Good steel."

"My thanks for the compliment." Darik sounded pleased. They arranged themselves—the *adai* in the three chairs near the window, probably, the *s'tarei* standing behind. There was another long silence, I felt eyes on me. I finished another braid, moved on to the next.

They started exchanging names. I did not listen. I finished the last braids and twisted them all up, running the ribbon through with practiced ease. Then I simply sat and looked into the fire, wishing for my *dotanii.* Twas braced next to the bed, and I chided myself for leaving it there. But I could not risk their eyes upon me while I stalked to my sword, though my hand ached for it.

"—begging for your return." the older *s'tarei* said, and I slumped further, cupping my chin in my hand. "She sent this, sealed for you, and you alone. Will you accept the message, at least?"

I heard a sigh. Darik's voice came from the window. He would be standing, looking out over Hamarh Street. "The situation is...complicated," he said, slowly, and I might have smiled if I had not been so busy trying to be invisible. He used the word for a difficult, long-drawn out battle in which there are no clear victories, with the inflection made it only an incredibly complex problem. Twas neatly done, and managed to convey more than most people could have with a long speech. "I am not interested in the Dragon Throne. I was *taught* to have no interest. I did not think I would be missed."

"G'maihallan needs an Heir," one of the *adai* said. An older woman—probably the twin of the older *s'tarei.* I listened intently. "The Hatai have opened peace negotiations, since the Border is renewed, but the strain is telling on the queen. She grows old, and has lost her prize. We all know how much she loved her daughter." She used the word that could mean *daughter*, but was in reality the word for *pride.* Twas a nice touch.

"I know better than most how much she loved her daughter." Darik used the same word, and his inflection was not kind.

A long embarrassed silence filled the room like wine in a

cup. I felt something curious—an urge to turn and meet Darik's eyes. His gaze was a weight against my shoulders, more a comfort than an irritation now.

I studied the polished wooden floor, the tips of my toes, my battered, callused feet. Sellsword's feet that had seen long leagues in boots and hard campaigns. There was a blister under the nail of my left fourth toe, a gift from the duel or from the last fight with bandits. The urge to meet his gaze with mine wrapped inside my brain, teased at my eyes.

I managed to stay still.

"You have a duty," the older *s'tarei* said, reluctantly. "Please, Your Highness, will you not at least accept it? Tis only a message."

Darik's silence became very much like the quiet I had felt from him as he moved through the woods, night-hunting.

I wished I could speak to him. *What does it matter? At least read it. Then you may decide.*

There was a gasp, and I turned before I could stop myself. The three *adai* stared at me. Their *s'tarei* did too, but with decidedly less stunned expressions. The young *adai* I had seen before the duel—Janaire—reached up to touch her own braids, looking at mine.

"Very well," Darik said. "I shall read it, and give you an answer, Hadarik. I warn you, though, my *adai* is even less enchanted with the idea of returning to G'maihallan than I."

One *s'tarei*—a lean older man with a sprinkling of salt and pepper in his hair and the sharp features of an Insharimir—produced a scroll-case, an elaborately carved ebon cylinder. Twas chased with silver, an elaborate filigree of the royal Dragon breathing fire. Darik took two steps, plucked it from his hand, and half-turned, facing me. He was smiling, but it was a faint hurtful smile, his armored expression.

I did not think on it, simply found myself on my feet with my hand extended. "I will." I heard my own accent, the lilting song of Anjalismir. I could be placed easily from that voice, but none of them knew me, did they? I was a stranger to my own House.

The third *adai*, motionless in her chair, was a small thin woman with very long braids bound with silver and a silver *dauq'adai* flashing against her chest. She seemed familiar, but I did not examine her too closely. My own *dauq'adai* was hidden, a warm lump against my breastbone, and I met her wide dark eyes only briefly before I took the scroll-case from Darik.

"As you like," he said, in the personal inflection, and I heard his relief. Maybe none but I would have heard it; since I had traveled hard leagues with him without speaking at all.

I clicked the scroll-case open and retrieved a thick roll of parchment. Twas sealed with the queen's personal seal, a reclining dragon over a black Sun. I broke the wax with no ceremony at all and unrolled the top half.

"To Tar-Amyirak Adarikaan imr-dr'Emeryn, Dragaemir-hai, my son and Heir, greetings from the hand of An'Dragaemiran Tayanikaa imr-Yadorikaa, Dragaemir-hai, queen anointed of G'maihallan and blessed one of the Blessed Ones, Moon on Earth." I did not let my lip curl. Twas a struggle. "Our son." The writing was a firm, clear calligrapher's hand, obviously the queen's. It was not the carefully round script of a *kafa'adai*, an *adai* scribe. "Far have you traveled from Us, and without a message to warn Us of your intent. We were told you had survived the attack on your royal life and traveled to the Dravairehai Temple of the Blessed Moon to receive your *dauq'adai*, and We congratulate you on your foresight." I glanced at Darik's face. His jaw was set. He watched the fire. I moved a step closer to him, continued reading.

"We are saddened to report to you the loss of Our body-Heir, your cousin Kallistaa. The last attack of the Hatai upon Our westron borders took her royal life. We are saddened by this event more than We can express, and yet are thankful the Moon in Her mercy has left an Heir to the House of Dragaemir." I swallowed dryly, thought longingly of the soup cooling on its tray.

*Kaia...*Darik's voice, laid in the shell of my ear like a gift. I stayed my course, reading aloud.

"We ask that you return, to take your rightful place at Our right hand, to act as Our advisor in all things, and to prepare you for the weight of the crown resting so heavily upon Our head."

Twas a space, and I unrolled the scroll a little more. The tone of the letter changed completely, from the formal inflection to the most personal of family inflections, used between mother and child. I scanned it, and inhaled sharply. *Oh, gods.*

"Adarikaan, bright blade of your mother, I know you hate me. You have reason to. None knows the depths of the harm done to you more than I, and none knows the price you have paid for your bloodline more than I. I thought only to enforce policy and unify G'maihallan. I thought only of the good of the people of the Moon. Surely you cannot blame me for that?

"G'maihallan needs you. Please, by the mercy of the Moon, come home." I glanced up at Darik again. His jaw was set, and his eyes were burning black.

The tone shifted back to formality, the queen addressing a subject and Heir. "In Our hand, and with Our seal, we seal this letter and bid you farewell, hoping to rest Our eyes upon you soon. An'Dragaemiran Tayanikaa imr-Yadorikaa, Dragaemir-hai, queen anointed of G'maihallan and blessed one of the Blessed Ones, Moon on Earth."

I unrolled the rest of the scroll. Just another seal, the imprint of the royal House. Darik stood straight as a lance, his shoulders rigid, and his face was terrible in that moment.

The room was completely silent.

I reached for him, touched his shoulder. I could find nothing to say.

"G'maihallan needs you—" the older *s'tarei* began. I remembered his name: Hadarik.

I spun to face them, these six G'mai. They resembled me, except for my golden eyes. Twas unnerving, faces so much like my own. I had grown so accustomed to the faces of the Lan'ai Shairukh coast. "Leave him be." My voice could have cut the window-glass.

Hadarik stopped, and I turned back. "Darik?" I rolled up the parchment, slipped it back into the case, and closed the case with a snap. I touched his shoulder again. The material of his shirt was soft, the brocade a different texture under my fingers.

He finally gazed at me, not at the fire. *Well?* he asked. *What say you, my* adai*? Command me to go back, and I will. But not without you.*

His eyes were awful, black holes in his face. My fingers

closed involuntarily, digging into his shoulder. *I would rather roll in pigshit than go back to G'maihallan.* I opened my mouth to say it.

Tis the queen, Kaia. A muscle in his jaw flicked. *Speak to me privately, Kaia. I swear to the Moon, your voice is the only thing that could stop me from...* His voice ceased, yet I understood. Twas rage filling his veins, the rage of a *s'tarei*, not something to be trifled with. *Please, please, speak to me thus.*

Very well. You do not wish to return, and neither do I. I am bound for Shaituh. Rik needs me. If you are determined to go with me—

Why must you even ask? Fury colored his words a deep purple-red, the color of a deep fresh bruise. *You know I will follow wherever you tread. You are my* adai.

I cannot leave you and the barbarian here, then. I swallowed dryly. For a dizzying moment, I felt something I recognized in his mental voice.

Loneliness. A loneliness and hurt, aching anger at least as violent as my own. I knew that feeling, shame and fierceness and stubborn pride mixed together until the resultant stew stopped the throat and choked the heart. We were akin, Darik and I—me shunned by my House, him shunned and trained harshly by his. If any G'mai alive could understand what I felt, my own fury and shame and bitterness, he could.

Very well, I repeated. *You've sworn your oath to me, let it be. Let it stand, flawed or not. We shall go to Shaituh. Do you wish to tell them, or shall I?*

He closed his eyes, his throat moving as he fought for control, found it. When his eyes opened he was himself again, and he nodded slightly, his eyes locked with mine. I do not know what he saw in my face, but I saw his jaw relax as if he found what he sought.

I know what you feel, I told him, silently. *I truly do.*

He took the scroll-case, his fingers gentle. Then he turned on his booted heel and faced them. "Do you know of the attempt on my life?"

All six of them looked on with blank incomprehension, except the older *adai*, the one in the chair Hadarik hovered over. She folded her hands primly in her lap. "I would guess," she said softly, "it was not a palace coup, since the body-Heir was not attacked. It is rumored, Dragaemir Adarikaan, that *you* were the target."

A faint smile returned to Darik's face. I saw the shadow of some deeper sorrow on his face. "Then you will understand why I will not risk my *adai* in a return to a viper's nest. Look elsewhere for your sacrifice to the throne of G'maihallan."

"Are you uncertain of your ability to protect your *adai*?" She lifted one elegant eyebrow, an insult to match his.

I could not help myself. "I am *more* than capable of defending myself, thank you," I informed her in sharply polite G'mai. "I was thrown from of my House and he was very nearly thrown from of his. I may have deserved it, but *he* certainly did not. So the queen requires him now? She should have thought on this before she barred him from the festivals. He might have found a true *adai* at the festivals, but instead he was forced out of G'maihallan on a coney-chase with a flawed *dauq'adai*. Now he has a flawed *adai*, and dueled me seeking to prove it. All this because the queen was too short-sighted to see mistreating him was not the way to ensure her succession." I had to stop to breathe. They stared at me, the three *adai* slack-jawed with what looked like amazement.

"There is no need for—" the older *s'tarei* began.

"Do not lecture me on what there is need for, *s'tarei'sa*." Twas terrible manners to interrupt, but I cared little. "Where were you when I was thrown from of my House, to tell what there was *need* for?"

"Anjalismir," the third *adai* said, suddenly. The *adai* who spoke like an Anjalis-kader, with a slight lisp. "You are from Anjalismir. Anoritaa's daughter."

I studied her. Wide pretty face, dark long-lashed eyes, a pretty chiseled mouth. Her accent almost matched mine.

Oh, no. "Darminaa." Disbelief tinted my voice. I *knew* her. She had been a few summers older than me, not one of my age-mates but close enough. *Mother Moon, no.*

"The Heir?" Her *s'tarei* looked like a Kamarimir, from the northern mountains, a face like a pale stone carving now brightening with interest. "Truly?"

"Kaialitaa." She pushed herself to her feet. "I almost did not recognize you. You are alive—and you are *speaking.*" Her dress was deep rich red, velvet worked with embroidered, interlocked crescents. Twas a beautiful gown, and I remembered the pattern from Anjalismir when I was a child.

Did you expect me to creak and coo like a ratbird? "Of course I am speaking. I could always *speak*. Nobody cared enough to listen."

Darminaa did not care for my objection. "When her mother died, she went mute. She would not speak. The Yada'Adais tried everything to reach her, but she was cloaked in silence."

I found my voice again. "Cease this. He does not wish to go, I do not blame him, now leave us *be*."

"Where did you learn to fight like that?" Janaire's lovely young face was solemn. "I did not think an *adai* could do such a thing."

"She took a wooden practice sword to the practice ground," Darminaa supplied helpfully. "Her mother's brother trained her. He said it was not against the Law, and at least she had at last shown an interest in living. The entire House was in an uproar. None knew where she slept, or how she ate. She was a ghost in her House."

"Leave us alone," I said, but none listened to me anymore except Darik, his black eyes thoughtful. There was no further trace of the awful rage. He reached down with his free hand and took mine, his fingers warm and hard, callused from sword practice.

Like mine. How alike were we, this princeling and I?

"They sent for trackers, but she simply *vanished*." Darminaa tossed her head as if she still had her child's braids. I remembered her more clearly now—she had fostered at the House but never lost her soft lisp. "Took only a sword and her clothes. She had retreated to a cellar—once they found it, they moved her to her mother's chambers. She had carried even her books down to the damp little hole."

It still hurt. I had created a sanctuary for myself in the cellar, true. Returning to its womblike dimness and finding my belongings gone had been a violation, one I still felt the sting of. I had not stayed longer than necessary in one place since, always moving away, and yet I still felt the thump of fear under my ribs and the unsettled feeling that nothing truly belonged to me, that something had been stolen and I would never regain it.

"Mother Moon, *enough.*" Darik's voice cut through hers. "My *adai* requires rest." He held up the scroll-case. "As for this, Hadarik, you may take my answer, written on air. *No.* Let my lady aunt, the queen, explain my refusal to her council however she chooses. I want none of it." It was the voice of royalty again, and the other two *adai* slowly rose to their feet, unwilling to disobey.

"You will not reconsider?" Hadarik asked.

"No." The single syllable, in all its curtness, was more than a simple refusal. Twas utter negation. "I crave your pardon for your trouble, Karaiimir Hadarik. *Adai'sa*, accept my thanks." He was drawn up to use every fingerwidth of his height, his hand caught in mine. I could not seem to make my fingers let go. He was not pale, but his face was set and his eyes blazed. He looked like a statue of a Dragaemir prince, carved out of something warm and utterly stubborn. Steelstone, perhaps, or heated marble.

Darminaa seemed as if she wished to say aught else, but I glared at her and her *s'tarei*—the Kamarimir with the pale stone face—closed his hand over her shoulder, murmured in her ear. She bit back whatever she intended to say.

Janaire lingered behind, her *s'tarei* Atyarik seeking to urge her for the door. "You have a great gift. You could be a healer." Her flawless young face was pale and determined. His face, even and unremarkable for a G'mai, was just as set.

I could find nothing to say. Her *s'tarei* finally took her from the room, speaking to her in a low voice.

"I care not," she said finally in fluid G'mai, as he pulled her out the door. "She has such Power and she does not *use* it, simply lets it fester—"

The door closed. I heard his voice, low and resolute, and hers answering him. The sound of *s'tare'atan*, the young, cautious *s'tarei* and the young, headstrong *adai*, something familiar from my childhood. I had heard that exchange many times in the halls of Anjalismir, always listening from the edges.

Darik squeezed my hand. "My thanks, K'li."

The top of my head reached just under his chin, and his

extra size had told on me during the duel. I am built slight, as were all G'mai women. I have extra muscle from years of hard campaigning, but he was *s'tarei*, and had several muscle-ropy pounds—and several inches—more than I did. "You have let the marshcat free now. Are you absolutely certain—"

He laid a finger against my lips, gently. Was it wrong that every nerve in my body leapt at that touch? "Do not ask me again. Where you go, I go, Anjalismir Kaialitaa. Now you should rest. You are trembling."

"I am *not*," I objected immediately, but let him lead me to the bed.

He did not press the point. "Tomorrow will be better. The *jada'adai* has mostly faded. The longer we stay close, the faster you will recover."

I did not argue. What was the point? I had thrown my lot in with his, and defended him in front of a collection of G'mai just as if I was his *adai*. Twas too late now. Flawed or not, it was done.

A Street-Troupe

We left Vulfentown a little before dawn, Darik leading the gray gelding, Redfist the packhorse. I asked him if he wished to stay with Kesa, who was a little piqued with me for taking some of her custom and her new lover away. Redfist had merely grunted, and kept saddling the packhorse.

I took it as a good sign.

Riding out through the East Gate in the early-morning darkness, we were greeted by the sight of two fine black horses, Atyarik and Janaire riding them. I pulled the gray to a stop, cursing inwardly.

Behind them, perched on a rawboned brown nag that hung its head with shame to be seen next to the beauty of the G'mai, was a lanky, light-haired Pesh minstrel, clothed in wild tatters of red and yellow sewn together with more enthusiasm than skill. A lute-case was strapped to his back with wide rough twine, and he looked very pleased with himself. His dark eyes glittered in the predawn gray.

"Well," I said finally, in commontongue. "We have seen you. Now you may leave us be."

"We shall accompany you." Janaire's lovely face settled into unaccustomed determination. "You require training, and I am *yada'adai's'ina.* I can help you." She wore a travel-dress of blue velvet, and a light summer cloak draped her slim shoulders. Her braids were neatly done in a fashion I had never seen before. Of course—twould change with each new generation of *adai.*

Darik dropped his face as if hiding a smile. I could not tell for certain. "I need no training," I said, shortly. "And you, minstrel. You have made enough coin from me. Go elsewhere."

"Iron Flower." The minstrel almost stammered. "I am bound for Shaituh, and I need protection on the road. Plenty of bandits, and some bad trouble. I am told you never deny a traveler in need—"

Mother's tits. Who told you that? "I am about to. What do you *want*?"

"Merely to accompany you." He shifted uncomfortably atop his nag. "I am handy with a blade, and—"

"Then why do you not carry one?" I sounded like an old, cranky sellsword. I *felt* like one, too.

He had no answer. Darik looked up at me. *What does it hurt, Kaia'li?*

Plenty. I sought to reply quietly, but Janaire flinched atop her black horse. *I will never be free of him and his silly songs.*

Darik shrugged; a beautiful movement expressing resignation. I wondered how I could tell. Then again, he was so fluid, so expressive, twas hard not to.

"Safety in tribes, lass," Redfist piped up. "You said it."

"Mother's *tits*." I examined all three of them. Atyarik sat motionless on his horse, and I sensed he wished nothing more than to have me refuse. He did not look at me, though, he watched Janaire, who simply sat and waited, something strange shining in her dark G'mai eyes.

"Very well. Only as far as Shaituh. Then you go your own way, and good riddance." I eyed the minstrel, who grinned, suddenly delighted. Pesh usually have wide faces and big bones, and this boy had hands the size of troutfish and a few fingerwidths of space between his sleeve and his hand. His wrists and ankles poked out from tattered clothes. The lute-case was lovingly polished, but just as threadbare as the rest of him.

"My thanks, Iron Flower." Relief shone in his face.

He is about fresh mischief. I rolled my eyes and sighed. "Tis *Kaia*. I shall thank you to stop that Iron Flower business. What sorry stable did you steal that bit of horseflesh from?" I touched my heels to the gray's sides, and he moved forward. Darik followed.

"I did not steal." The minstrel actually sounded offended. "I paid for it in song."

And received your song's worth, too. "I lay my bet you did. Why could not I have Bard Teodok or Illessi Damatria chronicling my exploits? Instead I have one broken-down Pesh lutebeater. The Iron Flower and the King of Thieves—you made that song, did you not?"

His mouth firmed, and his dark Pesh eyes sparked. He had a hooked nose and a wide generous mouth, fine blond eyebrows that looked a little like Kesa's. A shadow of dark blond scruff was part of a beard, and he pulled in the nag's reins. The horse looked old and tired, but it perked its ears and moved forward. The G'mai fell into line. "I heard the story in—"

Gods above. "It did not happen. I actually never met him. He is too small a fish for me to bother netting."

If I had told him the Moon was not made of silver, he would have looked less chagrined. "But I heard it from a good source, a man who said he knew you."

I was about to reply when my ears caught the sound of a galloping horse. Vulfentown was quiet this early in the day, except for the caravans and the docks. Here at the East Gate there were no caravans, I would swing north around the bulk of the freetown and join the Road further north. I could avoid the witch, and give myself some time to think. I had also thought anyone seeking to catch Darik and ask him again to go back to G'mai would wait at the North Gate.

Darik looked up at me, his eyes depthless. "What is it, K'li?"

"Leave the road. All of you, over there." I pointed to a small grassy area set to the side of the gate. It was a staging area for infrequent caravans going east to Pesh. My nape tingled. Trouble coming, again. I heaved a sigh.

Redfist, thankfully, led the packhorse over to the grass. The early-morning mist muffled the hoofbeats. *Close now, and quick. What else could possibly go wrong?*

Do I even dare to ask?

Atyarik's horse pranced a little bit, and crowded Janaire's. She tossed her braids and guided her black horse over to the grass. The minstrel's eyes were wide and dark. His nag followed, far more sprightly than I would have believed.

"D'ye need me there, lass?" Redfist called.

I reached up, touched the hilt of my *dotanii*. "No." I looked down at Darik. "You should retreat a step or two, princeling. A runaway horse—"

"I am equipped to deal with such, Kaia'li." Leave it to him to sound utterly unmoved. But his mouth compressed, as if he sought not to smile.

The galloping slowed. The guard at the East Gate—a lone burly freetowner who looked to be half Shainakh, half mongrel—stepped out of his hut.

The horse came into view on Tamarakh Street, a bay, slowing to a trot. It pranced—a fine parade-show move. Clinging to its back was a small ragged figure. "What now?" I said, half to myself.

A beggar on a horse that expensive? Darik's voice whispered in my ear. *Tis strange indeed, K'li.*

"How do you know tis a beggar?"

"No saddle. And no saddlebags. My eyes are not yet clouded."

I should not have asked.

The horse trotted through the gate, tail flicking. The guard leaned on his pike, regarding the spectacle. Twould make even more fodder for gossips, if he recognized me.

The urchin clinging to the horse's mane looked vaguely familiar. I kept a loose hold on the gray with my knees, ready to guide him out of the way. Darik let loose of the reins and moved away a few lengths to give me room to maneuver. The horse trotted up to us and finally stopped, head held proudly.

A child, his greasy lank hair falling forward over his face, clutched the horse's mane with white-knuckled fingers. He was barefoot and malnourished, with large, staring black eyes. Looked like a Shainakh. I waited, easy in the saddle, my hand on a knifehilt.

He stared at me, this little product of the streets, and I cast back in my memory for that face. Why did he look so familiar?

I remembered. The pickpocket I had tossed the *kiyan* to. The one Darik had cuffed on our arrival to Vulfentown. Had I not been so disarranged from twinsickness and the aftermath of the duel, I might have recognized him immediately. Tis unlike me to ever forget a face.

Silence stretched brittle. The gate-guard watched, interest shining on his broad face. I let my eyes move over the thin child clinging to the horse's back.

"Lady." He had a thin piping voice "I brought a horse."

I could not let my smile show, but my mouth wanted to twitch. "So you did."

"I'm fair with pockets." He glanced nervously at the other G'mai, the giant, and the minstrel. Last of all his eyes flicked past Darik, and he flinched. "And quiet. Not like that lot."

What is it you wish of me, child? "True," I agreed. "Did you steal that horse?"

"I'm too small to steal a horse." Now he was all injured innocence.

My mouth twitched once more, I kept my face expressionless with an effort.

The horse bridled a little bit, stamped. I examined the boy again. He put his chin up, and I saw the shadow of a bruise on his sticklike throat. It reminded me of Darik's scar.

"What is your name, *cha*?"

"None. Call me Rat, *cha*."

"*Cha*." I took my hand away from the knifehilt. He was no threat. "Well, what do *you* want?"

"Travel with you. See the world. Travel with the Lady Kaia." He gave me a gamine grin, but there was something too panicked about his wide eyes and his clenched hands. "Doan want to be wharf-rat no more. See the world, learn to fight."

"Are you wanted for murder or robbery?" *You are far too young for my world, little one.*

"*Cha,* no. Just pick pockets, steal a meal."

"What of the horse, then?" *You stole that, young one. But from who?*

"Travel with you, *cha*. Got to keep up."

Mother's tits. When did I become a home for traveling halfwits? What did one more burden matter now?

It had been the hardest thing for me to learn to ignore, the hard usage of children in cities. Inside G'maihallan, even shunned children are fed and taught. They are too precious to waste, among us.

I felt the weight of other G'mai eyes on me—Darik's, and the pair on their black horses. If I did what I should and refused the child, they would think less of me.

Why did I hesitate? I did not care one whit for Atyarik or Janaire's disapproval. But Darik's...that was another thing.

The guard watched closely, too far away to hear but close enough to be interested. "Do you pick the wrong pocket a-traveling with me and I shall strike all your fingers off." I tipped my head in Darik's direction, a braid falling over my shoulder and swinging to add emphasis. "Or he will. *Cha?*"

"*Cha*, yes, lady. I swear."

I kneed the gray forward, came side-by-side with the bay. Twas a big horse—not big enough for the Skaialan, but very fine. I ran my eye down the horse's legs, noted the depth of the chest. I offered the boy my hand.

We touched fingers to seal the agreement. "I expect you not to steal except when I ask for such." I held his dark eyes with mine. "You could cause trouble, picking the wrong pocket."

"*Cha*, lady, I know that." At least his teeth were good. I checked his arms. None of the rash that came with dreamweed, and the whites of his eyes were not yellow with *vavir*. He saw me checking. "I do not chew weed or *vavir*, lady. Clean."

You are a quick little thing, are you not? Quick, and with brains enough to know quality when you see it. "Good. Would you mind if Darik rides the horse? You may ride the packhorse, with our Skaialan." I watched him carefully. Darik was moving up slowly, his eyes cold and dark. *What am I doing? I cannot care for a little one.*

Still, the horse was a fine one. The boy might be hanged if I sent him back inside the walls. And the eyes were upon me.

G'mai eyes. The codes of my childhood rose to constrain me once more. Had I ever truly escaped them?

"*Cha*." The Rat slid down from the horse's back. He landed on both feet, with admirable grace, and staggered. I reached down, caught a handful of his ragged shirt, and hauled him up into the saddle. The gray sidled a bit nervously, but I had my knees clamped firmly, and he relaxed.

Darik caught the bay's face, patted him. The horse made a low whickering sound. G'mai *s'tarei* are good with animals—Darik spent a few moments murmuring in G'mai. Baby-talk, to ease a four-legged cousin. I rode over to the group clustered in the grass, then hefted the child into the packhorse's saddle. "Shorten those stirrups on the packsaddle, Redfist, if you please."

"Aye, lass," Redfist grumbled. "Ye and yer soft heart."

"This is Rat." I ignored the jibe. "He travels with us. I might as well make it a complete Rijiin streetshow. I know not how I am to feed you all, with winter coming, but I suppose it matters little. Come along, we waste daylight."

"Should we not find him a proper saddle?" Janaire's eyes were on Darik, murmuring to the bay. The horse shuddered, its sides heaving and its muzzle dropped. Darik patted his neck, smoothed his mane, and kept speaking softly. I watched, and finally the horse's head came up and he nuzzled Darik affectionately.

Darik took a fistful of mane and was on the bay's back in one graceful movement. My heart banged against my ribs, subsided. I tried not to show it. "How hard can you ride him, D'ri?" I called.

"Maybe half a day, hard. Longer if we stay below a trot," he called back in G'mai. "He is tired, this cousin. Been mistreated—not by the boy, by someone else. The boy has some *adai'in*, it seems."

Perhaps he has more than me. What will happen next? "Lovely," I muttered, and wheeled the gray toward the dusty ruts of the road. "I would ask how this could become any stranger, but the gods might seek to show me. We shall travel swiftly to outrun such luck."

I was certain none could hear me, for I spoke under my breath. Yet I heard Darik's half-smothered laugh, and it made my frustration all the sharper.

Travelsong

I rode at the head of my little group as we trotted around the walls of Vulfentown, following a track I found years before through a belt of marshland. Twas wet going, but the Sun shone out from behind veils of low scudding cloud. We joined with the road going north to Shaituh midmorning, and Darik brought the bay horse up to pace behind mine. Like most G'mai, he did not *need* a saddle, though a bridle might have been well. I would have to trade for one, and for a pair of boots for the boy.

"Why the boy?" Darik guided the bay closer, so my own horse blew out a whinny. "Does he seem a fine traveling companion?" His mouth quirked, firmed.

I could not deny a child with you looking on. I shrugged. "He has nowhere else to go, D'ri." I scanned the horizon again. The north road ran between a pair of bluffs here, scrub twisted by the salt wind on one side and trees rising on the other, going inland to the forest, which would begin to take on less moss and more pines. "I remember being that young, and hungry."

The barbarian's voice lifted behind me, growling through a drinking song. The piping of the boy—he could not be more than eight or nine summers high—lifted as well, giving sweetness to the bawdy lyrics. The minstrel's mellow tenor put them both to shame. That did not deter them, though; the Skaialan merely growled more loudly.

I waited until they ceased, the boy laughing, then I sang to keep from speaking.

My voice rose between the bluffs, something all the G'mai would know. Twas the Lay of Beleriaa, the daughter of the

Moon and Haradaihia, who had met the Silver Ships and returned to teach the First Folk of the Law and the bond between twins. Twas a lovely lilting air. I sang alone through the first verse, wind rising and brushing through the trees on either side. I smelled salt sea and the marsh to the west, and had almost forgotten I traveled with a whole cadre when a second female voice joined mine, taking the harmony line.

I had forgotten what it was like, to sing with other G'mai. Janaire's *s'tarei* joined in too, after a brief hesitation, taking the male part; Darik began to sing too, quietly at first. He had only a middling fair baritone, flexible and well-trained, and he gave the song no false decoration.

Twas a relief to find something he did not do perfectly.

I began to enjoy myself, my voice loosening, silvery instead of rough in the upper registers. Janaire kept the harmony, and the wind through the treetops sang too. Its voice was lipless, tongueless, but still part and parcel of the harmony.

With the fourth repetition of the chorus, I decided to play. I took the higher melody, my voice slipping between the *s'tarei* like a silver ribbon between dark clouds. It rose, fell, caroled out between the branches and flashed forward on the road, showing me a caravan ahead. It moved slowly, we would overtake it probably by tomorrow. Dust hung in the air, and I heard the bellowing of oxen, saw pots hanging from the back of a waggon, heard the crack of a whip and a caravan travelsong. Horses moved between the waggons—the caravan crew, fully armed and watching in all directions. Too many horses—had a caravan master been frightened by the tales of trouble on the road?

I came back to myself holding the last long sustained note of the first canto, Janaire's harmony cascading away below me. I held as long as I could, let it fall, and filled my lungs as Janaire brought it to a close.

The second half told of how the Darkness came from between the stars to make naught of what Beleriaa had wrought. *Darkness without a soul, evil without a name*; the G'mai fought with Beleriaa, grateful for the gifts she had brought and honoring the woman who had taught them so much and ruled so well.

I sang through the death of Beleriaa's *s'tarei*, Anjalismir Tarikaan, from my own House. And Beleriaa's survival—

unheard of in later times, that an *adai* or a *s'tarei* would survive the death of the other. We had been bred to it, the twinning, we did not survive its breaking.

I sang of the duel between Beleriaa and the embodiment of the Darkness, where Beleriaa—with Tarikaan's *dotanii*—broke her first sword inside the Darkness and worked the greatest sorcery of the First Age, binding the Darkness into the remaining blade she named for her twin—*Tayrikaan*, Darkness-in-Service.

I repeated Beleriaa's promise to the G'mai: She would watch over the sword, keeping it in the Sacred Mountain, Anjalistirimakan. If the Darkness ever rose again to threaten the world, the G'mai were to use Tayrikaan to defend themselves. *Only that born of Darkness can stop Darkness, so it is sung, sing and remember, remember the song.*

I often sing while I travel, and this was no different. I sang alone, and the Sun shone on the road in thick golden waves. The rain had fled. I had been right—today was good weather. We should just make it to Shaituh in a week's time, if it held.

I finished the second canto with Beleriaa assuming her place among the gods in the Eternal Halls, as the guardian of the G'mai. There in the Halls she was reunited with Tarikaan, in a descant all but the most experienced singers fumbled on, one I did not assay, simply took the lower and easier harmony.

There were four more cantos, but I finished the second and stopped, watching the road. Dust rose in the distance—that caravan I had sensed ahead. I saw the column and thought it hung a bit low in the sky. Twas slightly westward, where the beaches would be soon. Had they stopped? Why would a caravan stop less than two days from Vulfentown? Or was it farther, and the distance deceiving me? Telling distances with a song was tricky, and I had learned not to trust it overmuch.

I pulled the gray to a halt, Darik right beside me. The rest of them straggled up, and I lifted my hand for silence, forestalling questions. The bay whickered and subsided, and I heard the minstrel shift in his creaking saddle.

Perhaps a ship had run aground. That did happen, not very frequently, but enough to make it a possibility.

I half-turned in the saddle. "Rat." I heard him twitch in the saddle. "What gossip, about trouble on the north road?"

His short nervous silence added to my own. "*Cha*...bandits and other trouble. Shainakh army detachments, I think. Heard so on the wharves."

"We came out this way earlier," Janaire said. "I did not trust the air. It seemed fell, so we turned back."

Aye, you turned back in time to make my life miserable, adai'sa? Yet I had other concerns. "Shainakh army detachments." *Why? The Emperor knows better than to trouble with the freetowns.* "Well, nothing to do but find out. I've nothing against the Shainakh army, though they are generally ill-tempered."

"Oh, aye lass," Redfist said behind me. "I hae never met a good-tempered army yet. What are ye planning t'do?"

"Satisfying my curiosity." I gathered my reins. "And mayhap finding a way to feed you lot through the winter."

"But—" Janaire started, and her *s'tarei* murmured something. Whatever it was, it quieted her, and I started the gray up a long shallow hill. The road ran north and curved a little east, and from the rise we might be able to see a fair bit ahead.

"What do you think?" I finally asked Darik, grudgingly. He rode next to me, the horse obeying the pressure of his will without a bridle needed to tame it.

He did not disappoint. "Trouble. The dust in the distance hangs too low, and tis mixed with smoke. Either a caravan has stopped travel, or something has befallen it. Both are not entirely appetizing thoughts."

I nodded, my braids falling forward. "I saw a caravan ahead, though tis hard to tell how far. Probably the same one."

"I know. I felt it, while you sang." The bay plodded on. Twas a good horse. The streetchild had known what he was stealing, or had been lucky.

Too much luck flowing in this river, both good and ill.

Reminded of the child, I pulled the gray gelding to a stop and half-turned. The boy held onto the saddle, his face pale under dark Shainakh coloring. His eyes were half-closed, and his mouth gaped slightly. Still, he kept hold, and I recognized the look he wore. Determination.

I glanced up, checking the Sun's stance in the sky. A trifle before nooning. "We stop now."

"But tis not even noon!" Janaire, protesting. Of course. "We just left Vulfentown."

"You may return hence, if you like." I cast around, found a shallow grassy area to the left and guided my horse down. "But as long as you travel with me, *I* tell you when we stop."

The minstrel coughed nervously, but held his peace. He was wiser than he looked, at least.

The Songs Are Wrong

I dug another piece of dried fruit from the bag. “Easy, little one.” He had already wolfed the journeybread and the dried meat. I offered him a drink from my waterskin.

The rest of them gathered a little space apart, speaking quietly while they took their nooning. Darik separated himself from the group, paced across the grass to where I stood guard over the young pickpocket. His fingers had not been into my purse, but I did not wish to risk the others. It was too soon to tell if he was trustworthy or not, even if my instincts spoke for him.

Even if the G'mai would think less of me for chastising him, did his hands itch for the wrong pocket.

“S’good,” Rat said, barely stopping to chew. He perched on a fallen log, his legs pulled up to either side like a frog. I smiled at this, then frowned at his battered and callused feet. I had no idea how to care for a child. I had never frequented the nurseries of the House as some other G’mai girls did. On the other hand, a young one who could survive alone on the wharves of Vulfentown by picking pockets would hardly be a child anymore, no matter how few summers he had drawn breath.

“If you do not slow, you will make yourself sick like a horse.” I had suffered the belly-gripes myself after breaking a long fast, wished to save him the discomfort.

Darik’s hand dropped to my shoulder. I did not push him away, I was too busy thinking how I was going to care for a little pickpocket. “How is the little one?” he asked in G’mai.

"*Cha.*" Rat looked up, his face bright and interested. "Tis true you are a prince?"

"Of a sort," Darik replied in his fluidly accented commontongue. "I am Kaia's protector, small one. Take care to stay on her good side."

A thin thread of pleasure wormed below my breastbone. I tried not to feel it. I did not remark the fact that I needed no protection, either.

"*Cha.*" Rat nodded vigorously. His greasy hair flopped over his face. "'Sides, I saw her fight."

Darik nodded. He glanced back over his shoulder at the others. "Kaia?" His tone held a question. *What shall I tell them?* His voice brushed against the inside of my head, silently, a prayerbell's sonorous tone.

"Does it matter what you tell them?" *Because I truly do not care.* I thought it as quietly as I could. Darik still winced as if I shouted.

"It might. The G'mai are here because I am here, and will obey me if necessary. Redfist and the minstrel, who knows? If we are attacked, Atyarik will protect Janaire, and I am responsible for you. But the others..." He shrugged, a movement I could feel through his hand on my shoulder. The touch was oddly comforting.

"*I* am responsible for my safety," I reminded him. "I have done well enough until now."

"True. You have. An honor to fight beside you, then, and guard your back. Which still leaves us the problem of the others."

Very graceful, princeling. "Redfist can protect himself," I said, dismissively. "It would probably be a blessing if the minstrel dies."

"You do not mean that." It was a quiet statement of fact. "What of the little one?"

"We shall watch him, you and I. I have taken him under my protection, *s'ai adai.*" I dared not look up at him. I had never in my life said the traditional words that stated an *adai*'s wishes.

There was a long moment of silence. "*Insh'tai'adai.* If you wish it, it shall be done. Consider yourself under my protection, child. Unless you disobey Kaia."

"Does he have to do everything you tell him?" the little pickpocket asked, his eyes wide and round. He had finally stopped stuffing himself, for which I was grateful. A belly-griped child would be no Rijiin holiday.

I have not seen anyone yet outside the Blessed Land who would understand, small one. "Obedience born of affection, tis the rule." I sought to explain. Wind came over the bluffs guarding the road and ruffled the little one's hair, touched my braids. I looked down at Rat, wondering how in the name of the Moon I had ended up with a *s'tarei*, a ginger-furred barbarian, a half-rate minstrel, two G'mai, and a child pickpocket. Perhaps I could teach them all acrobatic tricks and play for coin in Shaituh. "Now you, little one, are you part of the Thieves Guild?"

His eyes could not have stretched any wider. "*Cha*, no. Too young."

The wind shifted, and I tested it, sniffing cautiously before relaxing. Nothing out of the ordinary. "Well, I am of the Guild, and I may sponsor you. But you must be very careful."

He nodded so enthusiastically I thought his head might snap off. "I will. I *will.*"

"Good." I turned and looked up at Darik. "My thanks, D'ri."

His face was pure G'mai; he smiled a little. Twas not his faint ironclad grimace. It was a genuine one, and his black eyes were warm. There was a faint rough blush on his cheekbones from the wind, and his hair lay against his forehead in messy tendrils. He ducked his head slightly, accepting the thanks. "Tis nothing, Kaia. Truly." Did he sound...no. He *could* not sound uncertain. Twas just the personal inflection, transforming his words into something tender. A shared secret.

I reached up without thinking and smoothed his hair back from his forehead. It was rough silk, the texture of it very much like my own—perhaps a little coarser, twas all. I patted it into place, examining the way it reflected the light with a blue-black sheen. D'ri looked down at me, quietly, his Dragaemir face harsh and beautiful, his jaw set with something like pain. Was it pain? If it was, had I caused it?

I did not wish to cause him pain.

"There." My voice sounded strange, softer than I usually

spoke. "Now you look more the prince."

His *dotanii* shifted against his back as he moved. He studied my face, intently, searching for something.

I found my fingertips against his cheek. His skin was warm. His eyes held mine for a long breathless moment.

The little pickpocket shifted on his seat and I started, taking my hand away. There it was again, a sharp needling pain when I broke eye contact with Darik. "A little less hungry now, *diyan*?" It was a pet name for a trained *farrat*, especially when accented right. Twould serve the boy as a use-name, I decided, as small and quick as he was.

He nodded. I handed him the waterskin again. He took a long draft, his young throat moving as he swallowed. His shirt was too big for him, and dirty gray. His trousers were ragged, held up with a bit of cord. The weather was not right for such thin cloth, I would have to find him aught else to wear.

"I will tell them," Darik said, a little hoarsely, from behind me. I had not asked him to tell anyone aught.

"My thanks," I said, automatically, and the pickpocket gazed up at me.

Such trust in such a young-old face. "Is he *truly* a prince?" The very idea would seem exotic to a freetowner, with their disdain for any but elected officials.

I nodded. "Truly. Heir to the Throne now." *And bound to me, it seems.*

"Why is he here?" The boy's eyes were a little less wide and hungry now. "Because of you?"

I shrugged, a gentle movement. The familiar explanation rose to my lips, altered only slightly by Darik's presence. "*Cha,* no. They threw him from our homeland, just like me. They tossed me away because I have no magic, young one, and Darik was a threat to the succession to the Throne. So we are two outcastes." I took my waterskin back. The boy's fingers were thin, marks of malnutrition showing around mouth and eyes. "Let us hunt you some warmer clothes, *cha*? A bath would not do harm either, but I see no bathhouse here. We will have to find you some shoes."

The boy dug in his ragged shirt. "I have coin. Can pay."

For some reason, it sent a bolt of hot lightning shame

through me. "*Cha*, keep your coin, *diyan*. You shall have a share just like anyone else here, as the Thieves Guild dictates. I do not need your coin."

He dipped his head forward, as if ashamed. "*Cha*, lady." The hurt and uncertainty in his voice scored my own heart; had I ever been so young?

No, I had left G'maihallan when I was sixteen, scarce more than a child but still more handily equipped than this young one. "Why did you wish to come with me? And steal a horse as well?" I gave him another piece of dried cirfruit.

"*Cha,* needed the horse to trade so you let me come." He had eaten three times what I would have and still looked hungry. "Wanted to come with you. You told him not to hit me, in your profession. Tossed me a *kiyan*. I knew who you were, and the gossips said you were...well, there's songs."

"There certainly are." I lifted him down, my hands under his arms. He was light, too light even for a child. "Most of the songs are wrong, though. A lesson for you, *diyan*, most of the songs are *very* wrong. Come, I think I have a heavy shirt that may fit you."

Starseed

We camped that night in a sheltered waystation bearing evidence of the caravan passing before us—scuffed dust, a doused campfire, a broken doll laying at the very edge of the grassy space. Whoever the caravan master was, he or she was a good one—even the beast-dung had been shoveled to one side. There was firewood in a small stone shed, recently replenished, and the cistern was clean and clear.

Atyarik picketed the horses while Redfist brought deadfall, and Janaire kindled a fire by sitting before the pile of tinder and small twigs and staring fixedly at it until a thin curl of smoke rose up and small flames began to dance. It was one of the oldest G'mai skills, fire-calling, and I surreptitiously slipped my tinderbox away in a saddlebag.

I walked the perimeter of the waystation, checking for weaknesses, before Janaire called. "Kaialitaa?"

I looked over. Atyarik had put down a *tavar'adai* for her, and she fed wood to the newborn fire. Redfist passed me, his arms full of fuel. "Minstrel went to find meatroot an' spice," he said, over his huge shoulder. "I'll hunt fer fresh meat. Should I take D'rik?"

Why ask me? "If he wishes to go."

The boy hovered near Atyarik, who was teaching him how to picket a horse. The *s'tarei* was gentle, at least, and the boy—dressed now in one of my heavy linen shirts, the sleeves rolled up to his wrists, and a pair of short trousers I had cut down for him—looked almost civilized. *Tonight I should use the extra material and some felt from my clothpurse to make a pair of soft shoes. He sorely needs them.* "What, *adai'sa*?"

"Oh, none of that," she sang in G'mai, her young face bright and open. "Come, sit down, your first lesson."

"I have no interest." I stalked to the fireside. "I have little Power, if any."

"Then you have naught to lose," she answered, logically enough. She tossed two braids back over her shoulder. "I am *yada'adai's'ina*, and I need practice in training so I may become Yada'Adais. You could aid me."

I bit my lip, gazing at the fire, then at her. The softness of Gavridar in her face; she was young too, as young as the boy in her own way. "Do you think so? I know *yada'adai's'ina* must train for years before they are allowed to apprentice."

Her slim shoulders moved under dark blue velvet, hunching. She was indeed beautiful, her caramel skin flawless and her eyes large and deep over a pair of sculpted cheekbones and her pretty chiseled mouth. I felt graceless and callused next to this girl. Had she ever been hungry? I doubted it.

"I wish to be Yada'Adais. Tis the way I've chosen to be of service to the G'mai. I have no skill with blades like you, or knowledge of weapons and tactics like the *s'tarei.* All I have to offer is my skill as a teacher, and I have not much of that either." Sadness tinged her tone, and I felt a small twinge. I had not been kind to her.

You are turning soft, Kaia. Soft as a spoiled fruit. I dropped down next to her, cross-legged on the grass. "Well. If you require practice, I can provide. I warn you though, I am likely to be a difficult student."

"The best kind, for practice." She dug in a pouch hanging from her silvery belt. "Here. Try this." She extracted a small silver sphere about the size of a small Hain oil lamp, easily cupped in a woman's hand. It appeared made of bright but inert metal, but I knew better, my skin prickling with gooseflesh. Twas a *taih'adai*, a starseed, a teaching sphere. "Tis the first lesson. Take it from my hand."

I examined her face. There was no hint of mockery or cruelty. I struggled with the urge to rise and leave her to it, retreat from another failure. If she could not teach me, would she shun me as well?

I have said I will, so I must. I steeled myself, took the

sphere.

It vibrated slightly in my hand, starmetal warming to my touch. As I cupped it in my palm, it birthed a silvery soft glow, brighter than an oil lamp.

"This is the first *taih'adai*." Her voice was more authoritative, its Power contained and irresistible. She was certainly a teacher, for all her youth. "There are three sets of seven, and they comprise the basic education an *adai* needs to control Power. They are used when an older child or an *adai* cannot take direct instruction, and should work well for you. This one will teach you the basics of keeping your *taran'adai* to yourself. As you've no doubt noticed, you are extremely loud when you try to speak to your *s'tarei*. This shall also teach you some little else."

I stared at the *taih'adai*. The light intensified, a cold breeze touching my skin as if the wind from the winter sea had come to rest against me. "Why does it glow?" My voice sounded very far away.

"Once activated by a *yada'adai's'ina,* it glows in response to the magnitude of an *adai's* Power. Your talent is immense, Anjalismir Kaialitaa, and so..."

Her voice faded as I stared into the light. The *taih'adai* shone fiercely now, white-hot silver pouring in concentric waves. I felt a dozy sense of panic—I was slipping into a trance, dangerous if there were enemies nearby.

Ease yourself, K'li. Darik's voice, distant but still audible. *I shall stand guard. Do as you must.*

Comfort filled me, and the light took me. I could no more stop it than I could stop breathing.

A True G'mai

Darik stroked my hair, gently, touched my forehead. The fire had died down to a low glow and Redfist was asleep, judging by the audible snores. The minstrel—he had given his name as Gavrin—picked out a low tune on his lute. He had a fair hand with spices, and the coney stew tonight had been far more savory than expected. The boy was curled into a small ball next to Redfist. I did not blame him—the barbarian was warm even if ripe, and the night would be chill.

Atyarik's arm was around Janaire, who leaned against him, hugging her knees. Every so often he murmured to her and she would wake enough to laugh softly, a counterpoint to the minstrel's wanderings. Eventually she slid down to sleep curled on the *tavar'adai*, and Atyarik pulled a blanket over her, gently.

The Sun had gone down behind the bluffs to the west, dyeing the sky with veils of deep furnace red and purple. I had lost the better part of a candlemark in the silver light from the *taih'adai*.

After a long while, Darik spoke. "Better?"

The nausea had quieted. I leaned against him, my head on his shoulder. The shaking in my limbs faded. Janaire had taken the small silvery sphere back and passed her hand over it, murmuring as the light died. Tomorrow I had another. Another episode of screaming silver light and Power compressing itself, arrowing into my mind.

I have Power. I am G'mai. "I never knew," I whispered. "They never told me."

"With a silence like yours, Kaia, I can understand." The lilting sound of G'mai was infinitely soothing. Darik's voice was low and private. "How old were you when your mother died?"

"Five summers high. Just before my Test, she caught the fever and died. When I was Tested and...the silence came. Nobody spoke to me." I sighed. The *taih'adai*. It had...what had it done? I felt quiet, and very calm. Calmer than I could ever remember.

I have Power. I am G'mai.

Darik's arm tightened over my shoulders, a comforting touch. "You must have loved her very much."

"She was..." I closed my eyes. The memory of my mother was pain and pleasure in equal parts, her braids falling over me as she kissed me goodnight, her *s'tarei*—my father—a quiet presence behind her. He had been always willing to play with me, often carrying me on his chest in a child's sling or teaching me hand-tricks and rhymes as my mother worked in her study. She was the Heir of the House Anjalismir, and often busy. I remembered his voice, and how he would let me tug on his hair and play with his knife-hilts.

She had always smelled of warmth and fresh perfume, my mother. "She was very kind." It could not encompass what I felt when I remembered her, but I sensed he understood.

"Hm." A soft, companionable sound. I had surfaced from the silver light to find him behind me, his hands on my shoulders, bracing me as the nausea struck. When I had turned to him, tears trickling down my face, he had touched his lips to my forehead, gently.

I was not certain what to think. We had finished dinner in silence, both of us.

The minstrel tossed fresh wood on the fire, edging a bit closer to us. "Tis a lovely night." Tentative, as if he expected me to dispute such a thing. "My thanks for allowing me to travel with you, Lady Kaia."

"Tis merely *Kaia*. And you are Gavrin." I was shocked enough to feel some kindness for him.

"I earned my name." He lifted his chin, pride showing through the raggedness of his garments. "I was a bondslave in Pesh until the man who owned me died. His will was a manumit, but I could not stay in Pesh without falling into slavery again. I had the lute from my father, so I began to sing.

Tis a good life. Hard, but good."

"Your hands." They were so disproportionate, caricatures like a Rijiin puppet pageant. "How old are you?"

His fingers stroked the lute strings. They responded with a low chord. "Oh, fifteen summers, I think, though tis hard to tell. The life of a bondslave's a hard one." He smiled as he said this, a smile mixed of pain and gratitude combined. "I was glad to leave it."

"Tell me what a bondslave's life is." For I had never wondered before, simply been glad I was *not* of their ilk.

His fingers wandered on the strings. A slow rill of melody sounded, inexpressibly sad. "I did make a song of it." His dark eyes half-closed staring into the fire. "But nobody wishes to hear. They wish to hear of the Iron Flower, and other heroes."

Heroes? I have never met a hero, young one. If they exist, they are well hidden. "I wish to hear." And I did. "If tis awful, I will tell you."

His fingers kept up their wandering. It was a beautiful melody. "You truly wish to hear of it?"

"Oh, certainly. Tis bound to be better than the tale of the King of Thieves." I wanted to hear more of his lute playing, to stave off the coming of sleep. Darik would take the first watch, but if I slumbered, I would dream of silver light and my mother's voice. She had been a teacher, my mother, and a singer. The silence that had descended on the world with her death was still only a breath away.

No, Darik whispered into my mind.

Twas as if I was standing in a vast cavernous empty space now. The *taih'adai* had erected a wall between me and the screams of other minds, and I felt naked without that constant chaos washing against me. As if I had been swimming in a sea all my life, now plucked out and shivering on a rock, hearing the waves outside but no longer buffeted by them. *The silence will not return as long as you hear me—and if it does, I will still be here.* S'tarei *and* adai, *bound together. Does the silence return, I will not leave you, K'li.*

The minstrel cast me an almost despairing glance, his eyes those of a child seeking approval. "Do you really wish to hear it?"

I yawned. Darik trailed his fingers over my cheek, and I sighed, leaning against him. I would never have thought I could find comfort in his nearness. "Yes, I wish to hear it. Either play it or go to sleep."

The Pesh nodded. His hair was the color of dark honey. Now that he had his growth, he was lanky and just a little ugly, but he must have been an attractive boy. Perhaps once he achieved his adulthood he would be easy on the eyes, if he did not use his minstrelsy to seduce the wrong woman and gain a slash on either cheek from enraged relatives.

The Pesh liked boys. I had spent some time there, as a guard for a merchant's house, finally leaving with a caravan bound for Tak-Himor. It was a strange city, citizens cloaked in yards of blackcloth secrecy, but the holy men and women naked in the streets, singing their devotional songs to their god. Shaal was his name, a god of stone and caged fire—open flame was not allowed inside the Pesh borders. It was disrespectful to the god.

"I will give it to you, then." Gavrin struck a low discordant chord on the lute.

He began to play. It was a sad, limping tune, and when he began to sing I understood why.

Pesh is a broken tongue full of clicks and hisses. I had not gained much of it in my time there, but I had a rough idea of his speech and listened intently. He had some talent, this raw-boned minstrel, when he was not inflicting kettlecrock hero-tales on his listeners.

Gavrin sang of the cold of early morns in Pesh, rising to start the caged fires, scrubbing floors, backbreaking work for children and adults alike. He sang of families broken at the auction block, sold into slavery to pay for debt, of the lash of a whip and the cruelty of auctioneers. He sang a slave's lament and a longing for freedom, and of the extinguishing of hope by hard work and the lash. He sang of bruised hands and knees, of the iron at the throat of a slave, collar and cuffs. He sang low and long against the grief and the agony, and I was surprised to find fresh tears on my cheeks as he finished with a low moan that could have been a heart breaking and life fleeing a weary body.

There was utter silence afterward, and his fingers plucked

a silvery trill from the strings. The firelight painted his face a shadow showing what he could become, given enough time. The hush continued until he coughed nervously. "Tis a bit rough," he said, defensively. "Needs more time, and work on the descant."

"Tis wonderful." I wiped the tears away. "*That* is what you should be singing, minstrel."

He laughed, a small bitter sound. "None would pay coin for that, Lady Kaia."

I moved a little, restlessly. Darik was still next to me. "I would. It reminds me of the mountains, back home. Harsh, and beautiful. Do you have more?"

"A few." He stole a glance at me from the corner of his dark eyes. I could see this in the uncertain light from the fire. "Laments, mostly. Things I play while traveling, for my own pleasure. I know a few Gemerh songs, too, from the Tsaoganhi. Spent a whole year traveling with them, learning everything they would teach me."

I nodded, felt Darik shift his weight slightly, leaning in toward me. I have never traveled with the Tsaoganhi, they think G'mai are bad luck, and women not of their own kind especially unlucky. Their women are fierce with knives and words, but shy and retiring when the men speak. They travel in waggons, brightly painted and strung with glittering things to keep away the *malende*, the bad spirits. It was a pity—they felt the same way about magic as I did.

Or the same way I had.

I have Power. I am a true G'mai.

I still did not believe it. Twas as if something precious and fragile was placed in my hand, and if I breathed upon it, it would melt. "Play, then. At least one more song before sleep. Tomorrow is another long day of travel."

"If you ask it, lady, I will play." He had a fine courtly air spoiled only a little by the wide disbelieving grin on his face. "I shall give you my favorite of the Gemerh songs, then. I learned it traveling with the Tsaoganhi and they did not know what it meant, just that twas a traveling song."

He struck the first chord and began to play, and I smiled. Twas a child's song, a teaching rhyme about the night sky, and

I hummed along. It was a naming of the stars the Elders came from on the Silver Ships, the Everstar and the Red Star, the constellation of the *dotanii* and the Bracelet, Beleriaa's Door and the Plough.

I fell asleep in the middle of the song, sliding down, my head pillowed on my arms, and Darik laid a cloak and a blanket over me. Music followed me into darkness.

I am G'mai.

I fell asleep believing it, for the first time.

Mystery

The gray cantered up the rise. This was the last high sandstone hill before the bowl of the coastal plains, the Road wheeling eastward toward Shaituh. Darik's bay matched my horse stride for stride, and we reached the top of the hill. I pulled the gray to a halt and surveyed the plain below.

Darik had fashioned a bridle of sorts—no bit, just a loose twisted contraption giving the appearance of reins. The bay pranced and snorted, throwing his head up, and Darik calmed him with a murmur.

"Mother Moon." I whistled, a long low sound.

Darik said nothing, merely looked.

The Plain below was empty, rolling sweeps of chedgrass the Road cut a channel through, a pair of ruts ground by countless waggon wheels and horse hooves. I looked to the west, over the broad sweep of grass-spotted sand that replaced the marshes.

Marooned on the sand were two caravans. I saw the waggons, but no oxen—and no cooking fires. And the shape of the waggons was wrong. They were only charred skeletons.

My vision is excellent, the G'mai are gifted with good eyes. I saw nothing living among the wreckage of the caravan. The mystery of dust and smoke was at least partially solved. We had not seen or passed the caravan since, for there was no caravan to be seen.

"What will you do?" As though he did not already know.

"I shall satisfy my curiosity." I touched a knifehilt as the gray stamped, catching my nervousness. I swung down from the saddle, stiffness from long daily riding biting at my back and thighs. "Tis my greatest flaw."

"Mh." He did not rise to the bait. "I will accompany you, Kaia."

I considered this, looping the gray's reins over my arm. "There is no danger." *Nothing moves there, Darik. And if someone is hiding in burned-out waggons, they may mean ill, and I do not wish to risk harm to any member of this merry troupe.*

"True," he agreed easily enough. "Still, I shall accompany you."

My sigh was a gust of wind. "Very well. Have Redfist keep them out of sight, and follow me. Agreed?"

"Wait for my return." For one moment he was every fingerwidth the prince, an unconscious air of command hanging on him. It did make him handsome. "Please."

I blew out a short, impatient breath, handing the reins up to him. "You are more trouble than you are worth. Hurry."

"I do not think the waggons are likely to escape." The bay turned, prancing, and cantered back to the small group waiting below. The gray followed, without a look back, its lead attached to Darik's hand. It would be easier to take the horses, but I did not wish to risk the four-footed cousins. Something did not feel right here—and if aught happened, I wished to be certain the others could return easily to Vulfentown. Besides, I could not see if the sand was firm enough, closer to the caravans.

I stood on the hilltop, clearly silhouetted for any crossbow bolt, and felt Darik's worry. He felt he should be with me, not playing messenger. But he obeyed.

When he returned, loping for the top of the hill, he stopped next to me, the wind fingering his hair. He touched my shoulder, and the contact was pleasant. Comforting.

"The barbarian says to be careful," he said in G'mai. "The little one says he wishes to come, and Janaire argues with Atyarik about following you, and the minstrel is generally keeping his head out of the bickering. In other words, all goes as it has these past few days."

It won a smile from me. "I am glad tis unchanged. Come with me then, princeling. Shall we solve this mystery?"

"An honor to guard your back, *adai'mi.* If we uncover anyone living, shall I kill or simply disarm them?" His black eyes were level and serious.

I still did not like the thought of him among charred waggon skeletons, but I started down the hill. "Do as you think best, D'ri. You have seen a battlefield before."

He walked beside me, or slightly behind, moving silently. I took care with my steps, though we were clearly visible. His silence—the silence of a *s'tarei*—spread out to enfold both of us.

Of course, he did not know what waited amidst those shattered, smoking waggons. Nor did I. Bandits were unlikely, they would not stay after stripping the waggons and taking survivors for sport or slaving. Scavengers were likely, human and animal. Yet scavengers would have been moving about, unaware of our presence, focused on their food.

Twas likely the scene was deserted.

Yet if there is anything I have learned in more than a decade of sellswording, tis that no situation is entirely predictable.

Why are the waggons still burning? Vaguely disturbed, I eyed the caravan again. No, more than vaguely disturbed.

Very disturbed. Bad trouble on the road to Shaituh, Ammerdahl Rikyat asking for me, the Shainakh Emperor crazy enough to start jabbing at Pesh in addition to the Danhai, and my nape crawling with the feel of danger.

I do not like this, Darik said privately. *It feels wrong.*

I agreed. It rubbed every instinct against the grain. Yet passing this close to a mystery without investigating it was beyond my strength. The more I knew of this, the better prepared I was to keep us all safe on the road to Shaituh. Also, the knowledge might be worth something. I needed all the coin I could gather to feed myself and the others through the winter.

I can bring us coin, if necessary, Darik offered. *I have certain skills considered valuable.*

I stopped, examining the line where the grasslands merged with sand. Confused tracks here, something long and dragging. Scorching, padded feet.

I whistled again, a nervous note added to the sound of waves and wind against sand. "*Ya'hana.*" The word rode a long wondering breath. "Tracks."

Darik was examining them. “I have never seen these before.”

“I have.” I fell back into speaking G’mai, as I often did with him. The only change was my intonation, as equal and intimate as his ever had been. “Wyvern. Three of them, maybe more.”

He cursed, quietly and passionlessly. We have all three varieties of wyrm in our country—the long fiery wyverns, the dragon, and the dragon's smaller more-dangerous cousin, the wingwyrm. Some *s'tarei* even go wingwyrm-hunting, when their population needs thinning.

There are no songs for wyrm-hunting except laments.

Darik spoke the same question immediately occurring to me. “Why so close to the sea?”

“I do not know.” I shivered, examining the tracks. Now I could see a clear line of charring the lie of the grass had hidden, striking up and away from the hill. “They are solitary creatures, unless tis a mother with little ones. But the tracks are too big. And they will not come close to bodies of water, tis poison to them. They are dry-mountain creatures.” I chewed my lower lip gently, checking the Sun in the sky. “Mother’s *tits*. We shall find a waystation tonight. I like not the thought of facing a wyvern in darkness.”

He nodded. But he examined the waggons. “What of the oxen?”

“Wyverns would eat them.” I studied at the closest waggon, at once seeing what he meant. The traces were perfectly intact, not broken as if a wyvern had torn them or an ox sought to bellow free and escape. I looked at a few more waggons and saw they were all the same.

I smelled conspiracy, or witchery. Or some combination of the two.

My eyes met Darik’s. “So the caravan stops here, sees three wyverns, and looses their oxen to meekly hand them over? Or bandits strip a caravan and wyverns come down from the hills to burn it for no apparent reason? Or...” I shrugged helplessly, spreading my hands.

“A mystery.” He used the particular term in G’mai for a riddle that had no answer. It was also the word for a fool’s riddle, the kind that was ridiculously simple once a fool told you the answer. I had to smile. His tone was light, but with a sharper edge, and I turned to look at him. His mouth was a straight line and his black eyes warm with something I had seen before on a man's face.

I swallowed dryly, lay my hand against a charred and shattered waggon-box. "Is there any cargo left?"

He did not look away. "No. Whatever this caravan carried is gone now."

I closed my eyes, and tried to imagine.

Why would a caravan come to the sands? No fishing, no hunting here. Had the caravan master seen wyvern traces and decided to be near the water despite the risk of sinking the waggons? It seemed unlikely that bandits had driven the caravan down onto the beach. So for some reason, the caravan had come here. Then the oxen were taken, and the wyverns happened later.

No caravan would gladly lose all its waggons, though.

When I opened my eyes, Darik's eyes were still on me. He watched.

"Let us return to the others. Unless you think it profitable to look further." My tone was a little sharp.

"Enjoyable, at least. There is profit in enjoyment," he fired back. I had forgotten the richness of G'mai, the complex wordplay. He had just neatly outdueled me with words.

I do not recall drawing this duel-circle. "There is also a tax on enjoyment in this part of the world. Tread carefully, princeling."

His eyebrows lifted a fraction. "I can think of no tax that should be levied on this enjoyment." It was a formal pun-session now. He had challenged and I had answered. "The Sun, the sea and a pretty *adai.*"

Clumsy, for one so adept. "Two out of three is good odds, at least," I offered obliquely, running my hand along charred wood. Intense heat, for a short period of time. The board underneath was still fairly sound. Definitely wyvern fire. But *why*? They do not like people, staying as far as possible from civilization. Why would they seek out a caravan that stank of humankind? And where had the cargo gone? There were tracks, too blurred to be of any real use, unlike the wyvern trail.

"I see no cloud in the sky." But his intonation was just imprecise enough to imply he *did* see a cloud—trouble approaching—in the conversation.

"Lightning does sometimes descend from the blue." Twas an old line of poetry, so well worn it was almost cliché. Not my best effort, but twas only a warning.

"Absolutely. Like a *dauq'adai* on a whitebark branch."

I had two choices, now. I could make another witty pun and embroil myself even deeper with a palace-trained master of wordplay, or I could be rude.

I chose to do both.

"Whitebark repels evil, I am told," I said sweetly. "As does silver."

He nodded slowly, his hair falling forward over his forehead. "So does...steel." The word he used was a pun for a sword—and a *s'tarei*. In particular, the more...ah, intimate aspects of a *s'tarei*.

I decided to use the same term. "I have little known steel to *repel* evil." I turned away to look toward the hill we'd come from. "Sometimes a bright blade can be wielded by a black heart." I used the word that could be interpreted as his name, *darikaan*.

"Take care how you use yours, then." He followed me as I quartered the charred waggon, wrinkling my nose once or twice against the smoke.

"I have wielded my blade for a long while." I used the driest academic tone possible, to forestall the double meaning inherent in the word for *blade*. "I do not need instruction."

"You are a pinquill, K'li." The amusement in his tone warned me. "I should know better than to give you a pretty word."

"You should. I do not like pretty words." I used the word for useless frippery, with a savage intonation, weary of this game. I had grown up listening to wordplay, to the singing rhythm of G'mai, but I suddenly had no taste for it where Darik was concerned.

"Perhaps a bright blade can be more useful than pretty words." The word he used so softly—*darikaan*—was so blatant as to need no explanation.

Why are there no bodies? No arrows. No chopped bits of waggon. Where are the people who drove this caravan? "Perhaps. Yet I will keep my own blade. I have no use for another."

There. That was just vague enough for him to take as a compliment or a brush-off. Twas a nice touch, as it effectively closed the game. I had won.

"For someone who did not speak for years, you have a facile tongue." His tone grew serious. "Why are there no bodies? No carrion?"

"I may not have spoken, but there is nothing amiss with my ears." I touched my knifehilt again, running my fingers over the familiar soothing smoothness. I was doing so too frequently, lately, searching for comfort. After so long without, comfort seemed both useless and craven. "There are no bodies because the people did not die here."

"You think they died elsewhere? And I rather enjoy your ears, Kaia'li." There it was again, that intimate tone.

I could have blushed all the way to the sharp tips of said ears, coughed slightly. "I find it hard to believe anyone traveling with this caravan is still alive. Let my ears be."

I finished quartering the smoking waggons. There was not a single usable thing left in this ruin of a perfectly good caravan. It had been picked clean, or the people had left a-carrying their load like turtles.

The horses. There were too many horses. Perhaps they fired the waggons and loaded the horses? But...wyverns. Whatever answers this riddle is beyond my ken.

"Not even a touch?" Darik asked. "Or a look, or a sigh?"

I *gave* him a sigh, a deep one. *Why now?* "We are in the midst of a ruined caravan, the tide approaches, and there are three wyverns on the loose, behaving as wyverns should not. I do not think now is the time to court me."

"If not now, when?"

I spared the caravan one last sweeping glance before setting off for the hill. "I know not, Darik. I trained myself rather effectively not to even *think* of G'maihallan ever again. Then you bring your flawed *dauq'adai* and drop it in a barbarian's pocket, and I find myself as the leader of a street troupe and fostering a

Vulfentown wharf-rat. Truly the ways of the gods are strange."

"If pretty words will not help, and being a blade at your back will not help, what will? Help me, Kaia. I have never met a more difficult sparring-partner." He sounded as if he meant it.

That was a compliment, and twas unintentionally warming. I actually half-turned and gave him a smile. "Well. Tis nice to know. I thought I was losing my skill."

I might not have seen the flash of pain that crossed his face if I had not turned. I stopped short. He stared straight ahead, for the top of the hill. I heard a horse neigh—Atyarik's black gelding, sensing our approach.

What if the waggons were abandoned? But why would they be left here?

That question was enough to warrant further thought. Yet I was distracted. "Darik?"

"I swore I would not push you, K'li." Dismissive. He still looked at the top of the hill, his eyebrows drawn together and his mouth tight.

I sighed again, touched his shoulder, the one I had repaired his shirt over. My fingers met black G'mai cloth, brocade against my fingertips, and he gave me a startled glance.

"Patience, D'ri. I am learning to be an *adai*, and the *adai* of a Dragaemir at that. *Adai, s'tarei*—we are thrown into this by the gods, who are probably having a right hearty laugh at our expense this moment. In any case, I have accepted you. There is no need to court me."

"What if I feel a need?" His black eyes were less guarded now, raw and open. "Am I not *allowed*?"

I am not a toy or a courtesan, princeling. "I am fond of you, D'ri. Do I have to share your bed now?"

Did he look, for a moment, a trifle exasperated? "No. Not a bed. But it would be kind of you to share some small part of your heart. Even the Skaialan receives more regard from you than I do."

"I am sorry, if you think so." My throat was full of something difficult to speak through. "I..." My voice failed me, and still I touched him, unable to take my hand away. He was motionless under that touch. The wind rose, ruffling through grass, bringing the faint smell of smoke. A mystery to add to all other mysteries crowding my life now. I had been so utterly successful at avoiding entanglement before, sometimes at the cost of bloodshed. It mystified me to be caught so neatly and effortlessly now.

He nodded, slowly, once it was apparent I could not say more. "I will wait, K'li. As long as necessary."

I found my eyes meeting his. Even my own gaze betrayed me—their gold would always mark me as flawed, among my own kind.

Darik made a small restless movement. As if he wanted to say aught else, stopped himself.

"I would not have you harmed, D'ri." Quietly. Twas all I could give. "Now we must return to the others."

He nodded. I walked past him, my skin sensitive to his every movement. But something made me stop. I turned to face him again.

"D'ri." I noticed for the first time that I had shortened his name to a G'mai use-name, a mark of companionship. "I will try to hold you in higher regard." As soon as twas out of my mouth, I regretted it. It sounded snide and unhelpful.

He nodded thoughtfully, glanced over my shoulder at the still-smoking caravan. "Then I am happy."

I swore to myself and stamped away from him. I had wanted to see the burning caravan, not get entangled in a discussion with him about—

What precisely had we been speaking of, anyway? I no longer knew.

Rage and Fire

We camped as the Sun was almost below the rim of the horizon. I had remembered there was a waystation here, a sheltered one, high stone walls we could defend if necessary. Two entrances—a large gap in the wall toward the front, and a smaller wooden door leading out the back. The enclosure held a well and a shed full of firewood, and the packed earth of the campground looked relatively free of rocks. A scorched circle of stones waited for a campfire, and I set Janaire and Diyan to building one. Redfist bolted the back door with a massive beam that looked near as long as my body, and Atyarik and Darik, both hunters, disappeared into the coney-filled grass. The minstrel and I occupied ourselves with unsaddling and caring for the horses, who had their own pen inside the packed-earth enclosure. We had plenty of grain, thanks to Atyarik, I would have been picketing the horses outside if I had not seen wyvern sign.

I kept my silence as I worked, thinking. I had turned the mystery over and over in my head most of the day, and was no nearer a satisfactory conclusion.

The only logical explanation ran somewhat thus: Some traveling-group disguised as a caravan had left the waggons on the beach and the wyverns had happened by. Who would travel disguised as a caravan?

Shainakh army detachments, on the road north, someone's voice rose in my memory. If twas a puzzle, I lacked a crucial piece; and that is enough to make any sellsword cautious.

"You are quiet, lady," Gavrin offered as he brushed down one of the sleek black G'mai horses. They liked his gentleness—one sniffed his light hair, lipping affectionately. "The caravan?"

Ordinarily I would have bristled, that the minstrel could tell what I thought of, but this was no ordinary event. Three wyverns? Working in concert? And why, by the gods, were the waggons empty?

Indeed, that the caravan had been abandoned was the only logical explanation. But *why*?

"Yes, I am thinking on the caravan." I drew the brush down the bay's broad haunches. He shifted to lean into the stroke, and I leaned a bit more into him. "Three wyverns working together. It bodes ill."

"Is that why you sought this place?" He pushed the horse's nose aside, gently, patting the broad neck. Against the slender grace of the G'mai beasts, his ragged red and yellow looked even more torn and faded, yet still cheerful. Was I thinking of dropping coin on clothing him, too? He sorely needed it.

"If I were alone, I would pass the night in a tree. Or atop a large rock, and risk losing my horse. Wyverns are nothing to dice against. Three of them working together could mean sorcery—or worse." The bay stamped, and I pushed against his side, keeping his hooves from my feet. "I do not like sorcery, and I like even less the thought of *worse*."

"I thought all Gemerh were sorcerers."

"No. We—*they* use Power. Tis not the same." I drew the comb down. "The sorcerer enforces his will on the world, and so does the witch. Though in the higher levels, they say, they simply run with the natural flow and reorder the world. Tis complex." The horse dropped his head, flicking his ears, enjoying the combing. I felt Darik's silence coming back to camp. Twas exceedingly strange that I missed his presence.

That flatters me, K'li, his voice whispered in my ear. *I miss your presence, as well.*

I did not reply. If I had Power, as Darik and Janaire said—and especially a great deal of it, though I did not think it possible—the risk of *jada'adai* was very high. I could not be away from him for any considerable length of time without falling ill. After the last bout of twinsickness, I had no desire to repeat the experience.

"It *sounds* complex." Gavrin interrupted my musings. He looked interested. "The other lady Gemerh, is she a witch?"

"No, she is *adai*. A twin. She holds a great amount of Power, and Atyarik is her defense. Tis so, the *adai* and *s'tarei*, twins. One to hold the Power, the other to defend. The *s'tarei* makes certain the *adai* does not drain herself into death, and the *adai* makes certain the *s'tarei* is not attacked from behind." I finished and patted the bay's neck. He whickered with pleasure, and the gray crowded close, hungry for attention.

"Are there Gemerh men born with Power?"

I do not wish to explain this. I wish even less to think on it. I turned to the gray. "The *s'tarei'sa* have some inborn talents, like speaking to animals or a sense of danger, or the silence. Tis said the gods only gave the *s'tarei'sa* certain gifts, because of the risk of a man using them in anger. Rage is a risk for the *s'tarei*, and the *adai* must hold them to mercy. Tis an old tale, that the Elders in the Silver Ships gave the G'mai the task of protecting the Blessed Lands, and gave them the gift of Power to do so—but there had to be something to save them from hubris, and the twinning does so. For every G'mai, a twin. Except me." I drew the comb down, picked the loose matted hair from it, did so again.

"But you have a twin." He moved to his bony, biscuit-brown nag. "The prince."

I shrugged, glancing at the walls, each stone fitted carefully. The wind would come chill off the sea tonight, if my nose told me aright; I was glad to have the shelter of walls. "It appears so."

"He must feel for you, Lady Kaia. I saw him, after the duel. He was pale, and—"

I do not wish to make my uncertainty fodder for your songs. I was unable to think of how to extricate myself from this conversation politely. "What did you think of the duel?"

"Twas magnificent," he said immediately, and I winced to think of another song born. "But when the barbarian carried you from the dueling ground, I stayed to watch the prince. He appeared to be weeping without tears. He simply sheathed his sword and—"

Oh, Mother's tits. Cease this. "Gavrin. I do not wish to hear more."

The minstrel shrugged. "As you like, lady."

"Tis *Kaia.* Not *lady.*" I saw Darik and Atyarik come back into the waystation. They were both carrying fat glossy coneys. "Look, there they are."

"Twas quick."

"G'mai are good with bows. We have sharp eyes." *And sharp ears. And sharp words, even for each other.* The childhood proverb rose in memory, and my shoulders hunched. I had spent so long seeking not to think of my homeland, but now G'maihallan was pursuing the least of its daughters even across the Lan'ai.

"Truly a blessed people," Gavrin murmured.

I made a short noise, not quite disagreement but close. "Other peoples are free to love where they will. G'mai have a marriage forced upon them. Tis not so much of a blessing, sometimes."

"Is that what you hate him for?"

Hate who? Darik? "I do not hate him." I found it true. I did not hate Darik.

I did not hate him at all. There lay the heart of the problem. He deserved a finer *adai* than I could ever be.

I blew out through pursed lips as the horse whickered, and looked to the sky, checking the weather again. Janaire waved a greeting to Atyarik—she and the barbarian already had the stewpot out, and something simmering. Adding the coneys would make a fine dinner. Her soft Gavridar face lit up.

Twas beautiful to see, Janaire and her *s'tarei.* She touched his shoulder when he reached her, softly, and light entered his spare Tyaanismir face. He seemed to truly care for her. Of course, she was a beautiful G'mai girl, and was all the things a G'mai girl should be—a pretty *adai,* talented with Power, and soft in all the ways a G'mai girl was trained to be.

She was not silent, harsh and flawed.

I think you are exactly as you should be. Darik's voice caressed my cheek, my hair. *I could not have asked the gods for more.*

Tis a nice sentiment, I replied, *but I do not believe you. And cease listening to my thoughts without being invited. Tis rude.*

He made no reply, giving his brace of coneys over to Atyarik and turning toward the horses. He crossed the packed earth gracefully. I looked over the gray's back, my eyes meeting his across the distance. Despite my sharpness, twas a look of silent accord—his worry matched mine. Something did not seem aright. I had not said *sorcery* to Darik, but I thought on it, and he could certainly feel the direction my thoughts were wending. A sorcerer unleashing pet wyverns on a convenient set of waggons—destroying something?

Enemies? But there were no bodies. Evidence?

Evidence of *what*?

He reached the horses. The bay nosed him, affectionately, and he scratched the bay's face. "*In'sh'ai, ataraun,*" he said, quietly, to the animal. "And a good evening to you, *adai'mi.*" He spoke G'mai, and his inflection was as intimate as possible.

"Good evening, Your Highness," I answered formally, in commontongue. "I see your hunting went well."

"Well enough." He changed to commontongue as well. Was it courtesy, or unwillingness to let me have the upper hand? "Dinner?"

"Soon." I kept combing the gray, watching my hands move. Darik's gaze was a weight I could not shoulder just yet.

The minstrel made a low sound that might have been a laugh. I glanced at him, daggers in my gaze. Gavrin dropped his gaze to the nag's back. "I think I should help the boy." His voice was choked with something—laughter, perhaps. I hoped it was not—I was already in a black mood, growing blacker by the second.

Like Darik's eyes.

Diyan scampered between the barbarian and Janaire, laughing. He seemed at ease, and I caught sight of Atyarik performing a small hand-trick for him. Janaire ruffled the young one's hair, and he ducked his head, shyly.

Darik simply stood, watching me. His eyes were quiet and depthless. A slight breeze played with his clothing, touched his dark hair.

I might as well tell him what I fear. "I wish you to take watch with me tonight. Atyarik and Janaire can have the first watch, and we shall take the second. Redfist and the minstrel should take the third—the closer to dawn, the less danger."

He nodded, his black hair falling softly forward. "You think the wyverns will come during the second watch, in the deepest part of night."

I drew the comb down the gray's neck. He made a low horsey sound of pleasure and leaned into the stroke. Darik's eyes were still and flat as a painted surface. "I think if something has forced three wyverns to act so contrary to normal wyvern behavior, why not an attack during the night? And the second watch *is* the most vulnerable."

He nodded. "You wish me to watch with you?" He used the word that could have meant "wish" and could have meant "trust".

"Of course." My eyes locked firmly onto the gray's mane. "You are my *s'tarei.*"

He said nothing, but when I looked up through my lashes he smiled. It was the slight upward quirk of his lips I had seen before, a shared expression, something tender and amused I had never seen him practice in anyone else's presence.

Only with me.

"You are a continual surprise, Kaia'li." Soft and intimate, the words just brushing the air.

I ducked under the horse's head and turned my back to him, starting to comb the gray's other side. "If the wyverns attack, the best we can hope for is to hold them while the others flee."

"We have two *adai.*" Thoughtfully, a strategist's tone. "Surely that counts for something. I begin to think sorcery is involved with this."

"It certainly stinks of *something* unnatural. We have one *adai*, and one not-even-half-trained, severely flawed *adai.*" My voice, for once, held no bitterness. *I am G'mai. I have Power.* The thought was a wonder, again.

"Nevertheless."

"I am not certain I wish to go further with Janaire and her *taih'adai.*" Somehow, with my back to him, twas easier to speak of. "I know she needs help, but..."

"It cannot hurt, to aid her. Can it?" He sounded uncertain. I felt his fingers brush one of my braids.

"I do not know. Tis strange, to have the *taih'adai* speak to you. I almost feel I am shapeshifting to someone else—I am not *myself* anymore." I drew the comb down, the horse whickered and flicked his ears.

He said nothing.

"I think it frightens me." My neck and shoulders were tight. Me, the sellsword Kaia. *How long have I lived without fear, or simply denying it? Running from fear does no good, as Kesa says; it only pursues you faster. And now that I have admitted my fear to him, what will happen?*

"I would ease your fear, if I could." He spoke in G'mai, and I could not imagine him speaking otherwise.

I blew out between pursed lips again, whistling in place of speaking. Silence bloomed; I finished brushing the gray and turned to face Darik. He stood with his feet braced against the earth and the twin *dotanii* rising behind his shoulders, a tall, thoughtful man with all the harsh beauty of the Dragaemir.

Too much beauty for this part of the world. He belonged *home*, in the Blessed Land, where he would not frighten me with the weakness I had fought so long to overcome and conceal.

I stepped close to him, fascinated by the play of failing light against his black hair. "Ah, D'ri. You are not to blame." I found my hand touching his shoulder again—the one that had been wounded. The first wound of his I had ever felt. "Watch with me tonight, then. We shall see if the wyverns come."

He looked down at me, wearing that small smile again. "My thanks for your trust, Kaia'li."

My fingers caressed the brocade of his shirt. Such a small thing, the feel of fabric made by others of my kind. Homesickness I thought I had banished forever rose in my throat, pricked behind my eyes. "My thanks for your patience, D'ri." I studied the shape of his mouth, the arc of his cheekbone, the harsh beauty of his face balanced gracefully against the tensile strength of his body. I had noticed his beauty before, and his deadliness, and his patience; but I had not noticed them together, all at once.

He was truly a *s'tarei*.

"What will you do, if we have three wyverns to deal with?"

My hand cupped his shoulder, feeling muscle tense under my palm.

"Defend you as best I can. As a *s'tarei* should."

I nodded, my braids falling forward over my shoulders. He touched one, lifted it, the rope of hair slipping against his fingers. He pushed it back over my shoulder and paused, looking down at me.

"Keep your distance from the wyverns," I said, softly. "Let me deal with them."

"Kaia—"

"You will be responsible for making certain the others escape. I can face anything short of a wingwyrm, princeling." My intonation took the sting out of the words. "I am worried for their safety."

"I will *not* leave you to face wyverns," he said softly, but with great force. "Is that clear to you, Kaia?"

I sought for a conciliatory tone. "D'ri, I need to know you will care for the others. It will free me to fight effectively."

"You are not the only one with a blade," Darik said tightly. "Three wyverns may prove even a match for you, Kaia'li."

I have fought wyverns before, prince. I even killed a sorcerer terrorizing a village after I left G'mai. For a moment I felt panic rising, the unsteady terror that drowned me whenever I thought of the caves under the earth, the sorcerer's soft laughter and the hissing of flame.

I had thought it luck, the chance stumble that saved me from the trap of the sorcerer's eyes. What if it had been untrained Power, or some other difference? What if I was not nearly as strong as I thought?

I shook myself free of memory. I do not like to think on that time in my life. "I have faced wyverns before, and left the fight whole. I wish you to care for the others."

"No." Stubborn to the last. "I did not take my oath to them."

"Please." Twas the only weapon I had against him. Sharp words had not worked, and ignoring him had only made me sick with fever. "Please, D'ri. If the wyverns come tonight, you must protect the others and take them to safety. Then you may return and fight beside me, but I *need* you to do what I ask.

Please."

He shook his head, his jaw set stubbornly. "Kaia. I *cannot* let you face three wyverns—or possibly more—alone."

Mother Moon, do not push me, princeling. "I am *requesting* your aid. You seem only to obey when tis advantageous, *s'tarei mi.*"

Twas an unparalleled insult, even from me. For a moment I thought he was about to strike me. He certainly looked angry enough to do so. His hand even twitched, though I was not sure what he intended—to slap me, or to merely brush his hair back from his forehead.

Then his Dragaemir face opened into a smile, and I almost took a step back. I was not ready for such an expression from him—tender, pained, and wry at the same moment, his black eyes dancing and his mouth relaxed into a grin. "It cheers me that you would take me to task, *adai'mi.*"

I realized I had spoken in G'mai, and addressed him just as an *adai* would. My heart leapt inside me, traitorous piece of meat that it was.

It almost managed to distract me. Almost. "Good. Then you will take the others to safety, and I will deal with the possible wyverns. Should it become necessary."

Now we hit the snag in the reel of silk. "You cannot command me to leave you. Tis against the Law."

"You are quick to invoke the Law to your benefit." A scorch of anger rose under my breastbone. "You are not commanded to leave me. You may return and aid me against the wyverns if you like—*if* they even show their snouts tonight!"

My voice hit a pitch I had rarely heard before, and I heard a sharp intake of breath. I glanced behind Darik and saw the boy staring across the packed earth of the waystation, his dark eyes wide and frightened. Janaire and Atyarik watched, Atyarik's face dark with anger and trepidation, Janaire's hand to her soft Gavridar mouth. The Skaialan stood with his legs braced wide apart, staring at the sky, apparently lost in thought while fingering his axe. And the minstrel? He stirred the stew for our supper, pretending not to notice. It was the first sign of tact he had shown.

I swallowed roughly, took a firm hold on my temper, and

took a firm hold as well of Darik's shirtfront, wrapping my hand in G'mai fabric. "You *will* listen," I hissed through my teeth. "You may be a princeling in G'mai, but here, in my life, you are nothing more than a problem I cannot solve short of my own death. You will *not* bandy words with me. *I am the leader.* This little troupe of street-performers is under my protection, and my direction. If you wish to disobey me, *go* through that door and do not return." I jerked my head toward the aperture in the front wall leading to the outside world. "I have not come through war, hunger, sorcery, and thievery to have some jumped-up princeling tell me when he will and will not obey. You may return to G'mai and die of twinsickness on the way, for all I care."

He did not look at me. Instead, stared down at my hands caught in the front of his shirt. I shook with something too complex to be called rage. "No," he said, and nothing more.

I made my fingers tear free from the cloth. "Go to the fire," I said, harshly, in commontongue. "I do not wish to see your face until the dawning, *s'tarei.* You are a disgrace."

It took a physical effort not to draw my *dotanii.* If I drew on him now, I would not be fighting coldly, with calculation. I would strike to kill, and he would not stop at defending himself.

I would make it impossible for him to stop at defending himself.

A faint inner voice reminding me of Kesa's sought to tell me to calm myself. I could not. For the life of me, the man could irritate me just by breathing. Was he not satisfied that he had entirely ruined the life I had made for myself?

Though I could not blame him. After all, I had picked Redfist's pocket, and plucked the *dauq'adai* out neatly as could be. The fault was mine. Who was to say the gods had not had a hand in gifting him with a flawed *adai,* for some purpose only they knew?

Even if I had Power, I was still none of what a G'mai woman should be.

I could not blame Darik for that, but it did not stop the furious pain in my chest. It did not salve my need to hurt him, a simple extension of my need to hurt myself.

I put my hands flat on his chest and shoved him. He moved

back, gracefully, his face closing with an almost physical snap.

I turned on my heel and stalked for the gap in the wall. I had almost reached it when the boy pounded across the packed earth and nearly collided with me. "*Cha,* do not leave!" he yelled. "Do not leave!" He clutched at my belt and I found I had locked his wrist, stopping myself from squeezing roughly with an awful sweat-prickling effort. His eyes were wide, his thatch of hair was wild and tangled.

You are in a fine stew, Kaia. You must calm yourself. "No fear, little one. As long as you are loyal, I shall not leave you." Too late I realized I spoke in G'mai, something this little one would not understand.

I did not understand myself now either.

"Do not leave!" he repeated, hysterical strength in his small arms. I could only imagine what he thought I intended.

I took him by his thin shoulders. It was an effort to speak in commontongue. "Go back to the fire, Diyan. Now."

Something in my face made him obey. He stumbled back, his eyes locked with mine.

"Kaia—" Twas Janaire. I set my jaw. If I paused to speak, I would call her something so filthy her *s'tarei* would never forgive me. Not that I cared, but twould be impolite. And a G'mai should always be courteous.

Even a flawed one.

Twas not courteous at all, Kaia. You are wrong. He is right to insist, it is his duty.

The thought only fueled my fury.

I stalked out of the waystation and made for the small stream the watermark on the wall told me should be near. Chedgrass swirled around my hips once I left the beaten earth of the small track. I was so angry I barely noticed the way the grass swirled and flattened, my anger a silent wind touching the stalks.

Power. I had Power, of whatever uneven quality, and it threatened to escape my control.

Why am I so angry? Because he will not leave me? Because I have lost control of my own life? I shared my bed only with loneliness before, and wished for him, even if I did not know it was him I wished for. Why do I balk now?

I set my teeth in my lower lip. Twas pain that was needed, to restore my restraint. What was it about the man that could drive me to the very brink of my self-control? It did not bode well. I had never thought there would be a *s'tarei* for me, since I had no Power, so I had never paid attention to the finer points of the Law dealing with relations between a *s'tarei* and his *adai.* Twas very true I could not shun him, unless he directly did something to make himself *sharauq'allallai,* outcaste. Which he had not—he would merely not leave me to the wyverns. I could not blame him.

But twas more important to let the others escape than to have him prove once again that he could force himself into my life.

And just this afternoon I had felt...

What exactly had I felt? Did I even *know*, anymore, what I was capable of feeling?

Kaia, you must cease this. I found myself at the stream without knowing how I had arrived, walking with anger covering my eyes.

I was even *thinking* in G'mai again, my birthtongue slipping to the surface with an ease that belied long absence. I had learned commontongue quickly, not wishing to be reminded of anything resembling my native land. I was a sellsword, an assassin and a thief, something no G'mai girl dreamed of being.

Something no *s'tarei* would want

I went to my knees and dipped my hands in the water, seeing a patch of meatroot off to the side. I did not want meatroot.

I did not know what I wanted.

I cupped cool water in my palms, brought it to my face. The shock helped clear my head. Here in the bowl of the plains, low scrub bushes clustered around the streamlet, providing some cover. The hills rose and pleated gently away, covered in chedgrass, a sea that bore the ships of caravans toward Shaituh and the other coastal cities, a sea that held a few wandering nomadic tribes and the ever-present grasscats and coneys. Not at all a wyvern's hunting ground.

The caravans were still smoking. Yet I saw the smoke

before.

That was what bothered me. The caravans were still smoking and scorch-hot when I reached them. Fired once, or fired twice? But the wood underneath had been sound, still.

I sighed, dipped my fingers in the water again as the light failed in the sky. Night here on the plains fell swift, like a hawk from the sky's blue vault.

What could I do? Leave them to their own devices and return to Vulfentown on foot? It would not be long before Darik tracked and found me. And the others were my responsibility now. I had taken on the burden of being the captain of this small detachment. I did not wish to steer the ship of others' fates. I had enough trouble steering my own.

I have never sought command, but sometimes the only thing to do is guide those too tired or inexperienced to guide themselves, especially in the wilderness, where a misstep can bring death. Or in a battle, where death is quicker, striking like a foulmouth-serpent, with not even a hiss to betray its intent. I had suffered hard for the ability to *survive* no matter where I found myself; to deny those who trusted me the benefit of those harsh lessons seemed unworthy of even a flawed G'mai.

I splashed my face again. I was not accustomed to this. I was accustomed to traveling alone or with a caravan, silent or singing as the mood took me.

Lonely, even if I did not acknowledge it.

The hissing sound startled me—a snap and crackle of flame, and I glanced up, startled, before I dove to the side, rolling.

Twas sheer instinct, learned on so many assassinations and silent thieving attempts, not to mention scouting against the Danhai. When a bolt streaks for your head or heart, the safest thing to do is roll away, blindly, even if you are not sure the bolt is meant for you. To hear the whistle of the arrow cleaving air is of no use unless you act, at once, without thinking.

I gained the safety of the stream, blindly, thinking of wyverns. Water was poison to them.

My *dotanii* left its sheath with a low singing note. I stood knee-deep in the stream, water dripping chill down my back, and stared wildly at the gathering dark, breath coming harsh and fast. The hissing sound circled me. I smelled burning, a dry sour lizard-smell wedded to the sharp odor of navthen, a combined scent that dragged me back to caves under the earth and whispering, chittering laughter.

Memory was pushed away. I could not fight battles both past and present. I could only fight the battle *now*.

Instinct had driven me into the water. So, in the water I would remain. My boots were sound, even if they would be sodden before long.

I held my *dotanii* in the third-guard, followed the hissing with my ears. I could have turned to follow the sound, but that would have sloshed my feet in the stream and generally deadened my direction-sense. Best merely to wait, silent as an adder.

They do not name me Adderstrike, like that assassin in Pesh, or Swordsong like that redheaded mercenary. No, I am saddled with Iron Flower. Gods preserve me.

The hissing came again, and I felt a brush against the new walls separating me from the outside world. If not for the *taih'adai*, I might have felt the danger long before it approached me. Then again, I had been all but blind with rage, not usual for me.

I felt aught else then, a silence descending over me very much like the silence that came over the world when my mother died. But this was subtly different, the silence of a *s'tarei*, and I felt Darik's presence.

I had ordered him to stay by the fire. But all his attention was on me. He did not communicate with me with *taran'adai,* which was probably discreet of him given my temper.

In any case, I needed my concentration for battle.

I took a deep soundless breath, gaping my mouth to make it quiet. How could a wyvern hide in the scrub brush, even a small one? Twould be too large to remain unseen, and the smoke would give it away.

It streaked out of cover, low and furious, a long fluid shape scored with ropes of white-hot glow, bubbling saliva frothing between needle-sharp teeth. It looked like a quick running dog crossed with a serpent, tasseled ears lying flat against its

narrow head. I had just enough time to reverse my largest knife along my forearm and let out a short, sharp sound of rage before the thing was on me.

I went over backward, into the water, and steam boiled up. I thrashed in the knee-high water, fruitlessly, the dead charcoal husk of the wyvern impaled on my *dotanii*, when a line of fire slashed up the outside of my left leg from ankle to up over the knee, biting in and eating all the way down to bone.

I knew, even as water filled my mouth and nose and I struggled to heave the steaming body up off me, that it was Darik's pain, not mine.

I could find no purchase on the bottom of the stream. The water forced its way down my nose, burning through my throat. For a moment I was in the caverns again, bleeding and alone, bones shifting underneath me as the sorcerer laughed, taunting me. *You cannot win against me, girl. I am far more than you will ever be.*

And my reply, delivered from the depths of sheer stubborn refusal? Merely a curse, before I spitted him and freed the mud and wattle huts of Sidai from his depredations.

I lunged for air, desperate to fill my lungs and break through the wall of the past threatening to drown me. One last heaving effort and the wyvern husk moved slightly, enough for me to gain a little space, even with the current forcing me down and the wyvern's body weighting me. I surged up into the free air of the present, coughing and choking, and scrambled for the stream's edge.

Something whizzed past me, and I dropped. My ears strained and my fightbrain catalogued the sound, trying to decipher it. *Not arrow, not bolt, not knife...what in the name of Beleriaa was* that?

"Come out, weirdling." Twas a male voice, speaking in—of all things—lightly accented High Shainakh. "Come out, Kaia Steelflower, come out, cease your damnable elvish witchery and face me like the true abomination you are—"

Elvish? Gods, how I hate that word. "What the—" I began, and something else streaked toward me. It was a bolt of something that clipped the edges of my newfound mental walls and threw me to my knees again.

"In the name of the new God-Empe—" the voice started; I was hurriedly cataloguing my options and seeking to struggle to my feet.

"*Kadai a'adai allai!*" Screaming. It sounded like Janaire, her soft Gavridar accent blurring the crisp consonants. The battle-cry of an *adai.*

Silence, then, too. Probably Atyarik. Twas a fierce silence, not like Darik's cool, utterly impregnable quiet. There was a low, sliding grunt, and I heard Janaire's voice again, chanting low and furiously, one of the Lays. A particular phrase from the Lay of Destruction, about the Darkness—the words were laden with Power. She was fighting him on his own ground, this sorcerer, whoever he was.

Oh, thank the gods, I will never think of you as helpless again. A fully-trained *adai* is far from the worst help one could have against a sorcerer. There was another soft, chuffing grunt. My lungs burned, both from effort and near-drowning.

I threw my knife, steel cleaving air with a low deadly whistle.

It flew true, and the darkness resounded with a choked-off scream of rage and pain. Atyarik cursed, steadily and fiercely. I made my way with more luck than grace through chedgrass and blinked in surprise when Janaire flicked a small sphere of silvery light into being. The *zaradai*—witchlight—cast a soft silver glow onto the scene.

A thin, brown-haired man in the shifting gray robe of a sorcerer curled on the ground. No wonder I had not seen the wyverns.

A sorcerer. Gods above and below, I wish to go the rest of my life without facing another. I shook water from my *dotanii.* My leg throbbed. *Darik. He's wounded.*

"A witch," Janaire said. "And well-trained, at that."

"Sorcerer." My voice was harsh. "A witch would not enslave wyverns." My knife was buried in the man's throat, I had thrown true. His eyes glittered with death-fever. He was Shainakh, I judged, and saw his gaze fixed itself on me. A deathstare.

Why would he seek to kill me?

"Why would you seek to kill me?" I approached him

cautiously. How did he know my name? Was it by chance, or had I made an enemy I did not know of?

“’Ware, Kaialitaa,” Janaire said. “He is still alive.”

I shrugged. “No knowledge without danger, so the Yada’Adais always said.”

I lowered myself gingerly next to him and wrenched the knife from his throat. Blood gouted, black in the soft silvery light.

I noticed aught under the blood on his chest, through a rent in his robe. If Janaire’s warcry had not tattered the cloth, I would not have. As twas, I almost missed it.

There was a mark on the man, with a shimmer of Power over it quickly fading. Twas on his torn and bleeding chest, right over his left nipple. The glyph meant “hand” in Shainakh, done in faint blue ink. The tattoo and the small sorcery covering it made my mouth fill with copper.

A Blue Hand. Here, in sorcerer’s robes, with three wyverns, and two destroyed caravans?

“He is dying.” Janaire’s hand was at her mouth again.

My leg burned again, and I looked up at Atyarik. His long face was grave and distasteful.

“Ease his passing.” I gained my feet in one stumbling rush. *Darik.* He was concentrating fiercely, shutting me out perhaps without realizing it.

Water dripped from my clothes and *dotanii.* I was soaked to the bone and would start shivering soon, and by the time I reached the waystation I would have two raging wyverns to deal with, if they had not fled at the sorcerer’s death.

It did not matter.

Darik.

My leg threatened to buckle underneath me.

I ran.

A World without You

I skidded into the enclosure just in time to see the last wyvern scuttle up the barred wooden door. Wood smoked, charring, the wyvern's claws made solid *chuck-chuck* sounds. It scurried over the top of the door and leapt from the wall, freed by the sorcerer's demise.

Redfist, his beard singed and a murderous gleam in his green eyes, hefted his axe. The boy crouched behind him, two thin *stilette* glittering in his hands. The minstrel—I could not see the minstrel.

I did not care.

Darik stumbled and I caught his shoulder, holding him up as best I could. The left leg of his breeches was smoking, and I lowered him to the ground. "A blanket!" I yelled. "Fetch a blanket!"

Diyan scuttled over to me, one of Janaire's blankets in his hands. "*Cha—*" he started.

I did not give him lee to speak. "Waterskin! Where is the minstrel?"

"Hit on th' head," Diyan tossed over his shoulder, before pelting over to a scatter of gear. He came back with a waterskin as I wrapped the blanket around Darik's leg. D'ri hissed out through his teeth in G'mai, an oath I had rarely heard except on the practice ground. "Th' barbarian tends him."

"Good." I tore the waterskin from the boy's hands. My leg throbbed, especially down near the ankle. I flipped the blanket cautiously up and doused his boot and ankle, seeking to abate the burning of wyvern venom and heat-violated skin. "More water! Redfist, the minstrel?" I pitched my voice to carry through the enclosure.

"Clean out," the barbarian called back. "Hit wi' a stray knee, I think. Saved the wee lad from untimely death. What of D'rik?"

"I shall live," Darik said. "Merely a burn." But he spoke in G'mai, and there was a dazed quality to his voice I did not like.

I slapped him, sharply, and sense returned to his eyes. The crack of the blow echoed against the walls of the enclosure, and I let out a sound closer to a sob than I believed myself capable of. "Do not *dare* to leave me, D'ri!" I told him, in singsong, furious G'mai. "Do not! Stay here!"

His head swiveled back to face me, his eyes finding mine through an ocean of pain. His black gaze focused. "Kaia'li? The wyverns?"

"Two dead, one fled. Your leg—Janaire should return soon. A sorcerer." *A Blue Hand,* I added silently, and poured more water over the burn. It went all the way up his leg to above the knee, along the outside, as if a fiery whip had been pressed against the skin. "A sorcerer was there." I babbled in G'mai. My hands were impossibly hot, and I shivered so hard my teeth clamped shut. My leg gave an amazing flare of pain, echoing Darik's injury. The burn was deep but narrow. A wyvern's claw, perhaps, or tail.

Even wounded, he tried to calm me. "K'li, gentle. Ease yourself."

My fingers loosened from the empty waterskin, and I clamped them around his leg halfway up the calf. My hands burned, *burned*, and I shivered so hard my teeth threatened to splinter. Water dripped from my hair, from my soaked clothing. Darik said something else but I did not hear, I was too occupied seeking to yank my hands free.

They would not unloose. My hands were bound to him. The fire inside me rose, like a fever, like the twinsickness, a cresting tide of heat and weakness.

"Kaia—" Darik said, but the heat passed through me in one furious wave. The pain in my leg spiked, a tearing agony. I spat a shipboard curse that made even the barbarian blink.

Darik grabbed my wrists, forced my hands away. He looked better. The color returned to his face, and his eyes were no longer distant. “Kaia. Cease.”

How could I? I did not even know what I *did.* My hands were burning, burning, and so was my leg.

Hands came down hard on my shoulders, fingers digging in. A great cool weight washed through me, filtered by Janaire’s touch. “I think she sought to heal you, Adarikaan.”

“I think so too, Gavridar. And she did a fair job of it.” He let out a sigh. “Pity, another pair of breeches ruined.”

“Atyarik will give you another.” She sounded calm, at least. Then she said something low and fast in G’mai, something about Power-sickness and sorcery.

“Kaia.” Darik came up to his knees; his arms were around me. “Are you wounded? You are soaked.”

“I am well enough.” The pain roaring down my leg gave one last crunching flare, extinguished itself while Janaire said something else. I had trouble understanding, her Gavridar mouth turning the words into liquid song. Or was it that I was in shock, staring down at my glowing hands? A blurring line of silver outlined my fingers.

I tried to shake it away. It would not go.

Come out, weirdling. Come out, Kaia Steelflower, come out, drop your damnable elvish witchery and face me like the true abomination you are—

What had he meant? Why would a Blue Hand want me dead? *Why?*

“K’li,” Darik said, quietly. “Stay with me.”

“What did he mean?” My entire body seemed to break out in shivering gooseflesh. *Elvish. I hate that word, they use that word and have no idea what they mean.* “The door—the back door. Is it burning?”

“No, merely charred.” Darik spoke calmly, but his eyes were dark and wounded. “Ease yourself, *adai’mi.*”

“Carry her. Set her down here. She killed a wyvern and faced down the sorcerer—he almost netted her like a fish.” Janaire’s voice caught, but she did a fair job of giving orders. I had not thought she had the sense to do so.

Atyarik appeared, moving into the enclosure with a swift stride, his face full of thunder. Of course—I had told him to kill the man. *Ease his passing.*

Had he done so? Of course he had. He was a *s'tarei.* He would not falter to do what must be done.

I shook like a windblown leaf. Gulped down breath and forced control.

I am Kaia. I am sellsword, thief, and assassin, the Iron Flower, I need no one. I am strong, and I stand alone. My body shook, slipping, something hot and barbed rising under my skin.

"You will lose control and fall ill," Janaire said. "I could help you, if you would but let me."

I shook my head, gasping, and tried to free myself of Darik's hands. The smell of burning hung heavy in the air.

The others gathered. I finally succeeded in pushing Darik away. He gave in after a short struggle, and I made it to my feet. Then I offered him my hand. He gained his feet too, a little less gracefully than usual. The blanket fell aside. The smell of charred flesh was gone. His leg was healed and whole.

"You were wounded." The words tore my throat. I gazed up at him, the unsteady tremor returning to my bones.

His face was thoughtful. "You healed me, Kaia'li. My thanks."

I took in another shuddering breath. "Redfist, find something to close the front door. Janaire, tend the minstrel. Atyarik, check the back door, and if tis safe, help Redfist."

Atyarik actually looked to Darik first, and the Dragaemir nodded. His hand held mine. A clean, calm warmth slid up from his hand into mine, up my wrist. "Do as she says. I will care for her."

The Tyaanismir gave his assent and stalked away. Janaire stood for a moment, watching me, before she shook her pretty head and attended the minstrel. Diyan stood frozen, thin and quiet, his eyes owlishly large. Redfist examined the front opening, his massive back turned to us.

"I crave your pardon." I spoke quietly, in G'mai. "It matters little, less than nothing. Forgive me, D'ri."

He shrugged. "No matter. Tis enough that you—" He examined my face. "Thank you, K'li."

It was not what I wanted. I wanted to lean into him, rest my head on his shoulder, and convince myself he was hale. "Do as I ask, D'ri. Twill make everything easier."

"I should not leave your side, K'li." He brushed one sodden braid out of my face, tucking it aside. My heart leapt. "Do not ask me to do so."

I shook my head. "D'ri—"

"Please. Do you know what it is, knowing your *adai* is under attack and being unable to aid her?"

I opened my mouth to say aught, stopped. He was, again, correct. It was the nightmare of every *s'tarei,* to be unable to help an *adai* in peril. I bit my lip, feeling like a small girl in Anjalismir again. Instead of arguing, I closed my mouth tight enough to lock back any word.

What could I say?

"Come to the fire. You need dry clothes, and a blanket. And chai, I do not know how to make that awful kafi of yours." He pushed his hair back. One of his knives was missing.

Two tears spilled out of my eyes and tracked hot down my cheeks.

Kaia? He sounded alarmed.

I waved it away. "I am well enough." I swallowed against the lump in my throat. Darkness pressed against the borders of the waystation. I knew two wyverns were dead and one was fled, and the Blue Hand sorcerer was dead too. But still, my body shivered and leapt at the slightest sound.

Combat-sickness. I had been too close to death. My body did not still realize I was alive.

I dropped down in a sodden heap next to the fire, staring into the flames. Wyverns and a Blue Hand sorcerer. The Emperor, wanting me dead? Why? I was too small a fish for an Emperor to cook. A religious fanatic? Some races hated G'mai for their bred Power, considered us abomination. But what would a fanatic have to do with me? Had I made an enemy? How had he recognized me, had he been watching the waystation? But nobody knew I came this way, except Kesa and Jett.

A Blue Hand. The God-Emperor was an absolute ruler, of course, but true power resided in the bureaucracies and the priesthood. Azkillian was cannier than most Shainakh Emperors in that he had tamed the priests and pursued his war against the Danhai with little resistance, grasping control with an iron fist. I was only a sellsword and a thief, with some little fame. Why would a Blue Hand wish to kill me? His duty to the Emperor should have kept him from indulging in bloodsport on the side, even if he was a priest's dog or had a personal duel with me.

Darik brought me fresh clothes, and held a blanket while I struggled out of my sopping-wet gear next to the stone wall. I was grateful for that. He disappeared behind a stack of firewood and returned with a fresh pair of breeches on, borrowed from Atyarik.

We gathered at the fire. I still trembled, wringing my hair out, my sword-harness too damp to buckle on properly. We divvied up the stew, and I ate with shaking hands. We did not speak overmuch, but Darik's eyes met mine several times, and I was grateful for his company.

I need the taih'adai, I thought, blankly, staring into the flames. *I must learn to control this or it will eat me alive. Perhaps it was Janaire that healed him. I do not know. No, I know. It was me. I have Power. I am G'mai.*

But the thought beating under my mental thrashing was stark in its simplicity.

Darik. He could have died. He faced two wyvern alone. The idea of a world without him frightened me. Me, Kaia Steelflower, who was said to have no fear; I who hid my fear so well.

I did not speak. I did not need to. The shaking in my body spoke for me, and took a long while to fade.

Trouble on the Road

Four days later we reached a shallow ridge in the bowl of the coastal plains, the Road wheeling eastward toward the great river-trade center of Shaituh, the power of the plains and a pearl in the Emperor's crown. Darik's bay horse matched mine stride for stride, and we reached the top of the hill, where I pulled the gray to a halt and surveyed the gently rolling expanse of chedgrass falling away below.

"Mother Moon," I breathed.

Darik looked. He said nothing.

The Plain was marked by an army. Sunlight glittered on mail and pikes, I heard the familiar cries of a Shainakh drill instructor barking, borne to us on the wind. I looked to the west, the broad sweep of grass replacing the marshes this far inland. There was a silvery rill of the Shaidakh River wending toward its great fan-tail of marshland before it reached the sea, if it ever did.

Adrift on the grass were three caravans. I saw the waggons, but no oxen—and no cooking fires. The shape of the waggons was wrong. Charred skeletons, again. I shivered. Had the wyverns been here, too?

The mystery was at least partially solved. We had not seen caravans before us—because there were, again, no caravans to be seen. How many had passed this way? Five were lost, two we had seen on the beach fired and left without oxen. Trouble on the road to Shaituh, indeed.

I slid off the gray's back and tossed my reins to Darik. "Get below the hilltop," I told him, and he obeyed without argument. "Go down and keep the others there."

He nodded. I dropped down to my belly like a wyrm, hoping nobody had seen us. The camp continued below, far enough away that guard detail probably had not spied us. We were too far out for sentries, and this hill was not high enough to be a strategic point.

Or so I hoped.

I examined the lay of the army. Standard Shainakh camp, the commander's tent in the middle, a guard network like every other guard network I had ever seen. The standard flying over the commander's tent, though, was something new.

Twas not the Emperor's standard. Azkillian's device was the Invincible Sun, wreathed with a serpent. This was a white horse silhouetted against the Sun.

I knew that sigil.

I turned over onto my back and gazed at the blue sky. Chedgrass waved gently above me, heavy with silken seedpods. A white horse was the symbol of the Ammerdahl kin, and Ammerdahl Rikyat had been asking for me.

The caravans. Two of them, circled on the beaches, victim of wyverns. And now these three, empty land-ships on the grass in three distinct circles. Fired, the oxen and the people gone. How many caravans had left Vulfentown in the last two or three sevendays? Easily ten or a dozen. So some were let through, and others were not.

The sky was a deep cloudless blue. I smelled a faint breath of salt wind and the overpowering greenness of chedgrass, heard the soughing of the waves lapping the shore, the tides of a grass ocean.

What did I owe Rikyat? We had suffered together, through battles and raids, not to mention the thirst and the screams. When you fight so closely with another the bond is deep, no matter how unwelcome. He taught me of standing watch, and of military discipline, and gave me a passport into the rough circle of the Shainakh irregulars. One did not last long on the Danhai frontier without battlemates.

I had paid part of that debt already, had I not?

Clash of steel, the battle yell caroming and sliding between my dry lips, the screams and howls of the wounded. Rik's face, glazed with blood and battle-fury. "Fall back! Get back, woman!

Fall back!"

The horrible whistling sound, Rik's agonized scream as the quarrel buried itself in his chest. I screamed with him, grabbed his surcoat, and dragged him backward as four more crossbow bolts whistled through the air, thocking solidly down in blood-soaked earth.

He had taken the quarrel for me.

"Leave...me!" Blood striped his lips, he spoke under the noise of sudden chaos. "Tis an...order, Kaia!"

I screamed wordlessly, dragging him with hysterical strength, my boots slipping in blood-mired earth, grass trampled, the ululating of the tribesmen growing ever closer as I dropped him and drew my bow. The Danhai would not take either of us today. Not if I could gainsay them. I nocked the first arrow, my dotanii *quivering in the earth where I had driven it; the standard of my division-of-one. Clenched my jaw, drawing the string to my ear as shapes became visible through the smoke, my teeth grinding so hard my jaw ached. When I spoke it was the calm voice of one who faced utter disaster. "I shall not leave you, Ammerdahl Rikyat, orders or no. You owe me at dice."*

Then the first rider, yelling as he bore down on us at a gallop, longsword out. The arrow, released and whistling, bow sounding thrice more before I had to drop it and grab my dotanii, *because though I had killed four of them there were six left, they were too close and I had nothing but my sword and my fury to protect the man lying wounded behind me.*

It would have to be enough.

I exhaled, shuddering. What did I owe Rikyat? Only a life. Redfist *thought* he owed me his life. He was wrong, of course—I had been half-asleep, reacting on instinct when I killed the Hain, and Darik had not been a threat.

Still, the debt felt was the debt paid, among those who lived by the sword.

I slid down the hill a few more bodylengths and made it to my feet in one motion. The rest of them were gathered just out of sight. Janaire was pale, and Atyarik watched her, his face a little chalky under its caramel tone. The barbarian tapped his axe-haft with one blunt finger. The minstrel, his eyes wide, looked from Darik to Janaire in obvious confusion.

They were all nervous. I could lay no blame. *I* was nervous. The wyvern attack had made us all wary. Travel had become quiet and tense. Last night the *taih'adai* had made me so exhausted I had slept through all three watches.

The boy met me halfway between the hill and the others. He was sweating. "The lady says she feels bad about this. The prince, he says *cha,* they can turn back, but he goes with you. The barbarian says he willna turn away from a fight. Is there a fight, Kaia? Is there?" His voice piped, reminding me again of how young he was. And how he had stared at me for the last three nights, fear and awe mixing heavily.

For better or for worse, he had chosen me to fix his course by, and I could not set him adrift.

"I do not think so, small one." I ruffled his hair, taking a light tone with an effort. Darik had made him a pair of soft, felted shoes, I was too exhausted by the daily *taih'adai.* "We shall see. Come along."

He fell into step beside me. "If there is a fight, what should I do?"

"Stay near me, or D'ri. We shall watch over you." We reached the others. Darik sat easily on the bay, his black eyes fixed on me.

"Well, lass?" Redfist said. "Do I need me axe?"

Not a word of leaving, Redfist? For a barbarian, you are honorable. I felt a sharp prick of guilt for calling him "barbarian", even to myself. "No. Tis a man I know, Ammerdahl Rikyat. I owe him my life once or twice, and it seems he needs aid. Either he or a member of his kin, tis almost the same thing to Shainakh." My eyes traveled over them, but what I saw instead was yellow dust, yellow grass, and the last twisted face of the Danhai tribesman as I landed on my back, his heavy bulk atop me and his eyes already dimming with death. I had, by some miracle, fought them off and dragged Rikyat out of that hell.

I remembered little enough of that desperate fight, and I wished it to remain so.

"I do not ask any of you to accompany me. I do not know what an Ammerdahl does with this army, but I suspect tis likely to be unpleasant. None of you owe me aught. You may return to

Vulfentown and go about your lives. I have a personal debt to pay, and you need not involve yourselves."

Redfist snorted. "I'll be going with ye, lass. I owe ye a debt too, in case ye've forgotten."

"You owe me nothing," I said irritably. "Darik was never a threat, and I did nothing but pick your pocket and bring you trouble."

"Ye fought beside me." He patted his ginger beard, combing it with blunt fingers. "I go wit' ye."

"I am not much use in an army," Gavrin chimed in, the wind blowing his shoulder-length hair into a wild mess. "Yet I would be a poor minstrel if I left now."

The boy leaned against my side. His head only reached my ribs, and the left side of my body twinged. Twas a memory, nothing more. Darik's eyes still held mine. That black gaze held more secrets than I cared to learn.

"*Cha.*" Diyan blew out the word between his lips.

Janaire looked at Atyarik. Her lips moved a little. I sensed she was using the *taran'adai.* It was impolite to listen, so I looked down at the ground. Darik still said nothing.

"Well," Janaire said finally. "I promised to teach you. This changes nothing. We shall go."

I shrugged. "Darik?"

He moved a little, restlessly. The boy leaned into my side a fraction more.

"You need not even ask, Kaia," Darik said softly.

"Fools, the lot of you." I pushed the boy toward the packhorse. "Go, mount up. Let us go." I swung myself back into the gray's saddle and waited while Redfist lifted the boy up into the saddle. "Now, *nobody speak*. Any questions, I answer them. Let me deal with the Shainakh. We will be lucky to get through the guard-rings with the horses." I wheeled the gray toward the crest of the hill. "Remember, *nobody* speaks except me."

"We shall remember," Janaire said. "*You* remember you are the *adai* of the Dragaemir Heir to the Throne."

"I do not need reminding of what I am, Gavridar Taryarin Janaire." I touched my heels to the gray's sides. He was more than willing.

We crested the hill, and I gathered myself. The gray picked down the hill, and my braids bounced against my back.

Perhaps Rikyat would know why a Blue Hand had sought to kill me.

We rode through chedgrass, and I heard the Shainakh sentry-call. Twas a little different than the one I remembered, and by the time I urged the gray into a trot I scented the familiar smoke and metal and unwashed bodies of the Shainakh army.

Armies everywhere smell the same.

I pulled to a stop right at the first guard-circle and leaned forward in the saddle. The guard presented his pike, and I heard the gallop of scouts and sentries to either side. *Sloppy. Rikyat should know better.*

Then again, if he was doing what I guessed, he need not worry about the approach from Vulfentown. He needed to worry about the east, where a chain of cities and fortresses commanded the fertile lowlands of Shainakh.

The sentry examined me, and I could not believe my luck. A broad squat Shainakh with close eyes and a long narrow nose, his chainmail painted red. He tipped his helm back, peered more closely at me. "Tartak roast me in hell," he said finally, in commontongue spiced with Shainak, a pidgin I could have spoken in my sleep. "I owe Havadain Nikros ten *kiyan*. He swore you would come."

"I pay my debts," I answered, casually, in the same language. "Ammerdahl Rikyat has summoned me."

He spat to the side. "Ay, ya, he has. Hard to find you on the Lan'ai Shairukh Coast, Kaahai."

"I was in Hain." I leaned against my pommel, eyeing him, as the rest of my merry troupe gathered behind me. "Did you know they have stopped sending spices from Otterei? Some sort of famine out there."

"Bad news." He lifted his pike. The sentries, seeing this, went back to their rounds. The scouts, however, came to a stop and waited, four of them ringing our little group loosely. "Pass by, Kaia. Your lot, are they trustworthy?"

I shrugged. "Sellswords. Trustworthy enough. Rikyat will decide."

"Oh, ay, he will." He grinned broadly at me and reached up. We both made fists and touched knuckles, the Shainakh soldier's salute to a fellow. "Good to see you, Kaahai." Twas Shainakh for *pretty mare*, and they called me that because I had carried a wounded Rikyat through the battlefield on my back. There was also the not-so-pure connotation that Rik and I had been bedmates.

"I cannot believe you bet against me, Jadak."

He guffawed, showing a missing tooth. "Nor can I, prettybit. Nor can I. Pass on!" He snapped me a salute that I returned, and he guffawed again as I kneed the gray and trotted past him.

A Gods-Touched Man

The scouts accompanied us to the central tent, warding aside challenges. I had just dismounted in front of the huge round commander's tent, kicking aside a tuft of dusty grass, when Ammerdahl Rikyat roared out of the tent at full speed. He wore leather armor and boots, and carried a Danhai longsword. That gave me a bit of pause, but I shoved the gray's questing head aside and ran for him.

I met him halfway and caught his arm, socking my hip into his and throwing him. He hit the ground and came up rolling, and I saw Darik leap down from the bay. *No!* I almost shouted, flinging out my hand to stop him. *Trust me, I am in no danger.*

Darik's jaw set. He stood, tense, holding the rope bridle. The bay, catching his nervousness, sidled and stamped.

Rikyat turned and grinned at me. His lean, tanned Shainakh face was fey, and his red-brown hair was pulled back into the soldier's braids, one on either side of his face, ending in bone beads swinging back and forth. He looked fit and thin, as if drilling hard for at least six moonturns.

We circled, warily. Rikyat had a handspan and several pounds of soldier's muscle on me. I smiled, shaking my braids back. The yells started, the sentries leaning on their pommels, chanting Rikyat's name. A few of them chanted mine, too, and the betting started.

He leapt for me and I moved aside, sweeping his legs out from under him and rolling under his strike. I came up, whirled, and closed with him, grappling. I punched him in the belly and was rewarded with a huff of air.

We separated again, and his hand twitched toward his sword. I grinned at him. "Want to?" I asked, in gutter Shainakh. "Knife or sword, soldier. Come on."

"Remember S'tai?" His voice was the same, hoarse and excitable.

"How could I forget?" I watched him warily. We circled, every move countered by the other before it could be launched. The yelling intensified. I paid no attention.

His hand flicked toward his sword, and my *dotanii* sang as it cleared the sheath. Darik said something, tense at the edge of the crowd, but I could not be bothered with it. Rikyat was dangerous, and I needed all my concentration.

Steel clashed and chimed. My *dotanii* whipped up and blocked his strike, and we fought, both of us panting with exertion, blades blurring.

But Rikyat was not G'mai. And he was not Darik. Darik I could not have overmatched so easily. Was I doomed to measure all men by a G'mai princeling now?

I knocked Rikyat's blade down and used my shoulder to send him sprawling, my sword at his throat as he lay supine. The cheering crested, washed over us both. Rikyat grinned. We were both sweating by now, dust streaking his face again. "Welcome, Kaahai."

"Tis good to see you, Rik." I sheathed my *dotanii* and leaned down, offering my hand. "Where did you find that pigsticker?"

"Won it in a dice-game. Got a good reach." He took my hand and I hauled him to his feet. The longsword vanished, and he threw his arms around me, hugging me so hard my ribs almost cracked. "I knew you would come. I *knew* it."

"So I am told." I held him at arm's length. The losers were paying the winners, and the crowd thinned, dispersing rapidly, returning to the business of running a camp. "What is this, Rik? If I did not know you better, I should say you are about to do something suicidal."

"Sha." He shook his head. The bone beads danced. "Who did you bring with you, prettybit? Looks a sorry bunch."

I spat to the side. "Ah, sha, you know, people keep following me around. I grow tired of killing them."

Rik's eyes moved over the group, lingering longest on

Redfist. "A giant, a Pesh lutebanger, a git, two stonefaced elvish, and another pretty bit. She fight like you?"

I shrugged. *Elvish again. I hate that word, Rik. You know I hate that word.* "Witchery. Useful."

"Ah." His thin eyebrows went up. "Well, come, the *adjii* will take the horses, and you will have a tent. Who is the dark one? His eyes follow you."

"He is mine." I spoke still in Shainakh. I offered no other explanation, and Rik's eyebrows went up even more. There had been a joke making the rounds that Kaahai welcomed no man except her own sword-hilt before the last battle on the S'tai Plain, the one that had lost me my taste for the Danhai war.

"Well, no matter. Ammerdahl Rikyat welcomes you and yours, Kaia Kaahai Steelflower." He clasped my forearm and I clasped his, digging my fingers in. He grinned, but there was a feverish sparkle to his eyes I did not recall. "Come, and clean up. The dust here is not so bad, but not so good either."

I motioned for the rest of them to follow. Redfist lifted the boy down from the saddle, and Atyarik dismounted. The *s'tarei* lifted Janaire down, his hands at her slim waist, and Darik approached me cautiously. The minstrel lowered himself from the bony brown nag—which seemed to be as tough as travel leather, I had to admit—and made it to the ground safely. He had a purple bump on his head from the fight with the wyverns, and looked as sorry as his horse.

Darik's face held nothing but interested pleasantness, but underneath he was tight-strung as Gavrin's lute. Rikyat measured him from head to foot, looked at me.

"Decorative." His tone was dismissive. "Can he use those things?"

I shrugged. "Trained in strategy and tactics. He won a few battles in my home country." I gave the words an ironic twist, to keep Rikyat guessing.

"Ah." Rik's eyes lit up with comprehension and distaste. I wondered why Darik's presence should displease him, and felt a faint stirring of worry.

He led us into the command tent, and in short order we sat on rugs in the Shainakh style, food spread before us. I took a cup of *haka* and lifted it for a healthy swallow, watching Rik over the rim. Darik sat next to me, with the silence of a *s'tarei*. He took a sip of *haka* and set his cup down. *Kaia?* His voice whispered in my ear.

Quiet, I replied. *I am negotiating.*

"So." Rikyat settled himself. He scooped up his eating picks and took a bite from a dish of fried stretchlegs, and I did too. The others waited until I nodded, and began eating as well. Janaire scanned the interior of the tent, her dark lovely eyes wide as she took in the gold hangings and silk swathes. I saw Rik's gaze settle on her and I reached out with my boot to tap at his knee.

"Forget it. She is wedded to the long-faced one." I watched Rik's face fall.

"Pity. So you guess what I am about."

"You are in rebellion." I picked up a stretchleg, bit into it delicately, chewed. He had a good cook, at least. "What brought this to pass?"

"Azkillian." Rik's lip curled. "Raising taxes on staples. Riots in the interior, and the temples are closing their doors. He is hiring mercenaries. Planning an offensive on Pesh. Can you believe it?"

"I guessed when I heard the news of the taxes on rice, flour and salt. And the lowering of tariffs—metal, leather, liquor. Just what one needs for a fresh offensive."

"Should have known you would guess, Kaahai. Always that sharp mind of yours." He picked up a bowl of rice, and we began in earnest.

"So why were you offering a reward for someone to carry a message to me? Yes, I heard. I can only guess it has something to do with rebellion." I did not speak of the Blue Hand. If twas common knowledge that he was asking for me, and he was in rebellion, no wonder a Hand would be sent to dispatch me. Would Azkillian spend any time on signing that order himself? Had the Hands found out Rikyat was in rebellion? Who knew?

Still, something did not ring quite true. How could a Hand have slipped past Rikyat's army? Was his guard-ring sloppy in *every* direction? Twas not like the man who had managed to bring a raid party through the Danhai territory more times than I could comfortably recall.

"Guessed right." Rikyat took another gulp of *haka*. "We were lucky, Kaahai. Too lucky. You dragged me through mud and blood to the healers and stood guard over me when the army retreated. You took me from the Plain under the nose of the Danhai. Remember?"

I shrugged. Of course I remembered. Why else was I here? "You took the bolt meant for me. I remember."

"Fight beside me." Rikyat's eyes all but glowed. "We can topple Azkillian, withdraw from the Danhai. The people are weary of the war against the barbarians, they long for peace. I can stop the killing and make Shainakh great again. You said it so often—more to be gained with diplomacy than with the sword."

He looked down into his cup, his brown face lit from inside. I watched this, a little unsettled. "I felt a great stillness come over the Plain when that bolt hit me." His voice was too quiet. The *adjii* brought more plates of food in—roast hanta, sweet tarka in red sauce, fish and roasts. There was the spongy flatbread the Shainakh like, and plenty more *haka* and wine and tea. Janaire and Darik did not drink of the liquor, just tea. Atyarik took one drink of the *haka* and coughed. Rik paid no attention. "Some may laugh," he said, in Shainakh. "I saw Hashai, god of fire and retribution. He came from the heavens like a thunderbolt and spoke to me. Told me I was His chosen one, sent to purge the empire from the sickness of Azkillian."

"And your mother's mother was an Imperial concubine's daughter." I settled myself in the cushions. "Therefore you have a claim to succession."

His eyes came back from that distant place. "Yesss..." A long hissing breath. "You saved me, Kaahai. You were Hashai's instrument, and you are lucky, gifted. I wish you to fight with me."

I leaned back, took another gulp of *haka*. It burned all the way down. "Well, I have all these mouths to feed."

"A twentieth of all loot." Immediately, the bargaining began. "Regular pay. I wish for you to *adjii* me. And your tactics-trained friend there. I can always find a use for such. Not only that, but I have a special mission for you."

"Ah." Politeness demanded I bargain, make a show. "I do not know, Rikrik. A rebellion. Tis chancy. And I am a foreigner.

If anyone does follow my orders, twill be a miracle. If you lose, I will hang."

"These are desperate men, already committed to treason in the eyes of Azkillian. They have little to lose. Most have lost family in the Danhai war, and they are levied to the neck with taxes to support the crazyman's dreams. They will follow—and if you are caught and hung, *I* will be quartered alive. We have popular support. *And* the support of the priestesses of Silesh. That counts for much, here. Shainakhum is the great god, blessed be His Name, but Silesh makes the rice grow, and She is not happy with Azkillian."

"How do you know?" I picked up a sweet rice ball. "Did She tell you?"

He stared at me for a long moment, as if gauging me for mockery, and shrugged. "Harvest has been bad. Drought in the interior. When is the last time such occurred?"

I leaned back against a round red bolster. The rugs were orange and red and yellow, Sun-worshipping colors. "Huh. And you think a backwoods provincial is more to their taste, your gods?"

He jabbed his eating picks at me. There was a glitter in his dark Shainakh eyes that made me wary. "Watch your pretty mouth, woman. I will have none of your mocking."

I let the corner of my mouth curl up. "You really think you can rebel against Azkillian?"

"We already have. This is but a quarter of the army. The remainder is in hiding near Shaithammuz, in the mountains."

"Why did you come here?" Though I already knew. I picked up a long strip of roast hanta, ate it delicately.

"To take Shaituh. Was waiting for you. Hashai told me you would appear before the New Moon. Two days to New Moon and you are here, with a raggle-tag group of sellswords and a lutebanger." He slapped his knee, laughing. "Hashai has a sense of humor."

I finished chewing, washed the hanta down with tea. "And once you have Shaituh, the supply routes are doubly secure. Have you already taken Shaivakh? Or are you waiting?"

"No need to take Shaivakh," he said. "The Shaikuhn there is one of ours."

Then this actually has a chance of working. A chill touched my nape. "Who? I have been away, and have missed the event."

His black eyes met mine for a long moment. "Ah, prettybit, I am half believing you are considering joining me."

"I never could resist trouble. Twenty Rams for a moonturn." Twas a fantastical sum, and I expected him to haggle.

Uneasiness twisted inside me. *Why did the Blue Hand know my name? And you, Rikyat, what game do you play?* It did not seem he was telling me everything. Of course, I could hardly expect him to—I was an outsider, even if I had saved his life.

Yet something was *wrong* here. Between Rikyat's feverish eyes and the persistent crawling of the skin between my shoulderblades, I was nervous as a sellsword before her first battle.

I could not tell quite what was wrong, but the gold would aid my inquiries. And if I had to, I could feed everyone in my troupe and outfit them through the winter with that coin.

"Done!" He clapped his hands, and an *adjii* staggered in with a small ironwood coffer. He laid it down next to me and bowed, hands together in the Shainakh way. I nodded. The casket flipped open, revealing Shainakh Rams. At least a hundred of them, more if I did not miss my guess. "Here, take it. Good faith."

I examined him over my cup. "What of the caravans? The burned ones."

"Loyal to Azkillian." He waved a dismissive hand, his dark skin webbed with thin white scars from drill and battle-wounds. "The women and children were spared. I am no monster."

"Comforting." My eyes narrowed. *What of wyverns, Rikyat?* "And the men?"

"Loyal to us, they are given pay and a position in the army. Loyal to Azkillian, beheaded. We have only twelve beheadings so far. Good, eh?"

"If you can trust those who convert at swordpoint." I reached out, hands loose, palms open. "I am with you, Rik. I owe you a life, at least. I reserve the right to command my cadre."

"Granted." He touched my fingers. "What else, Kaia? You never bargain this easily."

You are giving me too much gold. Why, Rikyat? What has changed you so much? "Safe passage back to the freetowns for my companions, at any time."

Rik leaned back, smiling sagely. "Now there is a flash of the old Steelflower. I will have safeconducts on the morrow. Anything else?"

"Who do you have in Shaivakh?" I set my *haka* cup down.

He threw back the last of his *haka* and slammed the cup down on the rug. "Yattokik Aveydrat. Made Shaikuhn by the grace of bureaucracy two moonturns ago. It was the last thing we waited on."

"Yatto's a Shaikuhn?" I was hard-put to keep stunned disbelief out of my voice. "Whose arse did he oil?"

"Evidently the right one. He is loyal—been stopping messengers headed east to the Holy City. Even the Blue Hands have been set at naught. What say you, Kaia?"

"I say you are mad." I poured him more *haka. I killed a Hand less than a day ago that perhaps knew of your plan, Rikyat. What say you to that?* "But then, you have always been mad, so tis no change. Very well, then. I fight in your rebellion. There is a debt between us."

"You carried me to the healer's tents." Rik's dark, slanted Shainakh eyes lost a little bit of their feverish glimmer. "I owe *you* a life."

"Then we are in debt to each other," I said. He tossed down more *haka.* "I expect to see your maps and supply lines tomorrow. And your sentries are sloppy. They should be watching the way we came."

"Ah, ya, Kaia." His eyes glowed like coals. "I knew you would come."

Honor Sold

I leaned on Rik, hiccupping, and painted a sloppy kiss on his cheek. Darik watched this with no evident amusement or dissatisfaction, and I waved him inside the tent. "You can' hold your *haka*," I informed Rik, who was weaving a little himself. "G'on, sleep t'off."

"Kaahai—" Rik's fingers bit into my shoulder. "Th' dark one. He your *bakaii*?"

Why do you ask? "S'mine." I hiccupped again. "G'to sleep, Rikrik. T'morrow."

He nodded and wove away, singing an old Shainakh drinking song. Night curved over the army camp, and his bodyservant—a young Shainakh boy with a terrible scar down the side of his face—gave Rik his shoulder.

Rik had spoken no more of special missions, and nothing more about the Hands. I, for my part, told him nothing of the Blue Hand dead by my knife, the one with three wyverns in his grip. *Why were those caravans fired, on the beach? Did the Hand need them for aught?*

Or had the trouble on the Shainakh road been army detachments, come to requisition supplies from the caravans? Had the caravans themselves been supplies intended for the rebellion?

I stumbled into the tent, making sure the flap was folded before I straightened, discarding my act and meeting several pairs of staring eyes.

"What?" I tied the tent flap closed with quick fingers. "Employment through the winter at a good rate, and if their rebellion goes sour we fight our way toward the hills and escape over into Pesh or the freetowns. Tis good work."

"You just sold your honor for coin," Atyarik said, softly. Janaire, standing in the middle of the tent, simply watched, her dark lovely eyes huge and liquid in the dim light from the lamps.

Braziers scattered through the tent, and twas warm enough that I shoved my braids back, wishing I could shrug out of my leather vest and open my shirtlaces. "I need coin to *feed* you. Tis harvest season, but I cannot feed you off chedgrass. If you are so insulted, there are safeconducts waiting in the morning. This could be far worse. The real fighting will not begin until spring, and if you are lucky you may leap ship to Antai and wait out this civil war. If, that is, the rebellion is not crushed before winter. Azkillian has not ruled Shainakh this long by being a fool. If one of his spymasters sent a Blue Hand after me, the God-Emperor is hardly uninformed of Rikyat's intentions."

I stalked to the central area of the tent and dropped down on a rug, groaning. *Haka* is hard on the body. Rik would have a sore head tomorrow. "Rik is half-crazy, but he is of the nobility and has a legitimate grievance. Azkillian has bled the peasantry dry to pay for this Danhai war, and has not had so much as a league of territorial gain for five summers. It has degenerated into a *lahai'arak*." That was the G'mai word for a complex mess of a battle where none won. I looked up at the giant, who had eaten more than all the rest of us put together and was now in the process of picking his teeth with a blunt fingernail. "What say you, Redfist?"

Green eyes twinkled under his eyebrows. I wondered why the gods had made his kind so hairy, if their country was truly too cold for lesser folk. "Aye, lass. Sellswording is nae honorable, yet tis an honor to fight beside ye. If ye say this man is just, then I'll wet me axe for him."

I gave him a weary smile, pleased and warmed at the same time. "My thanks. You may go back to G'mai, *s'tarei'sa*. Minstrel?"

The minstrel dropped down on his own rug and stretched, working his worn-down boots off. His nimble fingers seemed barely equal to the task, even if his hands *were* the size of small troutfish. "It seems to me there is more to this rebellion than Ammerdahl Rikyat will tell you."

I stretched my arms over my head. “Precisely, Gavrin Silvertongue. Which is why I shall go night-hunting. If he hides aught, who better to find it than a thief? And they all know my face, I will hardly be challenged if they see me.”

“You will allow this?” Atyarik turned to Darik, who stood by the tent flap, his arms folded. The heir to the Dragon Throne simply looked thoughtful. His hair was mussed over his forehead, and his eyes were black enough to lose a soul in. He had said nothing at all through dinner, and watched his *adai* touch another man with no sign of anger or displeasure.

He had slept beside me for weeks now, and I had allowed it. I now *needed* to allow it, for the *taih’adai* sent me into a sleep so deep it was like death. And whom did I trust to guard my back or my slumber?

Only him. How soon the world of my trust had expanded to include him.

“I can hardly halt her,” Darik said. “She is my *adai*. You may leave for G’mai in the morn, do you disagree.”

“We are not leaving,” Janaire said firmly. Diyan dropped down next to me and put his head on the rug, curling up like a beetle.

“*Cha,* neither am I,” the boy piped up. “Swore to come with Kaia.”

“You cannot—” Atyarik turned to Janaire.

“I can, and I have,” she said, firmly, in G’mai. “This is my *student*, A’rik. A Yada’Adais does not abandon her student.” The girl’s chin came up. She was dusty from traveling and pink-cheeked from one drink of *haka*, and she was lovely as only a G’mai could be. It would cause some problems if she could not handle herself.

“J’ni. Please. You will be in danger.” Atyarik’s inflection was unbearably intimate. My eyes found Darik’s. He was still very quiet. Too quiet. What was he thinking?

I did not want to know. And yet, I could not avoid knowing. He had set himself to guard me with the all the fierce dedication of a *s’tarei*.

“And so will you.” Janaire's tone did not ease, soft and inflexible. “I did not take this quest to sit quietly by the fireside, *s'tarei'mi*. You wished to find your Prince, I wished a chance to prove myself as a Yada'Adais. This is the road the Moon has given us, this is the road we shall walk." She nodded once, smartly, cast her eyes around. "I suppose we sleep on the rugs?"

"They brought our gear in." I waved a languid hand at the back of the tent. "You can find your *tavar'adai* there."

"Good. You have another *taih'adai* tonight."

I would do much to avoid it. "Oh, lovely. Before I sally forth to thieve from a cadre of bloodthirsty Shainakh? Or after?"

"Before." Twas a sparkle in her beautiful black eyes. I bit the inside of my cheek to keep from swearing at her.

Diyan was already half-asleep, his breath whistling through his nose. I patted the boy's hair, and my eyes met Darik's.

"Does it strike you," he said, "that this Rikyat has another purpose for you, Kaia'li?"

I nodded. "It does indeed, D'ri. And he has not mentioned the presence of a Blue Hand sorcerer or wyverns either. Which is why I shall take Diyan with me tonight, his ears may catch whispers mine will not."

"I would accompany you," Darik answered mildly. *We still have not addressed the question of why you allow that man to touch you with your* s'tarei *standing by.*

At least he was being private about it. "I do not think you can be quiet enough, D'ri." *Sparring with Rik is the only thing he understands, tis the only thing that impresses the army. I brought all of us into their good graces with that display, including you. There are few female sellswords in Shainakh, most of them in the irregulars, and they are a hard lot. Word of this display will reach the few that count, and we shall have entry into their clique.* I sighed, rubbing at my forehead. My head hurt, the *haka* had risen from my stomach and was filling my eyes with vapor. *I have my reasons for what I do, D'ri, and none of them are to harm you.*

Darik paced over to sink down next to me, touching my forehead. His fingers were warm, and they helped with the pain. "Hmm. I would prefer to accompany you. The boy is tired."

"You cannot thieve." I closed my eyes.

"I thieved my life from the queen of G'mai." He brushed a braid back from my face. The touch comforted me more than anything else ever had. He stroked my cheek, softly, slid his knuckles over my cheekbone. "Surely that counts."

I sighed. "Very well. Wake me in a candlemark."

"I will," he promised. *Or Janaire will use her sharp tongue on me, and that I do not relish.*

I considered laughing, but I had already dozed off.

Witch and Power

"This *taih'adai* will give you the beginnings of fire-calling, which I do *not* suggest you practice anytime soon. You are likely to burn down a few of these tents. You will learn the beginnings of *zaradai,* too. Twill also begin teaching you what to do with your Power instead of letting it fester in silence." Janaire's eyes met mine. "If you go down into silence again, Anjalismir Kaialitaa, it will go ill with your *s'tarei.* You cannot afford to act thus. You are not a child now."

I bit the inside of my cheek to keep from replying, watching the small silver sphere in her hand. Atyarik sat behind Janaire, his face dark with anger. She ignored him. Her tone was one I remembered from hearing the Yada'Adais address large groups of G'mai girls, a firm, clear voice that brooked no disobedience.

Redfist sprawled on a pile of rugs, his green eyes winking between ginger eyelashes. He stroked the haft of his axe, meditatively. "Seems a bit of magic, K'ai," he rumbled, and I was grateful for the distraction.

"Tis G'mai." I stared at the sphere the way a bird might stare at a snake. The sight of the silver spheres caused a queasy not-quite-excitement right under my breastbone. "Not quite the same thing." *I am not certain I should do this in the midst of a Shainakh army camp.*

Darik lay the boy down on a rug and covered him with a blanket, tucking him in.

"What's the difference?" Redfist looked interested, almost inordinately so.

"Well, the witches push Power into people until they reach their capacity," Janaire told him. "It forces all the doors in their house open, so to speak. It takes intense training for a witch to deal with the trauma. G'mai are different. We are born and bred to Power, and our entire way of life fosters it. We grow slowly into using it—except for Kaialitaa here." She looked at me, her small teeth chewing at her lower lip, and I saw again how young she was. "She will be more like a witch, since she's denied herself for so long. Tis a hard road to travel. But she is G'mai, bred to *adai*. Twill only make her stronger."

Speaking of me as if I am not here. Irritation rasped at my throat. Darik dropped down next to me and touched my shoulder, a friendly contact.

She is explaining to the barbarian. His tone carried equal parts of amusement and concern. *You are pale.*

I do not wish to do this. Especially in a Shainakh army camp, with a riddle to solve.

True enough. I sensed he did not know quite what to say. The silence between us had grown delicate, fraught with unsaid things.

The silver light threatened to thrust me out of myself, to remake me into something more like Janaire—a sweet, fragile G'mai girl, talented with Power but helpless without a *s'tarei*.

Darik's response to this was a laugh he stifled with a cough. *None could ever consider you helpless, Kaia'li. Your* dotanii *will convince them otherwise.*

I had feared, three nights ago, that he had been wounded badly enough to risk death. In that moment, the prospect of life without a certain G'mai princeling had frightened me deeply.

Too deeply.

"Well, hand it hence." I interrupted Janaire's further explanation with all the grace of a criminal expecting execution. "I might as well do quickly, if I am to do at all."

She passed her hand over the *taih'adai*, and it began to glow. "Watch. Tis responding to me."

The silvery light was low and soft, and I waited for it to intensify to the customary blinding glow. It did not. "Why does it glow so differently?"

"Because your Power is so much." She offered the *taih'adai* with both soft hands. I glared at the vibrating sphere, smelling the peculiar tang of G'mai *adai'in*—something I had not had in so long I had almost forgotten the scent of it. "Take it, Kaia. It does become easier, I swear."

I did not believe her, but I cupped my hand and took the heavy silver sphere. It brightened immediately. Light streamed between my fingers, making shadows stand out knife-sharp and black as Darik's eyes.

I will keep watch, Kaia. Darik said, but I was already gone, locked in a world of silver light.

Be Discreet

Warmth, and softness. A persistent movement, shaking me, calling me out of the deeps of sleep. I groaned, softly, wanting nothing more than to burrow into the blankets.

The whistle of second-watch in an army camp pierced the night. I opened my eyes.

"Tis the second watch, K'li," Darik whispered in my ear. "The boy sleeps, and everyone else too. Shall we go night-hunting?"

I blinked, looked up at him. The familiar sounds of a Shainakh army camp sounded outside the tent's silken walls. He sat back on his heels, twin *dotanii* spiking up over his shoulders. "Second watch?" I remembered nothing but silver light, and the *taih'adai* whispering inside my head, light filling the space behind my eyes.

Memory, flooding back. Rikyat. Ammerdahl Rikyat was rebelling against Azkillian, the God Emperor of Shainakh. Except there was a wrongness in the pattern. Three wyverns, a Blue Hand sorcerer, and something Rikyat had not revealed.

Rikyat. A god, speaking to Rikyat. Twas not entirely impossible—but the fevered glitter in Rikyat's eyes, his preternatural self-confidence, was enough to disturb me mightily.

I have seen the goddess Taryina-Ak-Allat speak through her priestesses in their drugged trances, each woman speaking a different word in the chorus of the goddess, sometimes all of them at once, the High Priestess with her blank, pale eyes watching from a huge gray throne with its crystals glowing like moons under the huge fringed silken canopy. I have seen the ecstatic dances of the Hain, blank faces lost in contemplation of infinity as their bodies whirled through space. Gods do not use their mouthpieces gently. What did the Shainakh gods want of Rikyat?

I had little concern for myself—the Moon is jealous of Her children, and a G'mai, even a flawed G'mai such as myself, does not have much to fear from other gods. Yet Rikyat looked like a dreamweeder, his eyes too bright and his cheeks flushed, total foolhardiness and drunken confidence shining from him.

I pushed myself up, slowly, and yawned. "Can you be silent?" I murmured in G'mai. I found that it felt natural to speak to him with the most personal inflection possible. "I do not want us caught."

"I will not fail you." He whispered in G'mai as well, and his inflection was unbearably intimate. "I am used to discretion."

"So it seems." I pushed back the blanket he had settled over me. It was strangely satisfying to see him upon waking. "My thanks, D'ri."

"For what? Discretion?" He handed me my *dotanii*, encased in its sheath. I smiled, standing up and stretching, strapping the sheath to my back.

"For standing guard while I am in the *taih'adai*."

He turned slightly to glance over my shoulder, checking the tent as I stretched again, joints cracking. I found I had more to say to him. "What do you see, when the light takes me?"

"The light, and your face," he answered softly, turning back to me, cupping my face in his callused hands. He examined me, his mouth straight and severe. "You look peaceful."

He was perhaps as surprised as I that I allowed him such closeness.

I managed a shaky smile. His skin was warm and slightly rough. "Peaceful? Not I, *s'tarei'mi*."

He smiled, I saw it clearly even in the dark, and felt it against my skin like sunshine. The lamps were snuffed and the tent was full of shadows. I thought perhaps he would kiss me, but he did not. I had no idea what I would do if he tried. The thought of him seeking to do so was strangely pleasant, too.

"What do we seek, K'li?"

"I do not yet know. We shall see what we can find."

Outside, the night was full of the sounds of a Shainakh army camp. Faint music played somewhere, and the roar of men drinking and dicing—any excuse for a celebration, here among an army at rest.

I ghosted from tent to tent, listening, Darik drifting behind me. I made two discoveries in a very short period of time. The first was that our tent was loosely watched. Perhaps Rikyat was not as sure of me as he wished me to think.

The second discovery was that Darik would make a good thief. He moved silently, drawing the darkness over him as a good thief always does, taking his cues from my actions. When I ceased moving, he did too; when I stopped breathing, he did as well. He followed me like a shadow, like my shadow.

Like a *s'tarei*.

I quartered the camp, staying away from the well-lighted lanes and using the "bedmate's alleys"—the little avenues between tents only dimly lit and mostly deserted except for surreptitious visits between lovers. The army seethed quietly, as if my coming was a yeast added to it. Whispers held my name—that the gods looked with so much favor upon Ammerdahl Rikyat, even the elvish of the Blessed Lands came to his cause.

Gods, how I hate that word. Rikyat was indeed skilled in the art of rumor. It is impossible to be otherwise, in a Shainakh army. He had managed to turn my arrival into a mark of favor from the gods. Clever of him, if it did not turn against him.

There were other, darker whispers too.

Rumors of assassinations, the Blue Hands moving through towns and taking everyone suspected of rebellion. Sightings of strange lights to the west, over the sea. And faint whispers of two supply caravans carrying a cargo of gold through Vulfentown and leaving waggons on the beach for the tide to take, the rest of the caravan coming to rejoin the army and the oxen going to pay off a shadowy ally.

That gave me chills.

Rikyat would be moving on Shaituh next. Would the city defend itself, or would it welcome him like a Rijiin courtesan? And what of the supply by sea? Did he have a naval force? If so, who commanded it? Or was he relying on the fickle winds of commerce to keep him safe from naval attack? The Shainakh were not so fond of shipboard fighting, except against starving pirates.

I finally circled the guard perimeter of Rikyat's great tent, and found three different approaches I could use, if I was careful with the timing. I chose one and slipped up to a pool of shadow near the tent's back wall, listening intently.

"—dangerous."

I heard the strike of flint and steel, and the brief fizzle of incense tossed on burning charcoal. A moment later my nose flared sharply to catch the scent—shaina, the heavy, perfumed musk Shainakh preferred. Twas a heavy scent, unlike the clean smells of G'maihallan or the floral cloying of Hain.

"Of course she is." Rikyat sounded no more drunk than I, and I found myself smiling. The mere soldier I had known would not have used such craft, but of course his noble family had taught him well. A good head for drink was a prerequisite of an officer. "No sharp tool is fully safe."

"What of her companions?"

"Good fighters." Now Rikyat sounded a little peeved. "Dear gods, Brunhor, you sound like an old woman. Kaahai is to be trusted. I *know* her. Her word is given. It should not take much to ease her into our errand. The Steelflower kills for red gold, that is well known; I have never seen Kaahai to be overly squeamish. Azkillian is enough of a tyrant to satisfy even her conscience." He trailed off, meditatively.

My blood began to pound in my head. *Oh, Rik. Rikyat, how could you?*

"Killing an Emperor is unwise. The blood-guilt is too much." The voice sounded nervous.

There was a full handspan-of-moments' worth of silence. Then Rikyat said, very softly, "I will pretend I did not hear that mumbling. Azkillian has lost the protection of the gods."

"Tis a dangerous thing, to kill an anointed one." This was a hoarse female voice, one I knew very well. So Shammerdhine Taryana was here? A cool, canny fighter. What attraction could Rikyat hold for *her*? She was of one of the oldest noble families in Shainakh, intermarried with Azkillian's clan. An old, hard-line noble House. For a Shammerdhine to be here was a sign the God-Emperor had lost more popular support than I had ever thought possible.

Little pieces of the puzzle fell into place. I have never been stupid, or willfully blind. Well, perhaps once or twice. But now my eyes were opened, like a newborn child's. Ammerdahl Rikyat had sought to use me.

Use *me*, the Iron Flower, Anjalismir Kaialitaa. I had not survived beyond the borders of G'maihallan by being amenable to those who sought to use me.

"Unless he has lost the backing of the priestesses of Silesh," Rikyat said. "And *I* will not kill him. The Gemerh care little for our gods, Tarya. They worship the Moon, and some silver ships, tis said."

"What of the one that follows her? Gossip marks him a prince." Brunhor did indeed sound fretful.

"Good. As long as Kahaai is distracted by him, she will not notice she is our killing hand," Rikyat said. "Now pay attention to the maps, and stop twittering like a *boydhar*. Hashai has revealed to me the locations of the garrisons. The Burning One also revealed to me that the assassin Hrunmuth was killed last night, by steel, water, and fire at once. He brought the Steelflower into our arms as neatly as a beloved into a bride's embrace."

"Steel, water, fire—probably the only thing that *could* kill him," Tarya mumbled, and laughed. "Good. We are rid of one loose thread. Do you think she guesses?"

"It matters little," Rikyat said. "Is the second act in place?"

"Ready and waiting, my lord." This voice, male and very low, sent chills down my skin too. It spoke High Shainakh, a dialect I did not have much experience with, and every muscle in my body recognized it as a killer's voice. My spine turned to ice. I motioned Darik back. I had heard enough.

We retraced our steps to our tent, and slipped inside with none the wiser.

As soon as I reached that dubious safety, I found myself biting my lip again, gnawing it worriedly.

So. It explained much, and opened a gallery of yet more questions.

Had I killed Hrunmuth the assassin? Steel, fire, water—it

was passing unlikely twas someone else. And yet, how would Rikyat have known of it if a god—or a witch—had not told him, indeed? Hrunmuth the Blue Hand had known my name. *Do you think she will guess?*

Rikyat had set an assassin on me to set me against the God-Emperor.

Set him, and set him at a place where he knew I would be passing: it would not take much effort to find I was in Hain; even if I had been up the coast or coming in from Antai I would have had to pass Vulfentown, I arrived in Shaituh almost every harvest-season. All an assassin would have to do is wait; if that assassin was Hrunmuth he had also served Rikyat's purpose in keeping the coast-road clear of spies.

A cool finger traced its way up my spine. I turned to Darik. "He means to use me to kill the God-Emperor of Shainakh." The disbelief in my voice was only countered by the worry plainly visible on Darik's face.

Twas shocking enough, that my stone-faced Dragaemir could look worried at all, much less *this* worried, with his brow furrowed and his mouth turned down. "How? In open battle?"

I shook my head. "No, D'ri. I am an assassin. And a passing-fair one. He seeks to induce me to penetrate their Palace in the middle of their Holy City. Good gods above, what on earth could he—"

I stopped, surveyed my sleeping companions. Surely Rikyat would not harm them?

I was not naïve enough to believe he would not.

In the morning I would send them away. Rikyat might seek to use them against me. *I will stay, with D'ri, and see what must be seen. I owe Rikyat, and if the coin I must use to repay that debt is the life of a crazed tyrant, so be it.*

Yet Rikyat set the Hand on me, if I understood this aright.

Gods above and below, that does not cancel out the debt. The gods are playing with me even now.

"I cannot believe you are seriously contemplating this, Kaia." Darik looked even more worried.

"If I take this commission, I will have an Emperor indebted to me. Unless it is too much a risk to let me live or Rikyat fails, in which case I will have to escape the Holy City and the entire land of Shainakh, overrun by civil war." I whistled softly through my teeth. "Gods, G'maihallan might actually be a holiday, compared to that."

"Kaia—" he began.

I lifted my hand to still him. "I have accepted coin in good faith. We shall see what he seeks to 'ease' me into. If there is anything of the old Rikyat inside that gods-burning shell, he needs me." My jaw set, and I felt Darik looking at me through the tent's darkness, his eyes moving over the planes of my face. "I have been called Kaahai, and tis perhaps time he found what a balky *kaahai* I can be."

My stunned disbelief still haunted me. I would have done whatever Rikyat asked, if he had merely *asked* me. *Had* he sent an assassin after me? A Blue Hand sorcerer? But how had he seduced a Blue Hand, since they were largely thought to be incorruptible?

Then again, if the Shainakh gods were with him, twould be no large matter for Rikrik to find a Hand that could be bought. Even in the God-Emperor's service there were men less-than-honorable.

Especially in the service of power were such men to be found.

"If you do indeed owe a debt, I shall help you pay it. And what after that, Kaia? Would you return to G'maihallan with me? I have little taste for the palace, but we may find a small House, in the mountains, and live perhaps unmolested." Twas the most fantastical thing I had ever heard him say, but I was too worried about Rikyat—and the tale of Hrunmuth the assassin—to muster any anger. Or even to remind him I never wished to see G'maihallan again.

I chewed my lower lip, sliding my weapons-harness off. "Gods. I had not thought...the *Emperor.* Gods, D'ri. That would almost be a commission worth taking, if only to see if I *could.*" *And if Rik had not lied to me.*

"The others will not leave." He spoke in G'mai, and his tone was worried and intimate in equal measure. *And I do not believe you would kill a man merely to see if it were possible, Kaia.*

Not even if I was starving? The silent speech between us rode a different path than the words we spoke aloud. "I may convince Janaire to leave, if I take all the *taih'adai* as soon as possible. Redfist and the minstrel, too. Tis madness to accompany me on this. Especially for coin, as Atyarik would say."

Even if you starved, Kaia, you would not do such a thing. "The boy?" Darik sounded so utterly certain of me.

Was this what it was to have a *s'tarei*? To feel a man's faith in me?

"If I may watch for myself, I may watch over him as well. And you gave your oath." The reality of what I had heard hit me like a mailed cestus to the pit of my stomach.

I could not believe it. Rikyat had betrayed me.

Betrayed *me*.

Yet I had sworn, and my companions would be hostages to his pleasure, led blindly into the trap by me alone.

I had to follow Rikyat, at least until I had repaid the debt or found some other way to ease us from an army's hold. Then I was free.

"I did promise my *adai* I would watch over the small one. It pleases you, I will do so." He unbuckled his own weapons harness, slowly. Something tight in my throat eased a little. Darik looked intent, thoughtful. "Shall I stand watch?"

"We are safe enough tonight." I toed back the blankets someone—perhaps Janaire—had thoughtfully piled for a sleeping-nest. The braziers did a more-than-tolerable job of warming the air. In winter the plains would be miserable with coastal rain, even if the presence of the seawind kept snow away. "And I sleep lightly in an army camp, always."

I settled down, working my boots off, and Darik stood, watching me. Indecisive.

I knew what he could not ask me, unwilling to press.

I patted the rugs next to me. "Tis a chill night." It could have been interpreted as an invitation or an explanation. Either would do. I had almost forgotten we conversed in my birthtongue.

He eased himself down, more gracefully than I had, and laid his *dotanii* within easy reach. He yanked off his boots with quick, hard movements. "You are a mystery to me, K'li. Where has all the armor gone?"

As soon as he said it, he tensed, perhaps wishing he had not reminded me. I shrugged, yanking on my boot. "Do you wish me to keep you at swordpoint? I will, if you like. We are surrounded by potential enemies, and Rikyat seeks to use me as a knife to the heart of Azkillian. I have been betrayed by the one person in this camp I was certain I could trust. I would much prefer you to guard my back than have to set myself against you as well." I finished working my other boot free and stretched out, yawning. The *haka* pounded in my head. *Haka* and some other, deeper pain.

Darik lay on his back, his hands laced behind his head. It was a strangely vulnerable position, and I settled myself down on my side, carefully not touching him, but able to see his face in the darkness when I propped my head on my hand. My braids were twisted up out of the way, a heavy weight.

"I will tell you, I do not like to see you used thus."

"I do not either." I yawned again. "Rikyat is gods-touched, though." My eyelids were heavy, I felt them dropping. "And this whole quest seems gods-touched as well. Too much luck flying about, both good and bad. I have grown used to traveling alone."

"Well, no more." Darik settled himself more securely, relaxing muscle by muscle. "Now you have a *s'tarei.*"

Indeed. And glad I am of it, though I wonder why the gods saw fit to bring you now. I dropped my head down onto the bolster, and Darik pulled the blanket up over me, tucking me in. "So it is. Sleep, D'ri. Who knows when we shall sleep again?"

He did not reply, but I felt his watchful silence. In that darkness, before I let myself sleep, it was more than I had ever wanted.

It was enough.

Another Knife in the Dark

I woke to confused motion, the sound of steel meeting steel, and the wet thud of a body against unforgiving earth. I gained my feet, my *dotanii* clearing its sheath before I finished waking. I found myself staring down at the remains of a Shainakh man bleeding out on the rug. Darik pushed me aside, his face full of rage.

"What the—" Redfist struggled to his feet, grasping his axe.

I wiped the sleepsand from my eyes and stared uncomprehendingly down at the Shainakh. He was not dressed as a guard, and there was a stray breath of sorcery on him. Something I had smelled too recently for my comfort.

I wanted to bend down and pull back his tunic, to see if he had a small blue glyph tattooed on his chest. Yet as soon as I moved Darik moved too, crowding me back with his body until I almost stumbled over the blankets.

"'Ware." Atyarik stood guard over Janaire, who stretched and yawned as prettily as a snow maiden, her black hair falling down in a series of dainty braids. "Are there more?"

"Just the one, and he wanted Kaia. Or at least he walked straight for her, through the rest of you." Darik's eyes were flinty, burning black.

I re-sheathed my blade and moved as if to kneel by the dead Shainakh. He had stopped bleeding, and his sloe eyes were glazed. I did not recognize him. "You killed him." I sounded sleepdazed.

Darik moved again, shoving me back from the body. It had all the quickness of a reflex action. Of course—twas the reflex of a *s'tarei*, pushing me away from danger. "Darik, he is *dead.*

Cease this."

He stepped aside, unwillingly, and began cleaning his *dotanii.* He had only used the one. "Your pardon, Kaia'li. I am a little disarranged, this early in the morn."

A laugh boiled in my throat, but I bit it back. "Perhaps we should brew you some kafi." I knelt next to the body, avoiding the large pool of blood. Darik had opened the man's throat, quietly and effectively. I tweezed down his shirt, grimacing as hot blood slipped against my fingers.

There, on his chest, the small blue tattoo. A Blue Hand.

Gods above. I chewed at my lower lip.

"What is it?" Janaire yawned again. I suppressed a flare of irritation. Would she sleep through a pitched battle?

The minstrel did not snore, which meant he was awake and listening. Diyan curled into a tight little ball. Atyarik's eyes moved over the interior of the tent, slowly, and he finally re-sheathed his knives. "An assassin," he said, flatly. "Meant for the princess."

He spoke in G'mai, and his tone held a faint challenge. The word he used was reserved for the *adai* of a male Heir, a term unused for many summers. I pushed my braids back, I needed to twist them up out of the way again before I faced the official inquiry into this event. My mind began clicking through alternatives as my fingers, nimble and habitual, commenced searching the assassin's clothing.

"Now you rob the dead?" Atyarik, shocked, in G'mai. "Truly you are a—"

"Hush." I used the rudest possible inflection. "Aught I find will tell me who he is, and what he wanted here. Armed with that knowledge, I may keep all of us—including your *adai*, honorable one—safe and alive. Were I pretty and useless, I would have remained in G'mai and you would be still searching for your princeling. Take a little more care in how you speak to me, Tyaanismir." I cut the assassin's purse free and my fingers found several other small items, all of which I swept into a hank of cotton cloth from my clothpurse. "Redfist?" I switched to commontongue. "When I give the word, go outside and strike up a bellowing about an attack. Janaire, look as shocked as you can. Atyarik, *do not speak*. Your tongue will cause us all trouble. D'ri—" I looked up to find his eyes on me. His face was set and white, and he made a small movement, as if seeking to touch me. "My thanks, *s'tarei'mi.* Collect the boy. Wake him gently."

He nodded, his jaw set, and Redfist yawned, stretching. "Ai, K'ai, yer a fine general. What should I bellow?"

"Something about an attack, then switch to Skaialan and rant as filthily as you like." I swept the entire bundle—cloth, purse, and one of the man's knives—to the side, tossing it against the side of the tent, right next to my saddlebags. "Go, now."

He rumbled to his feet and lumbered outside. Darik spoke softly to the boy, who murmured a reply. *Darik,* I said to him privately, *my thanks. My thanks,* s'tarei'mi.

You are most welcome. The set of his shoulders eased. *I am happy to have defended you.*

What was he seeking? How did you wake?

I woke upon hearing him enter the tent. Darik threaded his fingers through the boy's hair, murmured to him in G'mai. Diyan blinked sleepily, still a child in waking. *He unerringly chose you as his target, Kaia, and approached with his blade already drawn.*

I nodded, flipped out one of my own knives. Darik half-turned, hearing the sound of metal clearing the sheath. Janaire said something, low and fierce, to her *s'tarei,* who rumbled a response.

I steeled myself, motioned to Atyarik. "Come here, if you please."

He obeyed. I handed him my knife. "Here." I pointed at my left shoulder—that side had been closest to the door. Once outside, Redfist began yelling, his barbarian voice booming in commontongue. "Cut me, a shallow slice. Now."

He glanced at Darik, who went white under his caramel G'mai coloring. Janaire gasped.

"Lady—" Atyarik began.

"I do *not* have time to bandy words!" I snapped. "Do it!"

Darik, his face chalk-pale, nodded once. "Mind you cut her shallow, if at all, Tyaanismir." Yet his voice was strained. Diyan blinked, his eyes round and dark. The minstrel lay still as death.

The strike came as a lick of fire. I seized my knife from him, flicked a little blood onto my bedding, and motioned Atyarik away. "Go tend your *adai.* You have my thanks."

"For a prince you give insults, and for a blow you give thanks?" His tone was sharper than I thought even *he* could muster. "You are truly strange."

"Go to your *adai.* D'ri, come here."

"That was not courteous of you." Darik's jaw set.

"No. It was not. However, now you truly appear frightened." I watched as he picked his way across the tent, moving stiffly. When he reached me, I threw my unwounded arm around him. He jerked in surprise and slid his arm around my waist, holding me close. The physical contact helped, eased the tension in him. My left arm throbbed. Atyarik had sliced true. "Have I not earned your trust, D'ri?"

He nodded, once, shortly, his sleep-tangled hair falling over his eyes. "Indeed you have, *adai'mi.*" His arm tightened around me, steadying me as I took an experimental stagger.

The clangor of alarums from outside reached a high pitch, and Redfist burst back into the tent, Rikyat on his heels, steel drawn. "Kaahai!" Rik bellowed, and stopped short, seeing the body and my blood-sopped shirtsleeve. Four of his personal guard, with the white horse badge on their leather jerkins, piled into the tent after him.

I shook free and crossed the tent in four strides, Darik shadowing me, until I reached Rikyat and grabbed his jerkin, shaking him. I knew my golden eyes were wide and full of fury. "Is this your hospitality?" I raged. "A Blue Hand, here? In the midst of your camp? The *second* Blue Hand I have seen in two days? What says your god, Ammerdahl Rikyat?" Five more sentries crowded the tent door. "*What game do you play with me?*"

I reached a screeching pitch to make an Antai fishwife proud. Rikyat looked at the assassin, at me, at Darik's white-lipped fury, at Janaire's wide-eyed paleness and Atyarik's stone-set jaw.

He sheathed his sword. "I crave your pardon, Kaahai," he

said, with far more dignity than I expected. “You are right to be angry. I have not told you all.”

“This is true. Tis very true. I am not happy, Rikyat. Why would your Emperor send his Hands after me?” *Was this your “second act”, Rik? The one meant to push me into your arms, as a tool to do your bidding?*

He considered me for a long moment, I let loose of his jerkin with a final shake. “How badly are you wounded?” he asked, anxiously. But not nearly anxiously enough.

My temper snapped, coldness spilling through my stomach. He could have told me the truth at that moment. Instead, he chose to turn the question aside.

“Not badly enough to matter,” I said. Darik tensed behind me, responding to the clipped brittleness of my tone. “You have *much* to tell me, Ammerdahl.”

He nodded once, a short sharp movement. The bone beads danced. “My apologies, Kaahai.”

I showed him my teeth in a grimace nowhere near a smile. “Remove this waste from my sight. I will tend my wound and have breakfast and perhaps some decent kafi, *then* you may tell me what this is about. And mind you hold nothing back, Rikyat. My temper is none too smooth this morn.”

Ammerdahl Rikyat put his palms together and bowed, in the Shainakh way. His twin braids, with the bone beads in them, swung forward. “The army will be on the march soon—two days, if all goes aright. If I cannot convince you by then to stay with our cause, you may keep the gold and go whither you will.” His gods-touched eyes did not speak to what his mouth was saying. Those eyes...

I did not shiver, but twas perilously close. This was not the Rikyat I had known.

The first Hand I could understand, to make me think the Emperor wanted me dead or merely to unbalance me. Would Azkillian truly wish me dead, though, if he received word from his spies that I was commissioned to assassinate him? Though I had taken commissions and proved myself one of the best assassins on the Lan’ai Shairukh coast, twas still not enough to trouble an Emperor. Declaring me anathema or setting a bounty on me inside Shainakh borders would have kept me away from even Shaituh for long years, if not forever. Twas not even necessary for Azkillian to be bothered, one of his spymasters could have sent out the orders easily enough.

How many other assassins has Rikyat sent after the God-Emperor, that he would find me necessary? Would he have told me of another assassin's death? Or am I intended as a distraction, whether I succeed or fail?

I nodded, my right hand clamping over the shallow slice Atyarik had gifted me. My own blood slipped hot against my fingers. The four sentries sheathed their blades, set to work lifting the assassin's body. "You may merely tell me who you wish to contract me for. Two Blue Hands in two days will be a brew easier to swallow once I know *what* they wish to kill me for."

Admirably, he showed no sign of surprise. Rikyat shrugged his lean shoulders. "Are you certain you are hale, Kahaai?"

"Very certain, Rikrik." Now I sounded tired, and Darik's hand closed over my left shoulder, over the pressure I kept on the wound. It hurt to prove Rikyat had betrayed me. I could not let the hurt show—I was practiced at keeping the agony of betrayal from showing in my eyes. Darik was a solid, warm presence behind me.

He *will not betray me, at least.* Twas a strange thought.

"I think she requires kafi," Darik said mildly, and Rik's eyes shifted past me to touch his.

"I believe she does. It seems the flower has a sword to guard her." A line of Shainakh poetry, a little clumsy in commontongue but still almost a challenge coming from the leader of the army.

Had Rikyat planned seducing me into more than violence? It seemed likely. He had always been a companion of mine, and gossip had paired us several times. I had never been lonely or drunk enough to fall into his arms, and now I wondered if he took it hard.

I also wondered how neatly I would have fallen into Rikyat's plans had it not been for Darik, and the luck of picking a barbarian's pocket.

I felt the smile touching Darik's lips. "A sword is proof against trouble, indeed," he replied in commontongue.

Perhaps only I heard the disdain in his tone. Twas a good response—a little unimaginative, but just the subtle phrase a prince would politely say to warn a man away from the prince's consort. A G'mai would find Shainakh poetry crude, to say the least.

Rikyat laughed, and sobered. "My apologies, Kahaai."

The *adjii* carried the body of the assassin out, and someone muttered the man had joined from one of the caravans. I winced. If the Blue Hand had truly arrived without Rikyat's behest, the consequences could be severe. If Rikyat had brought the Blue Hand in himself through a caravan, my making a fuss here would make reprisals necessary for the sake of the army's rumor-mill. Rikyat would use this opportunity for a purge, if necessary.

Even in this, I was serving his purpose.

I nodded, seeming to accept the apology. Ammerdahl Rikyat had matured from a spendthrift noble in the irregulars to a true leader, and one that would not hesitate to use me without my knowledge if he saw fit.

If he can. If I were disposed to let him.

Rikyat took one last look at the tent interior and stalked out. I blew out a long breath between my teeth and turned to Janaire. "I need *hamarai*. Please."

She nodded, and closed her eyes. She was still far too pale, and Atyarik watched me as if I were an adder under a child's bed. Redfist was unwontedly silent and serious, his brow crinkled with thought. Mercifully, nobody said a word until Janaire opened her dark eyes and nodded. "*Hamarai.* We are enclosed in silence."

The *hamarai*—the wall of silence—was the best way to guard against prying ears. It took a little Power, and a little skill—both of which I lacked at this point. The air turned soft and motionless, heat suddenly collecting in corners and folds. I slumped, Darik caught my shoulders.

"Wha' was that, lass?" Redfist asked. "Ye bore no mark when I stepped out."

I nodded. "I needed a legitimate cause to blame Rikyat. Blood is the only thing that qualifies. He is the commander, so he is responsible." I shook my head, forcing myself to *think*.

"What a mess. What a gods-blighted *fuchtar* mess."

"Your Highness," Atyarik said, stiffly, "it appears I was mistaken."

I thought he spoke to Darik, so I took no notice. "I do not like being pressured into a contract. The bastard set two Blue Hands on me." I put my hand over my left shoulder again. "*Cha,* Diyan, bring me my clothpurse. I need to bandage this."

"Your Highness." Atyarik stood steel-straight to catch my attention. "It appears I was mistaken."

I measured him from head to foot. What was he thinking? Janaire peered up at him. She had not even pushed her blankets back, just sat up in her sleeping-nest and regarded us with her dark, perfect eyes.

Mother Moon, Atyarik, close your mouth. I am not in the mood to be baited now. "What ails you, Atyarik? If you seek another way to tell me I am an honorless outcaste, save your breath for singing."

"No." The Tyaanismir's long face was set and unwontedly thoughtful. "I can no more dispute your honor, Anjalismir Kaialitaa. I would not wish to be your enemy."

"Then you are wise." Oddly enough, his gruff approval mattered. "Thank you, Tyaanismir."

"Will ye nae tell me what is goin' *on*?" Redfist's voice hit a pitch just below a bellow. "I wake wit' the clash o' steel, and bring yon ant's nest of men in, and ye're bleeding to boot! What is it, K'ai?"

"I believe Rikyat wishes me to assassinate the God-Emperor of Shainakh—or use me as bait on a hook, somehow. And he was indiscreet enough to let the fact slip." I rubbed my forehead with my fingers. *I suppose I cannot consider it a compliment, though I am sorely tempted to.* "I am hungry enough to eat a hanta. Janaire, how soon may I finish the *taih'adai*?"

"Too quickly may cause sickness." She blinked, owlish in surprise.

The minstrel yawned and stretched, stirring for the first time. "I may walk through the camp," Gavrin said quietly. "Minstrels hear things. I can catch what is said of this attack, and who is reporting to whom."

If I ever considered you an empty-headed lutebanger, you

have my apologies. "Well enough. They will bring breakfast. D'ri, you should check the food for poison—though I doubt it will be used, tis best to be safe. Janaire, I need the rest of the *taih'adai* as soon as possible. Redfist, Gavrin, Diyan, tidy the tent and get everything stowed. After breakfast I shall visit Rikyat, and the rest of you will find what gossip you can. D'ri, you shall accompany me, and your task will be to play a barbarian elvish princeling. Can you do so?"

He shrugged, a fluid, lovely movement giving assent. "Come. Let me bandage your shoulder, *adai'mi.*"

"Very well," I said, as Gavrin hauled himself to his feet and stretched. His straw-colored hair stood in ragged tufts, and my own braids felt mussed. "We may yet see a way free of this trap."

I could not help but realize I might be lying.

Foreknowledge

Breakfast was light and poison-free, Shainakh spongy flatbread and dried fruit, *kimiri* cheese, kafi and chai and cir juice. It was brought by four wide-eyed *adjii,* their badges of Rikyat's personal staff. We were treated as part of the command staff, which might have made it easier to escape—or far more difficult. The *adjii* snapped their salutes, and I returned them. Nobody spoke overmuch, and I was glad of that, at least.

D'ri bandaged my shoulder, and I refused Janaire's offer of a healing for no reason other than I was too busy going through the assassin's personal effects. Twas a strange collection of items, including a cylindrical scroll-case I did not open yet. I wanted a measure of privacy to plumb its secrets, though I suspected already what it would say.

We were just finishing kafi and chai, the tent flaps pulled open to let the morning breeze in, when Janaire froze between one word and the next, her pretty facc draining of all color. I stood by the open front flap, sipping my kafi meditatively, D'ri a silent warmth behind me and Diyan crouched at my feet. The boy was unwilling to go very far from me. Redfist glanced up from his food—he ate as much as all the rest of us put together, and often remarked mournfully that he wished he had some ale. The minstrel was just finishing a cup of chai, slurping contentedly.

"J'ni?" Atyarik asked.

My head came up, alerted by the tentative shortening of her name.

She trembled, her eyes dilating, and dizziness spilled through me as if the world had halted its steady motion. In

Anjalismir, during my childhood, there were several girls gifted in *fatan'adai*—the telling of the future. They all twinbonded very young. I heard twas so because *fatan'adai* is so dangerous to an untwinned *adai*, the gods made certain to send their *s'tarei* to them as quickly as possible.

I recognized the breathless blankness of her face, all light emptied from her eyes and the gaze grown piercing, as if she saw below the skin of the world.

Her tone was light, queerly flat. "No...*no*...too much, the army, there will be slaughter..." More came, in G'mai, the words spilling from her pale lips too quickly for true comprehension, their urgency striking the air like a carrier-bird's wings.

My stomach dropped inside me, turning in midair like a Kshanti acrobat. *Army* and *slaughter* meant nothing good for us.

I set my kafi cup aside and opened my mouth to ask D'ri what was happening—twas reflex, since I knew perfectly well—when the alarums began to sound.

"Redfist!" My voice sliced through Janaire's. He bolted to his feet, no small feat for a barbarian the size of a small mountain. "Go fetch the horses! Diyan, stay with Gavrin. Minstrel, make certain everyone remains *here* unless the camp is breached. If tis, direct them—and the gold—*away* and set your course for Vulfentown. I shall find you there. *Move, damn you!*"

Redfist ran for the pickets, thundering out through the tent flap. I collated the battle-alarums—a large force approaching, certainly an enemy. I swore. The minstrel hurried to pack a saddlebag, Diyan aiding him with a cheese-pale face and trembling fingers.

Darik touched my elbow. "K'li?"

"An enemy force approaching means Rik has been found out. He will have to fight or lose three-quarters of the army and perhaps the leader of the rebellion too—Gavrin, pack up my saddlebags and take them with you. Make sure Redfist knows to direct you back to Kesa at the Sparrows Moon, *cha*?"

"*Cha,*" Gavrin replied.

Diyan's eyes were wide as a hanta's. "Is there gon be a fight, Kaia?" His face was wide-open and worried. This was a different wilderness than the one he navigated as a wharf-rat. I felt sorry for him, caught in such a large game.

"Blood will be spilled for certain. Do not fret, little one." I ruffled his hair, then set him aside.

I scooped up my bow and a full quiver; I could always borrow another from a Shainakh cavalry archer. Janaire had folded into Atyarik's arms, her mouth still moving with the future-telling. I had no time to listen.

Hoofbeats, yelling, more cries, more alarums. No panic tinted the sounds, which meant the army was fully drilled and in good morale despite the sloppiness of his sentries on the seaward side. The more I saw of Rikyat's work, the more uneasy I became. He was not the feckless young sellsword I had known.

He could have used me as a hand uses a glove if not for Darik. What would I have been willing to believe, had I traveled to meet Rikyat alone?

I ducked out the front of the tent and met the Skaialan leading the horses, taking the gray's reins. Late-morning sun drifted down thick and gold, and I could not see anything other than the camp's rising dust. I did not like not seeing what was bearing down on me.

I swung into the gray gelding's saddle, hoping he was not battle-shy. "Stay with them, barbarian." I jerked my head at the tent as Redfist handed the bay's reins to Darik. "Make certain the minstrel does not thieve the gold." It took a full-throat shout to be heard over the din. "If the camp is breached, flee for Vulfentown and go to Kesa's. I will come to meet you. *You must stay with them!*"

Redfist's face darkened, but he nodded, and I wheeled the gray's head around and touched my heels to his sides. He shifted into a canter almost immediately, and I heard another horse whinny behind me. Darik? Probably. I had other concerns. Redfist would care for the others, which freed me to think of how I was to survive through the morn.

I took the avenue leading to the central tent, and arrived just in time to see Rikyat mounting a huge white Shainakh warhorse trapped with armor. The beast pawed and snorted uneasily, a bad sign. It meant he smelled nervousness.

"How many?" I yelled, using the gray's weight to force

through the knot of *adjii* and support staff. There were grim young faces, and even grimmer old faces.

"Full battalion!" Rikyat yelled in return. "*Hamashaikhan!*"

A full battalion of the Emperor's Elect? I swallowed dryly. There was little chance of avoiding battle now.

Shammerdhine Taryana appeared, on another white warhorse. She was a tall, competent-looking Shainakh, corded with muscle, a good seat on a horse. Her long black hair was braided back and coiled in the Shainakh noblewoman's fashion, held with two long flexible metal pins. The smell of dust and horse rose with the din. She wore simple leather and chain, and also carried a Danhai longsword. Her red sash made her identifiable as command corps.

I cursed inwardly. There were other red-sashed Shainakh I did not know, but I had seen them yesterday. "How far?"

"A candlemark. They must have surprised some of the scouts." Taryana took care with each word, her features set into a mask. "Greetings, Kaia."

"And to you, Shammerdhine-ka." I well knew to be respectful of her. "Where do we meet them?" This I directed at Rikyat.

"We hold at the Towan Hills, less than a league from here. I have sentries posted and a group at the west hill to watch that goat-track, do they seek our flank. Kaia, are you hale enough to fight?" Rikyat's eyes blazed. The bone-beads clacked as he swung his head, accepting the salutes, his gaze moving, moving. There was a great deal of noise, which we all ignored. The other command staff were busy yelling, directing messengers, making decisions.

"I am," I said grimly. "Who else is command staff, and what am I to do?"

"I shall give you the *tamadine.*" He smiled his lopsided Ammerdahl grin. I compared it to Darik's faint ironclad smile and found Rikyat's lost its charm. "The shock cavalry are loyal, and—"

"—and if I am killed on the front lines you will be forced to explain nothing." My tone was not polite, and Shammerdhine's eyes narrowed. Rikyat's gods-touched eyes met mine, and I was glad I was not Shainakh. How much of the force of his gaze was diluted by my G'mai blood? If I were less of a child of my people, would I feel the swimming sense of languor a bird feels under a snake's hypnotism? "Give me the baton. North side of camp?" I snatched the silvery wooden cylinder he produced and tucked it away. "You *owe* me, for this. Who is the officer in charge?"

"Kevest One-Hand. I gave him orders last night."

I nodded, curtly. I knew Kevest, and more importantly, he knew me and would fight beside me. The *tamadine* were perhaps men I had fought with before, if I knew Rikyat. He would not send me into battle with a troop of Shainakh who would disobey my commands.

Would he?

If he would use me against the God-Emperor for a still-cloudy purpose—*use* me, instead of asking me—he was also capable of giving quiet orders that I was to be martyred on the front lines of a skirmish. Would Darik ruin those plans too?

My mouth dried, slick with dust. "Gods be with you, Rikrik." *Your own gods, for mine will be occupied looking after me.*

Rikyat leaned in his saddle, grabbed at my reins. "Let us not part in anger, Kahaai. I have an answer for every question. My thanks for your willingness to fight."

Ammerdahl Rikyat the spendthrift and fellow soldier I knew. This man, Rikyat of the blazing eyes and gods-touched brain and the smooth tongue, was not what I had expected. I snatched my reins away and offered him my fist. We touched, his knuckles to mine, as we had before every pitched battle against the Danhai. My skin crawled. He had set an assassin—*two* assassins—on me. "Send me a messenger or two. If tis possible, I shall win this battle for you." *It will free me from my promise to you, one way or another. Then we shall see who uses who.*

"What of him?" Rik jerked his chin at Darik, who crowded his horse right next to the gray. Redfist had apparently found a high Shainakh saddle for the bay, but the reins were still the loose contraption Darik had put together. His ability to speak-within to a four-footed cousin would be invaluable in a melee. Darik appeared cool and calm, every inch the prince—but his eyes flicked through the crowd, watching for danger.

"He is mine," I said, shortly. Let Rik make of it what he would. "He fights beside me."

Darik's attention was a thin thread of almost-silence in the middle of the crashing, heaving din. Less than a candlemark with a full battalion bearing down on us—Shainakh battalions were easily half an army. And the Emperor's Elect were well-trained.

Now I was implicitly given part of the command on the very front line of battle array. Kevest would be spitting with fury, he always was before a skirmish.

"Good hunting, then, Kahaai," Rikyat said. His command staff was waiting patiently.

"Watch yourself. Hashai guard you."

I do not know why I said it, but Rikyat's eyes lit up. "He will." He turned back to his staff. I touched my heels to the gray's sides and forced through a knot of *adjii* coordinating supply lines. That done, I settled the horse into a trot and started for the north side of the camp. No use in killing anyone with a headlong rush now that I knew what I was to do.

When I am done with this, all promises will be quits. I shall be free to leave Rikyat to his own foul work. Why did I ever promise to see this dice-toss through?

Darik rode next to me. The camp was a clatter of seething activity, and I blew out through my teeth, a familiar knot closing in my belly.

What was I to do? Help command the shock cavalry. Why had Rikyat not kept me close to him in the command staff? Kevest would fight with me, and any of the irregulars I knew personally, but the entire cadre could not possibly hope to trust me as a field-commander. Not in the din of battle.

Kaia, Darik said, and I thought distractedly it was a good thing we had the *taran'adai,* for he would certainly have had to yell over the noise if we had not. *It is not too late to avoid this.*

Negation rose in me. *And be struck at as we flee? No.*

His calm helped. His absolute trust in my ability helped, too. Another *s'tarei* might have been fussing at me about the danger.

I still might. Amusement tinted his tone. *You seek to give our companions time to flee, then.*

Among other things. I edged the gray around a knot of infantry exchanging battle-banter, strapping on their swords. A few of them recognized me, saluting. I saluted back. They seemed far more trusting of me than I believed possible. Then again, Rikyat had maneuvered them as neatly as he maneuvered me.

I shook the thought away. How had I arrived in the midst of a rebel Shainakh army with a knot of companions seemingly determined to follow me about and a gods-touched commander who tried to kill me—and then put me in partial control of his most important troops? Troops who had possibly not even seen me yet?

Darik's calm invaded my head again. *If they refuse to follow your command, we shall watch the battle from afar. Tis that simple. Now stop fretting, and start thinking of the terrain.*

I did.

Luck

Kevest One-Hand bellowed at a knot of men and women saddling their horses. I reined the gray to a stop and looked down at him, a grizzled Shainakh with threads of gray in his thick dark hair and a seamed, wrinkled face. He wore the crimson sash of a commander and a short Shainakh *machat* strapped to his belt. He saw me, and I held up the baton, waiting for his expression.

His eyebrows raised fractionally, and he nodded slightly. Just the same. I had a moment of memory so strong it seemed as if I was reliving a hundred raids and battles against the Danhai—the dust, the stench, the screams of the wounded and dying, and my heart staggering under the burden.

"This is what Ammerdahl sends me?" he roared, throwing his good right hand and his mutilated stump up into the air. The entire corps—three hundred strong, the central cavalry unit—would serve as a scout force and shock troops against the front line at whatever Rikyat decided was the weakest point of the attacking army's line. It was our task to shatter the line and push through to break the opposing army. "Kaia Kahaai Steelflower? *This* is what he sends me?"

I leaned on my pommel. "And good morn to you, Kevest." I tossed him the baton, and his good hand flashed out to catch it, instinctively. "I am to *adjii* you." I was lying. Those had not been Rikyat's orders.

Rikyat was not here. And he had tried to have me killed to boot.

My mind kept returning to that central fact, playing with it, pawing at it lightly like an inncat with a mouse.

Kevest stared at me with his mouth open in shock while my name was taken up on all sides, a chorus of yells. The *tamadine* crowded around, the ones already horsed gathering at the rear of the press. Tents flapped in the early-morning breeze.

"*Saddle up!*" Kevest bellowed, and caught my reins. "You *adjii* me, then. What is this you bring me?"

He meant Darik. "One of my kind. Good fighter."

"Well, see he stays out of the way," Kevest snarled, and a solemn-faced young Shainakh boy brought Kanhaainsal, a huge white stallion I remembered. Nobody else could ride him, he was ugly and bad-tempered—and he was vicious on the battlefield. Kevest's largest task on the field was staying atop the beast.

"A fine welcome." I watched as he swung himself into the saddle and stuffed the baton into the specially sewn loop on his red sash. "We face *Hamashaikhan,* One-Hand. The Emperor's Elect." My words carried—I pitched them to a crowd-filling volume. *The tamadine* quieted, watching. I let my mouth curl up into a smile, playing the role.

Kevest swore. "Who commands them?"

"We shall certainly find out." I stroked the gray's mane, soothing.

"They have never lost a battle. Except against the Danhai." His ruined stump of a hand rested on his high Shainakh pommel, his seamed face pale under its color.

I know, Kevest. Why do you say it? "I have never lost a duel. Ever. " I restrained the urge to spit to the side. "We shall see."

At that, a cheer rose and swelled through the *tamadine.* Roaring, bellowing, ringing their knives against their shields or clapping and stamping, the din was incredible. Morale was good. That, at least, was a blessing.

They are frightened, Kaia, Darik said. *I would not fight in G'maihallan under these conditions. You are not required to do this.*

I owe Rikyat. This is as good a coin as any to pay that debt.

You could die. And he has betrayed you, sought to use you. Darik did not sound happy. But he stayed with me as the rest of the *tamadine* mounted, and there was the last-moment confusion of sorting into battle-order.

How could I explain? I was bound to see this through. The same impulse that moved me to pick a barbarian's pocket now compelled me to join this battle.

Then we were trotting out to take our place in the long column to re-form less than a league away, where the two hills rose with the Shaidakh River running to the side to provide cover and a long slope into a marshy bog on the other. The road behind us crossed the Shaidakh at the shallow, chuckling ford named *Haigradabh*, an ancient word left over from the Darjani tongue, meaning something like *laughter*. The Darjani Empire had been shattered when the Shainakh under Rejkillos the Fire-Prince had come from the desert on their long-legged horses. It had been a long time, but evidence of the Darjani was everywhere—even in the Shainakh army's discipline and tactics.

We reached the site where the army massed; confusion and strained expectancy everywhere, horses shrilling and men yelling. Kevest bellowed orders at the top of his considerable lungs.

It was extremely familiar, like an old tunic. My heart eased into pre-battle coney-running, high and fast.

Messages flew in from all corners, by runner and horse. I wondered what the Shainakh would think of the great G'mai armies, moving in silence, the *adai* using *taran'adai* to relay messages, the *s'tarei* quiet and grim. The tribes that raided G'mai—the Hatai through the K'nea Pass, the Boyad and the Kheruski through the broad Varad Passage to enter G'maihallan—spoke in whispers of the women of G'mai, and killed *adai* when they found the chance. They know the way to kill the G'mai is to concentrate on the women.

I was more than busy coordinating the line of men. I knew or had seen most of them, some on the S'tai Plain, others from garrisons and border raids against the Danhai. They knew me, and many saluted as I rode by, giving orders and tightening the line. *The Steelflower!* they cried. *Luck is with us!*

I did not argue.

A dust haze rose in the distance. I marked it, the rest of the army did too, and fresh clamor broke out. It spoke well of Rikyat's capabilities that he had the entire army on the battlefield of his choosing, well-drilled, well-fed, and well-rested. It also spoke well of him that his network of spies and scouts had alerted him to the approach of the other force.

Of course, the only thing that could be said about the approaching battle was the soldiers had little time to be nervous. I hoped Redfist and the rest would be safe if the line broke and the camp was raided, but I had little time to worry over them either.

The dust cloud grew nearer as morning light slanted down. We were lucky to be fighting without the Sun in our eyes, as we had during most of the battle at S'tai.

I shook myself, reining the gray in next to Kevest, watching the dustcloud draw nearer and nearer. "They are fools if they attack between the Hills," I said, more to myself than to him. "No decent commander would do so." Darik stopped behind me and to my right.

"Unless they think us unaware." Kevest leaned over in the saddle and spat accurately to one side. "Rikyat is witched. He sees things, knows things. Either the gods have touched him, or some evil spirit has."

"Which do you lay your odds on, Kevest?"

There was a standard-bearer carrying the white-horse banner, seated appropriately on a white mare with a good deep chest. I would have laid money he was listening eagerly. An expression of awe drifted over Kevest's face.

"I know not. I only know that Azkillian, curse his House, cannot keep bleeding the land dry to pay for Danhai. We have lost too much already against those cursed nomads."

I made a slight noise, neither affirmation nor denial. Kevest watched the dustcloud and ran another critical eye over the *tamadine*, spread in a line two or three deep. Behind us, mail clashed and men shouted. The only din greater than a potential battlefield is the din of an actual battlefield.

I patted the gray's neck. The horse was remarkably calm. *If you are battle-shy, my four-legged cousin, we shall both have ill-luck. I crave your pardon for subjecting you to this. You have carried me faithfully and deserve much more.*

The *tamadine* were quiet now, the only sign of nerves an occasional hoof's restless stamping. Messengers waited tersely, men tapped their swords, a few of the women irregulars were humming. Someone whistled a common camp song about a girl with dark deep eyes and a faithless lover.

I am not calm at all. I glanced at Darik, who had held his tongue except for the occasional brief reply when Kevest threw a question at him. Kevest was fascinated by the silent, scarred G'mai who rode with me, barely speaking and rarely taking his eyes from me. I was all too happy to have Kevest diverted. If he survived this battle and discovered I had been ordered to take command, we might well come to a duel.

I patted the gray's neck again. "So you think Rikyat gods-touched?"

"It matters little." Kevest had once fought off four Danhai at once, in a raid turned into a melee near the A'taharh garrison. I remembered the sting of my last arrow against my fingers and charging down the hill screaming my battle-cry, Kevest's bellow like an enraged beast, Rikyat beside me matching me stride for stride.

I surfaced from that memory too, Darik tensing behind me.

Twas time.

A scout galloped between the Hills, and I had my bow and an arrow in my hands before I even knew it. "One of ours?" I asked as the Shainakh halted, his horse pawing at the ground, the rider's eyes visibly widening even at this distance. He hauled on his reins, attempting to turn the prancing horse back.

"Kill him," Kevest said, and I nocked and let fly in one motion, aiming high.

Twas at the very upper end of a bow's range, even a G'mai bow. And this was a Hain bow, larger and clumsier than the long sweet curves of G'mai. Yet the arrow flew true, its black and white fletching blurring, and buried itself in the man's back.

A collective murmur rose from our army. The gray stamped. I was justifiably proud of myself—archery had never been my finest skill. As a matter of fact, I was faintly surprised the arrow had flown so well.

I could not tell if it was skill or some breath of Power that had flung it so true.

The scout's horse pranced and fled, the body falling from its broad back in seeming-slow motion, folding like a toy. The first bloodshed of the day, and twas mine. "Gods forgive me," I murmured in G'mai, the traditional prayer. I heard Darik breathe the same words, our voices in unison. *Twas a good shot, Kaia'li.*

I accepted the compliment, silently. Tension, now.

The line of *tamadine* closed in front of us. It was a loose line, with the closer-packed squads of ten behind us to make a screen of initial cavalry. The infantry spread behind, light cavalry massed on the wings, where they had the freedom of movement to skirt the Hills on both sides and fall upon the opposite force in a pincer. More infantry crowded in quick-march lines, to take the two low gentle peaks on either side of the road—*towan,* of course, meant *breast* in the old Darjani. Swords were out now, glittering in the morning Sun. Rikyat would keep the heavy infantry and the *shadat* in reserve for the decisive blow.

No time.

The lone scout was followed by an advance guard of *Hamashaikhan.*

Things began to move very quickly.

They had to advance, because of the weight of other bodies behind them, marching. Yet they could not spread, because of the embrace of the Hills and the river. They marched under Azkillian's device—the Invincible Sun, circled by a serpent. Under that flew another flag—a field of red, a serpent, and a single feather. Someone related to the Imperial House.

A rustling flew through our army, swelling into a deep-throated roar.

I cast my eye over the field again. We had a quarter-league's distance to cover before we engaged, should we charge. They pressed forward, men in light leather armor with travel-packs strapped to their backs. Some threw their packs down and began buckling their helmets on. We had achieved a complete surprise. Word passed slowly in their force—the ones behind still pushed forth between the Hills, pressuring the ones in front.

"*Attack!*" Rikyat's voice? I could not tell. It did not matter, the order would come from him. Moving us all from behind a curtain, like a god.

Kevest raised his voice too, a single wordless yell, a battle-cry all the *tamadine* knew by heart. I did not scream, but I did slip my bow back into its casing and draw my sword. Steel glittered in the morning light. This would not be a battle.

Twas a slaughter about to happen.

The *hamashaikhan* marched in standard order, unprepared for ambush. I could not believe Rikyat's luck. Twas not customary of the Emperor's Elect to be so sloppy.

If it was luck, or his god. Did it matter?

I touched my heels to the gray's sides, and he started forward willingly. The entire line of *tamadine* shifted to a trot, the infantry behind us. The distance was not enough for us to seriously outstrip the infantry, who would be marching until the officers gave the order to charge, and the light cavalry would sweep in from either side around the Hills, acting as a bottleneck to keep the potential stragglers from escaping as well as pincers. It was brilliant, from a tactical standpoint, but all the same, I was uneasy.

Had Rikyat foreseen this? Had his god told him of it, dictated his strategy? Had he merely blindly kept us here, assuming the Elect would be marching in standard order? Or had his network of spies told him thus?

The line of *tamadine* met the mass of largely unprepared Emperor's Elect with a clatter and shout that reverberated through each horse. Oddly, the gray did not falter—I cut down two of the red-vested *hamashaikhan* and heard the screaming start. An arrow flashed past my cheek, buried itself in a *hamashaikhan* throat—Darik, protecting me.

The initial charge of the *tamadine* broke the mass of *hamashaikhan* into a disorganized rabble. *Where are the Elect cavalry?*

I saw them, forcing their way through the gap of the Hills. Riding in standard order, too, without heavy armor. In other words, geese for the plucking; if we held them in the gap the light and heavy cavalry on either side would sweep in and take them. Twas amazing.

The infantry engaged with another crashing shock. The sound of slaughter all around; the salt latrine stink of the battlefield, red blood and cut bowel, fear and aggression like rotting copper. Darik shouted as I cut down another *hamashaikhan*, and my taste for this was growing much less.

This was not a battle. There was no honor in it.

Their cavalry managed to reform and charge, and I was too busy to spare a thought for honor. Messengers were yelling once we had the space to listen to them, *adjii* using little silver whistles to transmit bursts of coded information, I heard the left wing was fighting through, there was a knot of resistance on the far left, that the—

There was no time to listen. I slashed overhand, kicked, the stirrup flaying a man's cheek and shattering teeth, and became aware of the gray, shuddering underneath me. Was he calm, or did my newfound Power merely ride him as I did?

I could not tell.

Screaming. Some had crossbows, and the presence of mind to use them, but they were few and the crossbows took much time to reload. The world dissolved into a thrashing mass of men and horses, swords rising and falling, lances snapped and thrown aside. By the time the line broke and we rode through, Kevest giving the order to hunt down the survivors and kill them if they did not surrender, I was nursing a bruised leg and the slash on my left arm was throbbing dully.

And I was still alive.

A Debt Repaid

The victory yell went up. I glanced at the sky, checking the location of the Sun and halting, my ribs heaving with deep starved breaths. There was no one left to fight, nothing left to do but offer mercy to the dying.

A candlemark. A single candlemark, not much more, for most of a battalion to be destroyed and death to visit a host. So much waste.

Rikyat, congratulating the troops, rode back and forth on his massive white horse. Screams still resounded, the infantry moving out and mopping up resistance. Darik pulled the bay to a stop. He was unscathed, his hair wildly mussed, his *dotanii* sheathed now. He looked grim. "Kaia'li?" His voice was hoarse from shouting.

I glanced across the field again. Something prickled just under the edge of my consciousness.

Power rose, spilled through my veins, a knowledge deeper than the body's instinctive knowledge of breath and pulsing blood.

Kaia, it whispered. *Now. Do what you must.*

The bow slipped into my hands. I saw it, then, the single red-vested body rising from behind a mound of dead *hamashaikhan,* the crossbow swinging up and leveling at Rikyat, unconscious and victorious in front of his troops. Shammardine Taryana yelled a curse.

The arrow left my bow, flashed in the still-morning sunlight, and for the second time that day, my aim was true. Darik let out a short, sharp cry—warning or otherwise, I do not know—and Rikyat's gods-haunted eyes flashed, startled.

The lone *hamashaikhan* fell, his face contorting with agony. I let out a long, sighing breath. Power faded, swirling between my veins, and a breath of wind touched the battlefield, lifting my sweat-soaked braids.

Well done, it seemed to say. *Well done.*

Taryana, her coppery sweat-shiny Shainakh face twisted with fury, began shouting orders to *make certain the bastards are dead!*

Rikyat's dark, gods-fevered eyes met mine for a long, painful moment. I heard his agonized scream again, so long ago on the S'tai Plain. The man I knew had died there. I had carried him on my back through mud and grass, over league upon league of the Plains, eluding the nomad bands of Danhai, back to the main body of the army that had given our entire corps up for dead. *That* man, the dead man, I could have killed an Emperor for—or tried, with every trick and scrap of luck I possessed.

That man would not have slaughtered half a battalion with such ease and apparent carelessness.

This man, I owed nothing to.

A life for a life, I thought, stunned and weary. Twas done. I was quits with him. My luck held—I had been given a chance to pay my debt.

The successive shocks—a *s'tarei*, two Blue Hand assassins, wyverns, the *taih'adai*—threatened to leave me a witless, staring fool. If not for reflex and a bolt of Power-laden foreknowledge, Ammerdahl Rikyat might be dead, and I forsworn but still free.

Luck, Kaia? There has been too much, both bad and good. Something has started here, like navthen mixed with ortrox.

I swallowed dryly, tasted dust. "Darik. We shall return to the tent."

"As you please." Calmly enough, his voice hoarse with dust and shouting, just as mine. I felt his exhaustion, and my own. Less than a candlemark of true battle wore the body worse than a day of drill.

I saw with some astonishment we had passed through the Hills. There were no survivors except those who had surrendered and given up their swords. They would no doubt be sworn to the new army, and the new regime.

I could not hope they stayed loyal, even for the man I had known.

Ammerdahl Rikyat was dangerous. He wanted me to attempt to kill the Shainakh God-Emperor, whether as distraction for another assassin or because his god told him I could accomplish such a feat. He would no doubt pay me good gold to do it, and would offer me more than gold if he thought it would tempt me. He had a tidy plan, as packaged and beautiful as a clothier's wrapping. Certainly his god would smooth his path.

I would not.

The gray was lathered and weary. A fine horse. He appeared none the worse, and unwounded beside. Another gift from the gods?

We trotted slowly through the wreckage of the battlefield. The infantry went from body to body, stripping and making certain they were dead. Good loot to be had, and the supply train would be taken too. Darik watched, the bay trotting and fretting at the makeshift reins. A good horse.

"Kahaai!" Rikyat's voice. "*Kahaai!* Wait!"

No. I felt Darik's silent agreement. We were in accord again, my *s'tarei* and I. He *understood,* a moment of comprehension as if we faced each other in the dueling ring again, our eyes locked and our hearts beating in unison.

The gray whinnied, and picked up his feet. Perhaps he was not too weary after all.

But I was.

Hoofbeats shook the ground, and I looked up. Rikyat and his *adjii* bore down on us. I pulled the gray to a stop. "Kahaai," Rikyat said, as soon as he could stop his huge white horse from stamping and pawing. "Kahaai, I can *explain—*"

The words broke free of me. "Did your god or your spies tell you this would be a slaughter? If your spies told you this would be a slaughter, why did they not tell you a Blue Hand would wish to kill me in my sleep last night? Or did it slip your gods-touched mind?" *Do not lie to me again, Rik,* I silently pleaded. *Tell me truth now.*

He shook his head, bone beads clicking. He was dewed with

sweat and covered in dust from the battle, but his clothes were still fine. One of his bone beads was speckled with blood. "Kahaai, I can explain—"

Weariness filled me like dark wine. "I do not want explanation, Ammerdahl Rikyat. I wanted truth, and you will not gift me such. I have repaid my debt."

He leaned in his saddle, his arm stretched out, fingers grasping as if to grab my reins again. I shifted, and the gray stepped away. Darik watched, his hand on a knife-hilt, his black eyes depthless. There was a stripe of blood up his flawless cheek. My *s'tarei*. He had fought as if possessed today. I had no worry for my unprotected back, safe in the knowledge he was guarding me.

I could not risk that for this gods-touched almost-Emperor. I could not risk him, having found him just in time. Had my own gods sent him across an ocean of time and distance to catch me before I fell prey to a mad man's quest for power?

Perhaps they had. Now twas my duty to guard his back, as well. There was nothing between Ammerdahl Rikyat and me but void.

"Kaia," Rikyat tried again, "stay with me. You are good luck. You would not rob me of my luck, would you?" He was using that fey smile again, the one I remembered from the Danhai wars, the smile that had called an answering grin to my lips more times than I could count. But he was no longer Rikrik, he was something else.

An Emperor? Maybe. But without my help.

Shammerdhine Taryana hissed an imprecation through her teeth, and my eyes met hers for a long moment. She ended by dropping her gaze to her pommel, but she did not look abashed in the least. My gaze was not something to be trifled with, especially now with the *taih'adai* burning inside me, teaching me the uses of Power. When I finished the *taih'adai* would I be able to fight with Power and steel both?

I hoped so.

"Farewell, Rikyat." My hoarse, colorless voice. "May your gods watch over you."

"Kaia, I..." The ghost of the man he once was struggled in the fiery lakes of his eyes, and drowned. "You know my plans.

Do not make yourself my enemy."

My lips twitched, and I stared at him. He was pale, and his fevered eyes were burning. A spark, carried into those dark depths. His gods would have no mercy for him. "How could I do so, Rikyat? You are gods-touched. I am not bound for Shaituh. Do not send another message—and *do not* send another Blue Hand."

His face changed. He knew, now. "You are far from your companions." He shifted in his saddle. "Surrounded by my army."

I glanced at Darik. He wore his faintest ironclad grimace of a smile, his eyes fixed on Rikyat. If Rik even so much as twitched for a weapon, D'ri would kill him. This I knew.

Oh, Rik. What changed you into this? "Do not dishonor your ancestors."

His eyes glittered, glittered. "Kaia. Reconsider."

I shook my head, my sweat-stiff braids swinging. "No, Rikrik. Farewell." I pulled on the gray's reins, and he turned gladly.

"You will reconsider. You *must.* You *will* fight beside me, Kahaai." But his voice broke on the last syllable. "*Kahaai!*"

Darik's bay fell into step beside me. *Kaia? Will he strike you from behind?* The line of communication between us turned taut and hot, the skin between my shoulderblades prickling with anticipation.

No, I answered. *At least, I hope not.*

The sounds of a trampled battlefield fell away from us, into Darik's silence, the determined silence of a *s'tarei.* I rode, my back cold with gooseflesh. There were crossbows, and other bows.

But it was not an arrow Rikyat hurled at me. "Kahaai!" he cried, across the distance. "*Kaia!*"

I had answered his cries once before.

I closed my eyes, continued on. Darik kneed the bay up to my side, to guide my horse.

"You are my luck! You *cannot* leave me! The gods told me! *My luck will turn against me! Kaia!*"

I did not pause.

"Kaia!"

"No," I said, only to myself, but I did not hear Rikyat cry my name again.

Bloodgild

The camp lay half-deserted, and the sound of Rikyat's cries did not ride to me on the wind. He had apparently decided to let me go—he would be busy enough mopping up the battlefield.

No. It had been less than a battle.

I had not thought he would slaughter a whole battalion. I had not thought he would use me, when I would have given him my strength willingly. I would have cheerfully planned to assassinate the God-Emperor himself, if Rik had not sought to use me without my knowledge. And he had put me on the front lines of slaughter—why? *Why*?

I had no easy answer, and I did not wish for one. What would have happened had not Darik pursued a failing Seeker from the borders of G'maihallan?

I had no easy answer for that either.

We reached the tent, and Redfist appeared, huge as a ship appearing out of fog. I had not thought I would be so gladdened by a huge, smelly, ginger-furred barbarian, but weary joy lighted under my heart.

"Fetch my saddlebags," I said, my voice throat-cut with yelling. "Hurry. We are taking our leave."

The Skaialan appeared equally relieved and curious, but he wasted no time with questions. "On the packhorse already, lass. Come."

Janaire ducked out of the tent, pushing her braids behind her ear. "You look terrible," she said in G'mai, her wide black eyes meeting mine. "You—oh. Oh."

Atyarik slid past her, holding a light summer cloak he wrapped around her shoulders. "We are leaving? Come, J'ni."

"He may follow you." Darik patted the bay's neck. "K'li?"

"There are other tasks to keep him occupied." I touched my braids, still tied back and coated with dust. "Let us *go*. I do not wish to stay here."

"In that you have my agreement, princess," Atyarik said. "The minstrel and the boy are with the horses."

Janaire followed him, her cheeks still pale and the fume of foreknowledge following her skirts like fine dust. She glanced back often at me, her unbound braids slipping forward over her shoulders. I urged the horse after her, Darik behind me. I clutched at the reins with nerveless fingers, my throat rasping. Redfist was already gone.

Kaia Steelflower, the Iron Flower, sellsword, assassin, thief. Now where do I wander? Antai, perhaps. I do not know. I took a deep breath. "Six rooms and seven waterclosets," I murmured. "A bedroom on the bottom floor. Linens hung in the Sun. Chai bushes out back."

Rest, Kaia. Darik's voice, calm and restful.

That won a tired laugh from my dry throat. "I cannot *rest.* I am responsible for you all."

"Let us decide for a day, Kaia. You have fought a battle." Darik urged his horse forward. The bay whickered as we reached the pickets.

Janaire was already in the saddle, Diyan's young, frightened face eased. Gavrin petted his brown nag and mounted with more luck than skill. He did not look well, pale and sweating.

"So have you," I pointed out.

Redfist led the packhorse, with Diyan perched in the saddle. Atyarik mounted his own slender black horse and made a low clicking sound of greeting. The minstrel, his face ashen, ran a hand back through his light hair, making it stand up like a bird's nest.

"Not the same one," Darik murmured. *Not the same battle at all, adai'mi.*

"Was it truly a slaughter?" Gavrin, bits of his mussed hair

sticking to his damp forehead. "They were bringing in the wounded—there was no news—"

So he had seen the cost of battle for the first time. I hoped the sight had sobered him out of wishing to make a drinking song of it.

"Hush." Janaire silenced him. When had she decided to speak so?

I put my head down, stared at the pommel of the saddle. My eyes filled with hot salt heaviness. My entire body burned with exhaustion; the horse needed a good combing and rubdown. I would not have minded one myself, as long as it was accompanied by a pot of mead and a hot bath.

Silence fell over me, the twilight of a silence I knew all too well.

"You did well," Darik said quietly. How could I still hear him? How could he stay so close to me? "You fought with honor, and repaid a life."

I shook my head. My braids, tangled and finally loosened, dropped forward across my forehead, swung down to touch my wrists. Ammerdahl Rikyat was dead, the thing living in his skin just an echo. I could have killed myself—and my *s'tarei*—in a battle that had no honor, against almost-unarmed opponents. I had been blindly determined to pay my debt to a dead man.

"You fought with honor," Darik repeated. His tone was formal, a prince recognizing his *adai*.

"You fought with honor," Atyarik echoed. I looked up to catch sight of him riding slightly behind Janaire, his back iron-straight. I could not see his face, but there was no sarcasm in his voice. For once.

I forced myself to *think*. They were still my responsibility. "The gold. Who has the gold?"

"I do, lass." Redfist's tone was carefully neutral.

"Leave it here." I urged the gray forward. "Pour it out and let Rikyat have his bloody coin."

"No." Atyarik sounded determined, but I still could not see his face. "Tis good gold. It will feed us through the winter, while Janaire trains you."

"Tis bloodgild. I do not *want* it."

"Then you are not required to spend it," Atyarik said. "You earned it nonetheless, princess. Keep the gold."

I closed my eyes, swaying in the saddle. "I do not want it."

"Then it makes no difference if *we* keep it, Atyarik and I. You will shatter yourself, Kaialitaa, if you fling yourself against a mountain." Twas a G'mai proverb, and for once, the sound of Janaire speaking the tongue of the Blessed People did not hurt me. For the first time, I found it comforting.

I wrapped my fingers in the reins. "You are all mad. Mad."

"Of course," Janaire agreed. "Why else would we travel with *you*? Darik, help her, she speaks nonsense." Her tone was forced and light, seeking to find some merriment where none existed. My back prickled with sweat, dirt, and danger. Would Rikyat send archers, swordsmen, to drag me back to his army? Or would he send an assassin to punish me for leaving his grasp?

A life for a life. I shuddered. The grip of battlefever eased. I simply felt worn, and suddenly old. The gray walked instead of trotting, his head drooping slightly. Wind brushed through chedgrass as we passed through sentry lines without a challenge. Everyone was at the battlefield except the healers and a few camp followers—and the wounded, returning from the slaughter.

We crested the rise, and I turned in the saddle to look back at Rikyat's camp. It shimmered in the gathering heat of day. Dust and smoke from the battle rose in the distance from the Towan Hills. More dust than there should have been. I heard a faint sound, carried on the wind—clashing, steel against steel.

More battle? But they had all been dead. Dead or near to it. Twas none of my concern now, anyway.

I drew in a long breath, and when I turned away from the camp I saw Darik had pulled the bay to a stop and watched me, black eyes thoughtful in a Dragaemir face. The scar across his throat drew my eyes again. Would I ever have the courage to ask him how he had received it?

Later. He tilted his head to the side. The wind played with his black hair, and I felt something in my chest ease for the first time in many years. It eased all at once, suddenly, and so completely I was half afraid I would fall from the saddle. *I will tell you later. For now, though...* "For now," he said aloud in commontongue, and I found they were all looking to me, even Atyarik, whose face was expressionless. "Where shall we go, Kaia'li?"

I set the riddle to my weary mind, which returned—thankfully—an answer. "Back to Vulfentown. From there we can decide where to winter." I pointed down the road. "That way."

Darik nodded. "As you like." The bay started in that direction. Redfist made an affirmative sound, very much like a grunt, and Diyan gave a sigh of relief.

Vulfentown, then. We could catch ship for Antai unless some other destination presented itself, and I could puzzle out a way to explain what I had just done. If Rikyat succeeded in his bid for the throne, I had possibly just earned his enmity. If he did not, what price would be exacted from those who had fought with him, even briefly? The God-Emperor had a long reach, even if I was only a sellsword thief of little account.

Where would I be safe—and not just myself, but the other members of my little troupe? Antai, Pesh, some of the other cities...who knew? I could not return to Shaituh now. I knew too much of Rikyat's plans, and he planned to attack the city as well.

I heard his despairing cry again. *My luck will turn against me!*

Gods grant it was true.

Where could I go now? How on earth could I keep them all safe?

Twas a riddle I would solve tomorrow, for I was far too tired to think, and we had a long weary journey ahead.

To Be Continued

About the Author

Lilith Saintcrow lives in Vancouver, Washington, with her husband, two children, three cats, and assorted other strays. To learn more about Lili, please visit www.lilithsaintcrow.com.

Between mage and man lies fire.

Touch of Fire

© 2008 Maria Zannini

Leda has been ordered by the House of Ilia to use her fae gifts to find an alchemist's bible, no matter what the cost. In a world where technology has been replaced by Elemental magic, this book is more dangerous than any spell or potion.

A ragged scrap of parchment is Leda's only clue and it leads her to the last man known to have had the book—a savagely handsome ex-soldier turned scavenger. Greyhawke Tams. He'll serve her needs nicely, in both her quest, and her bed.

The last thing Grey remembers is a bar brawl leaving him flat on his face. When he awakes, his situation hasn't improved. He's been bound in service to a contemptuous little fire mage with luscious curves and a deceptively innocent face. Grey's not fooled—he's hated the Elementals ever since he lost his younger brother to their brutal rites of passage.

But something about Leda tangles his brain faster than any woman he's ever known. And soon it becomes clear she needs more than his "services". A barbarous overlord wants that book and he's willing to shatter Leda—body and spirit—to get it.

She needs his protection. Whether she wants it or not.

Warning: Sex, sin and sauciness abound. This just in: Virgin butter not only helps nervous young virgins on their wedding night, it makes a damn fine hair liniment too.

Enjoy the following excerpt from Touch of Fire...

Grey slowed to a halt. He raised the palm of his hand and tilted his head to one side, trying to catch a whisper in the breeze. The forest had grown thicker, darker. They had traveled far in one day and dusk would be upon them soon.

"We should camp here, priestess. The forest will swallow us up if we continue in the fading light."

"You're right." Leda shivered. There was something in the air, like a bad omen looking for a host. She sensed it, but it had no form. Leda had been raised as an earth fae, but the elements knew their own kind. This forest did not welcome her.

Leda gripped the hilt of her sword. "Stay close to me, savage. These woods hold secrets."

Grey slid his sword from its sheath on Ghost's saddle. His fingers curled around its hilt, one by one. "Little fae, is that blade of yours sharp?"

Leda snarled at him. "Perhaps you'd like to test it."

"We sleep in shifts tonight." He threw their saddlebags at her feet. "I'll take first watch. If your magic works in this forest, I suggest you weave us a warding spell." He examined the broken limb of a bush. "We're being watched."

"From where?"

Grey shifted his gaze from side to side, looking for any clues of trespass. "I don't know, but I feel the glare of something dangerous. Someone is watching us."

Leda wove her spell though she wasn't sure it would take this deep in the wood. Earth realms didn't readily obey the will of a fire fae.

Grey gathered brushwood, stacking it high. No doubt, he intended for the fire to last all night. He pulled out his flint and struck it with the flat of his knife. The tinder sparked but refused to take life. Another spark, and the ember faded again.

Leda snatched the flint from his hand and flung it to the ground in exasperation. "Oh, for pity's sake! How do you plainfolk survive from day to day?" She passed the palm of her hand over the kindling and mumbled a chant, then pulled out several dried stalks of hay that had been flattened to the ground. She closed her eyes and rolled the sheaf between her thumb and forefinger in a rapid motion. A fragile ember emerged and she covered it with her free hand, then laid it on the rest of the kindling, lighting the papery bundle to hungry flames.

"Impressive. But we plainfolk managed long before you fae-kind rose from either hell." Grey walked over to the horses and ran his hands down Milke's back, showing more interest in the mare than the fire. "She's a fine one. I'll bet she can run all day without tiring."

"The Reverend Mother says we were born on the same cusp. She bought her for me six years ago. Milke and I have never been apart."

"I can see that. You bear a surprising resemblance to this nag." He cocked a teasing grin.

Leda tossed him an apple. "That's for Milke, not you," she warned.

"And what do I eat?"

"You're the servant. You cook." She pointed to the bag closest to him. "Supplies are in there."

He dug them out one by one, arching a brow at the well-stocked bag. Dried meat, cheese, and wine. "You travel well, priestess, but I see no bread."

She laughed. "This is where we test your cooking skills." Her hands rustled inside another bag and pulled out a small sack of flour and various herbs. "I trust a bachelor knows how to make flatbread."

They sat with their backs against their packs, watching the pita bread brown on the griddle. Grey offered her a swig from the wine skin. She shook her head dismissively.

"I don't drink alcohol."

He chortled. "What? Everyone drinks wine."

She wiggled her fingers in front of the fire, delighting in its warmth. "I don't. It muddies the senses."

Grey took the skin back and drew a big gulp from it. "You don't know what you're missing." He wedged the nearly full wine skin in the soft pine mulch between his legs. "Why do you carry wine if you don't drink it?"

"I find information flows more freely from the lips of a drunkard." She smiled at him sweetly.

He curled a lip at her. "Is there something more you want from me, priestess?"

"My name is Leda."

"And my name is Grey, so you can stop calling me savage."

Leda bit the inside of her lip. "I apologize...Grey." Her gaze wouldn't meet his, concentrating instead on the rice meal in her scarred wooden bowl. "I don't mingle with the plainfolk much, unless it's requested of me."

"And when you find this book, you'll take this collar off my neck?"

"I will. All we need is the book."

Grey grew strangely quiet and Leda noticed an aura of pale orange around him, the aura of secrets. She pushed her bowl aside and dug inside her vest for the single page of paper that had led her this far. "The book's not at your house, is it, Grey?"

He didn't meet her eyes.

"Grey."

"No. It was stolen from me before I even left the badlands."

"Who took it?"

"A madman. A fool. He came to my campfire after I had salvaged all I could from the stone crypt. He looked hungry and worn so I invited him to share my food. It wasn't until he sat down at my fire that I realized he was an untouchable."

"You let the unclean eat at your fire?"

"He was just an old man, hungry and lost. If he was infected with anything, I never caught the bad air."

Grey scratched the rough of a two-day old beard, his mind elsewhere. "Strange old man," he said, shaking his head. "He had the most peculiar expressions, nonsense, I suppose. When we bedded for the night, he blessed me for my kindness. Come morning, he was gone. So was my book."

"And was it the only thing he took?"

He ran his hand down the back of his head. "I don't know why, but he cut off a hunk of my hair. I had it tied with a short piece of cord. When I woke in the morning, my hair was loose and I was missing the knotted tail. I can't imagine how he got so close without me hearing him."

Leda narrowed her eyes at him. "You're sure he was an untouchable?"

Grey shrugged. "He had the sores on his body, though he seemed to move surprising well for a sick man."

"Then you have as much reason to find this man as I do. That was no leper who found you, but a shaman to the outcasts. They sometimes steal hair and fingernails from outsiders for their rituals."

"What kind of rituals?"

"Who knows? The shamans have a magic I don't understand, but if I were you, I'd want my hair back. There are stories that claim they can turn dead men into walking ghouls."

Grey jumped to his feet. "Buddha's balls! I'll have no heathen condemn me to the living dead."

"Since the book isn't at your home, we'll go straight into the badlands where you found your plunder."

"No. We go to my homestead first."

"Out of the question," she said curtly.

Grey loomed over her. "I wasn't asking, Leda. If that pleasure woman was killed for want of a piece of paper, then they will go to my home next. I intend to protect what's mine. We'll go after the shaman once I've secured my keep."

"Damn it, Grey. You have no idea what you're dealing with. Those weren't brigands who killed that woman, but trained assassins." Leda shoved her bowl into his hard belly. Grey didn't budge.

"And you think I am safer under the sword arm of a woman-child? You can barely lift the blade you carry now. I'll be saving your hide more than my own."

Leda tossed the bowl to the ground, and then slid her sword out of its scabbard, flashing it in front of his face. "I am a true fae of fire. And I can challenge any man in a fair fight."

He walked toward her, forcing her back step by step. "Who said fights were fair, mistress? Have you ever drawn blood, or even tasted it on your lips?" He slapped the sword from her hand and caught it with his left hand, then leveled its tip against her throat. “You have no idea what it is to fight, to bleed…to die. You witches prefer to butcher young boys in their sleep with your potions and brews.”

Leda looked down at the blade, surprised that he had disarmed her so quickly. A sword master, and one with a vendetta in his craw. His barbs were personal.

Most plainfolk distrusted the fae. But this one despised them.

“Your hatred is obvious. Did someone hurt one of your kin?”

Grey spat into the fire. “My younger brother dreamt of becoming a fire mage.” His eyes turned cold and distant. “He didn’t make it.”

“And you blame me for this?” Leda’s words were soft, a hint of regret in its delivery. Many children failed the rites of passage.

Grey turned toward her, the look of a man still seeking vengeance. For a moment she saw the real savage beneath the soldier. He narrowed his eyes at her and then she noticed his shoulders relax. The savage was buried once more. “He would’ve been your age…had he lived.”

“I’m sorry for your loss.”

Grey sneered at her. “The fae aren’t sorry for anything.”

He turned to walk away but her fingers touched him on the arm, stroking a long, wide scar. It was a wonder he hadn’t bled to death. “Where did you get this?” She nodded to the old wound, disturbed by its brutality.

“The battle of the Twin Rivers, a battle with the mages.” He smiled sardonically, rubbing the injury like a trophy.

“Many of my clan died in that battle.”

He nodded to the crest on her cloak. “You wear the crest of the earth realm, but you’re a fire fae. I didn’t realize they shared bread with one another.”

“Normally they don’t. The Reverend Mother of our clan bought me from a family who couldn’t afford another mouth to feed. She sensed I had the gift, but our talent rarely manifests before puberty. She had hoped I was an earth Elemental, like many born in our region." She kicked a tuft of grass. "But I was born of fire. By the time they realized it, Mother thought it best to keep me with the earth clan. She has no kindness for the elder of the fire clan."

"Lord Senosai."

"You know him?" Her eyes widened with renewed interest.

"I know of him. The warlord has placed his trust in him. Where the warlord leads, I must follow."

She scoffed at his blind faith. "You still have a soldier's allegiance."

"Even the drudgery of farming can't dull the blood of a soldier. I miss the life, but not the killing... There was so much killing."

His aura changed to something cooler and sad, a hint of lavender. The blush of regret. He handed her back her sword. His colors shifted again, mingling remorse with something new. *Deception.*

"Be a good girl, Leda. Take this collar off. You shame me for ill reason. I offered to pay for damages in good faith."

"If I remove the collar, the law cannot bind you to me. The collar stays."

He moved closer to her and fingered the curls along her face. "Come now, sweetness. I won't run from you. I'll help you find your book. Just take this iron cuff off my throat."

His eyes looked deep into hers, and she flinched when she caught her heart longing for this stranger's touch. She'd been alone too long.

Grey smiled at her, making her feel like a wicked little girl out on her first bed tussle. *Allah's mercy!* Did he think he could woo her for his freedom? She had been weaned on every secret of seduction. She was supposed to be the master here.

Leda pushed him away. "The collar stays. Savage."

58350636R00192

Made in the USA
Lexington, KY
09 December 2016